VLOGENTIA

A TALE OF SECOND WORLD

WM W SOMERS

"Any sufficiently advanced technology is indistinguishable from magic."
Arthur C. Clarke

AUTHOR'S COROLLARY
*Any sufficiently misunderstood or incomprehensible
technology is indistinguishable from magic.
It does not have to be far advanced, just not recognized as technology.*

ISBN: 978-1-7357879-0-9

Printed in the United States of America.

Cover Design by 100Covers.com
Interior Design by FormattedBooks.com

ACKNOWLEDGEMENTS

This book would not exist without the support of many people.

First, to my loving wife for her patience and encouragement during the writing and especially during the revisions.

And many thanks to Joan and Camilla for their support in provoking me into actually putting this story on paper.

A special thanks to Dylan Newton, my coach and editor, who helped guide me through the surprisingly difficult process of revision.

The comment by one of the bystanders to Juan and Bianca in Chapter 1 about the cowardice of the king is not original. It came from the old television program, *Bonanza*, circa 1965.

CONTENTS

CHAPTER	TITLE	PAGE

PREFIX

Sixty five million years ago a comet crashed into our earth. It caused one of the catastrophic extinctions in the history of this world. It also created a gateway to a virtually identical alternate universe, a small black hole surrounded by a self-replicating magnetic field that kept the black hole stable. This other universe differs from ours in minor details. The sun and the galaxies appear the same. But the earth has a slightly different geography. And it has two moons of equal mass to our one.

If a creature or object got just the right distance from the black hole's event horizon, it would be shifted to the other universe by way of its companion gateway, caused by the crossover disruption of the comet. And the return could also occur.

So, although life never started there, life migrated from here to there over eons. Some of this life evolved in different directions, over millions of years, and became the creatures of legend. Some of it changed only in size. Others remained the same as they were in their original habitat. Life in this second world prospered for ages and then people stumbled across the gateway.

FOREWORD

The Yucatan
Gregorian calendar: November 12, 1585
Mayan calendars: Tzol'kin: 6 Ik'
                         Haab: 0 Yaxk'in

Father Sebastian Vlogentia Garcia Lopez of the Dominican order knew this was going to be a very bad day despite the fact that it was the Mayan Tzol'kin day to pray for peace and domestic tranquility. He raced along the uneven jungle path, his heart pounding in his chest like the blacksmith's hammer and his breath coming in labored, painful gasps. His legs ached and felt as if they would turn to rubber. The day was hot and humid and the sweat formed beads across his face and soaked his clothes. As he ran the branches of the underbrush slapped across his face and assaulted his body. He wished he was a little less portly than he had become. He feared he would collapse into a heap of bones and skin at any instant. Despite his pain he found the willpower to keep going.

He had been visiting the nearby village when Diego de Landa's men arrived and started their pillaging. Homes and personal belongings were burning throughout the town. The church was ransacked and its library added to the flaming pyre in the town's center. Smoke from the fires burned the eyes and made breathing difficult. Cattle and other livestock were slaughtered in their pens or in the street. Villagers who failed to get out of the way were beaten and kicked once they were down. Sebastian knew he could not allow them to reach his people. It was vital that he reach his village before those minions of de Landa did.

He had been performing missionary work among the Mayan Yucatek people for almost ten years. The conversion was nearly complete and his parishioners were now peaceful and happy and he meant to keep it that way. But the plunderers were bent on force and torture. Obviously de Landa had learned that Sebastian's parish church and those of the neighboring villages had kept many of the old codices of Mayan literature and that simply could not be allowed. De Landa had written much about the Maya culture and language, but he also believed that their culture, with its history of human sacrifice, had to be violently and totally obliterated. He had even been recalled to Spain to be tried for his level of cruelty that was preposterous even to the Spanish conquistadores. But he was exonerated, reinstated to New Spain, and allowed to resume his inquisitions.

Sabastian, winded and sore, managed to arrive at his village before de Landa's company. Stumbling to the nearest home of one of the town's elders he pounded on the door. Ekchauh, the wizened village chief, pulled the door ajar with a puzzled, and sleepy, visage. "Que?" he asked, proud to show Father Sebastian that he had learned a little Spanish.

Father Sabastian could hardly speak since he was gasping as if it were his last breath, but managed to blurt out, "They are coming! They are finally coming! Gather everyone with their most prized family heirlooms, but no more than they can carry on their backs, their horse or burro. But tell them to hurry. We must leave now!"

Having delivered this urgent message Sebastian rushed to the church's library to collect the books and codices and documents in the library. He loaded them on the backs of the horses and burros stabled behind the building and returned to the central plaza. The entire village was there, most still in their nightclothes. Men brandishing what weapons they could find on a moment's notice. No swords or crossbows, they were a peaceful farming village, but lots of pitchforks, cudgels and other farm implements. Women milling around with children clinging to their skirts or babes bundled in their arms. The elderly mounted on the backs of burros or wedged into small carts. Everyone was talking or shouting to be heard over the others. It was pandemonium. They needed to be calmed before panic set in.

Sebastian climbed onto the side of the central well and held onto a vertical beam to keep from falling. He motioned to Balam, one of the other elders, to quiet the crowd. He was recovering his breath and strength, but still could not produce his normal Sunday volume. "My children, we are in grave danger. The forces of de Landa, the forces of the Inquisition, are coming to our town. We must leave before they arrive for they bring nothing but ruin and sorrow. But there is hope, much hope. We will find a place away from here, away from these destroyers, where we will continue our peaceful lives. Where we can raise our crops and livestock. Where we can rear our children. There is such a place and we will find it. But for now we must make haste. Finish gathering only the necessities," he believed his books and codices were necessities, "and follow me to the coast. From there we can hire ships to take us to safety. Hurry! We must start!"

With that he plopped down from the well, once again wishing he wasn't quite so plump, and led his laden animals to the edge of the village and waited for everyone to fall in behind. It seemed like an eternity, but was just a few minutes before the entire village was ready. They followed Sebastian out of the village with their few possessions, horses, burros, carts, wagons, and some other livestock. They left the town without looking back, certain there would be no return.

Trekking through a jungle with several hundred people and their belongings was difficult. Rapid movement was not possible. Side paths and misdirection were the order of the day. Sebastian knew they had to leave the Yucatan, so he made for the coast. There were merchant ships there that could be hired to flee to one of the small, uninhabited Caribbean islands where they could take temporary refuge.

As he hoped, there were four caravels at the small port ready to return to Spain. They'd delivered supplies to the various colonies, but were destined to sail home with empty holds. The captains were eager to accept any sort of cargo, no matter the amount of the payment. Sebastian's villagers crowded on board with everything faster than the sailors expected and immediately set sail.

It seemed like no time before a lookout spotted the perfect location. A small island with a good cove. The ships anchored and offloaded everybody and everything. The crews even left four single-masted skiffs for the new colonists to sail back to the mainland, should they ever wish to do so. Sebastian, Ekchauh, Balam and Cuauc got busy organizing their new home after the caravels departed for Spain, with strict orders to never mention the new settlement to anyone. A significant bribe insured their silence.

Everyone in the colony immediately set about arranging their belongings and erecting shelter, both theirs and Sebastian's. The new village, as yet without a name, was taking shape so he decided to take this time to learn more about this new home, whether temporary or not, and set off exploring. Wandering into the center of the island he discovered something amazing, in a clearing about thirty feet across floated a glowing orb about three feet in diameter and four feet above the ground. It emitted a strange blue light and was surrounded by a faint golden aura and the air nearby resonated with a low, constant hum. The first image that came to his mind was the burning bush when God spoke to Moses in the wilderness. Was this God? But it didn't speak, it just hummed. Perhaps it was a manifestation of God's favor. Perhaps it wasn't. He fell to his knees, "Dear Lord, please let this be a sign of your blessing and protection for my humble villagers. Help me to understand what we are to do with this sign. Give me strength and guidance. I humbly ask."

He rose and began to walk around the sphere. Nothing different, nothing happened. So he crept closer. Still nothing. Closer yet. Now he felt hotter and heavier and he started to get very uncomfortable. It felt as if he was turning inside out.

In an instant and without any warning he was in a different place. He was further from the globe than he had been just seconds before. The trees were different, the clouds were fewer, and the ground beneath his feet had a different contour. The air even smelled different, fresher and somehow richer than before.

He looked up and once again fell to his knees. "Dear Mother of God, there are two moons in the daytime sky!" he exclaimed, crossing himself several times.

This was definitely someplace else. Confused, he rose and wondered around for half an hour or so and noticed he was on an island, just not the one he was on a previously. Scared and afraid he was alone he returned to the manifestation and approached it as before in a vain hope he'd be back to where he started. He felt he same awful sensations and then he was definitely back on the original island. The trees were the same as before, the ground was the same as before, and the air felt the same to his skin and nose. He could even hear the villagers in the distance. Wonder of wonders. What was this thing and what was it doing here? He then remembered that the gold cross he wore around his neck had started to vibrate and float toward the globe as he neared it. Yes! It was definitely an omen from God. That gave him an idea. He backed away and took off the chain holding the cross and wrapped it around a stick he found. He then held the stick in front of him and slowly approached again. This time it felt different. The stick seemed to vibrate gently, and the sensations of heat, heaviness and discomfort were not present. So far, so good. He kept cautiously approaching the object and all of a sudden he felt a tingling sensation over his entire body, not the discomfort of the first attempt. He looked around and discovered that he had returned to the different island. Bewildered, he approached again with stick and chain before him. He felt the same sensations and, lo and behold, he was back where he started. He tried it again. And again. He transported back and forth several times, each time exploring a little farther from the orb. This other island was definitely a different place from where the refugees were camped.

He sprinted back to the beach flush with excitement. "You must come see what I've found! You must see this! Come Balam, Cuauc, and Ekchauh! This is amazing!"

The three town elders looked at each other, puzzled. He grasped Balam's hand and led them up to the top of the island, which really wasn't very high. In the clearing they saw what he had seen. It was as he described, a glowing blue ball three feet or so across floating in the air. The ground under it was bare, but a few feet away the grass grew nearly knee high. The clearing was open to the sky, but surrounded by a dense copse of trees, almost a jungle.

All of them were beyond astonished. "Is it deviltry, father?" asked Balam.

Sebastian said, "No, I believe it is an omen from God. It takes me to another island, far from here, most likely not even our world. A place where we will be safe from the conquistadores. Watch, I will go to the other island and then come back." With that he circled the globe with his stick pointed at it as before and disappeared. The three elders were more than astonished, and a little afraid.

After a few seconds Sabastian reappeared right where he started. "It takes me to another island every time, the same place each time, and then returns me to this island. What if we moved the entire village to this other island? Wouldn't it be safer than staying here so close to the Spanish and Diego de Landa? "

Considerable persuasion on Sebastian's part was necessary, but finally the other three tried to visit the other island. They each tried to hold the stick with the gold chain wrapped around it, but did not travel to the other island. They just got very hot and nauseous and needed to retreat. Finally, Sebastian tried holding each of them by the hand, one at a time, and leading them. That worked. They returned to the original island more excited than they had been for years. With God's blessing safety seemed at hand.

A few days of experimentation taught Sebastian how to use the globe. Wrapping a gold, or silver, chain around a wooden rod seemed to focus the magic. Much to Sebastian's surprise a cross was not necessary, just a bit of gold or silver around a stick of wood. Since the glowing ball took them to the same new island each time, much like a door to a new beginning, they decided to call it a portal. As it turned out only a few of the people could use the portal but they could take others with them to the new island. If several of them worked together they could take larger items, even the boats. They could leave de Landa and the conquistadors behind. The decision was easy, they would go to this second world and take all they could with them. It required all the skill the adepts and their magic wands, as people started calling them, but in less than a day and a half everybody and everything was through.

A few of the adepts noticed something odd. If they brought something of considerable weight through to this second world the weather in both places would cloud up. If the object was large and heavy, such as a boat, a brief but intense rainstorm would ensue. It even seemed as if the portal briefly shrunk a bit in size when that happened.

When they brought this to Sebastian's attention he dismissed their concerns. "Don't bother me with your ridiculous worries. The portal is clearly a gift from God. Would you tell the Israelites not to eat the manna from heaven? Of course not. Would you have told the five thousand not to partake of the fish and bread from our lord Jesus? Of course not. This is the miracle we need to save our people. How dare you question His generosity! If you persist in alarming my people, I will tell you to leave. Take your foolish qualms elsewhere."

Supervising the shepherding of the villagers and the livestock and belongings and boats to the Second World, as he and the elders were calling it, wore him down and made him cross, tired and testy. His anger was not usual for him and the malcontents, as Sebastian started to call them, decided to obey his demand and leave before he turned the rest of the colonists against them. They struck out on their own in one of the boats and were not heard from again by the rest of the village.

That evening over their first full supper in Second World, Sabastian was meeting with Balam, Cuauc and Ekchauh. Cuauc asked, "What would happen if people we do not want here would find the portal? What if the Spanish find it, and find us? Do we want to risk such an unwelcome disruption to our lives here? What should we do?"

"That simply cannot happen. It must be sheltered and access to it must be restricted to ones we would welcome," said Ekchuah. "We need to call a gathering of the people to decide how to protect us and this land."

Sebastian thought this was an excellent idea. "I will tell everyone to meet tomorrow after supper to discuss our fears."

The next night, after a considerable discussion at the conclave of the people, Sebastian came up with an idea. An order of protectors made of the people who were most adept at going back and forth between the worlds would be formed. Only they and those who they approved would be allowed to cross between worlds. In addition, during the jumps to their new home they discovered that if they excavated around a portal and then dug under, it would settle into the hole. Construction over First World's blue globe's pit would shield it from view. The protectors would guard the portals and limit contact between the two. It was settled, the Order of the Portal would protect their secret and their new secure lives could begin.

The next morning Father Sebastian stood on the beach and viewed his flock busy at work settling in their temporary quarters. He was pleased. As it turned out the island was not large enough to support the entire village so they'd need to use the skiffs to find a more suitable permanent home, but that would come. He would serve as the moral compass for the congregation and he and his successors would lead them and their descendants for many years to come.

Until one day a new king would put his plan for fame and glory into effect.

CHAPTER ONE
BIANCA'S DAY

Capital City, kingdom of Vlogentia, Bianca's room
Gregorian calendar: January 1
Mayan calendars: Tzolk'in: 9 Ik'
              Haab: 15 K'ank'in
The ninth Calendar Round since the founding of the kingdom of Vlogentia

B ianca knew this would be a great day. Not like the day before when she had noticed men following her as she made her way through the city. Not always the same man but there was continually someone behind her the entire day. She was, as always, armed with her dagger but the constant surveillance made her so apprehensive that she cut short her visits, retreated to her room and secured the door for the rest of the day and night.

"But today will be different. I will not allow my silly fears to spoil this day," she told herself. It was the Church's New Year festival day, the first for the new king, the Tzolk'in day for positive outcomes, and the day her team would play pitz in the grand ballcourt. It was going to be the perfect experience for a young girl such as herself to play the sport she loved with her friends.

Heady anticipation kept her from a restful sleep so she rolled out of her hammock well before dawn, threw on a night robe and raced down the stairs to the dining room. In her hurry she left off her shoes, she ran barefoot and didn't even care. Much to her surprise her stepmother and stepbrother were already sitting at the ornate wood table eating corn porridge, called 'atole' with a side of fresh fruit. It was one of Bianca's favorite morning meals.

She danced to the foot of the table and greeted the two of them, "Good morning and a fortunate blend of days to both of you." She nodded a greeting to the cook, who returned a brief curtsy.

All she got back was an insincere and mumbled reply from her stepbrother, "Nice days to you."

"And if it isn't Bianca the Bizarre. So nice of you to join us," from her stepmother.

She was used to the insult. She hardly heard it anymore. "Well I do think this is going to be a great day. I am so looking forward to the game this afternoon. I can't believe we get to play in the Grand Ballcourt. Are you coming?"

"No, we have other, more important for us, festivities to attend."

Bianca was determined to maintain her positive attitude despite her family's even more disconcerting behavior this morning than usual. Normally they didn't care what Bianca was going to do that day, or any day for that matter. Her stepmother, Andrea, devoted her time and devotion toward her son, Bianca's stepbrother, and that seemed fine. Andrea had allowed Bianca to continue the studies started by her real mother, she let Bianca traipse through the capital city at leisure, and she didn't push Bianca into very many of her numerous social functions, which was just the way Bianca liked it.

But Andrea was even more condescending and dismissive than usual. Bianca decided that she wasn't going to let Andrea ruin her day. The negative atmosphere destroyed her appetite however.

"I don't think I want breakfast today," Bianca declared, "after class I want to visit the city and enjoy the New Year festival and then go to the ballcourt."

"Do whatever you want," said Andrea, "what you do today won't matter... will it dear?" The latter comment addressed to her son. She barely glanced at Bianca.

"I thought you would be interested in our game today, after all we are representing the city. Our team doesn't usually get such a great opportunity."

"Not really, you just go play your game and we'll take care of our affairs." Andrea was now focusing entirely on her son, who had a very self-satisfied smirk on his face.

Bianca had never liked her step-brother, he was too self-centered and spoiled. When he did deign to speak to her he used the most condescending tone, as if she had no intellect. And on the rare occasions he would forcibly grab her arm to 'guide' her she would feel a cold shudder of revulsion. He had not always been like this. At first he had tried to be friendly in his own conceited way, but after a while he quit trying and grew brusque, distant and obnoxious. They now mostly went their separate ways, but today he acted even more haughty than usual.

"Fine, I'm going for a walk along the shoreline and then attend class. Have a wonderful day." Even Andrea noticed her sarcasm. Bianca spun on her heels and stomped out of the room.

No matter, an early morning stroll would calm her frustration. She would attend class, wander the festival in the city and then go to the grand ballcourt to play pitz. The cool damp ground felt good to her feet. The sky was clear, the storm of two days previously was long gone and left only a stiff west breeze in its wake. The three-quarter Haab moon was high in the sky and the full Tzolk'in moon was starting to set into the western sea. She made her way to the pavement along the shore of the inland sea, the breeze blowing her hair to her side.

The walkway this early was devoid of others, except for one man wearing a maroon hooded cloak standing near where she entered the paved walkway running parallel to the shore. It had a low brick wall on the seaward side.

"A pleasant blend of days to you," as she passed.

He merely grunted in return.

"*How rude*," she thought as she continued along the path. The lanterns illuminating the pavement that were filled with giant fireflies were beginning to fade as the insects started to go dormant for the day. She continued along the path relishing the scent of fresh air and paid the stranger no further notice.

A few yards farther along the route she saw one of the royal guard standing by the retaining wall looking out over the waves. She hoped, in fact she had planned, that he was Juan Alejandro, her closest childhood friend and boyfriend. He wasn't. He was Enrico, a close friend of Juan Alejandro's. But she stopped to talk anyway.

The guard noticed her and turned to greet her. As he did so he spied the stranger rapidly closing in on Bianca.

"You, what are you doing? Get away from her!"

Bianca turned and saw the man halt in mid stride, do an about face and hurry away. As he left he threw over his shoulder, "I was just walking along the path. I meant no harm."

"Well, that's settled. Good morning and a fortunate blend of Tzolk'in and Haab days to you." Said Enrico to Bianca with an elaborate bow to his friend's devotee.

"*So formal*," she thought to herself. "And a lucky blend of days to you, Enrico," she replied. "Thank you for chasing him away. I had enough of stalkers yesterday. What do you think he was up to?"

"I have no idea, he just looked suspicious. Perhaps he meant what he said."

"I suppose you're right. I'd feel bad if we chased away an innocent early-morning stroll." She paused for a second and looked out over the sea. "By the way, why were you staring so intently at the waves? They seem quite calm to me."

"Look closer. There are merpeople swimming beyond the breakers. We've had to issue a warning to the sailors tied up in port. Don't want anybody disappearing due to lack of caution."

Bianca now noticed the people of the deep traversing the waters. She saw their long, brownish-grey hair trail behind them in the light of the two moons as they dove under the waves, followed by a splash of their flukes. "Why are they here? They never get this close to the city. I thought they always stayed near the boundary isles of the inland sea."

"The recent unusual series of storms coming from the portal isle must have forced them close to our shores," replied Enrico. "Hopefully they'll retreat to their usual haunts in a day or so. Until then we've been detailed to keep a close lookout for them. We don't want any difficulties from them, especially today."

"Certainly not. The less trouble from them the better. What do you know about the storms? Are they truly originating from the portal isle? And why?"

"Well, that's the rumor. The why is a mystery to everyone I know. That's all I can say. It does seem suspicious though."

This wasn't turning out to be the pleasant pre-dawn tryst she'd anticipated. She had anticipated Juan would be on duty and they'd be able to spend some private time together. Unfortunately that was not to be. "Why isn't Juan Alejandro here this morning? I thought this was to be his duty station."

"He traded duties with me so he would be free later this morning. He said he'd meet you after your class and attend the festival with you before the game."

That was very good news. So she bade farewell to Enrico and continued along the walkway for a while still enjoying the warm breeze and the brilliant starlit sky filled with the two moons. After a while the sun started to rise beyond the kulkulcanland mountains far to the east as the Tzolk'in moon set in the west. She turned and hurried back to her room and dressed in her festival finery for the day.

On her way out of the room she checked her appearance in her full length mirror. The dress was her pride and joy, off-white with elaborate embroidery she had sewn along the hemline, neckline and sleeve cuffs. A blue sash was wrapped around her waist. The worst problem was her hair. It wasn't the dark brown or black of everyone else in the kingdom. It was white, the pure white of a frothy summer cloud, it hung down to her waist. It looked like the hair of a wise elder, not the hair of a twenty year old girl. It was the first thing anyone noticed about her. She tried to not let its lack of color bother her, the way she ignored her stepmother's insults, but that was almost impossible. She sighed in resignation, tied it in the back with a bow and put a sprig of fresh flowers above her left ear. "*That's the best I can do,*" she told herself.

She took one last look in the mirror, straightened her dress and hurried to the academy for her history class. She got there a little late, as usual, and tried to sneak in before Father Adames noticed. No chance. "Glad you could make it," he said. The other girls in the class merely nodded politely as she entered.

She took her seat next to Renata, one of her pitz teammates, as the teacher continued his lecture about the history of Vlogentia and Saint Sebastian, the founder and namesake of the kingdom.

"Are you excited?" she whispered to Renata.

"Of course I am. I can't wait," she whispered back.

"Ladies, please, pay attention. Now, who can tell me how we came to this great kingdom?" he asked.

Bianca raised her hand, but Father Adames chose Renata instead. Punishment for being late.

Renata sputtered for a few seconds. She seldom got to answer questions about history, probably because she seldom had the correct answer. Her strength was in arithmetic, especially with the Mayan system of base twenty numeration.

"I think Saint Sebastian sent out expeditions once our ancestors arrived on the portal isle. One of them found this land on the coast of the inland sea. It took a while to ferry everyone and everything here, but they made it. They were so grateful for their deliverance from the persecutions of de Landa and for Saint Sebastian's leadership that they decided to name our realm after his second given name. So we call our kingdom 'Vlogentia.'" She bounced up and down in her seat and giggled. This time she had the correct answer.

"Very good, but you left out that it took several months, not just a while. They had to construct a larger boat to ferry everything here." He liked precision, and he liked correcting students. "And what about the other nations on Second World?"

This time he let Bianca answer.

"Once the Order of the Portal was founded they restricted and monitored access to Second World to keep out those like the conquistadores. But occasionally they'd allow other persecuted groups to settle here. So we have refugees from the African slave trade, some English who fled from the religious strive of home, some poorer Spanish just wanting a better life, a small flotilla of Japanese fleeing the Tokagawa regime that somehow miraculously made it around Africa and into the Caribbean Sea of First World and some recent arrivals, the Chinese, fleeing from indentured servitude in the Americas."

Father Adames said nothing but merely nodded. She was right and he obviously missed having a chance to correct someone. He started to lecture on another topic, but Bianca raised her hand so insistently that he had to acknowledge her. "What is it, Bianca?"

"Father, what about the recent spate of storms that seem to originate from the portal isle? Is there trouble with the portal? What would that mean for us in Second World?"

"We have no information from the Order of the Portal that there is anything amiss with the portal, or anything unusual on or near the island. The storms are merely a coincidence. There is no danger to us. Stop worrying about them and please don't spread rumors. The populace doesn't need that."

"But there are already rumors flying through the city."

"As I said, don't worry. The Church and the Order will calm everyone."

"Yes, father." Bianca, unsettled due to her conversation with Enrico, was less than mollified. But she decided further argument with Father Adames was fruitless.

He continued with his lesson plan and the class went on for another hour or so before he felt satisfied and dismissed them.

Renata called to Bianca as they left the academy and went their separate ways. "I'll see you later, at the ballcourt. I'm going to see my family. If you see him say hello to Juan Alejandro for me. Don't be late."

Bianca turned from waving to Renata and almost ran into her boyfriend.

"Juan, a very blessed pairing of days. I'm so glad to see you. I missed you this morning but Enrico told me you'd meet me here. Let's go, there's so much to see and do today. Will you be at the pitz game this afternoon?"

"And a great twosome of days to you. Of course I will. Nothing could make me miss watching my favorite pitz player. But I won't be able to see you afterwards. I'll be on duty then, that's the deal I made with Enrico. So let's make the most of what day we have. Right now I'm hungry. If you are too, let's get something to eat and then roam the festival."

This was the festival of the Christian New Year. The sun was bright and clear. The city was alive with residents and visitors alike. Color was everywhere. It almost seemed as if a rainbow had fallen from the sky and settled like a blanket over the entire city. People were dressed in their finery and the sound was a multitude of voices blended together into a festive symphony. Somewhere in the distance a band was playing a song that carried over the crowd.

"After we get something to eat, I want to go dancing," she told Juan.

He nodded agreement.

They wandered up and down the main causeway through the city taking in the sights. They had to wend their way through the crowd, often bumping into others with a quick "sorry". Occasionally, an out of town visitor would stop to stare at her. The locals who knew her simply nodded a greeting, sometimes with a slight bow of greeting. She and they were used to her different appearance, and the sights along the avenue were so splendid the occasional reaction didn't bother her as much as usual.

"Isn't this wonderful?" she asked. "The two of us enjoying all this."

"I wouldn't want to be anywhere else."

The roadway was lined with the usual shops adorned with bright and multicolored decoration. All of them had their doors open with the owners out front hawking their wares or food. Often the décor included a three to four foot tall replica stele with Mayan glyphs on it to commemorate their heritage that long predated the arrival of the Spanish. Bianca had never done well learning how to read or draw the old glyphs in class, so she had resorted to asking one of the priests who had spent many years studying the old glyphs what the steles said. He told her that they were mostly gibberish, just meant to look authentic.

The smell of food cooking from numerous eateries permeated the air. Since she'd missed breakfast Bianca thought her stomach wondered if her throat had been cut. It seemed to her that Juan had forgotten his initial suggestion. She was starving.

"Let's stop here," she said as she pulled Juan's arm toward her favorite café, Joaquin's.

He offered only token resistance to her touch. Joaquin boasted that he had the best chicken in the city. Bianca suspected that sometimes the 'chicken' was really iguana, but she had yet to grow a long, spiny tail. So they bought two tamales apiece and a slice of honey-flavored corn cake to share. They each had a cup of hot chocolate. Juan's was spiced with chili peppers and Bianca's was flavored with vanilla. Juan made sure her cup had been poured back and forth several times so that it had a lot of foam on its top.

"See," he said, "now there's proof you're a good person."

"Thank you, so are you."

While they were waiting for their food, one of the crowd cautiously edged next to Juan. His face was a picture of worry and concern. His brows were raised, pupils dilated and his lips quivered. He wrung his hands like they were on fire. His voice wavered, in trepidation or anger Bianca could not tell.

"Excuse me, sir guardsman, and madam, but can either of you tell me what the king is planning? Our taxes are increasing every Haab month, conflicting edicts are issued from the palace daily and there is talk of raising an army. Why?"

Numerous others who were standing nearby nodded agreement.

Someone else chimed in, "What is the Duke of Ki'pan up to? Where is the king? We never see or hear him. Why is he hiding?"

Another added, "What about all the storms from the sea lately?" The anxiety in the peoples' faces and in their nervous comportment was clear.

Bianca was proud of Juan as he took a second to steady himself.

He made his voice as calm and steady as possible. In truth, Bianca knew he shared their concerns. "I am just a corporal in the Royal Guard. The king and his advisors haven't bothered to tell me their plans. I can't speak for their actions. As for the storms, as far as I know they're just an unusual circumstance. Please, the lady and I are here to relish the festival as are all of you. I'm sure all will be fine. Now, go and enjoy the day."

The people started to disperse, their demeanors showing a lack of satisfaction. As they turned Bianca heard one of the mumble, "I think the king is afraid of facing his populace. I think he's such a coward that his shadow is afraid of the dark." She didn't know which one said it, and didn't want to know.

She was glad Juan had taken the lead in responding to the crowd's questions. When politics or the king entered a conversation, she preferred to say nothing and keep her thoughts to herself.

They gathered their food and hurried along the avenue, not wishing to be confronted again. Juan was quiet in thought. Bianca was busy searching for the festive band so she could go dancing and cheer him up. The music came from somewhere nearby but she was never able to locate it.

They continued their exploration of the festival. Juan was looking around and listening to the crowd's chatter and apparently trying to assess their level of disquiet. He turned to Bianca and said, "There seems to be a man following us. He seems unremarkable, average height and build, dark hair of course, and wearing a maroon cloak. Have you noticed him as well?"

"Not today. But I thought some men were following me yesterday," she said, "but after I got back to my room and slept on it I finally decided my imagination was getting the best of me. It's odd that you mention the cloak. I saw a man wearing a cloak like that this morning when I was going for an early morning stroll to meet you, but he turned and went the other way when I met Enrico, who told me of your trade of duty assignments. I like our get-together today almost as much as this morning would have been." She smiled at him. "But, cloaks like that are quite common, so don't think anything about it."

"If you think so, then I suppose we're alright."

After they finished their quick snack and stroll through the festival they headed toward the city center where the grand cathedral, ballcourt, palace, and government buildings were located. Along the way the mysterious follower disappeared.

She wished she could stop and admire the various stores and homes along the way but the day was progressing and she risked being late for her game. They had to pick up the pace.

They passed buildings that had brightly painted red, blue and yellow stucco walls with tile roofs for the well-to-do merchants and artisans, usually with two stories, and thatched roof single story homes for the less rich. But it was all so bright and cheerful.

"Do you ever get tired of patrolling such a beautiful city?" She asked.

"After a while it all starts to look commonplace, especially at night. But I like my duty and being a corporal of the Royal Guard is quite the honor. But perhaps someday I can get promoted, all the way to lieutenant even. Wouldn't that be great?" He puffed out his chest at the thought.

"I like you the way you are."

The streets here were paved with brick, although the outer sections of town had cobblestone pavement, and sometimes just well-packed dirt. The city center had a low wall around it, not to keep people out since it was only about three feet high and had numerous gateways. It was there to mark the center as the ceremonial heart of the capital. In ancient times the city center was where the Maya built enormous pyramids to honor the pagan gods, but now there were no pyramids. In their place were the National Cathedral and Grand Ballcourt placed beyond the center's front wall and between them a grand plaza for ceremonies and processions.

The National Cathedral was full of congregants celebrating the solemnity of Mary, the Mother of God. You could hear the singing of the hymns across the city center. After the mass the local Mayan shamans would bless supplicants with their charms and rituals for luck and health. This mix of practices had been a tradition of Mayan/Spanish culture since before coming to Second World. After the Catholic mass and the Mayan rites in front of the house of worship the focus of the day would shift to the ballcourt and the holiday games.

Finally Bianca and Juan arrived at the ballcourt. He said, "I'm sorry we never found the band playing dance music. Some other time. But I'll be in the stands watching you today. Best of luck. As I said, I won't be able to see you after the game but plan on getting together tomorrow."

"Until tomorrow then." She squeezed his arm as he left.

Renata, as promised, was waiting outside the door in the side of the grandstand that led to their changing room. Standing with her was Julieta, the team captain. Daniela, the other teammate, was engaged in what appeared to Bianca as an intense conversation about twenty feet away. Lots of hand waving and pointing of fingers but not loud enough to overhear what the argument was about. The man was wearing a maroon hooded cloak that looked similar to the one worn by the stranger she passed on the walkway this morning as well as the man Juan had noticed in the festival. *What an odd coincidence,"* she thought. *"That design of cloak must be more common than I realized."* Finally the discussion ended, the man stalked away and Daniela hurried to the changing room's entrance.

"Are you alright?" asked Bianca. "Is he trying to meddle in our game. If so, we need to inform the guardsmen."

"No, it's nothing like that. Our game is fine. Just a family matter. Let it go." Daniela shrugged her shoulders and entered the changing room. Bianca decided to let it go, for now.

"Are we ready? This is going to be our big moment. I've been told the king's representatives and Vice Pope will be in attendance with the senior cardinals and many of the cathedral's priests." Julieta, the team captain, was almost literally jumping up and down with excitement.

"Don't get too excited," said Renata, "we still have to play a game."

"Yes, and most of the priests are there to make sure there isn't any gambling on the outcome, not to watch us," added Bianca. "There won't be many silver or copper coins changing hands today, although you might see some cocoa beans being given from one friend to another." They all knew that cocoa beans were the traditional currency prior to the Spanish arrival some four hundred years ago.

The three followed Daniela through the elaborately decorated door into the changing room where they changed into game gear from their festival dresses, white knee-length frocks with colorful embroidery around the neck, sleeves, and hem. The game could be hazardous and they needed to wear the kneepads, elbow pads, gaily decorated leather helmets with parrot feathers dyed with their team colors, and the heavy belt to guard their midriffs. Underneath the gear they wore simple unadorned frocks that went down to their knees. The festival garb would not survive the rough and tumble game of pitz. They were barefoot. The girls were eager to get the game started, although Bianca noticed that Daniela was unusually quiet and avoided looking at her.

"Are you sure you're alright?" She asked Daniela. "Is that argument still troubling you? Or are you as nervous as the rest of us? No need to be too jumpy, the other team will be just as anxious as we are."

"No, I told you I'm alright. Don't mind me." She turned quickly away, as if embarrassed.

The tone in Daniela's answer still didn't sound right. Something was amiss, but there wasn't time to address the issue.

The trumpet sounded to call the teams to the court. The blue and silver entered from their end of the court, the green and silver of Xantich from the other. The spectacle was amazing. The bleachers along both sides of the court were full, a crowd of several thousand at least. Many of them wore the blue and silver in support of Bianca's team. A large contingent at the far end of the seats wore green and silver, and gave a raucous cheer when the Xantich team entered. The blue and silver fans responded with an even louder cheer.

The veranda was crowded with the Vice Pope and his cardinals. Seated next to him was the king's representative the Duke of Ki'pan, looking very official and impressed with his importance. Situated in front of and below them were the city officials and the wealthy elite.

Bianca felt short of breath and her knees started to shake. They usually played on the smaller ballcourts around the city against local teams with much fewer spectators. This was definitely a big deal.

Before the game could start the Vice Pope, the man who represented the true Pope situated in the Rome of First World stood and offered a benediction. He was magnificent with the tall, conical mitre of white with gold filigree. His cassock was white but the stole draped over his shoulders was golden with golden embroidery. All agreed that his voice was melodious and could carry to the far reaches of the stadium. Mercifully, his prayer was short. He gave the signal for the game to begin.

The game official stood on a platform in front of the dignitaries at the edge of the spectator stands in line with the three foot tall post in the center of the playing area. The teams stood behind their identical markers a quarter of the way toward their end of the field. The ball, a rubber ball about twenty four inches in circumference and hollow, a recent change to make the ball bounce more and hurt less when it hit someone in an unprotected part of the body, was tossed into the air, the ceremonial conch shell was sounded, and the two teams rushed at each other.

The game and rules were fairly simple. To score a point a team had to propel the ball beyond the other's end line. The ball had to cross the goal line in the air, a rolling ball required a restart. Or, a team could score a point if they got the ball to bounce more than once off the surface of the playing area on the other team's half. If, however, a team hit the ball through one of the masonry hoops on the walls, they scored seven points. In the old days that score actually ended the game. In actual fact that became the sole focus of the teams and the game would degenerate into a melee at one of the rings with both teams just standing there, bouncing the ball endlessly trying to put an end to the contest. So, the rules were recently changed to encourage a more open, back and forth style of play. The trick was that hands, forearms, feet and shins and heads were not allowed to hit the ball. A player could use shoulders, knees, hips and midriffs to keep the ball in the air passing it back and forth until they found a way to bounce it where the other team couldn't reach it or just smash it beyond the end line. A really good team could keep the ball in the air, passing it back and forth for a long time until they could score or lose possession of the ball. An hour was not unusual. Anytime a point was scored, or a foul hit was declared by the official the conch shell would sound and a restart was needed. The first team to score the necessary points won the game.

Today's game for Bianca's team would be to fifteen points. Their game was the precursor for the men's game, which would be to twenty one points. Bianca's team were all amateurs, but the men, as were most men's teams, were professional players supported by wealthy patrons.

The first player to get to the ball was a Xantich. She caught it on the upswing from the bounce and bellied it toward one of her teammates sprinting down their left side. Daniela got to the ball first and directed it with her shoulder back toward the center. Renata bounced it far off of her hip, and Julieta smashed it with her knee and it flew toward the Xantich end line. One bounce past the goal and a point for Vlogentia.

"That was wonderful, Julieta," shouted Bianca "Let's do it again!"

The next restart resulted in Renata getting to the ball first and she bounced it off her belt toward Daniela, but she missed and the ball bounced in the blue and silver half of the field. Just before it could bounce a second time, Bianca slid under it and propelled it off her stomach into the air. The Xantich forward got to it first and directed it off her shoulder into the ground and toward the Vlogentia line.

One more bounce and a point would be scored either for a second bounce or by passing the endline. Bianca got up and raced, side by side, with her opponent. They both arrived at the same time with a resulting massive collision, which is actually not common in pitz since passing the ball to a teammate trying to score is the objective. They fell in a heap as the ball hit one of them on the foot before reaching the ground.

A foul and restart was declared by the official.

As they got up the forward said, "Let's not do that again. That hurt."

Bianca nodded in agreement. She was already hot and sweaty and out of breath.

The game continued. Both teams were evenly matched, but Daniela seemed distracted and not up to her usual level of play. She rarely would even look at Bianca, much less pass the ball to her. She spent considerable time looking into the crowd for some reason.

Bianca tried to follow her gaze to see what so preoccupied her. Nothing or nobody stood out.

Daniela even made several egregious mistakes allowing Xantich to score points. That was not at all like her.

Back and forth. The score was twelve to nine favor of Xantich. Bianca hadn't done too much lately since her role was as a defender. She constantly intercepted balls directed toward her end line and propelled it back toward the center, usually toward Julieta, the forward. It was not as glamorous as being a forward, but Bianca had an inner sense of accomplishment whenever she prevented a ball from scoring against them.

But a fortuitous bounce at her end of the field allowed her to shoulder the ball high before a second contact with the ground, and use a second bounce off her hip to propel the ball toward the left ring. A surge of excitement filled her. She saw a free path to the ring and charged forward, her heart racing as she neared. The ball hit the wall, missed, and bounced off the side of the ring and back. A Xantich player coming from the opposite direction tried to direct it toward her forward, but Bianca got there first, cut her off, and jumped as high as she could and hit it again with her shoulder. The ball ricocheted through the ring.

Seven points. Victory!

It had been a good game until the surprising ending and even the Xantich followers were not excessively disappointed. Both sets of fans gave their side a roar of approval, but the Vlogentia supports were again the loudest.

"This is the greatest day ever!" Julieta was this time literally jumping for joy. So was most of the crowd.

"Just a little bit of exaggeration, don't you think?" Bianca asked. She was just as excited but her normal reticence exerted itself. Now she just wanted out of the court and away from the throng.

"Yes, this is great! Now let's go make the other team sacrifice!" Renata was getting into the spirit. "Fortunately for them, all we make them sacrifice now is their purses, they have to buy us a meal."

In the days before the Spanish arrival human sacrifice of some players was occasionally practiced. Because of the ministry of Saint Sebastian Vlogentia were a Catholic people now, such things were unthinkable.

The captain of the Xantich team approached them. "Good game, but you got lucky at the end."

"Perhaps so, but it counts. What about our food?" Bianca felt like she was starving again, having missed breakfast and barely eaten lunch. She wanted to prod the Xantich team into fulfilling their obligation.

"My farther found a really nice eatery today before the game. Its run by a fellow named Joaquin and the food is really good. Let's go, I don't feel like standing here waiting for the men's game to start."

Julieta, Renata and Daniela all had a silent moan. They knew Joaquin's reputation for his chicken. Bianca was elated, she liked the café. But the offer was genuine, so after changing back into their festive garb, off both teams went. Bianca wanted to talk to Daniela about her unusual attitude today, but Julieta had gotten to her first and berated her severely.

"What's wrong with you? You could have cost us the game. Are you alright?"

Daniela looked away and replied, "I'm just fine. Let's go eat."

Once at Joaquin's, he greeted the eight of them like he was meeting his long lost rich uncle for the first time. "Welcome to our visitors, and welcome to the blue and silver. We can prepare for you a feast worthy of your exploits this fine day." Bianca suspected he had quite a few more cocoa beans than he had this morning. They would prove useful for the café.

He led them inside and put together three tables to make one large table. He gave each of them a cup of hot chocolate and asked what they wanted to eat. The Xantich team all ordered the chicken, Bianca's team all ordered poc chuc, a grilled pork dish on a tortilla with lettuce, tomatoes, avocado, onions, cilantro and marinated in a fruit juice.

The usual small talk about the flow of the day's game and pitz in general. Then the discussion gravitated to more weighty topics.

One of the Xantich girls wanted to know, "What is the new king up to? My father said he heard locals talking that the king is preparing the royal guard for battle. Why would he do that? Just who are our enemies? Why does the Duke of Ki'pan need a mercenary company? What is going on?"

Julieta, Daniela, and Renata all looked at Bianca. She knew that they were aware of her political leanings, or rather lack thereof, and were obviously curious about her response, if she would even offer one.

"I'm afraid I don't know and I really have no interest in knowing. The affairs of the king and his entourage really don't interest me. I like my studies, I especially like my friends," with a nod and smile toward her teammates, "and I like playing pitz. We do know that the Duke of Ki'pan is the king's uncle so we have to assume they are working together to some end. What that might be is their business, not mine."

The rest of the team nodded in agreement, even Daniela despite her still obvious level of distraction.

After dinner, the group separated and went to their various homes or inns for the night. All that is except Daniela, who pulled Bianca aside as everyone was leaving.

"Would you walk with me for a while? I need to tell you something, and it's important."

"Couldn't it wait until tomorrow? We need to have a long talk about what's bothering you."

"Oh, no. We have to talk now."

"Very well, lead the way." Perhaps now Daniela would relate what had been bothering her all day.

She led Bianca across the main road, now nearly empty as night was falling. Through a side street to yet another lane leading from the port. As they reached the road Bianca saw a carriage pulled by four horses coming toward them. The carriage carried unfamiliar livery. It was white, not recently washed, with red and gold trim.

"What is so important? What's going on?" asked Bianca.

"I'm so sorry Bianca, I really like you. We all like you. You are a real friend. But he said he'd harm my family if I didn't help him."

"What are you going on about? Make sense Daniela!"

"I'm sorry"

That instant Bianca noticed that the carriage had stopped alongside them, there were three people inside, two of whom appeared foreign. The two foot-men got down from the back and shoved a kerchief in her face. She started to fight back using the skills she'd been taught. At least one of the assailants received a broken nose. But the kerchief had a very strange odor.

Then, all went black.

CHAPTER TWO

JASON'S AND MARGARET'S DAY

Miami, Florida, Jason and Margaret Blankenships' home
Gregorian calander: December 28
Mayan calendars: Tzolk'in: 5 Etz'nab'
               Haab: 11 K'ank'in

J ason Blankenship knew this was going to be a good day. He and his wife, Margaret, were finally going to meet Xander, the venture financier that had been courting them. They were far too excited to sleep, so they rose well before dawn, threw on their traveling outfits, packed their luggage and raced out of the house. They didn't even take time for their usual breakfast. They tossed down a croissant, some orange juice and a banana on their way out the door.

They were dressed alike and their appearance made some who didn't know them think they were brother and sister. They were both about five feet nine inches in height, slender but with an athletic build, due to many hours in the gym, with black hair, dark brown eyes and tanned complexions. Jason had the current trendy hair style for the young urban professional. Margaret's hair was cut just above her shoulders. They were wearing identical brightly colored Caribbean shirts, sunglasses perched atop their heads, matching shorts and sandals. They had the appearance of a well-to-do young couple on their way to a Caribbean party cruise.

The sky was crystal clear, last night's rain was gone, leaving small puddles on the walkway as they splashed their way to the curb like two youngsters going out to play. The moon was just past new and not visible in the early predawn sky allowing the stars to shine like millions of fireflies in the heavens. They got in the cab they'd ordered for the ride to the airport.

As she settled into her seat next to Jason Margaret asked, "Are you sure about this? What do you know about this Xander fellow? I know you're excited about this trip, a professional opportunity and experience for you, but for me it's just a well-earned vacation. Is this something we should do?"

"Yes, by all means," replied Jason. "Last month when Xander contacted me by telephone, he said that he had a proposal, a lucrative one, for me. He had hired a headhunter firm and they recommended me for a problem his people are having on a small island in the Caribbean. They're desperately in need of someone who can design a medicine to alleviate some sort of an ongoing stomach ailment. He said he was very impressed with my resume and that I was the perfect person for the job."

"But, are you sure this is legit? Where is this island and why haven't we heard of it?" asked Margaret.

"He said it was a small isle in the Caribbean. Too small to be noticed except by the inhabitants. It's not even on the cruise lines' itineraries. And he is willing to pay very handsomely. He even said you were welcome to tag along as a guest. In fact, he insisted you accompany me. You get to have your much needed respite from your law practice while I finally get to do some good outside the laboratory and get paid as well."

"I hope you're right. You did go over the proposal with a fine toothed comb, I hope? Did you do a check on this guy? You're right about one thing though. I am looking forward to a nice beach for a week or so. Contract law is tedious, I do need this vacation."

"He checked out and the proposal looks straightforward to me, the details all appear correct. We will have a grand time and be home in a couple of weeks. Plenty of time to recuperate from our adventure before we have to go back to work. Relax, it'll be a blast for you. Just don't drink too many island cocktails with little parasols in them."

Jason had been eager to start his own company, determined to hit the "big time." The sooner the better. Jason would be the "brains" of the operation, designing new and effective medicines and lotions, and he'd have Margaret's expertise for the legal and financial side of the firm.

"Xander's proposal sounds almost too good to be true," Margaret said, then shrugged. "But it is an opportunity to start our own business. And to be on a remote island sounds like a great place for my vacation!" She sat back in her seat, a smile playing on her lips.

Jason fidgeted the entire ride. He was too excited to sit still.

The cab left them off outside the airline check in. Airport security was the usual drudgery, but finally they boarded their plane. The flight to Key West was short, but felt like an eternity. From that airport they took another cab to the marina to meet Xander. They exited the cab and got their suitcases out of the back and started to walk along the dock toward the slip number they'd been given. The island could not be far since he had informed them that they were taking a small boat to it.

Xander met them at the slip. He looked nothing like them. He was a little shorter but thin and weathered. He appeared to be a very tough fifty years old. His hair was very dark brown and his eyes deep brown as well. He wore a crisp white shirt with tan trousers and what looked like leather shoes. He wore no sunglasses.

The boat in question, a fifty-five foot vessel named the *Vlogentia* waited for them. The boat, or ship, they really weren't sure what to call it, looked more or less seaworthy. It was an inboard cabin cruiser with light blue and silver trim, a covered lounge area amidships, what appeared to be a cabin forward in the hull and an open aft deck. Nothing seemed wrong, but it didn't look as clean and shiny as Jason expected, especially considering the pay he'd been offered.

"Don't worry," said Xander with a wry grin, "she is as seaworthy as you could possibly want. Come aboard and settle in the forward cabin while we get underway. But first, meet my crew: Santiago and Pablo."

They boarded the boat and unpacked their suitcases in the cabin's minuscule closet. There were small nightstands either side of the bed, and what they hoped was a typical marine bathroom. The bed was larger than he expected and the woodwork and furnishings actually appeared quite lavish. So, he and his wife settled in while the boat got underway.

The travel was surprising smooth. Seas were calm, the sky was bright blue and the wind was fresh and gentle and from the west. The *Vlogentia* made good time to wherever they were headed. The trip seemed relaxing to Jason, but he felt bad for his wife. She spent the entire time perched on the edge of the bed, gripping it with her hands and making sure there was a clear path to the commode. She appeared much paler than usual At least she had yet to rush to the commode or the side rail of the boat.

After a while Jason got bored and went up the stairs to the main cabin to look around. It had a very small kitchenette and a lounging area. Forward of that was the inside bridge.

Xander sat there steering the boat. Nothing seemed out of the ordinary so Jason went out to the rear, open, deck and approached one of the crew, he couldn't remember if it was Santiago or Pablo, and asked, "What is the significance of the boat's name?"

The crewman just looked at Jason with a puzzled look. He was big, burly with the copper/bronze complexion of the Caribbean or Central America. He looked more like a stevedore than a sailor. He said something in a language unfamiliar to Jason. It certainly wasn't Spanish or French or Creole or any language Jason had heard before.

Puzzled, Jason backtracked to Xander at the interior helm. "What is the significance of this boat's name, and what language is the crew speaking?"

"Vlogentia is the name of our destination. The language is Yucatek, a Mayan dialect." Xander replied. He started to fidget with the throttle, he appeared quite nervous.

"Wait a minute. I thought we were going to an island in the Caribbean. I have never heard of Mayan being spoken on the islands. I'm not even sure it's spoken on the mainland"

"Oh, I assure you Mayan dialects are common in many places in what you call Mexico and Guatemala. But we will be arriving at our island destination shortly. Please stay below until then." Xander appeared very nervous now, and he motioned to one of the crew to approach them.

Jason took the hint. Santiago or Pablo or whatever his name really was appeared quite capable of making sure there would be no trouble. He went below and told Margaret what he'd learned. He added, "I not sure we've made a good decision. Xander is behaving very strangely. For what reason, I have no idea."

Margaret managed to reply through clenched teeth, looking as if she might need a trip to the head soon. "Don't panic now. There's nothing we can do. Once we get to shore we'll yell and make such a scene the police will have to be called. And, by the way, this was your idea."

"You agreed, don't forget." Jason plopped down on the bed and sulked.

Finally the boat slowed almost to a stop and crept forward in near silence. A half hour or so after that it tied up at a dock. There was a lot of discussion above deck, in the Yukatek language Jason had heard earlier.

Xander came below, along with who they now realized could only be a bodyguard. "It is now night but we will wait until sometime after midnight to debark. Santiago will provide you with some appropriate attire, you will not need your suitcases or what's in them. You will obey my instructions explicitly." The threat was implied and obvious.

"Well, we are not here, wherever here is, to do whatever your bogus contract said we were to do. Just exactly what is it you want from us?" asked Margaret. Once the boat had stopped moving and tied up she regained her composure and a quiet stomach. She was standing at the foot of the bed, Jason sitting behind her. Her arms folded in front and feet apart. Her face needed no interpretation.

"You will be doing pretty much what we discussed. Jason will be developing a drug, albeit a poison, not a medicine or a treatment plan. Trust me, he will very much want to make such a potion when you see the situation. You, madam, will stay quiet and out of the way. Enjoy your time off. If Jason performs as I know he can, you both will be allowed to return to your home in Miami, and the payment will be as discussed."

"I don't believe you. I want to see the local police. This is a kidnapping!" Her eyes were wide with fury, her voice loud and strained.

"Be quiet! I told you to not make a fuss. Sit down!" Xander motioned to Santiago, who produced a knife and approached Margaret.

She tried to step back, but fell onto the bed behind her.

Jason sprang up to defend her and received a punch in the chest and a knife at his throat for his effort.

With the two of them subdued, the bodyguard backed off, but kept his knife in the ready position.

Jason realized they could no longer trust Xander, but had no choice. The worry was how much he had told them was truth, and how much was lies.

'I told you that I would pay for your services, and I meant it. I also told you that you would be returned to your home, and I meant it. But you will follow my instructions or those things will not happen. Do I make myself clear?"

"I suppose so, for now at least," said Jason. He had his arms crossed and tried to look defiant. He wasn't sure if he succeeded.

Xander went back on deck, but left Santiago at the head of the stairs, watching.

Much later that night, Pablo gave them some dark grey robes trimmed in azure at the base, the cuffs and around the cowl. To wear underneath Jason was given a white cotton shirt, a pair of brownish trousers that buckled just below his knees, a jacket that reached halfway down his thighs and a pair of shoes. He felt like a pirate. Margaret was given a white cotton dress with lots of multicolored embroidery at the hem, neckline and sleeves.

They donned the unusual clothes and covered them with the robes that make them look like medieval monks, but with the wrong color robes. They were led on deck and told, "Make no sound, you are like mice sneaking into a pantry. Do not speak if spoken to by one of the brothers or sisters we might meet along the path, just follow me and let me do all the talking, if necessary."

Jason and Margaret followed Xander, who was also robed. "Santiago" and "Pablo", also equally attired, made up the rear, knives at the ready under their robes. They moved in the night as silent as ghosts along the pier and onto the island.

Xander allowed no lanterns so there was just a small amount of light from the stars in the sky. Enough to see the trail, but little else. Down to their left, alongside the dock, was what appeared to be a dormitory. It was obviously a small island since they could just make out the ocean to both sides. They crept up a winding path to the high point of the isle, maybe twenty feet above sea level. They encountered no one.

Xander appeared relieved. He whispered, "Good, all the staff are asleep or in their offices. They were expecting no one this evening or this night. They set no watch."

At the top of the rise was a trap door set flat into the ground. Xander pulled open the trap door and told them to go down the ladder. They had no choice, the two thugs were close behind. The ladder went down the side of an underground chamber. The chamber was about twenty feet across, round with featureless stucco walls. The floor was packed coral dust and sand. The ceiling was wood, with the trap door in one side. What was in the center of the room was not featureless. It was a glowing sphere about three feet in diameter, emitting a strange blue light and a low hum. Most amazing, it was floating unsupported about four feet off the floor.

Xander, looked up and said something to the two brutes above and they closed the door, probably to leave and take the boat away before anyone noticed.

"Really good security they have here," remarked Jason. The situation was so bizarre he was starting to regain his composure. Margaret, unusual for her, was mum.

"Look," Jason continued, "we don't want to be here. I don't want to do whatever you have planned. Let us go. We won't tell anyone, I promise. At least let Margaret free and I'll perform whatever you want. Just stop this nonsense before you get into all sorts of trouble with the law."

"Quiet! How many times do I have to tell you that you both will be fine, just do what I instruct you to do." Xander brandished his knife. "Now hold hands with me and follow me as we approach the portal sphere. When we reach the precise distance you will experience a subtle disquiet and the room will be gone."

Jason took Xander's hand and saw Margaret grab the same hand. Xander then took out what looked for all the world like a magic wand, and waved it in front of him. All at once, Jason felt both a chill and a warmth surge through his body, a sudden and brief sense of vertigo and he was standing in a clearing in a grove of trees, still holding Xander's hand. It was still the dead of night, however. The globe, or one identical to it, was now about ten feet away.

"We are here. You are on the portal island of another existence, another universe, parallel to yours. Let me explain. It is very similar to your world. We call where you came from First World. This is Second World. The portal has been here for ages. Over time many creatures from First World wandered close to the portal and arrived here in Second World. Then came various peoples."

"Wait just a minute!" exclaimed Jason. "What do you mean a parallel universe? I have heard of such theoretical ideas in my science classes, but no one really thinks such things exist." He turned to face Margaret. "Do they?"

She just shrugged her shoulders. Jason figured that the past few hours must have taken their toll on her. She appeared numb, or in shock.

"Keep your voice down! There are others here I do not wish to meet. To answer your question, there most certainly is at least this one alternate existence. If you doubt me, look to the sky."

Jason looked up. To his amazement there were two, yes two, moons in the firmament. One, smaller than the moon of Miami, was nearly full and overhead. The other, slightly smaller yet, was a waxing crescent near the horizon. As far as he could tell the stars seemed the same as what he remembered from home. *Yes, there's the Big Dipper, and there's Sirius and there's the Orion constellation,*" he told himself.

"This really is an alternate universe?" His voice was now hushed but pitched high, in near panic.

"Yes, it is. You are in Second World. Your return to First World depends on your fulfilling your task. Do not fail me. But let me finish."

"Eventually, the Order of the Portal was formed to protect Second World from the depredations of First World and to prevent unsupervised transfer of undesirables from one world to the other. My brother and I are/were members of that order, but we have decided we wanted to be more than monks skulking around on an island. We have been promised positions of influence in the kingdom of Vlogentia. In order to achieve our goal, and that of our benefactor the king, we need you."

"What are we to do? Will you really honor your promise? And what evils do you want us to perform?" asked Jason.

Margaret began to sob and wring her hands, "How are we supposed to do all you want? And how do we get off this island and back home?".

"How many times do I have to say that you will be allowed to return home, if Jason performs his task, and you stay quiet and out of the way. But for now follow me quietly. The members of the Order stationed here will still be asleep, as they are also not expecting visitors. There are vessels tied up to the dock like at the First World isle. Again make no noise. If you are caught, you will not be permitted to return to your world." He again waved his knife toward Jason.

Margaret looked Jason. "I guess we have to follow him," she whispered. "Talk to me later."

"I told you to be quiet. Follow me."

They moved stealthily along a winding path to the pier. This time they passed through a grove of trees. As they crept along the trail Jason saw a dormitory identical to the one on the original island. Tied to the dock was a single masted square rigged sailing vessel about fifty-five feet long also called *Vlogentia*. The deck was flat, no structures, with the wheel near the rear. The single mast was placed in the center of the ship, the gunwale was about three feet high and there was a hatch over the way down into the interior of the ship. On board were two more of Xander's henchmen, waiting for him.

There was another ship tied up nearby with a foreign name on the stern. Jason thought it looked Japanese or Chinese. A third ship tied alongside the second one was named *New Britain*.

Since the boat that had taken them to the first island was obviously named for their destination and there was a ship here with the same name, Jason reasoned that there must be other realms each with a vessel dedicated for travel from that land to this island. Plans for escape were running through his head. The two new crew complicated the matter.

Once aboard, Xander cast off and set sail. He had to instruct Jason on basic seamanship, so he could assist the other two. "Do what I say," said Xander, "and mind the sails. We don't want any luffing. If you're useful, I might make things easier for you."

Luck was with them. No alarm was raised, seas were calm, and the wind was behind them. That was fortunate since Jason had no idea of how to tack a sailing vessel. In fact, he had no idea what tacking was.

As the ship sailed across the night sea Jason looked up again and was amazed to realize there really were two moons, the one half lit moon almost directly above them and the crescent moon he had seen before. He was not mistaken. He had to blink his eyes several times to make sure he wasn't seeing double. It was true, there were still two moons. It had not been his imagination or disorientation from the encounter with the portal.

"OMG," he whispered.

Margaret was too distraught and seasick to notice.

Jason noticed air smelled different, both fresher and more invigorating. The wind behind him was cool and refreshing. He actually felt physically stronger and more energetic. The worry about their fate, and the threat from Xander and the two crew squashed any pleasure he might have felt. That defense mechanism wasn't working.

Two days into the voyage Xander summoned them to him. "I have a device that you will find indispensable. It actually was invented in your First World." He handed each of them a black plastic gadget that fit easily into the palm of a hand, or in a medium sized pocket. Attached was a wire about three feet long with an ear plug at the end. "This is a translator. Make sure the speaker is facing toward the person you want to understand, and it will convert the Yucatek speech into English in the ear plug. When you talk it will translate and project your speech to the listener. It took me quite a while to input enough Yucatek vocabulary and syntax for it to be useful. So, don't try the 'I can't understand' routine. Don't lose it, I don't have any more. Keep it on you and turned on whenever you are awake. Your lives may depend on comprehending the talk around you. The batteries should last for more than a month. Some of the sea traders speak English anyway. It won't help with any of our other languages. The official court language of Vlogentia is Spanish, however."

Jason and Margaret glommed onto the devices. At last, something that would be useful in this strange world. Especially if they were to be stranded here for quite some time.

The next day they arrived at and passed through a chain of low islands, probably sand bars accumulated onto shallow reefs. Once past those, they were in a large lagoon, almost a sea. While on a break Jason noticed strange creatures in the water swimming near the leeward shores of the islands and mentioned it to Margaret on one of the rare occasions she managed to make it to the rail without being sick.

"I think I'm going crazy, this trip is affecting me more than I thought. Those things look like mermaids and mermen! They have faces like people, long strands of hair and short arms, but flukes instead of legs. Please tell me I'm seeing things."

She replied, "Don't be silly, they're probably some kind of manatees. Those are what started the mermaid stories, after all."

Jason figured that she didn't want to believe what he'd really seen, this was all too strange and upsetting to her. She had obviously decided that denial was her preferred course of action.

Jason wanted to agree that this was all a mistake. Any moment now Xander would say something like "April fools" and explain everything and they would get on with the job he'd signed up for. Still, he couldn't shake the feeling that he wasn't seeing things even though that's what he wanted to be true. The moons proved they weren't in the Caribbean any more. Xander's story must at least be partially true. This was a Second World. What else would they see? He wasn't sure he wanted to know.

The wind in the lagoon died down and it took almost a full day before they tied up to a pier in a busy port. It was nearly sunset. There were numerous docks and warehouses and a large and elaborate Spanish colonial palace-like building to their right. They couldn't see much of the town, but could hear a lot of music and commotion.

"Welcome to Vlogentia. Wait here until dusk," said Xander, "When the festivities of the New Year celebration die down we will begin our journey to your destination." He left Jason and Margaret in the charge of the two sailors and went ashore to speak to another man leaning up against the side of one of the warehouses. He was obviously very pleased, he clapped the man on the shoulder and almost danced back to the ship/boat, Jason still wasn't sure of the distinction, nor did he care. It did occur to him however that today would also be January first in their "world."

"What if we don't want to wait?" said both Jason and Margaret as Xander came back aboard.

"You really don't have much of a choice do you? Do what I tell you or you're here to stay, if that's all the king feels inclined to do. Don't try to jump overboard and swim to another ship or the shore in hopes of finding help from the locals. My men will prevent that. Even if you would make it to shore, your wild story of an unauthorized use of the portal and your kidnapping would convince anyone you met you were mad. They'd turn you over to the king, who is in league with my brother and me. You would just waste my time and provoke my ire."

So much for the plan they'd discussed at night while locked in the hold. Xander's threat had to be taken seriously. They waited.

After dusk a large four horse carriage pulled up to the dock. It was off-white with red and gold trim, a door with ornate trim in each side, a driver on the front, raised, seat and perches on the back for footmen. Xander's two helpers, now wearing the robes of the Order, climbed on the perches. Jason and Margaret, also wearing the robes given to them days before, clambered inside with Xander and off they went.

"Keep quiet. Say nothing. I don't need any trouble from the two of you," said Xander. "We will be stopping in a bit and taking on another 'passenger'. Do not interfere." He took out his knife and held it prominently on his lap.

Jason was now more confused and frightened than ever before. The way Xander said 'passenger' sounded ominous. This man would one minute sound reasonable and promising great reward. The next he would be threatening their lives. He must be mad. He was a madman, but a madman with accomplices. Jason ransacked his brain for answers to their dilemma but came up empty.

A few minutes later the carriage was traveling along a cobblestone road between rows of buildings. They looked like more warehouses. It wasn't a very smooth ride. They bounced and jostled like a pair of bobblehead dolls.

Suddenly the carriage came to a stop, almost violently. The footmen jumped down, attacked one of the two women standing there and after a brief but violent struggle subdued her, threw a large fabric sack over her and threw her into the carriage.

Jason exclaimed, "What! Who is that? What are you doing? Why are you doing this? What is going on? Give me some answers, now!"

"In due time. But for now, I told you to be quiet and be still." Xander waved his knife in their general direction.

Jason looked at Margaret. She looked back at him with a face of resignation. He had no plan or idea what to do. He nodded and fell silent, gazing at the still form in the sack.

The two assailants got back on their stations and off the carriage raced. One of them did not sound happy. The translator apparently didn't have the vocabulary he was using in its memory.

As the carriage dashed away Jason and Margaret could hear through the translator the woman left behind sobbing and calling, "I'm sorry, Bianca."

CHAPTER THREE
FELIX' DAY

Capital City, Kingdom of Vlogentia, the palace
Gregorian calendar: January 1
Mayan calendars: Tzolk'in: 9 Ik'
               Haab: 15 K'ank'in

His royal majesty king Felix of Vlogentia knew this was going to be a very good day. His grand plan was going to start to come to fruition. Fame and glory were going to be his. The anticipation kept him from sleeping so he rose before dawn and rang for a servant.

The man arrived a moment later, still wiping the sleep from his eyes. "Yes, sire. What can I do for you?"

"Fetch me my most regal robe, I think I will go to breakfast this morning."

The servant procured a new blue and silver robe and Felix threw it on and paced back and forth in his suite until he was able to regain a measure of calm. Breakfast, usually one of his least favorite activities, was finally ready. Even that had been pleasant and amusing for a change. After eating he went to his office refreshed and ready to compose his speech to the Grand Conclave of Towns and Villages. That would be the culmination of his efforts to raise Vlogentia to the rank of The Grand Kingdom, with him as its monarch of course.

He went over in his mind how to begin the oration. "*I must impress upon them the dire nature of our apparent distress. Once they understand and agree with that the rest, the important part, will follow naturally,*" he told himself. That was good. Now he merely needed to wait for his agents to bring their news so he could coordinate their efforts.

Up until now, he had needed to rely on his uncle's advice and mentoring on how to run a kingdom. It was getting a little old. They shared the same vision and basic scheme to enhance the fame and glory of the realm, but Felix needed to put his own unique twist on things. He was, after all, twenty four years old now and it was time everybody started obeying his orders.

Felix was now in his study on the second floor of the palace. It was a large room filled with the mementos of previous kings. There were books, in Spanish and codices in Mayan. There was a suit of armor, never used since they had gone out of style before the Spanish and Mayan people had been transported to Second World to found Vlogentia. It was just for show. The woodwork was elaborate. Felix didn't really care about any of that. He did like the double door, now open, leading to his balcony overlooking the inland sea. But his favorite piece in the room was the ornate desk near the far wall.

He walked to and sat at the desk and rang the bell sitting on the edge. A servant, who had been waiting outside the large double door, entered. "What do you need, sire?"

"Find me a tailor of excellent repute. I will need new attire when I address the Grand Conclave of Towns and Villages after the delegates are assembled from across the kingdom. It must look inspiring."

After the servant left, he continued to work composing his speech to the Grand Conclave. It would have to be very persuasive to convince the Conclave to agree to his plans for the kingdom. Vlogentia had until now been at peace with the neighboring realms and had no need for a standing army. That would have to change. He needed a reason to raise a huge army. That should be the easy part, then he'd have to convince them to let him use the army for his real purpose. That would take some grand oratory to show them the grandeur that would ensue.

After a bit, another servant knocked on his study door. "Sire, there is a Member of the Order of the Portal at the palace gate who requests to meet you. Should I send him away or let him in?"

"By all means let him in." This was one of the people he had been expecting.

The servant opened the door a few moments later and Xavier, Xander's twin brother, entered. He was wearing the grey and blue robe of the order. He made a convincing pretense of bowing deferentially, "A fortunate blend of Tzolk'in and Haab days to you, sire. I have good news for you. I received a missive from my brother by way of one of our messengers from First World. He has found two excellent candidates for your scheme. One is a physician that is skilled in creating potions, hopefully fatal ones. The other is his wife who is a lawyer. We convinced her to accompany her husband for a holiday. Should it become necessary she may prove useful as an incentive. My brother should be here today with them, if all goes as planned."

Felix leapt from his chair and rushed around the desk toward Xavier, shaking his hand. "This is great news! Now we can start the rest of the plan." His speech was rushed and a little higher pitched than normal. "What about the kulkulcan? Have you been able to lure it into believing it should attack our border villages? The whole strategy rests on that. Were you actually able to speak with it? "

Xavier stood calmly, in opposition to the excitement Felix offered. "Yes. It can be difficult for a person to talk to a kulkulcan, or what our First World captives would call a dragon. They learned Yucatek from early explorers looking for gold in the mountains. But, the kulkulcano'ob have been reluctant to interact with humans since we have settled here. Perhaps some early prospectors told stories of brave knights slaying kulkulcano'ob left and right and they decided to stay in the mountains. But they will allow a parlay if approached carefully. This kulkulcan doesn't completely believe the old tales, his name is Ill'yx, and he has grand plans of becoming a feared calamity. He wants to become a legend for the ages and your approval for the attack gives him the incentive he needs to become the dreaded and venerated Grand Kulkulcan of the Mountains and Plains."

"But now that he knows you want some villages destroyed, he will coerce the other kulkulcano'ob to help him attack. We need to time events carefully. Then, our captive doctor must concoct a venom so powerful it will kill the kulkulcano'ob, but not until they have destroyed several towns."

"Doesn't he wonder why I want the villages destroyed?" asked Felix. He was now pacing around the study.

"No, he figures you have some unfathomable human reason and he doesn't really care."

"Has my other concern also been arranged?"

"Yes, sire. Please forgive my bluntness but the woman will no longer be a cause for your resentment," said Xavier. "As you ordered, I have arranged for her to be abducted and taken with our two captives to the village the kulkulcan is slated to attack. If the few survivors of the attack report seeing the kulkulcan killing a young woman, just like in the old tales from First World, how could they not want war with the kulkulcano'ob?"

"Excellent. We lose a few worthless villagers, I will be rid of her and we will then conquer the world! Let me know when your brother arrives with the captives."

"As you wish, Sire." With that Xavier bowed and backed out of the room to arrange the 'relief column' for the destroyed village.

Felix was pleased with himself. So far his vision for the future of Vlogentia was proceeding without a problem. And he would have vengeance on the woman who preferred a lowly corporal to his regal self.

"How dare she traipse around the capital with a mere guardsman instead of me? She pretends to ignore me whenever we are both about the city. What impudence! Well, I'll show her. People who offend me have to be dealt with," he said to no one but the nearby wall. "I'm the king. I can do things like that. Can't I?"

Satisfied, Felix went back to work on his speech. After a few hours the first servant knocked on his door again. "Sire, I have found a tailor who will make the suit of clothes you require."

"Excellent, send him in."

Enrique, a master tailor of the city, entered and bowed to the king. "Good days to you, sire. I understand you need a grand suit for the Conclave. I have a few samples of my work that you might find interesting." He then had his apprentice bring in several sets of formal attire. One of them, a maroon coat with brass buttons, definitely caught the king's eye.

"Let's try that one." Felix donned the coat and strutted around the room. He did in fact present a regal aspect. He was tall, thin with a fluid gait like a cat. He had the black hair, medium complexion, and brown eyes of almost all the population. He actually looked good.

"I like it," he said, "but can you add some more buttons? A king's coat should have lots of brass buttons."

"Certainly sire, but where should I put them? The coat already has all the buttons it needs to close the front and to keep back the cuffs." Enrique was puzzled. He stood before the king with his head tilted pondering just how to do this.

"Just anywhere. Try the sleeves, the shoulders, just anywhere."

"As you wish, sire." And with that Enrique gathered the coat, bowed, slowly turned and walked out of the study with his apprentice and the servant, subtly shaking his head the entire way.

Once the three had left, Felix hastened to the doors leading to the balcony. Throwing them open he stepped outside and stood proudly, his chest puffed out like a peacock. The afternoon sun had started to shine on this side of the palace and he felt like he was already the king of the world. He could hear the revelry from the city celebrating the New Year, which just added to his delight. This was a perfect start to the year.

Later that afternoon, his uncle, Ronaldo the Duke of Ki'pan, strode into the room. He didn't bother to knock or offer the usual polite greeting. "On my way here I learned from Xavier the plan is finally in motion. I hope you have taken care of everything."

Felix ignored the slight, as he always did. Ronaldo was his uncle, his mentor and the reason he held the throne after all. "Of course I have. In fact I have added a twist that will enrage the populace even more." He related his idea for the woman and the kulkulcan.

"Not bad, not bad at all."

"You must make sure your mercenary company stand ready should the people of the city start to grumble. And they must be present near palace when the Grand Conclave meets in case they question the wisdom of my edict. I don't trust the royal guard, too many of them have family in the city and they might side with them, the ingrates." Felix' voice rang with authority.

Ronaldo took a step back, surprise and admiration on his face. "It will be as you wish, sire." He bowed with considerable more deference than he had ever shown Felix before and backed out of the room.

Still later that day, the seneschal knocked, and entered the room with a stack of papers in his hands. "Your majesty, here are some papers and edicts that the ministers say need your approval and signature. What should I do with them?"

"Oh, put them here on my desk. I'll do something with them."

"Yes, sire. Forgive my interruption."

"No matter, you are just the harbinger of unwelcome news. You may go."

The seneschal bowed and left as quietly as he could.

This was the part of being a king Felix absolutely despised. Kings were supposed lead armies to victory. They were supposed to stand before the populace and make grand pronouncements. They were supposed to represent the splendor of the realm. They were not supposed to spend endless hours reading obscure documents detailing equally obscure goings on in the land. He hated doing this and he felt as if he was a captive. Isn't this what he had ministers for?

Let them do all the writing and just let him sign it. But they insisted he actually read them. What a waste of his time.

Nevertheless, he once again sat in his chair behind the grand desk, put his speech to the side and started to put ink to the papers. At least his doors to the balcony were open to let in the fresh night air. Neither of the moons were visible from his vantage point at this hour. Felix felt like a prisoner. A prisoner of paperwork. A captive of administration and boredom. He hardly even glanced and what he was signing. In his mind he was seeing his grand army sweeping everything in its path aside and he was in the forefront on his steed leading his soldiers to victory. That was what he wanted to be doing.

CHAPTER FOUR

THE RIDE FROM THE CAPITAL

On the road from Capital City, late night, kingdom of Vlogentia
Gregorian calendar: January 1
Mayan calendars: Tzolk'in: 10 Ak'b'al
　　　　　　 Haab: 16 K'ank'in

D arkness had fallen by the time the carriage with Xander, Jason, Margaret and the unfortunate prisoner had made its way into and through the city. Cobblestone streets combined with a single leaf spring on the axles made for an unbearably uncomfortable and rough ride. Sleep was impossible. In fact, Jason and Margaret had to keep chewing on some tasteless jerky-like snack in order to keep from chipping a tooth. Xander sat stoically the entire time, silent but continually fingering his knife. The woman who had been tossed into the sack and onto the floor of the carriage never moved or made a sound.

Xander's seeming unconcern about her plight alarmed Jason. "Is she alright? Is she even alive?" he asked.

"She should be alive and well, at least for now. She is merely unconscious, thanks to some First World ether," replied Xander. He casually glanced at the bulky sack lying on the floor between them.

"What about later, then?"

"We'll worry about that at the appropriate time."

That sounded more ominous for the woman's future than Jason liked. The situation was getting worse with each passing moment.

The roads were empty in the dark. Except that sometime before they left the city they passed what seemed to be a military patrol organizing for a trip. It had a troop of cavalry, a carriage much like theirs, and two supply wagons. Something didn't look right about the mounts, it appeared to Jason that they had pikes protruding from their foreheads. *"Are those unicorns?"* he asked himself. *"If so I better not tell Margaret. She has such a fixation about unicorns, ever since childhood, that adding that to everything else might send her over the edge."* He sat back and looked out his window at the darkness. Margaret did the same out of her side of the carriage.

Morning came, and the road smoothed out miraculously as they left the city. "This is so much better," said Margaret. "I thought we'd have our insides churned like a smoothie."

Xander looked puzzled at her reference. "We are on a sacbe, or white highway. This road is a marvel of Mayan engineering, and highways like this one had been in use in First World by the Maya well before the Spanish conquest. Long straight stretches of road connected major centers there and were paved with limestone. We do the same here. They are thirty feet wide and raised some eighteen inches more or less above the gently undulating terrain so as to maintain a smooth, flat surface. They have limestone sidewalls another eighteen inches high. Of course such construction is easier for us, we have draft animals and wheeled carts. Something our First World forebears lacked."

Jason was amazed at the sophistication of the construction. Based on her intense look, so was Margaret. In Jason's uneducated opinion the highway surpassed even the famous Roman roads. Every so often there was a small hut or building alongside the sidewall, obviously a rest stop.

Jason noticed that Xander had slipped back into his nice mode. Perhaps the man was schizophrenic, or tending that way. Jason wished he'd paid more attention to the psychiatric lectures in medical school.

A little later the carriage slowed and stopped at a sizeable pale brown stucco building alongside the road. Next to the building was an unpainted wood barn with a large corral in front with a dozen or more horses in it. This obviously was a livery where passengers could get out to rest and where the carriage could change teams.

Xander exited the coach. "Stay here, do not get out. I will be back soon." He motioned to the 'footmen' to watch them. Jason had even forgotten the goons were still on the carriage. He wondered what their ride and been like. They appeared to be as stoic as ever.

"But we have to get out, we have to use the facilities," begged Margaret, with Jason nodding in agreement. "And we need some water at the very least, and nourishment." Xander once again adopted a puzzled look, he obviously did not understand what 'facilities' meant.

Jason informed him of Margaret's intent.

"Very well, my associate will show you where to go. Do not delay. Get back in the carriage as soon as possible. Talk to no-one. No one here understands English, and hearing you speak and then hearing Yucatek issuing from your hand or pocket will arouse suspicion. We don't need that." He instructed one of the footmen/guards to accompany them and pay for their water and food.

Xander walked over to a man standing by the corral and spoke to him for a moment, gestured toward the horses and paid him something. He then strode past the open station door to a large wagon with yellow walls, orange gabled roof and a double door in the back. It appeared to have a fresh team. He spoke to the driver sitting on the front and seemed pleased with the response.

A few minutes later the station master lead out a fresh team of horses, unhitched the ones that had been pulling the carriage, and put the new team in place and led the first team to the corral.

After Jason and Margaret had been escorted back to the carriage, and just as they were climbing the step to get back in their seats, Xander came over and said, "Doctor Blankeship, you need to come with me. Mrs Blankenship you must get back in the carriage." With both guards now standing nearby no argument was feasible.

As Xander turned to go to the wagon Jason quietly whispered to Margaret, "When you get back in the carriage, check on the condition of the woman. She has been out for so long I am worried about her. If you can, see if you can help her."

Jason followed Xander to the wagon, where the driver unlocked and opened the doors. Xander motioned Jason to enter. Once Jason was inside he was flabbergasted. It had all sorts of very new and modern lab equipment still in the boxes stacked and tied down in the front of the wagon. There were numerous compounds and supplies secured to the shelves. It was almost a complete workshop. He took several minutes to perform a quick inventory of supplies and equipment. He tried not to be impressed, and failed.

Xander said, "We were able to acquire the supplies and equipment you indicated were necessary to fulfill your task. It was no easy matter to smuggle it past the other members of the Order of the Portal. Over the course of the month that I was in contact with you my brother and I had to make multiple excursions with easily carried packages, each time scheduling our return when the other brothers were not expecting traffic. So you see I am serious about you completing your task. You need to stop worrying me. You, and your wife, will come to no harm if you do what I need. Acquiring all this was not easy or cheap. I hope you appreciate our efforts."

Jason wasn't sure he did or expect to appreciate any of it.

They returned to the carriage and Jason started to get in. Xander did not. He said, "I prefer to ride in front with the driver, I need to be on the lookout for my brother and his entourage. My two footmen will ride with the driver of the wagon. I hope your concerns are alleviated now. However, don't even think of fleeing, you don't know where you are or where you could go. Just stay in the carriage, perform your duties when asked and I will honor our agreement. The prisoner should be awake soon and I assume you will tend to her. When she is fully conscious and fit you will tell me immediately, I will need to secure her. Do you understand?" They both nodded.

"Of course, we will cause no trouble at all," said Margaret. Her tone sounded less than sincere to Jason.

They clambered back into the carriage, careful to avoid stepping on the captive. Margaret whispered to Jason, "I tried to undo the knot in the sack holding the hostage, but could not get it loose. As far as I could tell her respiration seemed normal, I could feel her breathing. She was beginning to stir, she may come around soon."

"Thanks," he said, "I'll try to examine her once we get under way if we can unloosen the knot."

It was now close to midday and the heat was stifling. Both Jason and Margaret were sweating profusely, and Jason was worried about heat exhaustion or worse. He stuck his head out the open window and asked Xander, who had yet to climb next to the driver, "Can we please take off these ridiculous robes? We are about to melt."

"Very well, but fold them and keep them on the shelves above your seat. You will need them later." They thankfully got out of the garments, probably just in time thought Jason.

"Just a minute," said Xander, "on second thought, your voice, madam, did not convince me that you are in complete agreement with my needs. Without the robes you could move much faster. Guard, come here and secure these two to the carriage. If they tried to escape they couldn't go far, but I don't want to take the time to chase them down."

The guard/footman produced what looked like old handcuffs or manacles from somewhere. He secured Jason's right hand to the side rail of the seat. He did the same to Margaret's left hand. The each had at least three feet of chain so they could move around inside the carriage, but anything more than that was out of the question.

"*Great*," thought Jason, "*evil Xander is back.*"

Xander and his men took their places and the small caravan returned to the sacbe and headed further east. The road was perfectly straight as before except for an occasional sharp detour around a stand of trees or a hill. The terrain around them was mostly flat, but slightly rolling. Numerous fields of corn or other crops and pastures for the livestock surrounded the villages as they passed. In between the villages were the woods or fallow fields of grasses.

Margaret, who had taken some history classes in undergraduate school, remarked, "This is not the jungle landscape the Maya came from in First World. There are no great forests or jungles here they had to clear for their settlements. I don't see any of the cenotes, large underground water-filled limestone caverns so prevalent in the Yucatan, which were the entry to the underworld in Mayan mythology. The Maya of Second World seem to have adapted to this new environment quite well, however. I wonder what else is different from First World, and what is the same?"

Jason thought about telling her about the unicorns, but decided that later, once they were out of the restraints, might be a better time to do so.

After the carriage had gotten underway, they were able to organize their efforts despite the chains and work loose the knot holding the sack the poor woman was confined in and prop her on the seat in front of them. She did not seem to have been as affected by the heat as they had been. Probably due to acclimation, thought Jason. The activity had the beneficial effect of fully waking her. She appeared in good condition to Jason. Her pulse was normal and her respiration also seemed normal. He could detect no fever. She had no physical signs of injury. Her appearance was unusual for what their limited experience with the local populace led them to expect however.

She was of medium height, slender but obviously very physically fit. Her age appeared to be early twenties. She was wearing a three-quarter length dress with half sleeves that had incredibly elaborate floral embroidery along the neckline, sleeve cuffs and the hem. Around her waist was a light blue sash with white trim. An equally decorated shawl was draped over her left shoulder. Her complexion was the same as all the Maya they had seen, a dark tan. But her hair was as white as the summer clouds and fell halfway down her back. She had been wearing a flower sprig in her hair, but it was dried and disheveled. Her eyebrows and eyelashes were blonde. Her nose was not quite as prominent as most of the locals and she had wide mouth. Her eyes were her unique feature. She had pronounced oriental epicanthal folds. When she opened them they were not the dark brown Jason and Margaret expected, but blue. The brilliant blue of a perfect sapphire. They made an even casual glance appear intense.

She stared at them for a minute and seemed to notice the constraints around their wrists and the chains attached to the sides of the carriage. Jason and Margaret sat back on their seat and stared at her. Each tried to size the other side up. The Vlogentian said, "Buenas tardes! Mi nombre es Bianca. Quienes son ustedes y por que estan aqui?

CHAPTER FIVE

BIANCA AWAKE

On the road east of Capital City, kingdom of Vlogentia
Gregorian calendar: January 2
Mayan calendars: Tzolk'in: 10 Ak'b'al
                 Haab: 16 K'ank'in

B ianca had to sit for a moment, gathering her wits. The last thing she remembered was sinking into unconsciousness after being attacked while she was talking to Daniela. Now, it was daylight and she was in a carriage going who knows where with two strangers who were chained to the sides of the carriage. Their expressions might be showing concern for her situation or they might be evaluating her as an enemy, she just wished she knew which expression to believe.

They hadn't made any threatening moves yet. In fact she thought they were the ones who had freed her from the sack lying crumpled on the floor. They did not look like citizens of Vlogentia, they must be from one of the other realms of Second World, but which one?

She squirmed in her seat as a diversion while secretly feeling for the dagger she kept strapped to her thigh. It wasn't there, it must have been taken by one of her attackers. She decided that, for now, learning more about what was going on was more important than escape. They were restrained, escaping from them would be easy if necessary.

She said, in court Spanish, "Good afternoon, my name is Bianca. Who are you and what are you doing here?" She hoped Spanish was common enough among travelers that they would understand. They stared at her for a brief time and then introduced themselves.

"My name is Jason."

"And my name is Margaret."

They spoke the language of sea traders and pirates, a tongue Bianca knew. Then their introductions, in very imperfect Yucatek, were repeated from a gadget each held on their lap. Oh, this must be some powerful magic. No need to use their translating talismans, however.

"I am conversant in your language. It may actually be easier if you put away your magic speaking devices."

Both of them fiddled with their contraption, a look of relief and surprise on their faces, and put them aside.

Bianca was certain they were no immediate threat. She asked, "Where are we? Do you have any idea what is happening and why?"

Jason related his and Margaret's tale as briefly as he could. He added, "We do not know where we are since we know nothing of this land. All we know is that I was lied to about my purpose. The truth is that I am supposed to concoct a poison to eliminate a vermin of some sort. Margaret was allowed to accompany me as a holiday for her. However, that was undoubtedly also a lie. We fear she is here just as a hostage."

Margaret nodded assent and sighed. "We do seem to be headed east, toward where the sun rose this morning. What is your story? How do you know our language?"

"It's spoken by many of the sea traders who visit the capital's port. I really don't want to go into the rest. Like you I'm a prisoner of this Xander you spoke of and that is all that matters. Do you know what Xander, and whoever else he is in league with, have planned for me? I have trouble believing a couple of rogue brothers of the Order of the Portal could be as bold as this."

"No, but from what little Xander has told us whatever they have planned may not be good."

"Sadly, I have guessed as much." She paused, then added, "But would you mind telling me a little about yourselves?" Bianca was fishing for information, anything she learned about this situation could be useful.

"Well," said Jason, "Margaret is a lawyer who specializes in estate and contract law. I am a general medical practitioner as well as a biochemical engineer and chief pharmacological designer for a pharmaceutical company."

"I know what lawyers do. But as for your trade, that is a truly impressive string of nonsense syllables. Do they actually mean anything?"

"Oh, yes. Let me see. It means that I can make powerful treatments and medicines to cure diseases. It's actually very complicated. It took me years of study at universities and the use of complicated equipment and specific chemicals to create the drugs."

"Oh, you fabricate magic potions, then."

"No, it's science. Not magic. Everything I do is firmly based in science." He spent a few moments trying to detail how he used the learning he acquired at university to perform the complicated procedures necessary to manufacture modern medicines.

"I don't understand. You perform arcane rituals with special apparatus and secret ingredients. How is that different from magic? If anybody asks me, I will say you concoct magic healing potions."

Jason said nothing in reply. His expression was one of resignation.

"I'm sorry, I didn't mean to be rude," said Bianca. "I'm still rather dazed, disoriented and apprehensive. Would you mind if I just sat and recovered for a while?" She had decided her fishing expedition was going nowhere useful.

Of course, dear," said Margaret. "Take some time and rest. Xander told us to inform him the instant you awoke. But you have been through so much you need the time. Fortunately the sounds of the horses' hooves on the road and his constant chatter with the driver have kept him from hearing our talk. We can tell him about you later, if at all."

All three sat silently each apparently deep in their thoughts. Finally, the carriage and wagon came to a river, but the current appeared very swift. There would be no chance for fording. There was a cantilever bridge spanning the water that was under repair. The work crew had constructed a temporary one lane structure that spanned the torrent adjacent to the unfinished bridge. The caravan was halted by a signalman, who had already waved a team of oxen pulling a cart laden with maize across from the other side.

Xander was irate. He shouted, "May the merpeople take you. Can't you see we are on an important journey? Either make them go back, or make them hurry across."

Now that the carriage had stopped the three of them could hear his voice clearly. Presumably he could now also hear theirs.

"They're oxen. They don't back up and they move as oxen do," replied the signalman.

Jason leaned out his window to see what was happening. He reported back to the two women. "Xander is fuming, his face is actually turning red. Something I had thought impossible given his normal complexion."

Finally, they were waved across. Xander sounded surly. "We must keep to our schedule," he growled through clenched teeth. He spent the rest of the crossing infuriated and snapping at everybody and at everything.

The work crew was about forty men, dressed in short trousers or loincloths. There were a few women handing out water.

"Are those slaves?" asked Margaret in horror.

"No," replied Bianca, "our founder, father Sebastian Garcia, did not believe in slavery. He was leading our people away from slavery and the inquisition when they found the portal to Second World. Those are corvee workers. Each able inhabitant of Vlogentia is required to serve one Mayan month, twenty days, each year in public works, such as repairing this bridge. The crown assigns their task for the month, but supplies food, shelter and a small stipend for their labor. Often the wives accompany the men if circumstances permit"

"Isn't that the same as forced labor?" Asked Jason.

"We prefer to think of it as public service. And it keeps the crown from having to hire workers to do the jobs. Keeps taxes lower. It actually seems to develop the sense of community in the minds of the populace."

Jason and Margaret appeared satisfied with her explanation and returned to their contemplations. Bianca sat back, put her feet up on the seat and just stared out the window. Again deep in her thoughts, *"They are captives of Xander, as am I. If we can find a time and place to talk, perhaps we can devise a mutual plan for escape. They can help me get back to the capital, and I can help them contact honest members of the Order so they can return to their First World home."*

Xander had heard part of the exchange. As soon as the carriage cleared the makeshift bridge and before their accompanying wagon could finish he bellowed, "I hope the two of you have a moonless night! I told you to inform me the instant she awoke. I told you she had to be restrained. "

Finally, he had an actual target for his ill humor. He leapt down from the driver's seat, letting out a yelp as he landed awkwardly, and flung the door open so violently that it started to come off its hinges. Grabbing Bianca by her hair he yanked her out of the carriage and threw her violently onto the ground. Given the proximity of the guards, the driver and Jason and Margaret Bianca decided to swallow her pride for the time being and did not resist. If she fought and tried to run her new acquaintances would be in danger. She didn't want that. She might not escape in any event. She looked up from the ground and told Xander, "You realize no one will pay a ransom for me, don't you?"

"I am not interested in ransom," snarled Xander.

He had the driver toss him a leather thong and bound her hands behind her back. Once again she was picked up and tossed back into the carriage, but not in a sack this time. "Do not test my patience again, "he fumed at the Blankenships. "Watch her, don't let her try anything, and stop talking. "

Jason and Margaret apparently decided to stay mute for now.

Once the carriage was again under way, Bianca sighed, shrugged her shoulders, stood up then crouched down and let her hands fall down behind her to the floor of the carriage. Carefully, one foot at a time she stepped backward over her bound hands, then stood up and untied the thong with her teeth.

"He has the temper for a tyrant, but not the skill," she whispered. "We need to bide our time until we can plan an escape. I will try to devise a plan. You do the same. We must be in for a long ride, plan on talking this evening."

She sat back down, put her feet up on the seat, back to the wall and gazed out the window, attempting to concoct a plan based on the little information available. It didn't look promising.

CHAPTER SIX

THE ESCAPE

On the east road, town of Naats' Seebak Ha', kingdom of Vlogentia
Gregorian calendar: January 3
Mayan calendars: Tzolk'in: 11 K'an
              Haab: 17 K'ank'in

Bianca was already awake when Xander came pounding on her door to the room in the inn where the group had spent the night.

"Come on, it's time to get up! We have to get on the road, I have a schedule to keep," he shouted through the door. "Get your lazy self out here! The others are already stirring."

She made the pretense of tying her hands, as she had done the previous evening when she and the Blankenships had alighted from the carriage, and approached to the door. "I can't leave the room. My hands are tied and you bolted the door from the outside. I'm ready. Open up."

She heard the scrape of a brace being removed.

The door opened with Xander standing in the entry, arms akimbo and a scowl on his face. "Now, let's go," he said.

"No, not just yet!" She stamped her foot as forcefully as possible, then placed herself just inches from his face and snarled back at him, "First I want to know why I'm here and why I was abducted. You say you don't care about ransom, so none of this makes any sense. Jason at least has an idea why you tricked him into coming here. He's to make some magic potion to kill something. So does

47

Margaret, you wanted her as a guarantee that Jason would do your bidding. But what is my purpose? I don't do potions and I have no skills that I can see would be useful to you. Why am I here?"

"Your presence is vital to my plans," he replied as he jumped back a couple of steps. "Your purpose will be crystal clear soon enough. Quit complaining and come." A flicker of a sneer crossed his face as he spoke. He tried to assume a superior pose by looking down his nose at her. That was difficult since she was a couple inches the taller. He turned and limped toward the exit of the inn. "Come on, I'm tired of wasting my time with useless banter."

Bianca followed, still pretending her hands were bound. "*My presence is vital, but he refuses to say what it is. But it's important enough to justify kidnapping,*" she thought, "*that does not sound good. Margaret, Jason and I should make our escape sooner rather than later. I'll have to make something up, and do so now. I'll whisper to them that we need to flee now once we're back in the carriage.*"

Everyone else was gathering at the carriage where Xander had arranged for food to be brought to them. Bianca surmised that he didn't want her or the Blankenships interacting with anyone. He told Jason and Margaret that they were allowed to listen with their translators, but not to speak since that would cause too much curiosity in the locals. He then ordered Jason to untie Bianca's hands so she could eat. Fortunately for her Xander didn't try to do it himself.

After a quick breakfast, Xander retied Bianca's hands behind her and then prepared the vehicles. He was in a hurry. Bianca couldn't very well free herself in front of everybody, so she edged her way to a back wheel of the carriage. It was a very simple arrangement, just a cotter pin through the axle holding the wheel and a large washer in place. It was pretty shoddy manufacture. But it gave Bianca an idea. Pretending to scratch her back on the wheel, she managed to work the cotter pin loose. It would fall off at the first sudden movement of the carriage. The wheel would soon follow suit. Then the fun would start.

After Bianca, Jason and Margaret got in the carriage. Bianca leaned over to them and whispered, "Be ready! There is going to be a major accident right after we get moving. We should have a good chance of escaping." She stood and unbound herself as she had done the day before. "He doesn't learn, does he?"

This time the wagon led the caravan onto the sacbe, a driver and both guards on the driver's seat. Xander and the other driver were on the driver's seat of the carriage as it followed through the inn's gate. Just as soon as the carriage made the sharp turn to the left to start down the road, the left rear wheel came off and rolled down the highway by itself.

The carriage lurched to the left and immediately fell on its side.

Bianca and the Blankenships clambered through the now open door on the former right, now top, side of the carriage. On her way out Bianca grabbed one of the robes the Blankenships had put on the shelf the day before.

"*This might be useful as a disguise,*" she thought, "*at least it's less conspicuous than my dress.*"

As they paused to look around while atop the side of the carriage they saw that Xander and the driver had been thrown clear of the wreck. The horses had broken free and were following the wheel down the road. The crew on the wagon had not reacted yet, it was still proceeding along the road.

The three of them jumped to the ground and Bianca started to run around the back, out of sight of her captors. She motioned to Jason and Margaret to follow her. They didn't move.

"We're sorry," said Jason, "but we are not doing this. Staying with and working for Xander is our only chance of getting back to where we belong. Margaret and I discussed our situation at length last night. Following you guarantees us nothing but recapture or being stranded in a world we know nothing about. Whatever evil reason he had for lying to us, eliminating some creature or creatures causing harm cannot be a bad thing. Then he will take us back to that island and then back to Florida. We have to believe that."

Bianca retorted, "You're foolish, I don't think he has any intention of honoring his promise. But do what you feel you have to do." She was furious with them but had no time to discuss matters further. She continued running around the back of the wrecked carriage, across the road, and into the courtyard of the inn. Nobody had noticed her yet. Xander and the driver were still picking themselves up and wondering what had just happened. The wagon had yet to turn around, or even stop.

The courtyard was devoid of people and horses this early in the day. She made for the space between the inn and the barn to take stock of the situation. She donned the robe, waited for a few seconds and then cautiously looked to her left around the side of the inn. The Blankenships were nowhere to be seen, probably still standing on the other side of the carriage. Xander and the driver, having assessed the extent of the disaster, were running back to the far side of the wreck, undoubtedly to question Jason and Margaret. The wagon had finally slowed down to make the turn back to the scene, and the two guards had jumped off and were hurrying back to where Xander was obviously heading.

That gave Bianca a little time to think. *"First, I have to elude capture. Then, I have to somehow make her my back to the capital. After that I'm not at all sure what to do. There is no way of knowing who is involved in Xander's scheme, and why."* She considered contacting Joaquin or Julieta or Renata. But given the fact that Daniela had been complicit in her abduction, she wasn't sure she could trust any of her friends. *"Better yet,"* she thought, *"I could surreptitiously contact Juan, he's a corporal in the city guard and he would know who to alert to put an end to Xander's scheme. Maybe then, I'll ask someone to help return the fickle Blankenships to their home."*

But she had no money to hire a ride to the capital. So, if she couldn't find someone kind enough to lend her a horse, it would be a several days trek ahead of her. Better get started.

She ran toward the back of the inn, into the town and away from the highway. There was a dirt road running behind the inn which crossed the town's main street to her right. The road extended to her left and then curved off into a residential area. The dirt road continued in the other direction across the main street and past the church which sat across from the inn. The rest of the town was crowded with typical Mayan homes arranged in a haphazard fashion. Smoke was starting to come out of the chimneys as breakfast was being prepared. Beyond the town was a stream that fed the river the caravan had crossed the previous day. Beyond the stream was a small woods.

Deciding it would be a waste of precious time, she didn't bother knocking on doors and asking for help. She needed to get to the woods and cover before Xander's men spotted her.

Bianca hurried through the residential neighborhood, often running between or behind the houses. She quickly learned that strategy worked to her disadvantage. The sight of a stranger running through and around their residential area alarmed enough people that they started chasing her. Then the church's bell started tolling the alarm.

"Wonderful," she worried to herself, *"Xander must have alerted the innkeeper or the town guard. Now every resident will be chasing me. I must get to the woods."* She could hear that what had to be almost the entire town, along with Xander barking orders to his men, were on her tail. She kept heading north, away from the sacbe and inn, and kept the main street to her right. That was where most of the uproar was located.

Bianca continued dashing back and forth between homes in hopes of confusing the pursuit. The day was becoming warm and she was getting hot, sweaty and fatigued. If she didn't elude capture soon she wouldn't make it to the woods beyond the stream and then hopefully sneak her way back toward the capital.

She finally managed to put some distance between herself and the mob, but only for a moment. Sprinting to her right, toward the main street in hopes of confusing the pursuit, she ran into a small courtyard with a well in the center. Sitting on a bench near the well were two old women doing their embroidery and sharing the morning's gossip. They obviously hadn't yet heard about or paid attention to the news of the escapee and the chase.

Bianca ran up to them and pleaded, "Please, I need your help. I've been kidnapped and have to escape my captors. They're coming from the inn. They are led by a renegade brother of the Order of the Portal with his four helpers. Anything you can do would be wonderful. Please, please help me!"

The two women looked distrustfully at what Bianca realized they had to perceive as a strange girl with a mess of white hair, a dirty dress under a disheveled robe of the Order and a wild tale. They got up and scurried away, looking behind them and shaking their heads as they went.

"No, please don't leave. Come back," she pleaded with a desperate voice, "can you at least send a message to my friend in the capital, Corporal of the Royal Guard Juan Alejandro Gomez Mendes and tell him I've been kidnapped and have escaped. I'll wait for him outside your town."

The women continued to shake their heads and walk away.

Bianca tried to bury her disappointment.

It probably wasn't a good idea, but she had to stop and drink some water. Her situation was becoming desperate. With no relief in sight, Bianca had to continue her flight. So she turned north and dashed behind a few houses. After about fifty yards she ran out of the built up area and onto the grassy bank of the stream behind the town. It wasn't too wide but of unknown depth. On the other side of the stream was a dense woods made up of deciduous trees, mostly oaks, unlike the mostly palm tree groves near the capital. She was running out of time, the crowd behind her was growing by the minute and capture was imminent if they spotted her. Diving into the water she started to try to make her way across. The water was cold, bone-chilling cold, as it came from the mountains to the east, home of the kulkulcano'ob. Fortunately for her the current was surprisingly weak for a mountain fed watercourse and she was able to flounder her way across. Bianca was not a good swimmer. Once on the other side, and still fearing someone would spot her at any instant, she leapt up the short bank and into the woods.

Once in the woods she was able to rest for a while. But she was soaked, cold, and fearful. A prolonged stop to dry was not wise. The only choice was try to find a way through the woods to wherever the other side was, lose the pursuit, and start her trek back home. So, she got up and started through the woods. At first it was pleasant. The wood was dense enough to shield her from the town, the underbrush wasn't too thick and the smell was that of a fall harvest festival.

Then it started. This grove was home to a colony of what the people of Vlogentia called fairies, after the myths from the First World. She had hoped the grove was too small to harbor the pests, but obviously she was mistaken. They really weren't fairies, but some sort of wasp-like creature that had swarmed through the portal eons before people started to guard it. With time they had changed into the fairies. They actually did look almost exactly like a four inch tall person with translucent wings. They could sting, but over the years had developed a considerable intelligence that allowed them to harass and harry a person in their territory rather than attack immediately. The stinging would come later. She had heard legends that said they had some sort of sense about the portal. What that was the legends didn't say.

They came at her from all sides, and from above. Buzzing, diving at her, and swarming around to the extent that she had trouble seeing where she was heading. Worse, they emitted a piercing whistle and the multitude of wings cre-ated a loud droning sound, certain to alert the townsfolk of her location. She tried to shield herself with the robe as she ran, holding it over her head. That helped only a little, they still came after the robe. It blocked her vision which caused Bianca to fall into a shallow gully that led back to the stream. It was prob-ably intermittently filled with rain runoff. At the bottom of the gully was an old log butted up against a small boulder. Creeping between the two offered her a measure of shelter from the airborne attack. She curled up and did the thing she least wanted to do. She waited. Her patience actually paid off. After several moments the fairies flew off and left her alone. Exiting cautiously, Bianca crept out of the gully and toward the north, away from the town.

It was barely a few paces and the fairies were back, even more of them than before. But this time the high-pitched whistle sounded more like the words: "Portal. Danger! Portal. Danger!" She was too frightened to wonder about the legends.

Left with no choice, Bianca ran as fast as possible, losing the robe, falling back into the gully and being forced by the horde of fairies back to the riverbank and once again into the cold water.

This time there was no reprieve. The townsfolk had reached the stream by then and saw her flop into the water. She tried to swim downstream, away from the crowd until she could clear the woods. That was a futile attempt. It was a simple matter for a few of the better swimmers to retrieve her and haul her onto the town side of the water. The air was actually warm, but nobody could convince Bianca of that. She was shivering uncontrollably, and her hand embroidered dress she had been so proud of a few days before was soaked, torn and soiled beyond belief. Someone actually took enough pity on her to wrap her in a wool blanket. It felt good at first, but after it absorbed some of the water from her dress it felt almost as cold and it did reek the stench of wet wool.

She was marched through town down the main street to the church across from where the wreck was still lying on its side. Xander, having heard the commotion, was there. So were his henchmen, with Jason and Margaret. "That was a foolish action," said Xander. "You haven't accomplished anything except to anger me even more. I will tolerate nothing out of you from now on." He ordered a guard to bind her hands behind her as before, but also tied her feet and then wrapped a line around her waist and tied her hands to it. No more getting out of her constraints. The wagon was the only usable vehicle left, so she was tossed into it. She lay on the floor near the back. The door was open and the slight breeze made her chill worse. She was thoroughly miserable and dispirited.

Through her despair she heard Xander thank the townsfolk for their help in capturing the criminal. He didn't spend too much time on his praise, she knew he wanted to get going. Jason and Margaret and a guard rode in the wagon with Bianca. Xander and a driver rode on the driver's seat. The others were left behind to arrange repairs to the carriage. Since there was no opening into the interior of the wagon, Xander and the driver had to communicate with the guard inside the wagon with a series of coded knocks.

On they went, east toward the kulkulcanlands in the mountains. Jason leaned back, crossed his arms and appeared thoughtful. Margaret looked at Bianca with pity on her face. But Bianca knew the woman could say or do nothing due to the guard seated between them.

Bianca didn't know what the next days would bring. But she did know one thing: it couldn't be good.

CHAPTER SEVEN
MEETING ILL'YX

Approaching the town of Natts' Nohoch Muulo'ob, kingdom of Vlogentia
Gregorian calendar: January 5
Mayan calendars: Tzolk'in: 13 Kimi
                      Haab: 19 K'ank'in

J ason decided he hated traveling in the wagon. It was dark but not pitch black since there were four small windows and vents near the roof, two on each side. The shelves, racks and floor were filled with equipment and supplies. The three abductees huddled on the available floor space. The guard sat on one of the crates, but didn't act any more comfortable. At least the sacbe was smooth and the ride wasn't rough.

After the accident at the inn Jason and Margaret had said nothing to Xander during Bianca's attempted escape, feigning shock and confusion. But Jason understood that Bianca thought he and Margaret had betrayed her. So, hoping that Margaret could establish some sort of rapport to mend fences, he encouraged his wife to console Bianca and try to make her understand their decision.

He heard Margaret start by saying, "Dear, we didn't tell him anything, I swear. We hoped, and still hope, that he will let us go home after Jason does his job. We knew that trying to flee at that time would just result in recapture. As it did, I'm so sorry. We need to wait until we arrive at Xander's destination. If he does betray us, there ought to be better opportunities for all of us then. But, how are you feeling? Can I do anything for you? You look so miserable."

"I am miserable," said Bianca, her voice low but full of anger. "If you had come with me we would have had a better chance of fending off the fairies and escaping through the woods. All we had to do was evade capture until nightfall and then I could have led you back to the capital and safety for me, and return to First World for you."

"We honestly didn't think you, or especially the three of us, had a chance to escape. I'm truly sorry you feel we failed you. Still, can I do anything to make you more comfortable?"

"Another blanket to lay on, and get that guard to quit staring at me all the time." She paused for introspection. "I understand your decision, however wrong it was. I am certain Xander has no intention of letting you return home. I just don't understand why you'd pass up a chance to get out of his clutches. I'm not sure I can trust you anymore. Leave me alone for a while." She turned over to place her back toward Margaret.

"Very well, dear," said Margaret, "but I believe, I have to believe, there will be better chances soon if we need them. Trust me." She put a spare blanket over Bianca.

"Let's hope so," grumbled Bianca. With that she appeared to doze off for a while.

As Jason had hoped, the women did manage to become friendlier, although it took several attempts by Margaret to start a conversation. Both were naturally outgoing and cheerful, current circumstances notwithstanding, and they finally began to enjoy talking about nothing much of importance. There wasn't much else for them to do. Jason could feel the reluctance they all had about saying anything concerning their current state of affairs. But, Bianca seemed to warm to both of them. Jason hoped she was getting over her anger.

Jason spent his time in the wagon going over the inventory. Xander and his brother had acquired a lot of useful things if one was to treat a rash of injuries. Jason was much less certain what he could use to make a lethal potion. He searched through every box, crate and package in the wagon. The brothers clearly did not know the difference between a toxin and a medicine. He'd have to find a way to speak to Xander about that. He couldn't make a poison out of thin air, not even in Second World.

The journey continued.

The sun was setting behind them as the wagon moved along the road. Xander, in one of his good moods, had the door to the wagon opened and let Jason and Margaret walk alongside the wheels. He was now sure they would not try to escape. He did keep Bianca shackled to the back rail. She could walk along, but had nowhere else to go.

To their left was the stream they had been paralleling since leaving Naats' Seebak Ha'. Before them was Natts' Nohoch Muulo'ob.

"That's our destination," said Xander. "We're finally here. Now we can start on the next step of the plan."

Perhaps a mile or so beyond the town the mountains rose precipitously into the darkening sky, like jagged teeth. Between the town and the mountains lay a narrow steppe with occasional scattered clumps of oak trees. The stream flowed from a gap in the range, across the steppe, alongside the town and into the heart of Vlogentia. The town had a formidable stone wall surrounding it. The wall was constructed with fitted stone blocks, about ten feet high and four feet thick with a rampart along the top. It looked like the pictures Jason had seen of the stone walls found around Mayan ruins in First World. A wooden gate, now firmly shut, was set into the west face of the wall. That is where the sacbe ended. Jason could not see, but he surmised that the interior of the town was no different than the others they had seen.

Hoping she would be forthcoming, he asked Bianca, "Why does this town have a fortification around it? Is it a military post? Is there a threat? Is it some sort of special depot?"

He hoped that getting out of the confines of the wagon would make her friendlier and a little more talkative.

She did appear to be in better spirits. She replied, "Other than the wall, which surrounds both the town and a large pasture for livestock, it is a normal Vlogentia settlement. At the moment may appear deceptively peaceful. That is not always the case. The fortification is to protect the inhabitants, and whatever livestock they can herd into safety, from the occasional raids by the mountain trolls. They will every so often charge down from the valleys between the peaks to burn and destroy vulnerable buildings and slaughter livestock. If caught out of the town or fortified farmsteads, people would also be killed. Rumor has it, but nobody knows for sure, that the trolls harass the dragons, what we call kulkullcano'ob, as well."

"What! There are mountain trolls? There are dragons? Nobody told us about any of this. What is this place?" exclaimed Margaret.

"It's Second World, of course. You never asked, so I assumed Xander had told you about such things," replied Bianca.

"He never said anything about trolls, or dragons, or merpeople or fairies for that matter," said Jason. He glared at Xander sitting next to the driver.

Xander just shrugged and gave Jason a wry smile. "Welcome to Second World."

He ordered the driver to stop the wagon and continued, "It is too late to enter the town, but that was not what I had in mind anyway. We've done well and made up for lost time and this is exactly when and where I had planned to be. I have business with Ill'yx. Jason, some of your questions will soon be answered."

The driver and Xander descended from their seat and set to work moving the wagon off the sacbe. This entailed considerable grunt work from the driver, the guard and Jason with the aid of some levers crafted from loose tree branches lying in a nearby grove of trees to lift the wagon's wheels over the sidewalls of the road. Xander supervised. The women carried some of the less secured items. Bianca had to stay in sight of Xander and the driver or the guard at all times. Afterwards she was chained to the wagon once again.

After leveraging the wagon over the sidewalls, they skirted the far side of the grove, staying out of sight of the town, and made for another stand of trees at the base of the mountains.

Night had fully fallen by the time the wagon was hidden in the trees. Tonight would be a small, inconspicuous camp well sheltered from view of the town.

After a meager meal Xander made everyone lie down on a bed of leaves with a blanket over them. But he silently motioned Jason over before he could go to sleep.

"We are going to meet your victim. He's just a little way up the slope in his den and he is expecting me. He and I have plans that need to be finalized. You pretend you're my assistant. Be aware, he might be a little more imposing than you are expecting."

Now Jason was thoroughly confused. "If you have plans with him, why do you want to have me kill him?" Jason was horrified at the thought of actually being responsible for killing someone, but had tried to rationalize the action, without success, by convincing himself that this was a very evil person, even more so than the duplicitous Xander. Truthfully, he fervently hoped that he would not have to go through with the deed. The fact that the supposed victim was an associate of Xander's and that he was obviously going to force Jason to fatally double cross his associate made him sick to his stomach. "*I should join forces with this 'victim' and turn the tables on Xander,"* he thought. That idea made him feel much more honorable.

"Ill'yx is a kulkulcan, or what the provincials call a kulkulcan after the ancient Mayan feathered serpent of myth, you would call him a dragon. So don't have any qualms about your part. You need to see him to gauge how best to achieve your part. For me, I would consider putting poison in some cattle and luring Ill'yx and his clan into eating them. But you cannot act too rashly, we need Ill'yx, and hopefully the other kulkulcano'ob, to destroy this town and possibly a few others before you eliminate them."

"Wait, you can do business with a dragon? How is that possible? And what are you talking about? You want to wait until AFTER the dragons have destroyed one or more of your villages before eliminating them? That makes absolutely no sense."

"It makes perfect sense. If the kulkulcano'ob can level one or even several towns then the king can call on the population to raise a huge army to defend the realm. Of course, we would have little chance of defeating a horde of kulkulcano'ob. That is your part. Once they are eliminated the king will have amassed a great army the populace would not normally tolerate, and he can use it to bring fame, glory and conquest to Vlogentia. For our parts, my brother and I have been promised important posts in his government. But, between you and me, we have additional plans. As for you, if you don't do as instructed I have arranged a little demonstration of what you and your wife can expect. It should also help inflame the few survivors of the town to spread the alarm across the land. Now, let's get started, Ill'yx should be waiting."

Jason was aghast. Evil Xander was coming to the forefront. This was worse than anything he could have imagined. How in the world, in either world, could this be stopped? Something had to be done, but he had no ideas.

They went up the slope to a niche at the base of the mountain. Once there Xander called out, "I am here Ill'yx, it is Xander with word from the human king that he approves and encourages you to take your rightful place in the world."

From the back of the niche a head appeared. Definitely reptilian, or perhaps dinosaurian, thought Jason. More than four feet long and well over two and a half feet wide it looked like one of the velociraptor dinosaurs made popular in recent movies, but much larger. Jason couldn't tell in the inadequate light from Xander's hand lantern, but it appeared as if the dragon's head was covered in fine feathers rather than scales. He had a large feathered red crest atop his head. His eyes were huge, reptilian yellow, and set facing mostly forward. The teeth weren't visible until the mouth was opened, which was just as well. They were at least six inches long in double rows and gleaming like they were coated in steel.

Ill'yx spoke, "It's about time. I have been waiting for your report. You are sure the human king is in agreement with my ambitions. He doesn't mind losing a few of the settlements?"

The dragon's voice was not as deep as someone would expect from such a huge creature, but rather high pitched. It was also not as sibilant as people often assumed a reptilian voice would be. It further occurred to Jason that he wasn't even surprised that the dragon could talk. He'd been in Second World too long already.

"No," said Xander, "he does not. He has his reasons. These villages are beyond our area of interest. We have no interest in their fate. They are yours for your pleasure."

Xander, Jason mused, was an exceptionally good liar.

Xander went on, "Will you attack in the morning? Will the other kulkulcano'ob assist you?"

"No, they will not," Ill'yx answered, "they don't understand the need for fame and glory. They just want to stay in the mountains, fend off the hated trolls, and play and fish in the great ocean beyond the peaks. I couldn't even convince them to join me even after I killed one that was particularly vocal against me. That just made the rest of them cower in their lairs or fly to a lake. No matter, they will soon learn to follow me."

"That should be enough, "said Xander, "but I have one last task for you. We have a criminal with us, that's a person who has not followed one of our established customs. As punishment, I will lead her to the edge of the woods and push her out, you must dispose of her for us. The king will consider that a great favor. The people of the town must not see me however. Can you do that as well?"

"Certainly. We kulkulcano'ob can handle such mundane chores. Do not bother yourself with trivial worries. Tomorrow you will witness the power of our ancient breed."

Jason was now enraged. The reason Bianca had been brought was now crystal clear and he was ready to bolt to the campsite to warn Margaret and Bianca. The only reason he did not turn and run was that Xander was sporting both a rapier and a dagger tonight, and he was much quicker afoot than Jason.

Ill'yx went back into his lair, Jason and Xander went back down the slope to the campsite. "Say nothing or I will harm your wife," said Xander, "we need you, but we may not have as much a need for a lawyer. In the morning you better get started on a poison that will kill a kulkulcan. You may be in luck, we may need only enough poison to kill just one."

Back at the campsite, Jason was kept away from the women by the guard and driver, on Xander's orders. But deep in the night, when everyone was quiet and the guard was nodding off, Jason took a chance.

He surreptitiously crept over to Bianca to warn her. He was surprised, her blue eyes were wide open and alert. "You're in grave danger, you must risk another escape tonight, and there are no other options." He told her of Xander's plans for her and for the kingdom. He expected her to be terrified.

She was surprisingly calm. "Yes, I had figured out what he likely had planned for me. There was no other reason for my abduction and his reluctance to say anything about why I am here. There are always other options, good and bad. If I am right about Xander and about the curiosity of kulkulcano'ob, what you call dragons, I may have a good option. Does he still wear the rapier and dagger he donned today?"

"Yes, what of it?"

Bianca sighed, closed her eyes, and said, "We'll see."

CHAPTER EIGHT
ILL'YX CONFRONTED

Natts' Nohoch Muulo'ob, kingdom of Vlogentia
Gregorian calendar: January 6
Mayan calendars: Tzolk'in: 1 Manik'
                Haab: 0 Muwan

S unrise over the mountains took its time to clear the peaks, but the day was clear and calm. Bianca was awake, in fact she had slept little. The coming day and what might transpire and what she thought she could do about it kept her mind racing throughout the night. She had a plan if Xander did as Jason told her he would and if the kulkulcan was as curious as legends indicated.

Xander gathered everybody and announced at breakfast, "Today is going to be a great day. Manik' is the Tzolk'in day of destiny and the appropriate day for the onset of the grand plan. I can't wait for Ill'yx to appear."

The guard and driver applauded him. They raised their cups in a toast. "To a Greater Volgentia!"

Jason and Margaret, who had obviously been told about the 'grand plan' by Jason, sat with heads down, hands shaking in fear, and not eating anything at all. Margaret was silently crying.

Bianca took all this in, and tried to pretend to be nervous. Xander needed to believe she was terrified if her plan had any chance of success.

Finally the shadow of the mountains crept over and past the town and steppe, bathing the area in bright sunlight.

At last Ill'yx emerged from his lair and flew to the front of the grove where Xander and the rest of the group waited. Jason and Margaret appeared awestruck. Even the guard and driver seemed impressed. Bianca assumed that they had never seen a live kulkulcan before. For that matter, neither had she. He was, she admitted to herself, a truly awesome sight. Her level of anxiety increased twofold.

He was more than seventy feet long, almost half of that his tail. The most unusual alteration from the other creatures Bianca knew was that he had two sets of forelimbs. One set was slightly smaller than the hind legs and able to be used as either grappling or walking appendages. The other set of forelegs were wings, large wings. Ill'yx had at least a sixty-five foot wingspan when they were not folded alongside his body like a bird. She noticed, however, that he could use only one set of forelegs at a time. When he flew to meet Xander he had kept his forelegs curled up against his body. When he landed he could walk or manipulate things with the forelegs, but she saw that he had to keep his wings furled against its body.

Both forelegs and hind legs had large, six to eight inch claws, to go along with his iron crusted teeth. His body was thin and lithe, almost serpent like.

Bianca had read stories about kulkulcano'ob from the books brought to Vlogentia by Saint Sebastian and by later members of the Order. Ill'yx did not fit the description of a classic kulkulcan from European lore. The most striking difference from those stories was that he had downy feathers, much like a chick's or duckling's first feathers, intermingling with his scales. Ill'yx' back feathers were a deep blue green, and his underside feathers were a light blue grey. However his wing feathers were incredibly large, to serve as flight feathers. They were a deeper blue than his back. The underwing feathers were the same color as his underbody.

His tail was long, slender and rather stiff. It wasn't as flexible as lizard's tail but was semi-rigid. Bianca decided that was to balance and help steer him during flight, like a bird. His tail feathers were arranged horizontally, extending about ten inches from each side of the tail, and dark forest green. His head, blue green like his upper body, was as Jason had described to her the night before, there was a great red crest running along the top of his head. The crest turned into a row of ivory spikes running along his spine all the way to the tip of his tail. The spikes near his head and along the neck and back were four to six inches tall, shrinking to just a couple inches tall along the tail.

Bianca realized that a person who had stumbled from First World to Second World and then made somehow it back home would take tales of such an incredible beast back with them. Based on the texts she'd read she saw how someone could describe Ill'yx or his kin as the kulkulcan of European lore, or the Asian version of kulkulcano'ob, the Roc of Arabic legend, or the feathered serpent Quetzalcoatl of Mesoamerican myth.

Ill'yx walked to the spot in the grove where the caravan was hiding. The walls of Natts' Nohoch Muulo'ob were crowded with people. Bianca assumed they were wondering what a kulkulcan was doing there since she, and probably the townsfolk, were unaware of any history of contact between kulkulcano'ob and people.

Adding to the spectacle she could see twelve to fifteen other kulkulcano'ob perched on the mountain ridge behind the campsite's grove, just watching the scene.

Jason and Margaret were standing just inside the edge of the tree line near the campsite. Xander's men were watching them.

Bianca was standing next to Xander, on his orders. She was shaking and quivering in apprehension. She tried to tell herself that it was pretense for Xander's benefit, but that wasn't true. She no longer needed to pretend.

Xander, hiding just inside the grove, called to Ill'yx, "In order to have the greatest effect on the town and its people, you should burn the church first to demoralize them and then start to tear down the walls with your claws."

"I would think my presence hovering over you small talkative creatures would be frightening enough, but I will do as you ask. Just this once, mind you. What is a church? Why should I set fire to it? Fire is capricious and can have a mind of its own. It almost always flares out of control, cannot be stopped and destroys everything. Even we are cautious about using it."

"Don't worry about setting fire to the church, it is built well. You will only scorch it but you act will serve to further frighten the populace. It's a meeting place for the inhabitants. It will be the largest building in the village, near the center. Its front will be taller than the rest of the building with a bell in an opening near the top. There will be a symbol on its top that looks like this." He drew an image of a cross in the dirt. "I will stay hidden in the trees, I don't want them to know that anybody else is involved in planning and executing such a bold scheme. This is to be all about you today."

Xander continued, "After you start destroying the walls, I will shove the captive toward you from the trees." He grabbed and shook Bianca. "Stop the destruction for a moment and take care of her. Make sure it could be visible to any townsfolk that might be watching. Then go back and do your destructive best."

"I will do this last favor for you. I am not sure why one tiny creature matters so much when I'll be wrecking the entire town. You small talkative creatures are a mystery to me, I don't understand why you do some things. You will be beholden to me, however." He took a few steps back. "I best get started."

Ill'yx leapt into the air with a great downrush of his enormous wings, causing a gale like a storm surge from an approaching thunderstorm. He let out a loud, high pitched grunt as he lifted off and started to fly over the town.

The townsfolk appeared suitably panicked. They were screaming. Some jumped down from the wall and disappeared into the town. Some leapt over the wall and ran for the nearest copse of trees. A few dashed to the stream outside the wall, some to gather water buckets, but most to wade into the water. Probably, Bianca thought, in the hope of protection from fire.

She watched Ill'yx circle the town several times to locate the church Xander had described. She knew he'd found it when he stopped circling and prepared to exhale his fire.

His belly feathers rippled as he churned his stomach to generate the methane needed for the fire. A gnashing of his iron coated teeth sounded like a huge gong and created a spark. This resulted in an intense blue flame erupting from his mouth, and the church was soon ablaze. Bianca could see the flames from the edge of the grove of trees. Ill'yx then flew to the grassy expanse in front of the stone rampart. He landed, furled his wings, and his great front claws went to work tearing it down.

While all of this was going on, the other kulkulcano'ob stayed on their perches, but appeared visibly upset. They were jumping up and down, hooting, shrieking and furling and unfurling their wings like frightened chickens. It appeared to Bianca that they disapproved of the attack.

Some of the braver inhabitants of the town were still manning the rampart and trying to shoot Ill'yx with crossbows. The barrage had no effect on the armored scales under the feathers. After their bolts were spent they disappeared from the wall, most likely to seek shelter wherever they thought might be safe.

Jason and Margaret, standing by the wagon a few feet from Xander and Bianca were transfixed in horror.

Margaret was exclaiming, in a low quavering voice, over and over, "I don't believe this. I don't want to believe this. The old myths are coming to life."

Bianca stood next to Xander, still shaking but watching everything. The guards moved to stand behind her, ready to help Xander push her forward if necessary.

Apparently satisfied with Ill'yx' actions so far, Xander grabbed Bianca's hair.

This time she reacted differently. This wasn't Naats' Seebak Ha' all over again. She started to scream, whine and thrash about wildly. She tried scratching him. This visibly angered Xander, which is what she wanted. Her frantic twisting made it impossible for him to push her out of the grove without exposing himself to the town.

But by now all the townsfolk had taken shelter from Ill'yx. Nobody was left on the wall to see Xander carry Bianca down to him. So, he began to lug her closer to the kulkulcan before pushing her into peril. As he approached the kulkulcan she continued to writhe and scream, pretending to be panic stricken. But she was biding her time.

About twenty feet from the rear of the Ill'yx, Bianca suddenly stopped her wailing and thrashing. Using her hand-to-hand training, she stopped flailing her feet, straightened and planted her right foot on the ground causing Xander to stop and stumble. He was caught off guard, she had completely fooled him. She placed her left foot between his legs and twisted violently, throwing him over her shoulder and onto the ground with her on top of him. On the way down she smashed him in the jaw with her elbow. Then she began to tumble with him toward the kulkulcan. If kulkulcano'ob were as curious as she had been told, this would provide her the chance she needed.

Ill'yx was indeed seemingly interested about what was going on behind him. He stopped his destruction of the wall and started a turn to see just what was happening.

Bianca and Xander continued to roll down the slope toward the kulkulcan's feet, as she had planned. As they rolled down the grassy slope Bianca felt the rocks in the ground pummel her back. She felt Xander's breath on her face and saw the surprise, turning to panic, in his eyes. Both were now sweating profusely. While struggling with him, Bianca managed to draw the dagger from the sheath at Xander's belt. He continued to fight back, grabbing her by the throat and choking her. She couldn't breathe with his hands squeezing her neck, she was becoming desperate as well.

As they reached the kulkulcan's feet she managed to thrust the blade under the ribs and upward toward his heart.

Xander shuddered, and warm, rank blood spilled everywhere. She then saw a sight she never wanted to see again. His eyes grew glassy and lifeless as his soul left his body.

She felt his last breath escape and his limbs go limp. For an instant she was aghast at what she had just done.

While Bianca's brawl with Xander was ending Ill'yx clearly wanted to know what was happening. He continued his turn to assess the situation, now placing her and Xander's body by his front feet. This was the kulkulcan curiosity she needed and wished for.

Bianca recovered her resolve and, using all the strength she could muster, pushed Xander's body up and off her, stood and shoved the corpse at Ill'yx' face, obstructing his vision. As she did this, she drew the rapier from the scabbard at Xander's belt. When his corpse fell from in front of the now confused kulkulcan's face she was face to face with the monster. No more than a three feet between them, his enormous yellow eyes staring at her unblinking. His pupils were dilated, his mouth partially open getting ready to chomp her into pieces. His crest was fully raised. She could hear and feel his warm but not flaming breath and feel the air move as he fluttered his wings.

She was shaking like a leaf. For an instant that seemed like an eternity they confronted each other, Bianca knowing that the death of one of them was imminent.

Before he could recover his wits and fully open his great jaws for the killing bite she mustered all the resolve she had. She made a feint to her right with her hand but danced to her left. Ill'x y took the bait and lunged forward to where he apparently thought she would be. His jaws snapped shut with a thunderous clang as his iron-coated teeth met nothing but air. This put her alongside his great head and, with both her trembling hands wrapped tightly around the hilt, thrust the sword into the kulkulcan's right eye. She felt the blade pierce the eye and scrape on the bone as it passed through the gap in the back of the orbit and into the brain. Vitreous from the eye spewed from the wound, followed by a torrent of hot, malodorous blood. She twisted it back and forth as violently as she could.

Ill'yx let out a piercing scream, exhaled some fire and began to thrash violently.

Bianca, still holding the hilt, was tossed about like a sack of yams. One of his claws gouged her stomach sending a sharp pain along her right side. But she held on and continued to work the sword trying to sever the spinal cord.

For a few terrifying seconds the kulkulcan continued to writhe, then he fell lifeless with his head atop Bianca. She feared she would be trapped under him, but when she pushed the head up it was much lighter than she thought it would be. She heaved the head to the side, stood up and withdrew the sword from the eye. She stood unmoving for some time, taking in what she had just done.

For a few seconds, nothing moved as if time stood still. There was not a sound anywhere.

Then Bianca turned and walked slowly toward the ruined portion of the town barricade. She stopped just outside the large gap Ill'yx had made and spoke to the crowd now assembling at the ruined wall.

"I was a captive of the rogue man you see lying there next to the kulkulcan. He tried to have the beast kill me and then destroy your town as a pretext to convince the people of the kingdom to fight the kulkulcano'ob. He failed. I do not notice the other kulkulcano'ob eager to attack to avenge their fallen comrade. Perhaps they are now as afraid of people as you are of them."

She pointed to where the wagon was hidden in copse. "There are other captives hidden in those trees. They are from First World and strangers to Vlogentia. The sight of kulkulcano'ob terrified them. They are my friends and they need reassurance that they are now safe. Go help them, please."

She sat down on the ground, rapier still in her hand, both physically and mentally exhausted. She barely noticed when the wagon rolled by with Jason and Margaret walking alongside. Xander's men had fled.

While all this was transpiring, one of the kulkulcano'ob finally stirred. It flew down to the body of Ill'yx and cautiously walked around and sniffed it, then poked it with one of its forelegs. Satisfied that he actually was dead it turned to face its comrades still perched on the ledge and started speaking to them. The voice was a little lower in pitch than Ill'yx. It used kulkulcan speech, so no humans knew what was being said, but its actions implied that it was very pleased with the outcome. It hopped excitedly and seemed happy, if a person could comprehend kulkulcan body language. The other kulkulcano'ob reacted similarly. All of them appeared to Binaca to be elated at Ill'yx' demise.

The new kulkulcan turned and approached Bianca. It was slightly smaller, but not by much. It was colored identically. Perhaps a kulkulcan could tell one from another, but Bianca couldn't. She rose and stood still as a statue. She was no longer sure the kulkulcano'ob were as happy at Ill'yx' death as it seemed. Also, the realization of what she had just accomplished was starting to overwhelm her, and this possible new threat pushed her almost to the breaking point.

The kulkulcan spoke, in Yucatek, "Greetings to you, little one. I cannot tell you how pleased all of my clan is about the death of that tyrant."

Relief rushed through Bianca. All might be well after all.

It added, "My name is Ill'yonix. I am the first male egg from the clutch of the dam who is from Ill'yx' clutch." Bianca took several seconds to analyze this, and finally decided that Ill'yonix was Ill'yx' nephew.

She responded. "Greetings to you, sir kulkulcan. I am Bianca, a person of the kingdom of Vlogentia. I'm glad you are grateful for the death of your despot. If I could be so bold, why are you so glad he is dead? How do you know my tongue?" She was so taken aback by this turn of events, talking to a kulkulcan related to one that she'd just killed, that she forgot the polite way to greet someone. She hoped he didn't care.

"As I said, he was a tyrant. He wanted to terrorize all the lands beyond the mountains where our lairs are. None of us ever understood why. Any one of us who questioned him or defied him would be attacked. He even killed his own clutch mate. None of the rest of us want conflict with small talkative creatures. We ignore you and your ignore us. All we want to do is fly, swim, hunt for the great white fish in the sea beyond the mountains, and lay in the sun during the day. Our only conflict is with the mountain trolls who raid our lairs and steal our eggs and sometimes kill our young. We have no need for strife with you small talkative creatures. We give you our thanks and will return to the mountains. Good riddance to that one." He nodded his great head in the direction of the dead Ill'yx. "In answer to your second question, some of us learned your language from the occasional small talkative explorer. For now, may your wings find the gentle updrafts."

Bianca thought for a few seconds. "If I could have your attention, I have an idea. The mountain trolls will peer out from their holes and notice the damage to our town. They will undoubtedly attack tonight to steal livestock, wreck destruction, and threaten people since they can now swarm through the breach in our wall. What if you and your kin would help in our defense? It would help us, but also enable you to get rid of a lot of those vermin that would later threaten you. Humans and kulkulcano'ob working together could pose a serious danger to them. It would be benefit to you to fight them here, and not in your lairs where your eggs are at risk."

It was Ill'yonix' turn to ponder the idea for a while. After a moment, he said, "Wait here, little person. I need to consult with the others of my clan. I will return with an answer." With that he spread his wings, folded his forelegs, leapt into the air and flew back to the rest of the kulkulcano'ob still perched on the ridge.

Bianca had to duck from the downdraft of Ill'yonix' departure. Then she waited. So did the people of the town as well as Jason and Margaret. While she waited she turned to face the town. "Do not be afraid. The new kulkulcan, whose name is Ill'yonix, is friendly to us. He, and the rest of his clan are glad this one," she said, pointing to Ill'yx, "is dead. He will return in a moment. All is good."

Ill'yonix flew back to her position several moments later. "We think you have a good idea. Fighting the trolls in the openness before the town will be easier for us rather than in the confines of a lair. You small creatures protecting our flanks and wings will also be an advantage. Sometimes trolls can overwhelm us and severely damage our wings. They can even damage a young one enough to cause its death. I and four other of the older, more experienced troll fighters, will return at sunset. Be ready for us."

With that he flew back to the ridge, and all the kulkulcano'ob returned to the lairs in the peaks.

Bianca turned back toward the town and entered through the large gap in the defense created by Ill'yx. "The kulkulcano'ob are going to aid us in the defense of Natts' Nohoch Muulo'ob tonight if the mountain trolls attack, which we all know they are likely to do. As I said the clan are grateful that the one is dead. Apparently he was a despot. We will need their help tonight, since we cannot rely on an intact wall to keep the trolls out of the city."

This caused a wave of relief from the inhabitants.

"Trolls? The trolls you told us about will attack tonight? Will this nightmare never end?" moaned Margaret to Bianca.

"Trolls are the vermin for which our border cities need the fortifications," said one of the town's elders to Jason and Margaret, probably the mayor by his manner. "We have to deal with them often. They swarm out their holes in the mountains, gather during daylight and then usually attack at night. If we stay behind the walls and mount a defense, we are generally safe. But with this gap in our wall, we will need the kulkulcano'ob help to keep them out tonight." He turned to the crowd of townsfolk nearby and said, "But we can also help ourselves. Let's get busy repairing as much of our barricade as we can before they attack."

With that the folk started gathering the stone scattered by Ill'yx and putting it back in place. There was a lot of stone to replace, too much for the time left.

Bianca went to find the mayor and watch the repairs to the town's wall. She was clutching her side and walking with a noticeable hesitation in her stride.

She nodded to Jason and Margaret as they passed by her. They offered the barest of waves as they sat on the wagon looking terrified and lonely.

The setting sun lit the western sky with a red cast. Some of the townsfolk were saying that it portended an awful, bloody conflict. Bianca had to remind them, "A red sunset means tomorrow will be a beautiful, wonderful day. Have faith and courage. The kulkulcano'ob will be here. We will prevail."

The battle for Natts' Nohoch Muulo'ob was just hours away.

CHAPTER NINE
THE BATTLE FOR NATTS' NOHOCH MUULO'OB

Natts' Nohoch Muulo'ob, kingdom of Vlogentia, late afternoon
Gregorian calendar: January 6
Mayan calendars: Tzolk'in: 1 Manik'
                  Haab: 0 Muwan

Bianca was amazed. A large section of Natts' Nohoch Muulo'ob's fortification was a total ruin. Ill'yx had torn a gap in it about twenty yards wide all the way to the ground. A few townsfolk were frantically moving debris around trying to figure out how to rebuild by nightfall.

Having failed to find the mayor, she was sitting on one of the larger boulders located near the ruined section of the wall watching their desperate activity and trying not to notice the sharp and deep pain in her right side. Events had happened so quickly that she hadn't yet paid it much attention. Her dress was torn and completely soaked in blood. She had assumed that it was from Xander and the kulkulcan, but now she saw fresh blood oozing down her right side from a tear in the dress. A quick look told her what she feared, a gash about five inches long under her ribs, an injury she must have acquired from one of Ill'yx' claws during his death throes. She leaned back against the wall, closed her eyes and sighed. She didn't even notice she still held Xander's rapier in her right hand, the tip of the blade resting on the ground.

Someone touched her on the shoulder, and Bianca's eyes flew open as she leveled the rapier. Once she saw it was Jason, she lowered it.

He asked, "What's the matter? Are you exhausted, worried, injured or what? Margaret and I saw you sitting here and were worried about you. I thought I'd come over and see if I could be of any aid."

"Thank you. I have a deep wound in my right side. It's bleeding, I'm in pain, and I don't know what can be done." Her voice was weak and strained, even to her own ears.

"You know that I'm a healer, let me see."

She pulled the tatters of the dress away from the injury with her left hand and Jason examined it.

"A serious laceration to be sure, but it's treatable. I need to clean and bandage this. When the bleeding stops we can replace the dressing, close the wound and it should heal."

"There should be others with far less severe injuries who need treatment. Please take care of them first. We both know the frequent outcome of a deep slash to the stomach area. Despite cleaning and bandaging it becomes infested, the person develops a high fever and dies. Let me be for a moment. Tend to the rest. Then you can see to my wound." She closed her eyes again, leaned back against the wall again, and let out a low groan.

"Nonsense, you have forgotten that I specialize in magic healing potions." Jason's voice was filled with irony. "I can concoct a potion that will prevent the infestation and fever, and then I will close the wound so it will heal with hardly a trace. It's a good thing I made the guards abandon the wagon after you killed that kulkulcan. Among the supplies I found were several ointments and supplies that will be useful in treating injuries like yours."

"And you need care now. As I said there is an ointment in the wagon that will help. I don't see anyone else that needs treatment."

Bianca looked around and saw no injured people.

"Do you speak truthfully? If that is possible, I would of course be ever grateful to you. Can you make the potion now?"

"No, the potion can wait for a while. But I do need to clean and bind the wound to stop the bleeding. Wait here while I get supplies, and you need to have someone bring some fresh, hot water." He hurried back to the wagon as she requested a bowl of hot water from a nearby woman.

Jason was back at Bianca's side a few moments later with antibiotic ointment, scissors and gauze dressings. He cut away a portion of the ruined dress, cleaned the gash with warm water and a clean cloth, put some antibiotic ointment into it and dressed it as best he could. He used sterile gauze from the wagon but had to use a clean strip of linen around her midriff to hold it in place.

Margaret arrived at Bianca's side.

"Dear, you look terrible. I'm so sorry. You were incredibly brave. I'm so proud of you. You actually slew a dragon! I couldn't believe it at first. But look at you now. Your hair is a matted mess, of course. And your dress looks like a used surgical dressing. It's torn almost to shreds and is soaked in blood. You look exhausted. You poor thing!"

Margaret held her and wiped her face with a clean, wet cloth and made her let go of the sword.

When Jason was done, Bianca looked and felt much improved though still obviously in some discomfort.

She was able to stand, walk a few steps and look around her. She turned and gave Jason a careful hug. "Thank you both. I owe you so much."

"We're just glad you are feeling better and have a chance at recovery."

"You are a wonderful healer. God forbid, we may have need of your talent tonight. The healers' house is over there." She pointed to the house one of the women had indicated to her. "Please go help them and work your magic for us tonight."

Jason and Margaret nodded and gave Bianca one more careful hug.

"We're glad we can be of any benefit we can provide," said Margaret. "Please take care of yourself."

They walked across the street to the house, a new spring in their step. They appeared to Bianca that having something, anything, constructive to do raised their spirits. "*That's good,*" she thought. "*They may need their spirit tonight.*"

Now feeling stronger since the dressing was holding tight, she turned back to look at the ruined wall and the frantic activity of the residents attempting repair. The effort was totally disorganized and accomplishing very little. The coordinator of the effort, if he could be called that, was the man she had assumed was the mayor. He'd finally made an appearance. He was a stout, middle-aged man with the air of importance a mayor should have. He was raising his voice about the din but being heard by nobody.

She walked slowly to him, absently picking up the rapier, and said, "Excuse me sir, but it doesn't appear that much is being accomplished yet."

"No, you are right," he replied. "Everybody is running around and getting in each other's way. I don't know how to make this better. It has been years since the royal architects came here and directed the building of our defenses. We don't know what to do." He threw his hands up in frustration. "Oh, please excuse me and my poor manners for not giving you a proper greeting. I am at my wit's end. My name is Franco Estrada, although my friends call me Calhuka, my Mayan name." He needed no introduction from the woman who had slain the kulkulcan.

Bianca said, "Do not worry about formalities, sir. We have a crisis coming and our preparations are not adequate. If you don't mind, I have a suggestion that you could relay to your people. Call a group of workers over, five or six at a time, and organize them into a team. One person would be the assigned as the supervisor of that group, two or three of the others would be tasked to pick up a piece of debris from the rubble that the supervisor had spotted and bring it to their allotted site, and the others would fit the stone as best they could. While they are fitting the stone, more rocks would be spotted by the supervisor and brought to the site. They could even change roles every so often so everybody has a chance at being the boss. It would also be best if you concentrated on the sides of the gap. Building the walls there would narrow the access the trolls would have. As it is you are building everywhere, and the gap is still wide and the wall is low."

Calhuka thought for the briefest of moments. "This is an excellent suggestion. Thank you, thank you."

He immediately started gathering small groups of folks. "I've had a wonderful idea. I want you to start there…" and he repeated almost word for word what Bianca had said.

She didn't mind, let him take the credit if it made the walls of the fortification taller at the sides of the gap and the resulting opening smaller. She had to sit down and rest a bit anyway. She found her original boulder, which was not being used in the repair, and sat while still holding Xander's rapier.

Dusk was rapidly approaching. Repairs to the wall were finally progressing rapidly, but would not be finished by nightfall. That's when the trolls would attack. Finally Jorge Perez, the captain of the town guard, called a halt to the repairs, and started to organize the defense.

He stood in the middle of the work site resplendent in his guard uniform of light blue overcoat with silver epaulets, white trousers and a rapier at his side. Tall and very military in appearance, it was easy for him to command.

"I want crossbowmen on the ramparts of the wall, on either side of the gap. Do not form a solid line of defense across the break in the wall. Instead I want ten of the best crossbowmen spread out across the gap. When the trolls attack you are to fire no more than two bolts each and then fall back into the town. I want you to lure the assault into the breach. The town guard will be stationed in line here" –he stood about fifteen yards beyond the gap and into the town, near where Bianca was sitting—"and be armed with swords and wooden shields. The rest of you need to find any spears, axes, pikes or other useful implement and position yourselves in two lines from the edge of the intact wall to the shield wall of the guard. Gather what rubble or carts or anything you can use to form a barrier for you to defend. This will lead the trolls into a three-sided zone where they will be flanked on the sides as they are halted by the shield wall. We are going to make them pay for their audacity. Get busy, we have little time."

As the men organized the defense, Captain Perez noticed Bianca sitting nearby. He marched over to her and bowed. "Greetings and a fortunate blend of Tzolk'in and Haab days to you. Your actions today will long live in our legends. I must caution you, however, that this is a very dangerous place for you tonight. The trolls have an open invitation into our town. Normally trolls have a history of probing all sides of a town to find a weak spot. They circle the fortifications until finding a potential way into the city, and then mass for the attack. My goal tonight is to use our weakness and have them crowded into such a tight place they won't be able to fight effectively. But the tight place is where you're sitting. You need to move, I fear for your safety."

"And a pleasant blend of days to you, sir," replied Bianca. "I am where I want to be. The kulkulcano'ob should be arriving shortly and I need to greet them and position them for maximum effect. Had you forgotten they will be our allies tonight?"

"No, I had not. I welcome the aid. Their presence won't change my strategy, but will add considerable distress to the vermin." He bowed again and returned to his duties.

As he was organizing the men, the kulkulcano'ob arrived. It now was almost sunset and the trolls would be coming soon. Kulkulcano'ob rarely flew out of the mountain passes, and had never before seen in a group. They were impressive. Five sets of sixty-five foot wingspans side by side give the defenders a large shot of confidence. They landed just outside the wall alongside the body of Ill'yx with a noticeable tremor of the ground and the sound of five sets of wings slapping against armored bodies as they were furled. There they waited. Bianca signaled to the captain to accompany her to meet them. Her injury, due to Jason's ministrations, bothered her hardly at all. She walked with a normal gait.

"Greetings again, little person." said Ill'yonix.

Bianca recognized the voice, she still couldn't tell him from the others, especially in the gathering dark. "Greetings again to you and a fortunate mix to days for you," she said, "we welcome your arrival. How do you want to help?"

"If I may," interrupted the captain, "allow me to counsel such awesome allies."

Bianca was amused, he was clearly trying to be extremely polite to a creature five feet in front of his face that had two rows of eight inch long iron coated teeth.

"If you would fly just inside our wall, two on either side of the gap and behind the groups of men stationed there, and wait for the trolls to enter the gap. That will compress and disorganize any formation they might have," said Captain Perez. "Then you attack their confused mob. That would make best use of your talents. The fifth one of you should alight on a sturdy nearby roof and be ready to enter the battle where most needed."

"An excellent plan, please back up a bit so we can launch and fly to our spots." They did, and the kulkulcano'ob lifted off with a blast of wind and grunts.

The kulkulcano'ob had barely settled into their positions when the trolls swarmed out of the lower mountain passes and made for the town.

Jason and Margaret temporarily left the healers' house and walked over to see how Bianca was doing and to see what the town was up against.

"Have you ever seen these things before?" Margaret asked.

"No, I haven't," answered Bianca.

The three of them saw what looked like thousands of creatures, all about four feet tall. They had long faces and snouts presumably armed with sharp teeth. They appeared to be dark green in color, although it was difficult to tell in the growing dusk of the day. They walked on two short legs, and had short arms with clawed digits. They had no visible ears. The tails were long and snakelike. A sort of armor made of densely packed scales covered their bodies.

"Those aren't trolls," exclaimed Margaret, "they're just giant, armored, two-legged lizards!"

"Four foot tall lizards. Trolls. I don't see a difference," said Jason. "You need to come with us, Bianca. This is too dangerous."

"I'm alright. As I told the captain I want to be here in case what you call the dragons need my advice. I'll be fine. Don't worry. You need to get back to the healers' house. Go on!"

They hurried back to the temporary emergency clinic.

Onward the attack came. As Captain Perez had planned, the trolls saw the way into the city beyond the body of a dead kulkulcan. That should have given them pause, but it didn't. As the first wave reached the rubble at the base of the wall, the skirmishers fired their crossbows twice and retreated inside. Crossbow bolts then rained down on the trolls from the ramparts. Bianca could hear the clink of the bolts as they penetrated the armor of the trolls, followed by the grunts and squeals of the injured. Once the trolls were through the gap and into the town the defenders lashed out with everything they had.

The main defense line formed the shield wall about fifteen yards from the gap in the wall to halt the advance and began stabbing the trolls with short spears or cutting at them with swords. They were the city guard and moderately well disciplined. They held firm. The flank attacks from the other townspeople behind their ramshackle barricade caught the trolls by surprise and forced them into a disorganized mass trapped between the flank attacks and the shield wall. Then the surprise. Two kulkulcan leapt into the air and let loose with a blast of fire into the mass of trolls before furling their wings and dropping alongside the townsfolk and tearing into the vermin and taking vengeance for all the stolen eggs and dead young. Jaws snapped shut with a metallic clang, taking two or three trolls at a time. Their claws ripped every which way. The two others fell on the rear of the troll horde, compressing them even further into the trap.

Trolls fought back with a desperate ferocity. The stench from their mouths was like month old rotten meat, it could knock a man back by itself. A bite from of the lizard/troll could prove septic. They bit, they slashed with their claws, they flailed with their tails and they even tried to crush with their arms if a man got too close. They'd crawl over each other to get at a man.

Once the kulkulcano'ob were on the ground, they became vulnerable to attack from the sides. Trolls tried to rip off the wings and jump on their backs. The men would then attack while the trolls were thus occupied, killing them from behind.

The fighting was ferocious. After a while the flank battles became more disorganized as trolls managed to push through or clamber over the barricades. The humans pushed back. The trolls counterattacked. The combat degenerated into a melee. The shield wall was starting to yield ground under the constant pressure of hundreds of trolls. There was grappling, stabbing, slashing and biting everywhere and from all sides. The yells and screams of the men mixed with the grunts and hisses of the trolls and the near constant clanging of kulkulcan teeth biting a troll was deafening.

Ill'yonix, perched on the roof of a nearby house, saw a group of trolls pushing the humans' shield wall back into the residential area of the city. It was time.

He dove into the midst of the mass of trolls and began to wreck destruction of his own, his great jaws snapping shut and turning trolls into fragments. But five trolls seized the opportunity and latched onto his wings, which he had not had time to furl as he landed. This limited his fighting ability since he couldn't use his front legs with his wings extended.

Bianca saw his plight from the boulder she was now standing on, which up until now had been out of the fight. Ill'yonix was only a few feet away and in danger. She gathered whatever strength she had left and jumped into the fray, rapier still in hand. Her side sent a sharp pain along her body, the dressing had come loose and she started to bleed again. The stench of the trolls was nearly overpowering, like rotting flesh. It was no matter. She let out an incoherent battle cry, cutting her way through the mob and rushed to Ill'yonix and stabbed three of the trolls before they knew she was there. One of the others was skewered by a man just behind her. The last troll tried to attack the kulkulcan's head, but Bianca got to it as well and sliced it nearly in half. Fatigue swept over her, and her side continued to scream with pain.

But the trolls had finally had enough. The few remaining showed their tails and fled back into the mountains. The full Haab moon and the waning crescent Tsolk'in moon illuminating the rout. Crossbows sang with the few remaining bolts insuring the retreat. The only other sounds were the gasping of exhausted men and kulkulcano'ob and the occasional grunt or squeal of a troll as a bolt hit home.

Bianca looked around at the carnage. Troll bodies were everywhere. It would be a long time before they could mount another attack in such numbers. Human casualties were gratifyingly light. Captain Perez' plan had worked perfectly. Two of the kulkulcan had injured wings and one had an injured foot, from repeated biting by a very persistent, and now very dead, troll. Injuries that would heal with time. But the two would have to walk back to their lairs. For a kulkulcan, that was not a pleasant trek and they did not appear to be as happy as they should have been after such a decisive victory.

Ill'yonix once again approached Bianca, as he had done much earlier in the day.

"I now owe you a double debt, little one. One for ridding us of the tyrant, and one for saving my wings and possibly my life. This day should be remembered for a long time by both our kinds. Three of us will fly back to our lairs tonight. The others will have wait until daybreak for their walk home."

Bianca tried to curtsy, but her injury prevented anything except the barest of movement. "Before you leave, please consider returning tomorrow morning and bring as many of your clan as possible. I will try to assemble as many of the people as I can. There are things to discuss that should greatly benefit both kulkulcano'ob and humans and I think a grand meeting of all of us would be useful. Please come!"

"For you, we will come. But for now, good evening." With that the three took off and flew home. The other kulkulcano'ob simply curled up just inside the wall and rested. No humans seemed to mind.

Exhausted and in pain, Bianca once again slumped against the same boulder as before, with the rapier still clasped in her hand. She felt even worse than earlier in the day.

Margaret apparently finished with her duties in the healers' house, rushed over to her.

"Oh my, what happened?" She tried to help Bianca to stand. "You didn't get involved in the fighting did you? Are you hurt again? Do you have another injury? Tell me you're alright."

"I'm alright. I did get in a scuffle, but not a serious one. It's just that the dressing Jason applied has come loose, and I'm tired. Perhaps it would be best if I went with you to the healers' place."

Margaret called one of the fighters to assist her. While practically carrying Bianca back to the healers' home, he said, "You should have seen her! She waded right in and attacked a group of trolls assaulting the chief kulkulcan. Saved his life, too, I bet. He certainly sounded grateful." He had obviously overheard their conversation.

"What has come over you?" Margaret asked Bianca.

"I was trying to help my friend."

Once back in the house, Jason examined her. The dressing had come loose and she was bleeding again. Now he had the time and resources to treat it properly. He retrieved some of his "magic" pills from the wagon, and went to work. He carefully cleaned her wound again, put some more ointment on, and forced the pills down her throat. He then started to stich the wound closed.

Bianca lay on the cot watching him work. She felt weak and as if she were viewing Jason work on another person, like she wasn't the injured person.

At this point the town's chief healer interrupted him. "I have watched you work wonders this evening, but your sewing leaves much to be desired. Now you watch and learn from me." She went to her cupboard and retrieved a spool that looked like fine silk. "This is the silk from the great woods spider. It has its own magical properties. It binds a wound like nothing else, and it disappears after a period of time. No need to remove the sewing." She then went to work stitching Bianca's wound.

Jason watched her work. "I am amazed," he said to the healer. "I had no idea that all the vastly intricate embroidery you Mayan women do have uses other than decoration. I can barely see there was a gash there. Her wound is completely and beautifully closed. It might heal with a barely detectable scar, or no scar at all. And the stitches a self-dissolving. Well done."

He turned to Margaret, "I guess we're never too old or secure in our knowledge to learn something new."

"Got that right," she replied.

The healer took off what was left of Bianca's ruined dress and clad her in a clean, simpler one. It had less embroidery and a simple sash. There was no shawl.

It was now late, very late. Bianca laid back and was recovering. She learned from the healer that Jason and Margaret had worked tirelessly all day with the thankfully few casualties.

The healer added, "My name is Mia. This has been the most horrible day Natts' Nohoch Muulo'ob has had to endure. All of us, the entire town, are drained. Thank the good Lord for the help of the kulkulcano'ob. What a miracle! You cannot believe how quiet the town is now. Today was supposed to have been the Solemnity of the Epiphany, the arrival of the three magi, so it would normally have been cause for celebration. Perhaps tomorrow Father Reyes can perform a belated mass for us. He said the church was not damaged on the inside."

Bianca needed to sleep, but didn't want to hurt the chatty Mia's feelings. She was finally able to insert a phrase into the monologue, "I am glad to hear that," she said. "Tomorrow I have a surprise planned for the town, a good one I hope. Perhaps that will lift everyone's spirits. Now I need my rest."

"Will you be able to perform this surprise?"

"I won't have to do much, just watch mostly. For now, goodnight."

Mia patted her and put a blanket over her.

Jason and Margaret weren't in the clinic any more, they must have gone to bed before Bianca could tell them the surprise she had planned for the morning.

CHAPTER TEN
A NEW PACT

Natts' Nohoch Muulo'ob, kingdom of Vlogentia, the next morning
Gregorian calendar: January 7
Mayan calendars: Tzolk'in: 2 Lamat
                   Haab: 1 Muwan

Daybreak brought another bright sunny day, just as Bianca had predicted. Unlike the day before Bianca had slept well and rose late. She felt quite good, Jason and Mia had worked wonders on her injury and she was able to walk, carefully, outside to enjoy the morning. She could hear the church bell calling the townsfolk to the mass Mia had spoken of the night before. Attending church was something she ought to do, but she wanted to see to her friends first.

She found them by the wagon and they sat together for a while. She told them about her idea for a pact between humans and kulkulcano'ob. Both of them liked it. After a bit they started back to the healers' house.

Along the way they met Franco Estrada, the mayor, and Jorge Perez, the captain of the guard. The two of them wanted to start organizing the cleanup. It didn't take long for a disagreement to erupt.

"We need remove all these trolls from the streets and the wall before they cause a stink," said Franco. "This is disgusting and horrible, I want them out of here and burned outside of the city."

"Disposing of them in that way will make things even worse, "said Jorge. "Besides, the wall must be repaired before anything else. We don't want to be susceptible to another attack like last night"

"Nonsense. There aren't enough trolls left to attack anything. And if we repair the wall first, just how are you going to get rid of those trolls?"

"We'll toss them over the wall, and bury them."

"That will be a lot of digging and only after the wall is finished. You will take too long to accomplish all that. We must get rid of them sooner rather than later."

"Later will be fine, we need to defend ourselves. There are still trolls out there."

"And they will be licking their wounds for quite a while, we don't need to worry about them."

While the argument was getting more and more heated the residents willing to work had to stand around wondering what to do. From the looks on their faces it seemed to Bianca that the townsfolk had witnessed such a scene many times before.

Father Tomas Reyes, the parish priest, fresh from conducting mass joined the dispute and had to side with Franco. "He's right, Jorge, there won't be another raid for quite some time. You must get started getting rid of the dead trolls."

Jorge reluctantly agreed. Something had to be done. He just didn't agree with the sequence. But he also didn't want to argue with the priest. Neither he nor Franco had a good answer what to do with the trolls after they were removed from inside the town. For now, he ordered them piled up outside the wall beyond Ill'yx' body.

Bianca, Jason and Margaret shared a quite chuckle. The argument, probably the same one those two had every day, proved that the town was returning to normality, sooner than Bianca expected. The people of Natts' Nohoch Muulo'ob were incredibly resilient. That actually made her feel good.

Franco, flush with victory over his argument with Jorge, hurried over when he spied Bianca. "I can't tell you how glad I am to see you. I hope you are healing well." He was a lot more disheveled and filthy than yesterday, but in good spirits.

"I am doing well, thank you." She replied. "But, I have a notion to share with you. Yesterday the kulkulcano'ob and people worked together for the first time in our history and the results are astonishing. We defeated the trolls despite the destruction to the city wall. Can you imagine what might be possible if our two kinds would work together more often? As they were leaving last night I asked the them to return to Natts' Nohoch Muulo'ob today discuss the matter with you and the town elders. Was I too presumptuous? Or are you willing to entertain such a concept?"

Franco took a step back in surprise. "I have never contemplated such a thing. The kulkulcano'ob have always stayed to themselves in the mountains and no one that I know about has tried to venture into the great hills for generations. The only thing I thought we might have in common was a mutual hatred of the trolls, and I wasn't sure if that was true." He stopped to think for a moment. "Let me present this to the elders and I will give you our response." He went to find the town's leaders.

Back in the healers' house Margaret and Jason were cleaning up and gathering their supplies. While picking up unused bandages, she said, "I truly hope this is the end of this nightmare. I can't take much more. Please tell me that we're going to make it home in one piece soon."

Jason added, "I have no idea how we are going to get back to Miami. I honestly do not know where we are in relation to the capital and how to arrange a boat ride to the portal isle. I don't even know if anyone would care enough to help us."

Bianca heard them and chimed in, "Do not worry. I am certain that most of the members of the Order of the Portal are good, honest men and women. Not like that renegade Xander. Good riddance to him. Your presence here was not your doing and I think the Order will gladly return you to your home. Mayor Estrada or Father Tomas or Captain Perez can arrange some sort of transportation to the capital for you, and once there you will be able to contact the Order. I will imagine that they would require a solemn oath from each of you to never reveal the presence of the portal or Second World before they would arrange the return, however."

Both Jason and Margaret jumped for joy.

Margaret said, "Don't be offended, but it's time we are quit of this place. An oath is the least of our concerns."

They went back to work cleaning up and reorganizing the wagon for the expected trip back to the capital.

Bianca had nothing to do for the moment. She decided to go outside and sit on a bench near the road to rest and watch the workers doing the cleanup while she waited for Mayor Franco's response. She hoped she was right about Jason's and Margaret's imminent return to their home.

Work on removing the trolls and cleaning up the town had finally begun. She finally located Franco off to one side talking to some of the elders. After a while he strutted back to Bianca. "We think working with the kulkulcano'ob could be a promising development. What happens next?"

She was pretty sure the elders thought it was Franco's idea. Again, it did not matter whose idea it was as long as it happened.

"We wait for the kulkulcano'ob to arrive. They should land just outside the main city gate."

While waiting for the arrivals, Bianca walked gingerly through the broken wall to Ill'yx' body. Yesterday's terror was still fresh in her mind and looking at the dead creature somehow helped pacify the memory. She also saw Xander's body lying nearby. She knew she should feel remorse for killing him, both of them, and she did. The necessity of the deeds helped mollify her guilt.

Looking at Xander, she noticed a stick stuck in his belt. She hadn't noticed it before. Carefully removing it was easy. It was an ebony piece of wood about eight inches long, with a knob on one end for a grip, and it tapered slightly to the other end. It had gold inlay in the grip and the shaft had an inlaid gold spiral coiling toward the tip. It felt cool to her touch. When she held it she started to feel a strange sensation, like a deep vibration inside her body that traveled down her arm and into the stick. Not knowing what it was or what it was used for, she placed it under the wrap around her midriff that Jason had secured and vowed to ask Father Tomas about it. She started back into the town.

As she made her way through the wall, a great shadow passed overhead. It was the kulkulcano'ob arriving, a whole host of them. At least fifteen or sixteen. The sight of that many sixty-five foot wingspan creatures flying in formation just above them stunned Bianca and all the inhabitants of Natts' Nohoch Muulo'ob. It was a spectacle that no one would ever forget. The formation landed outside the main gate on the other side of the town and waited. Bianca tried to hurry to greet them while telling everyone she met that the kulkulcano'ob were still friendly and were there to negotiate an alliance. The news spread like a storm rushing down from the mountains and just about every soul in the town hurried to the gate to see what would happen. Work stopped on the cleanup.

Bianca was moving faster and steadier all the time. But she still needed assistance through the throng to arrive at and pass through the gate to greet the kulkulcano'ob. They were arrayed in two semicircles facing the town, one behind the other. One kulkulcan sat in front of them, facing Bianca as she went to greet them. Townsfolk poured out the gate behind her, along with Franco, Jorge, Father Tomas and the elders.

"Greetings yet again, little one," said Ill'yonix. "We came as you requested. What do you have in mind?"

"Greetings to you as well. I've had a wonderful idea. What if kulkulcano'ob and people could agree to help each other?" answered Bianca. "You have trouble defending your lairs from the trolls. Humans have trouble defending their livestock and themselves from the trolls. What would you say if humans would agree to travel to your locations and build defenses like the walls around the villages that keep the trolls out? Your eggs and young would be much safer. In return, you could fly over the foothills and villages and warn the humans if the trolls were mounting a raid. They could retreat inside their defenses sooner and stay safer. Such an alliance would benefit both sides."

Ill'yonix thought for a moment. "That sounds like a good idea. Why hasn't it been thought of before? Are your kind interested in such a pact?"

"I think so, but I need to confer with them. Can you wait here while I see what they think?" With that she returned to Franco and the crowd assembled just outside the gate. She repeated the entire idea to them.

Murmurs throughout the assembly indicated they liked the idea. Working with the kulkulcano'ob was a new and novel concept and it promised more security for the borderland settlements. Franco and the elders, noting the sense of the crowd, readily agreed. "Father Tomas can compose an agreement for both of us to sign," he said. "When can we get started? But first I do have some concerns that need to be addressed." With that he listed several things such as: how many people need to be involved, when would they work, how high and strong did the walls need to be, and more.

With a sigh, Bianca reported back to Ill'yonix with the demands, although she was careful not to phrase them as such. He thought for a moment and turned to talk with the other kulkulcano'ob. He returned to her. "Those are interesting points. We also some concerns. How often and how far should our aerial flights be? How many kulkulcano'ob need to be involved? Would you small talkative creatures be willing to let us have a few livestock if we fly far from the mountains? It's not as if their losses would be as much as if the trolls took them."

Bianca realized that negotiating agreements was far more challenging than she imagined. It seemed so simple in her mind. Both sides would benefit. She believed the pact should have taken no more than one or two attempts at compromise. Instead it was turning into a complicated mess. Then it occurred to her, "*Margaret said she specializes in drawing up agreements. Why don't I ask her to help me get these two fussy groups to one mind?*"

She looked around and saw Margaret, standing with Jason, in the crowd of townsfolk. She had to wave several times to get Margaret's attention, then motioned for her to meet. When they finally got together she asked, "You know what we need to do. The people and the kulkulcano'ob have to agree to work as allies. But both of them are making the process much more complicated than it needs to be. You told me this is your specialty. Please help me get an agreement. This is too important to let silly little details get in the way."

"When it comes to contracts and alliances, there are no silly little details," replied Margaret. "A detail to one side is often the crux of the matter to the other. Of course I will help. It is the very least I can do. Besides, I finally get to do something in Second World at which I am proficient. Lead on."

The day dragged on. First one side would discuss the latest offers at great length. Then the other. Bianca marveled at how Margaret could rephrase one side's problems into the other's solutions. They must have gone back and forth dozens of times. Bianca began to worry that either she or the day would give out before any agreement could be reached.

So many little details came up that she had never considered. The humans even wanted to know if they could search for the gold they knew was in the valley streams. The kulkulcano'ob wanted to know if they had to protect those humans. Kulkulcano'ob had trouble understanding why humans had any interest in such a useless metal. It was too soft to be used in building, too rare for amassing a significant amount, and too difficult to find in the first place. They did agree carry off the troll bodies to the great sea on the other side of the mountains and drop them in the water. That would attract and feed the great white fish the kulkulcano'ob relished so much. It would take a while, since a kulkulcan could barely carry two trolls through the high passes to the sea, but it would benefit both sides.

Nevertheless the negotiations progressed, albeit slowly. It finally occurred to Bianca that both sides were very much enjoying this game and were in no great hurry to finish.

During one of Margaret's lengthier human deliberations Bianca was chatting with Ill'yonix. She asked him how he came to speak Yukatek.

"Obviously, those of your kind don't know that a few of their fellows occasionally travel into our valleys to search for the useless substance they desire so much. As a youngster, I and a few other youngsters would meet them and learned your talk from them. Oddly, they were always very secretive and made sure no other humans knew what they were looking for or that they were even in our lands. What is it about that stuff?"'

"It's difficult to explain. If I have more time someday I will try," she answered.

Later, during one of the kulkulcano'ob' long discussions, she showed Father Tomas the stick she had found on Xander's body. She also told him about the strange sensation she felt when holding it.

He was instantly fascinated.

"That is a magic wand used by the members of the Order. It helps them negotiate travel between the two worlds. I have been told it also allows them to perform limited magic in Second World, but not in First World"

"I knew there is magic. Wait until I tell that science-minded Jason," interjected Bianca gleefully. "Won't he be surprised."

Father Tomas waited for her to stop giggling and continued, "Supposedly a member can create a brief but intense ball of light in the air, although it is very hot. With great effort they can also create an intense and narrow blast of air that dissipates after few yards. Such activities usually tire them greatly, so it is rare for them to try any of it"

"So there are limits on what they can do? How much can they perform before they tire?" she asked. She was serious now.

"It depends on the user. Some tire quicker than others. Except for travel at night when a short burst of light might be useful and when a limited defense is needed they don't bother with trying such things. When you killed Xander and got soaked in his blood you may have acquired some of those abilities. Or you have innate abilities and never knew it."

"You mean I might be able to do magic?"

"You need to approach a senior member of the Order to be trained in the use of the wand, if they will let you. I will write a letter to the senior bishop at the cathedral in the capital to introduce you to the head of the Order. That should help."

Bianca was stunned. Life was so different than a few days ago when she could enjoy playing pitz, meet with her friends, and not worry about what the king and his followers were doing. Now she truly despised what his majesty king Felix was planning for the realm and its people and she fervently wished it would all stop. She vowed to herself that she would do all she could to prevent Felix from succeeding. She now had a new, desperate, goal although she had no idea how to achieve it as yet.

While she was mulling all this in her mind, the negotiations finally reached an end. Margaret looked pleased with herself. Bianca was relieved.

Franco summoned Father Tomas, the unofficial scribe of Natts' Nohoch Muulo'ob, and had him transcribe the treaty. Franco, all the elders, and Jorge signed the document after making sure the populace concurred. Since kulkulcano'ob had no written language, Bianca had to read the entire pact to Ill'yonix for him to translate to the kulkulcano'ob that did not know Yukatek. She had to read it several times before they all understood and agreed. Kulkulcano'ob didn't write, of course, so she had each of them dip a claw in ink and put a little mark on the back of the treaty. She made sure both sides had a signed copy, although what the kulkulcano'ob would do with theirs was a mystery. She assured all sides that his holiness the Vice Pope took such agreements very seriously and would intercede to resolve any disputes. She hoped that was true.

Daylight was starting to fade, it had taken that long for the discussions to conclude. After the signing ceremony people and kulkulcano'ob intermingled and gawked at each other for the first time in known history. Nobody knew who suggested it, but a grand party was planned for the next morning. Neither side was worried about a foray by the trolls for the next few days, not even Jorge.

The kulkulcano'ob flew back to the mountains, with promises to return the next day with treats they thought the humans might like. Humans promised the same and retreated to their homes. The gate was shut and secured, which seemed sort of pointless since the wall had not been fully restored and needed a night guard. But it was the custom and nobody even noticed the irony.

Both sides were looking forward to putting the horror of the previous day behind them and celebrating tomorrow's festival.

CHAPTER ELEVEN

THE FESTIVAL

The town of Natts' Nohoch Muulo'ob, kingdom of Vlogentia, the next morning
Gregorian calendar: January 8
Mayan calendars: Tzolk'in: 3 Muluk
Haab: 2 Muwan

Margaret and Jason rose early. The night before had been the best they'd had in over a week. Mia had let then sleep in her house, in a real bed. There was no threat of Jason being forced to poison a dragon. There was no threat to Margaret. All they had to look forward to was a day to celebrate the town's deliverance from destruction and then their trip home. They dressed and went through the town gate to the field where the party was planned. They were eager to see a Vlogentian festival, finally something in Second World they actually wanted to experience.

It seemed to Margaret that the entire town was up early to prepare for the festival. People were pouring through the open gate behind her to the field. They were setting up tables, spreading blankets on the ground and carting well insulated cooking utensils to prepare food.

"You know I don't ever remember seeing an open fire or stove here," observed Jason.

"Well, we haven't been staying at the five star inns, have we?" said Margaret.

"No, of course not, but even along the road we ate cold food and I don't remember a galley on the boat from the portal island or a kitchen in the inn at Naats' Seebak Ha'. I wonder why that is?"

"If it bothers you so much, ask someone. I have other things to think about"

"Don't be so grumpy," said Jason. He proceeded to wander around the ground, careful not to talk to anyone, although Bianca had told everyone she met about their 'magical' translators.

Margaret enjoyed their bickering. It meant they were getting past the stress and fright of the past days and returning to normal.

She was amazed at the diversity of the apparel worn by everyone. The attire was a kaleidoscope of color. The men usually wore a brightly dyed shirt with a shorter sleeved overshirt that may or may not coordinate with the rest of his costume. Generally they wore white or cream colored pants that went down just below mid-calf. Finishing off the outfit was a cloth belt tied in front, and a wide brimmed hat. Occasionally one of the prominent men of the community wore a more formal outfit. It was much like the clothing Xander had given Jason, which he still wore It had a nearly knee length brightly colored coat, with lots of brass buttons, pants buckled below the knee, a white ruffled shirt, a leather belt and the ubiquitous brimmed hat.

Many women wore dresses similar to what Bianca had worn the first day Jason and Margaret had met her. They wore a cloth sash around their waist and some wore a brightly colored shawl over one shoulder. If the dresses were not embroidered, they were dyed in all sorts of patterns and colors. They wore their hair either long or secured with a ribbon across the top of their head.

The feast was varied with pork, beef, beans, yams and maize. The smell of carefully spiced food permeated the air like a delicious perfume. It made the mouth water even if not hungry. Several folks set up their musical instruments and started playing guitars, clay flutes, drums made from hollow logs, conch shells and horns. Sometimes one could make out the tune one group was playing, but mostly they clashed with a melodious din. It was just as cheerful as the New Year's festival in the capital had sounded to her on their carriage ride.

Shortly after the party started the dragons arrived. The first clue was a huge shadow coursing over the meadow, followed by the sight of fifteen or so dragons in two tiers flying wingtip to wingtip. They banked and turned by partially retracting their left wings and landed with a noticeable thump and high-pitched grunt as they hit the ground. They landed beyond the field occupied by the humans. Each of them carried a large slab of what appeared to be a very large fish cradled in their folded forelegs. One of them still had its head intact. "Oh, my gosh," exclaimed Margaret, "that's a great white shark's head, a very large shark's head!"

Jason tried to sound more debonair, "Dragons eat great white sharks. Seems about right to me."

He didn't fool her, she knew him and she knew he was actually just as impressed.

A few of the dragons flew to the other side of town and started to carry off the troll bodies two at a time to the sea across the mountains. They'd make a few trips and then join the celebration and some others would rotate to troll duty.

Margaret noticed that both people and dragons were enjoying the chance to meet and learn about each other. Two or three dragonets old enough to fly had come along, and they and the children had a good time chasing each other.

Bianca saw Margaret, waved and then scampered over and said, "Good morning and a lucky blend of days to you. I am so happy. Dragons, as you call them, and people are actually going to form an alliance for the benefit of both, thanks to your expertise and assistance. Let Franco have the credit for the original idea, I don't care. Besides, everyone knows it was you that got the two sides to agree. But the result is what's important. How are you enjoying our festival?"

"This is wonderful," replied Margaret. "I'm finally getting to enjoy my time here. Is this what all your parties are like? I must admit that I can't understand most of the conversation, though. Everybody is talking at once and in all directions. My translator can't separate the individual voices and it's mostly just garbled sound."

"Oh, I forgot about your injury. How are you doing? Do you feel good?" she thought to ask Bianca

"Don't worry, I'm doing well, even better than yesterday. Jason's potions and healing skills are remarkable. I cannot tell you often enough how grateful I am." Bianca paused to look around, "Just take your time and take in the sights. You'll figure things out just from the way people act. You must try the food, it's great."

"Oh, we have. It's delectable. We even like the shark meat. The people of Natts' Nohoch Muulo'ob are excellent cooks."

While the two women were conversing Margaret noticed the parish priest, she thought his name was Father Tomas, wandering through the crowd exchanging pleasantries with as many of his congregation as possible. At some point he stopped to look at a couple of dragons trying to talk to some of the people. He stood still for almost a minute before he stumbled back and fell onto a nearby stool.

"Did you see that? I think your priest has a problem. We need to check on him," she said as she pointed to him. They rushed to him, but not before one of the dragons got there first.

"I think that's Ill'yonix," said Bianca. "Maybe I am learning to tell them apart." They reached him just in time to overhear Illy'onix asking, "Are you alright, sir? Do you need help? Should I ask little one to come here to assist you?"

Father Tomas replied, "No, I will be fine if I can sit here for a few moments. But thank you for asking."

Ill'yonix said, "Very well, but wave at me if you decide you need help." He turned away and failed to notice Margaret and Bianca standing nearby. Once he was gone they finished their approach.

"What happened?" asked Bianca of the priest.

"I saw two of the kulkulcano'ob talking to some of my people. That started me thinking. Kulkulcano'ob are clearly one of God's creations. They are intelligent. They can talk. They can plan and understand theoretical concepts. They know right from wrong. Do kulkulcano'ob have souls? If so, should it or would it be possible to minister to them? How would the message of salvation be put in terms they would understand? The thought actually made me dizzy and I stumbled onto this stool. I'm not used to such deep theological questions. It didn't make the conflict any easier when it was a kulkulcan, and not a person, who came to me first."

He suddenly noticed Margaret's presence. "Surely you people of First World have answered questions like this. What is your answer?"

"I think a few of us may have broached a similar idea. But I have never heard about an answer. We are as mystified as you."

"I think I need to write a very long missive to his holiness in the capital with these questions. Perhaps he will have the answers."

Margaret and Bianca, sure that Father Tomas was alright physically, said their goodbyes and continued to wander through the crowd.

By now the townsfolk had their fill of food and started to dance. Some of the musicians got together and started a lively tune and the women began the circle dance, soon followed by the men outside the women's circle. They spun and their dresses and shawls flew in the breeze making a riot of color and motion. The men danced in the opposite direction with much leaping and spinning.

Ill'yonix and the dragons stood still for a bit watching the activity.

Based on the way that they looked back and forth at each other Margaret was pretty sure it made no sense to them.

After a little while of watching the dance Ill'yonix came over to the two woman and asked Bianca, "What are they doing? Are they ill? Do they need help?"

"No," she answered, "it is a form of celebration we call a dance people sometimes perform. It means they are well and very happy. Don't you have some sort of celebration like that?"

"Not like that. We dance in the air. We will sometimes congregate and make our version of what you call music." With that he called four of the other dragons to him. After a brief conversation in their language he told the girls, "This is how we celebrate."

The five dragons stood in a row and began to hum, first low and slow then higher pitched and faster. Then they repeated the process. Then they reversed the order and repeated that. They did this four or five times. It was actually melodic to human ears. All the people stopped to listen. Once the dragons were done they received a rousing round of applause. Bianca had to explain to Ill'yonix that was a sign of approval by the humans.

Around midday the party started to break up. Most of the populace of Natts' Nohoch Muulo'ob packed up and returned to their homes or shops. Several of the dragons united with the ones already on troll duty. There were still a few people and dragons left, including Franco, Jorge, Bianca, Margaret, Jason and Ill'yonix who were saying their goodbyes.

As they prepared to leave the field they heard the clop-clop of a mounted group proceeding along the sacbe. A few seconds later the procession appeared heading toward town. It consisted of a carriage, two wagons and a troop of about twenty royal guard cavalry, wearing their blue and silver uniform tunics, white trousers with blue side stripes, calf-high boots with long, sharp spurs and black hats with medium sized stiff brims. At the head of the column one of the guardsmen displayed the flag of Vlogentia. Each man was armed with a rapier and a crossbow.

When the troop saw the dragons and people mixing together outside the wall of the town, they stopped in utter confusion. The dragons and townsfolk also stopped to stare at the unexpected intrusion.

A man dressed on the robe of the Order alighted from the carriage and glowered at the people and dragons congregating in the party field. From a distance he appeared to Margaret to be a twin or clone of Xander.

He summoned the leader of the guard to dismount and accompany him as he approached Margaret's and her friends' position on foot.

While the two new arrivals were approaching, Margaret put her hands over her mouth in an expression of surprise and then exclaimed, "I don't believe it! I can't believe it! Those are unicorns. Those really are unicorns. I know we saw a group of mounted men that first night in the carriage as we left the city. But I didn't see the mounts clearly. I had no idea they were UNICORNS! Oh, I've always loved unicorns, and here they are. This is awesome! But they don't look anything like I expected."

"What did you expect?" asked Bianca. "They look like unicorns always look."

"I didn't imagine this," said Margaret.

They had jet black bodies, about sixteen hands tall at the withers, but with white manes, tails and fetlocks. The horn actually was an antler since it was made of bone. It was white as well. They had prominent canine teeth, like fangs.

Margaret, still agog with excitement, squealed, "Look, Jason, look. They have unicorns here. Isn't that wonderful?"

Jason acted unimpressed. "You've seen a portal between universes, what I thought were mermaids, learned about forest fairies, were attacked by mountain trolls and actually talked to a fire-breathing dragon. But you get most excited about unicorns?"

Margaret, reading his body language, was pretty sure he really was fascinated, but didn't want her to realize it.

"But Jason, they're UNICORNS!" She was literally jumping up and down in joy.

Jason stood and looked at his wife in amusement.

Just then Bianca managed to tear Margaret's and Jason's attention away from the unicorns and motioned for them to follow her to where Franco and the newcomer that looked exactly like Xander, even down to the robe he was wearing, were meeting.

The newcomer strode directly to Franco and said, "I am Xavier of the Order of the Portal and the emissary of King Felix. What is happening here? We were told by the king that a village on the border had been destroyed by kulkulcano'ob and the guard and I were to come to the aid of survivors and to fend off the kulkulcano'ob. Why are you cavorting with the kingdom's enemies? Are you all traitors?"

"No, one of the kulkulcano'ob did attack us, but was killed by the girl standing there." Franco pointed to Bianca. "It was a remarkable sight. The other kulkulcano'ob wanted nothing to do with the attack. They have, in fact, formed an alliance with us. They and we will protect each other from the mountain trolls. It seems you were badly misinformed."

"Only one kulkulcan killed, and the city intact? An alliance between humans and kulkulcano'ob?" Xavier appeared appalled. "She killed a kulkulcan. How could that be?"

Franco again pointed to Bianca and related her fight with the dragon and Xander and recounted the battle with the trolls and the part of the dragons. Xavier's reaction to this news fascinated Margaret. He appeared to recognize Bianca and, somehow, Jason and her. But the news about the renegade Xander and the death of Ill'yx appeared to hit him like a thunderbolt.

The guardsmen had also noticed Bianca and the Blankenships. One of them, a corporal, appeared especially stunned. Margaret assumed they knew Bianca from the capital, she had told Jason and her that she was well known there. They viewed Jason and her with expressions that said she and her husband looked like the unfamiliar and alien strangers that they were.

In the meantime the conversation between Franco and Xavier was finally starting to go Xavier's way. He had almost convinced Franco that they had been sent by the king to help with the aftermath of the assumed attack by the dragons.

Bianca had been listening intently to what he had been saying and appeared stunned. She addressed Xavier directly, "You said the king told you a village had been destroyed and needed assistance. That was seven days ago. Just how did the king know about the damage days before it was supposed to happen?"

As Xavier dithered trying to formulate a response she whispered to Margaret and Jason, "We know the answer. This man must be Xander's brother and a party to the conspiracy. I want you to watch the reactions of the rest of his party so we know which of this group is in on the plot, and which are innocent. It will also help remind Franco and Jorge that they were supposed to be pawns, dead pawns, in the scheme."

Xavier finally stopped fidgeting and said, "The king must be able to foretell future disastrous events."

"Nonsense," said almost everyone at the same time.

"No one can foretell the future of any sort," said Jorge. "Just what are you up to?"

Margaret could tell that the guard captain, his men and the drivers of the vehicles were just as surprised as Franco and Jorge. Good, they could be trusted to escort them back to the capital. She nudged Bianca and whispered back, "The rest of them can be trusted, I think."

Bianca nodded agreement.

Bianca asked Jason to tell everyone what he had learned from Xander about the details of the scheme to force Vlogentia into a nation at war. A war with everybody else in Second World.

It took quite a while for him to convince them, but they all finally accepted the existence of a deadly scheme. Not everyone was convinced the king was involved, however. It seemed entirely possible that a few devious underlings were using the king's name to further their ambitions. Even if that was the version of events they believed, Margaret felt that they would still safely escort Bianca, Jason and her to the capital.

Bianca turned to the captain and said, "If it pleases you, sir, perhaps you should place Xavier under arrest until we can get back to the capital. You should be able to sort things out then."

The captain, one of his men had called him Angel Mendez, appeared to be a career soldier with the bearing of a man of many years' service agreed, and ordered Xavier bound and held in the carriage under guard.

Since the town had undergone some actual damage from the attack, the supply wagons were driven into the town and unloaded in front of the church. The wagons and carriage were pulled by regular horses.

Margaret asked one of the troopers, the second in command she thought, if she could ride one of their unicorns. "Ever since I was a child I've wanted to ride a unicorn. Could I please have just a short ride around the field?"

"I'm sorry ma'am, but unicorns are reserved for use only by the royal family and Royal Guard."

For his part Xavier gave the impression of a man devastated by the news of his brother's death and the failure of the plan. He meekly accepted his capture and crawled back into the carriage, by all appearances a defeated man.

Sunset was now rapidly approaching. The guardsmen set up camp outside the walls, with Xavier trussed up in the carriage. Bianca, Jason, and Margaret said goodbye to their new friends from Natts' Nohoch Muulo'ob. They all wished each other well, knowing they might never meet again.

Ill'yonix and the few dragons that had been present when the column arrived had stayed around for the confrontation and were curious as to what was happening. Bianca told them about the plot to use them to start a war and then to have Jason kill them. He wasn't too happy about that. "Does this mean that some of you small talkative creatures cannot be trusted? Do we need to worry?"

"The humans you have dealt with yesterday and today are all honest and trustworthy and value your friendship. They will honor their part of the pact as you should honor yours. Should you ever have any questions about who to trust, confide in Father Tomas. He will not lead you astray."

"What are you going to do, little one? I don't want any harm to come to my new favorite small talkative creature," said Ill'yonix.

"I will return to the human great city to try to encourage them to halt the king's plan. That may be difficult. Should we not meet again, fly high and long," said Bianca.

"Thank you. Tonight we will return to our lairs. But tomorrow we will start our patrols looking for trolls. For myself, I owe you two great debts. One for eliminating the tyrant, one for saving my life. So I will try to watch over you on your journey to your great settlement. You may see me soaring over you frequently. If you need help, just signal."

"Now I am the one who'll owe a debt. But if I may, I should like to think that we are friends helping one another as friends do."

"I like that little one. I shall see you tomorrow as you travel."

With that he leapt off the ground and flew to the mountains with his companions.

Margaret and Bianca were blown back a few feet by the down blast as Ill'yonix took off. As Bianca staggered back she was caught by one of the guardsmen. She turned to thank him and let out a squeal of joy.

"By the fate of the failed old gods! Juan Alejandro, I can't believe you're here. I'm so glad to see you!" With that she threw her arms around him and kissed him soundly.

Margaret was astonished. She had no idea that Bianca had a boyfriend.

"And I can't believe you're here safe and sound," he replied. "When you disappeared from the capital after the pitz game I was frantic. No one knew anything about your whereabouts or what might have happened. I have been worried so much I almost didn't ride with this patrol, but thought I might find you wandering the countryside as you sometimes do. So I volunteered, hoping to find you. Why are you here, and what's this about kulkulcano'ob?"

Bianca gave him a short version of her adventures and kissed him again. The captain and the rest of the patrol went about setting up camp pretending they didn't notice.

Margaret looked on with amusement.

Juan glanced at his comrades. "Um, what about them?"

"They know we care for one another. I don't care what they think," Bianca said.

Camp was set up, pickets were posted around the horses and unicorns, which had to be kept separate. The night was warm enough that a few extra blankets from town were all Margaret, Jason and Bianca needed. Xavier was kept in the carriage.

Tomorrow the journey back to the capital would begin. Margaret wondered just how Bianca and Jason and she would be able to convince enough people of the criminal nature of the king's plan once they were there. Then she and Jason might be allowed to return to First World.

She hoped the journey would give them the time needed to concoct plans, perhaps devious plans, to accomplish their goals. The king had to be stopped somehow.

CHAPTER TWELVE

ON THE ROAD TO
THE CAPITAL

On the Sacbe, Kingdom of Vliogentia
Gregorian calendar: January 9
Mayan calendars: Tzolk'in: 4 Ok
           Haab: 2 Muwan

D awn once again came bright and clear. Jason was awake before anyone else, eager for the long awaited trip home to begin. Margaret was
a few moments behind him, also eager to start the journey. Bianca
followed suit a little while later. They all agreed that the physical dangers were
finally behind them and the trip to the capital would be routine. Then the trouble would begin.

The rest of the patrol rose a few moments later, prepared a light breakfast
and broke camp. They set off down the sacbe toward the capital. Leading the
way was the captain and his lieutenant followed by nineteen troopers. Then
came the carriage with the Blankenships and a bound Xavier inside. Bianca was
not riding in the carriage, however.

After a brief but intense discussion with Captain Mendez before breaking
camp she had been allowed to ride one of the unicorns whose rider had been
detailed to drive Xander's supply wagon. She spent most of the time riding
alongside Corporal Juan Alejendro with a smile on her face and occasionally

holding his hand. Jason realized it was the first time he had ever seen her smile. He also thought the rest of the troop seemed amused at the situation.

Margaret was jealous. "Bianca gets to ride a unicorn. We are stuck in this carriage with that"—she waved her hand toward the bound and mum Xavier— "criminal and traitor. We have been kidnapped, threatened with death, besieged by mountain trolls and I don't get to ride a unicorn. I don't care about their rules. We deserve a treat. It's just not fair." She sounded very close to pouting.

"Well, slaying a dragon does grant privileges, I guess," said Jason. His response, however true it might be, did not mollify his wife at all.

Progress was not as fast as Captain Mendez would have liked. "Can't you make that decrepit wagon go any faster?" he kept nagging the driver.

Jason counted him saying that six times during the first two hours of the trip.

But they made steady progress along the road and by dusk were near a small village. The captain decided to stop for the night and set up camp. He ordered the carriage and wagon to be left on the sacbe but the camp, horses and unicorns were positioned just off the side of the highway.

The night was mild and the sky was clear. The stars were intense. The Haab moon was just three days past full and didn't rise until just after the thin waxing crescent of the Tzolk'in moon had set. Bedrolls were laid out in a circle. Surrounding the campsite were lanterns with the huge lightning bugs glowing brightly.

While camp was being set up, the captain sent three troopers into the village to procure food for the evening. When they returned, they were animated and immediately spoke to Captain Mendez. Their speech was so excited and fast that Jason's and Margaret's translators failed them, just like at the party. They had to ask Bianca what the problem was.

She listened for a moment and then informed them, "The villagers told the guardsmen of a raiding party recently pillaging nearby towns and injuring some of the populace. They demand that the Guard pursue and capture the criminals, as is their duty. They are insistent that we must interrupt our return and end this pillaging."

"So much for a quick and uneventful journey," said Jason.

Margaret just rolled her eyes and threw up her hands.

Bianca continued translating, "After hearing the complaints of the villagers and collecting our food the soldiers regaled them with their secondhand version of the events at Natts' Nohoch Muulo'ob. They say an old woman listening to their tales of dragons and trolls had become especially interested when one of the troopers made an offhand remark about me finding a stick on Xander's body. She insisted on returning to the campsite with the soldiers to meet me".

The food was handed out. Some of the women and their men came from the village to help with the serving and to hear the gossip from the patrol.

Jason figured that it was a small village and hearing news from the capital and about the dragons and trolls would set tongues wagging for the next few weeks.

The captain took the opportunity to question the villagers and appeared to Jason to make a decision. He told his men that they would have to make a detour to stop the depredations. The news sounded as if the next village might be the place to start the search for the raiders. The translators worked well this time with only the captain speaking. Jason had been correct, the trip was going to be interrupted.

The old woman, whose name was Sacniete, sought out Bianca. She had to tear her away from the corporal and spent about an hour talking intensely with her.

Jason and Margaret, after being served by one of the village women, sat off to the side by themselves since the chatter around the campsite was in Yukatek and their translators once again continued to garble the combined voices of the guardsmen as they discussed the change in plans.

Xavier had been allowed out of the carriage to eat, but had a guard at all times.

After her long talk with Bianca Sacniete returned to the village. Bianca, noticing Jason's and Margaret's apparent isolation, excused herself from the corporal, gave him a quick kiss on the cheek, and came over and sat down next to them.

"I'm sorry you feel so lonely. I hope that in a few days you'll meet with members of the Order and they will permit you to go home and all will be better for you. That should not be a problem according to Sacniete. It turns out that she is a retired sister of the Order of the Portal and knows about their procedures and laws. All you will have to do is promise to keep Second World a secret and to stay in touch with the Order to verify your oath and they will keep you informed about us should you be interested."

This agreed with what Bianca had told them in the healers' house and both Jason and Margaret felt a wave or relief. Things were going to end well after all.

"Thank you very much," said Margaret. "But surely that didn't take over an hour to learn. What else did you talk about, if I could ask?"

"Of course you can ask. She heard that I found this stick on Xander and told me about it. They call it a magic wand." She took it out of her belt and showed it to them.

It certainly looked to Jason like the wand Xander had used when he took them through the portal to Second World.

"It allows one who has the talent to focus energies and use the portal safely. There was a lot of nonsense talk about how the wand works and how it allows an individual to pass through the portal. It sounded a lot like our conversation we had about your magic potions. To me, it's magic. The important thing for me is that, when I killed Xander I may have acquired some of his talent, or perhaps I've had it all along and did not know. In any event, Sacniete said I should contact the Order once we are back in the capital and find out. She was able to tell me how to make a light in the air with the wand, though. Maybe I can do magic."

This was interesting news to Jason and Margaret. It occurred to him that, if Bianca could use the portal, they might be able to stay in touch with her after they returned to Miami. He was also interested in the 'nonsense talk' Bianca mentioned and how the wand worked. He asked, "Can you remember what Sacniete said about the wand, as exactly as you can? Perhaps I can understand how it works."

"Why bother? It's magic. But if it will satisfy you, she said the Order had studied the science of the First World and they learned from there some of how and why it works. She made me write it down so I can tell a senior member of the Order what I know when we meet." She got out a slip of paper. "Sacniete said something about the laws of physics, if I get that word right, and how the electromagnetic force in our nervous system can be focused by some Second World adepts through the wand. It acts like an antenna and modifies the energy state of electrons. Does any of that nonsense mean anything to you?"

"Sort of. I think I have a vague idea of how it works. It is science, just as I thought it would be."

"No it's not. It's magic."

Margaret, in an obvious attempt to prevent an argument that neither side would win, interceded. "Actually you're both right. It depends upon your point of view."

"She then deftly changed the topic of conversation. "Just who is your friend in the guard? We saw the two of you embracing and kissing when the patrol arrived at Natts' Nohoch Muulo'ob and you spent a lot of time together today.

And you kissed him just now. You obviously know each other quite well." She sounded coy. "Won't the other guardsmen get jealous?"

"Over me. I hardly think so. His name is Juan Alejandro Gomez Mendes and he is a corporal in the royal guard. We have been close friends since we played together as children."

"How close?"

"Well, very close, he's what I think you would call my boyfriend, if I understand your language as well as I think I do. But he won't go as far as to formally court me. He is concerned about the difference in our social status."

Now it was Bianca's turn to abruptly change the subject. "I need to get some rest, we can talk again tomorrow." She went to her blanket and turned in for the night.

Margaret told Jason, "I understand. The difference between a corporal in the Royal Guard and a common and popular girl might be a problem in this society. I feel sorry for both of them. That aside, I still can't get over the fact that a commoner has been allowed to ride a unicorn and I was not. Can't you tactfully approach her in the morning and ask what I need to do to get a ride? Just a short one."

"If you really want me to I will," he said, not really wanting to.

Around midnight Jason was wakened by a noisy commotion by the parked carriage. "What's wrong?" he asked of no one in particular. Both he and Margaret got up and sped to the carriage. Bianca followed them.

As they got there they were able to overhear one of the men tell the captain, "I went to relieve Pedro at midnight, as you ordered. When I arrived at the carriage I noticed that one of the horses had been taken from the picket line. Then when I looked inside the cabin I saw Pedro lying unconscious on the floor. Xavier was gone. That's when I raised the alarm."

"What happened?" Captain Mendez queried Pedro after he came to.

"After dinner I was starting to put his restraints back on Xavier when he managed to pull a stick out of his sash and point it at me. I felt a blow to my head and I remember nothing after that," replied the woozy guard.

"May you have the fate of the failed old gods! Did no one think to search him for weapons or contraband items? Are you all stupid? Who was in charge of his capture? Does anyone know how long he has been gone or even which direction he took?" The captain was clearly not in a forgiving mood.

The guardsmen obviously decided silence was the better option.

It took a while to organize the search. They spread out with lanterns to scout the area to see if they could find Xavier or at least the direction he went. Bianca tried to use the new skill with the wand Sacniete had tried to teach her. No use. She reverted to using a lantern along with the rest of the group.

Finally, one of the troop noticed a path in the grasses leading north out of the camp. It did not look like a fresh trail, probably several hours old. Captain Mendez called for a conference of everyone, including some of the villagers they had to wake.

"We need to find this man. He is needed in the capital to answer for crimes we think he has committed. We also need him to clarify who is trying to damage the honor of the king. Lieutenant Gonzalez will organize a search party of five to chase him down. They will leave at first light so they can track him. The rest of us will continue to the next village to pursue the pillagers. That way we can do both our duty to protect the inhabitants of the villages and bring that criminal to justice."

"If we complete our mission and capture the raiders we will wait just outside the city at the Guard's usual assembly site for a few days until the party with Xavier returns. Then we will proceed to the palace as one and compare his account, that of the Blankenships and any witnesses we can find there. Thus we should be able to ascertain the truth about this plot."

"If we are detained in our pursuit of the raiders I want Lieutenant Gonzalez and his party to wait for us at the assembly site as well. If both parties do not meet within four or five days I'll take any captives to the prison and return to the barracks. If that happens we'll need a secondary meeting arrangement."

Jason sensed that the captain was obviously not as convinced as Bianca and he about the king's part in the plot. He probably wanted to keep Jason and Margaret close to him as well as recapturing Xavier. "*Well, we are foreigners,*" he thought.

Bianca whispered to Jason that his plan was a good one except that they knew the king was definitely involved. "We cannot convince the captain without Xavier's corroboration of your story," she insisted.

She turned to address the captain, "I need to go with the search party. I may be able to help find him. The kulkulcan, Ill'yonix, is grateful to me for what I did in Natts' Nohoch Muulo'ob, and has promised to search for me on our trip to the city. If I can signal him, he would be able to track Xavier for us. As for the alternate meeting plan, if we don't return in your allotted time, send someone to Joaquin's café every morning. If we arrive first and you are in fact delayed, we will take Xavier to the prison and I will stay in my accommodations. I'll then check with Joaquin every day. That way we will all be together, as you want, when we present our information to the Colonel of the Guard."

She whispered again to Jason and Margaret as the captain discussed her idea with the lieutenant, "I don't want to present our suspicions at the palace where the king would learn we know of his treachery. The Colonel will be a better choice to hear the evidence."

Everyone agreed to this change in plans. Fortunately the captain went along with her idea. They spent the rest of the night preparing for the division of the group. Bianca, Margaret and Jason spent some time saying a temporary goodbye.

"Enjoy your trip back to the capital, "said Bianca, "at least you won't have to share the carriage with Xavier. Take care of yourselves."

"And you be careful as well. Xavier seems as dangerous as his brother was, don't take any chances," said Margaret.

Jason just added, "Yes, be careful."

They parted for the rest of the night.

On the way to their bedrolls Margaret couldn't help herself. "Rats. Now I won't have a chance to ask her to get a ride on a unicorn. I was really hoping that could be arranged."

With so much to worry about Jason was getting a little annoyed with his wife's obsession with unicorns. "There will still be unicorns when we get back to the capital. You can ask for a ride then. Now let it go and get some sleep, we have a hard day ahead of us."

They went to bed, wondering just what could go wrong next.

The next morning Jason rose early again. He had not slept well with Xavier on the loose. Nor had anyone else it seemed.

Margaret joined him and they prepared the wagon for the excursion to the raided village. He fervently hoped this detour would not delay their arrival at the capital. Once there he feared that he and Margaret would be caught up with the intrigue over the king's machinations. That thought hung in the back of his mind like a curtain obscuring his and Margaret's ultimate goal of finally returning home.

But for now, they were off to chase down some looters. The king and their trip home would have to wait.

CHAPTER THIRTEEN
THE PURSUIT

Village by the Sacbe, Kingdon of Vlogentia
Gregorian calendar: January 10
Mayan calendars: Tzolk'in: 5 Chuwen
                  Haab: 4 Muwan

Bianca also rose early. Xavier's escape worried her more than anyone else in the party. Without him she knew there would be no way she and the Blankenships could convince anyone of the king's treachery. She had to make sure he was captured and able, even if forced, to tell what he knew.

Captain Mendez ordered the now useless carriage and its driver back to Natts' Nohoch Muulo'ob. He also sent one trooper with the driver as extra security for the partially ruined town. That left a unicorn for Bianca but forced Jason to drive the medical supply wagon and Margaret to ride with him. He then assembled his fourteen remaining soldiers, the Blankenships with the medical wagon and started on the road to the capital.

Lieutenant Gonzalez with his four troopers and Bianca had to wait for Ill'yonix to make an appearance.

Bianca was pleased to note that the captain had detailed Corporal Gomez for this patrol. That would make the search more pleasant for her.

The search party didn't dare to move far off the main road for fear that Ill'yonix would not spot them. So they waited, anxiety increasing with each passing hour.

Finally, just before midday, they saw his large wingspan soaring high just to east of their location. Bianca tried waving her arms without any noticeable success. One of the troopers tried firing a bolt from his crowbow at the kulkulcan, knowing the dart would not cause injury but might draw his attention. It fell woefully short, again with no success. As a last resort Bianca tried the light trick with the wand that Sacniete had tried to teach her. Wonder of wonders, it worked, sort of. The light was a tiny, feeble yellow-orange ball at the end of the wand, but it moved with the tip as she waved it around. The effort nearly drained her physically.

This time the kulkulcan reacted and turned to approach them as he lost altitude.

He landed to the side of the road a few yards from Bianca. The guardsmen, Corporal Gomez among them, were still not used to being this close to a kulkulcan and had to hold themselves and their unicorns in check. Bianca wasn't much more at ease, but was more used to conversing with a kulkulcan than they were, so she went to him and explained the situation.

"Anything I can do to help you find the clutch mate of the small creature who tried to goad us into such an irrational attack is no problem," said Ill'yonix. "I will fly over the fields and grasslands to the north and return to let you know if I spot him. Since I now know what your group looks like, I will have no trouble locating you as long as you are in the open. Your trick with the light caught my attention, but probably won't be needed any more. From altitude my vision is as good as an eagle's. I can fly every morning when the wind is from the west."

"That's wonderful, thank you very much. Your eyesight will prove valuable. The trick, as you call it, with the signal light used about all my strength for a while. I will save it for a more desperate situation. You better get flying, Xavier has a large head start on us. "

With that said, she returned to her group as Illyonix leapt into the air with the usual enormous downrush of air and headed off toward the north. The six of them followed on unicornback.

They left the sacbe and approached a mountain stream, the same stream Bianca had been caught in a week previously. A quick search up and down the water bank found fairly recent hoof prints. More hoof prints could be seen on the other side. Xavier had forded here. Once across they fanned out into a line abreast. Bianca in the center with Juan Alejandro to her left. Two troopers to his left and two troopers to her right. They separated about twenty yards apart to spot any change in the direction of his trail. The made a handsome sight with the troopers in their sky blue and silver uniforms astride the black and white unicorns. They were armed with rapiers, not sabers. They all had crossbows, lassos and two saddlebags with provisions for the trek. Bianca was riding in the center clad in the plain white dress she had gotten from Mia, which almost matched the shade of her hair. She wore the rapier she'd taken from Xander across her back. They started a quick progression through the grassland. But not too quick, the grass came up to the unicorns' knees and they had to be careful to not step in a hole or surprise an animal.

The land was nearly flat and covered with the high grasses. There were occasional small copses of trees, never more than five or six. Hiding in them was out of the question, so they didn't bother to waste time searching for Xavier in them. The sun was high in the sky but slightly to their backs as they headed north so the day was already turning quite warm. At least there was a noticeable breeze from the west to help. Every so often they'd see herds of grazing animals. Some of them resembled the rhinoceros from pictures in books from of First World, but their horn was shaped like a Y. The small groves of trees usually had giant sloth-like creatures, large enough to stand upright and graze off the branches of the trees. There were herds of small horse-like creatures, no more than a couple of feet at the withers. And large herds of antelope and deer. They saw no predators that day.

So far Xavier's trail had been easy to follow. His horse made a considerable depression in the grass as it walked through. They just had to follow the mashed down blades.

A little later Ill'yonix landed in front of them to tell Bianca he had spotted Xavier several miles straight ahead. He was heading north for the great river at the boundary of the grasslands, with the forest beyond that.

He said, "I need to return to my lair now, the afternoon winds are getting less favorable for soaring flight and I cannot sustain my altitude without them. I will start again in the morning from where I last saw him."

"Thank you. We'll see you tomorrow." Said Bianca.

After Ill'yonix took off they had to push through the matted grass where he had landed, but the trail was easy to find once they were past his landing area. They spent the rest of the day continuing to follow Xavier's track. At nightfall they made camp. Bianca was cautiously optimistic that they were gaining on him. He didn't strike any of them as a good horseman and he had no saddle in any event.

The next morning they arose at daybreak and began the chase again. It was too early for Ill'yonix to be airborne and over the grasslands, but the trail was still visible, though less so.

About an hour into the day they ran into their first big obstacle of the pursuit. Directly in front of them was a herd of the huge elephant like creatures that occasionally visited the steppe. Bianca had learned in her classes that they normally lived in the high reaches of the mountains where the climate was colder. But the grass here was new and too tempting to ignore. They had wandered across Xavier's path and blocked the party's progress. They differed from the elephants that the original First World Spanish knew. They were bigger, with a much longer and thicker coat of fur, dark brown in color. The tusks of the males were enormous. They almost touched in front on some of the larger males. Bianca's readings from First World books named them mammoths. The few Vlogentians that knew of them simply called them the great beasts.

Unfortunately, the herd decided that the best grazing they'd found in ages lay right across the path Lieutenant Gonzalez needed to follow. Either they would have to go around the herd and risk spooking them or losing the trail. The lieutenant decided to wait for them to move on.

Bianca hoped Ill'yonix would not pick this time to report. That would cause a stampede and no one could predict what direction that would take. Possibly right over them.

The small company waited patiently. The great beasts munched grass patiently. Then one of the herd's youngsters noticed the group and turned to look at them. His curiosity aroused, he started toward them. That aroused the ire of one of the females. She started to trumpet and wave her trunk wildly. That in turn attracted the interest of the large male. He also started to trumpet, wave his trunk, shake his head and start toward them, slowly at first but picking up speed with every step.

Lieutenant Gonzalez ordered everybody to back up, slowly at first. The tension in the patrol was palpable. Daddy mammoth was advancing at them, mama and baby were now behind him with the rest of the herd following. The unicorns were backing up unsteadily but not fast enough. Finally daddy started an all-out charge and the mounts started to panic.

Gonzalez shouted, "Fall back, fast! Run! Spread out and scatter. They cannot chase all of us. If you are the one being chased, make a sharp break to either side. I don't think they can turn as quickly as the unicorns." The company turned and ran. The female decided to chase Bianca. The male pursued one of the troopers. The youngster followed its mother. The rest of the herd followed randomly.

As instructed by the lieutenant, Bianca and the trooper each made a sharp turn and quickly lost contact with their pursuers. The unicorns were faster than the mammoths and soon outran them. For a brief time the situation seemed dire, but the great beasts soon gave up, decided the threat was over and regrouped. They went back to grazing peacefully as if nothing had happened.

Lieutenant Gonzalez signaled with his hand for the patrol to regroup and stand. The wait seemed interminable, but after about another hour the herd slowly moved to the east toward the mountains. The problem now was that Xavier's track had been totally trampled and unreadable. They had to fan out more than usual, with the risk of not being able to support one another if attacked by one of the great cats of the steppe. Once past the severely trampled area it took another hour but one of the troopers picked up the trail on the far side of the herd's original position. They were able to resume the pursuit with only the loss of two and a half hours.

About an hour after that, Ill'yonix finally appeared. Once again he landed in front of them. "Your prey is a farther ahead of you than yesterday. He has reached the great river but has not tried to cross it. He has turned west toward the coast. I have no idea what he is trying to accomplish."

Lieutenant Gonzalez rode forward with his chest puffed out and sitting stiffly erect on his mount obviously proud that he was able to approach and speak with a kulkulcan and said, "Thank you sir kulkulcan. That gives us valuable information since we can cut across his path and intercept him sooner than expected."

Bianca added, "Yes, thank you. If I could make a request, could you please land behind us if possible? When you set down you damage the trail he is leaving. If we are directly behind him we need to follow his trail. We need both your report and his path to make sure we catch him."

Ill'yonix said, "I understand. That is no problem and I will keep it in mind. I'll scout ahead for the little time the winds allow." He took off again to scout ahead before he needed to return to the mountains.

Gonzalez now ordered the patrol to turn northwest to cut off Xavier. He told his men and Bianca, "Xavier is following the Great River westward and must be headed for Puerto Norte, the fishing and trading town at the mouth of one of the branches of the river. He is probably looking to book passage to another land before we can capture and arrest him. This route is a little riskier than just following his trail, since we are cutting across the grasslands in an attempt to intercept him. My worry is that we will reach the riverbank either in front of or far behind him. The assistance of Ill'yonix is going to be essential to prevent the latter event. Let's get moving, if we're lucky we'll reach the river before him and be waiting to catch him."

The patrol headed northwest at a fast trot. Since they no longer had to spread out to search the grasses for the path, they could travel closer together and quicker. They needed to make up for the time that had been lost before they found out that he was missing and for the time lost evading the great beasts.

This suited Bianca and Juan Alejandro just fine. They were chatting away merrily and catching up with her adventures and his attempts to find her. She was feeling happier than she had for days. Her side was almost completely healed, and the terrible memories of Xander, Ill'yx and the trolls were starting to fade into the past, although they would never completely go away.

The clumps of trees were now more frequent and larger. Some of them were quite expansive. After a few hours of travel they approached a large stand of mixed trees, both deciduous and palm. From in front of the copse they heard loud pandemonium in front of them. There was roaring, snarling and squalling. It had to be a fight between the large, sickle-toothed cats of the woodlands and grasslands that the people of Vlogentia called the great jaguars.

Gonzalez ordered a halt, of course. Everyone stayed mounted in case the cats went after them. It was known that the creatures were not very quick of foot nor could they run very far so if the cats charged Bianca and the guardsmen escape was likely. The cats were ambush predators, leaping on their prey from the trees or from hiding and grasping with their front legs before using the huge canine teeth to sever the throat of their prey. They did not run down their prey like wolves and were not built for a chase. They were the most feared predators of the grasslands and the woodlands, however.

Since the fight didn't seem to be changing location, one of the troopers cautiously crept forward. He reported back that the battle was between two of the cats, he saw no others which was strange since they were known to be pack hunters.

Since Bianca nor anyone in the group had never seen a live indiviual of the great cats, their knowledge was from tales of those who braved the grasslands, they wanted to see what the fight was about. They snuck forward, prone on the ground, so they were hidden in the tall grass, but with the unicorns close behind and ready to flee.

The creatures were totally preoccupied with each other and paying no attention to the patrol or any of the large bison grazing nearby They were not as impressive as a kulkulcan, but fearsome enough. The cats were about seven and a half feet long with a short, foot long tail and slightly more than four and a half feet tall at the shoulders. The legs were proportionally shorter than a house cat's, but much more muscular, as was their head and chest. Their ears stood upright, were pointed and sported tufts. They must have weighed nine hundred fifty pounds or more. Their coats were short haired and mottled for camouflage. Their most notable feature was their huge canine teeth. These were more than a foot long, curved back and serrated.

The fight continued for several brutal moments. The two cats were fighting in a clear spot just in front of the copse of trees. The larger one was trying to brush the other out of the way, and the smaller one was desperately blocking it and holding its ground. There was no dead prey nearby, so the reason for the fight was not clear. The smaller cat appeared overmatched but fought with a ferocity of desperation. Finally, the larger cat, probably a male, gave up and limped away. The other lay on the ground, barely alive and defiant, but clearly severely wounded.

Nobody moved lest the large male return, but after several moments it was obvious that he was gone. The smaller cat, probably a female, still lay on her side gasping for breath, bleeding profusely, and moaning.

For a reason she could not fathom, Bianca felt pity for the injured predator and slowly approached. It tried to raise its head, but could not. Nor could it move any of its limbs, it looked like its neck had been broken. Bianca knelt down by the head and looked into the beast's eyes. She saw the same awful look she had seen in Xander's eyes five days earlier.

The life drained out of the cat and it died. All was quiet for perhaps a minute, Bianca kneeling by the dead beast and the men standing nearby. Then they heard the reason for the fight. From the brush in the woods they heard mewing and two cubs crept from hiding and went to their mother. They were only about a foot and a half long, and their sword-like canine teeth were only about four inches long. They nuzzled the dead body and sat down, clearly uncertain what to do.

"You were just being a good mother. Protecting your cubs from the male. You died saving them," said Bianca. "We won't let your death be pointless." With that she picked up the cubs, they were too young and confused to put up resistance, and carried them back to the men. "I want to bury the mother, and we'll take the cubs with us. When they get old enough they can be returned to their home in the grasslands."

Naturally, Gonzalez objected. "We don't have shovels to bury the beast, and why do we want to carry two wild cubs with us?"

"Then we will cover the body with stones and debris from the grove. The cubs can ride in my saddlebags. I hope they are old enough to drink water and eat some of the game we take for ourselves. When we get to Puerto Norte, we will surely find someone to care for them until old enough to release." She was putting on her most adamant face. She hoped it would work. She had decided not to let the mother die for nothing.

Seeing Bianca's resolve he let her have her way. He obviously thought that was better that than listening to her complaining the rest of the way. "Very well, but they will ride with you and you will be responsible for their care."

"Agreed. Let's get started."

Constructing a cairn for the dead cat didn't take too long, much to the lieutenant's relief. Apprehending Xavier was still his main concern. Bianca shared the contents of her saddlebags with Juan Alejandro since none of the other riders were interested in seconding her idea. She placed a cub in each bag with its head sticking out the top. They seemed to enjoy the ride.

The patrol rode until sunset and set up camp for the night. The cubs curled up against Bianca, apparently accepting her as their stepmother. She hoped she would be a better stepmother to them than her stepmother had been to her.

Fatigue and stress had taken their toll. She slept the night away soundly and was wakened only when the cubs demanded her attention. It only took a few bites to feed them from Juan's supplies and secure them in her saddlebags. They still seemed satisfied with the situation.

The patrol mounted and set off in hurried pursuit of Xavier. This would be the day they caught up to him.

CHAPTER FOURTEEN
XAVIER CORNERED

The grasslands north of Vlogentia
Gregorian calendar: January 12
Mayan calendars: Tzolk'in: 7 B'en
                 Haab: 6 Muwan

Bianca was detailed to ride behind Lieutenant Gonzalez as the patrol would trot in pursuit across the grassland.

He announced, "Today will be the end of the chase. This is the Tzolk'in day of triumph and I would like for it to live up to its reputation. Xavier has to be tired and low on rations. Let's go get him."

Bianca stowed her two new charges in her saddlebags and everybody mounted and started at a trot in column. About three hours or so later Ill'yonix flew in from the west where he had been doing morning reconnaissance. This time he landed to the side of the group. Bianca and Gonzalez went out to meet him.

"Your quarry is now just a few miles straight ahead of you. He is moving much slower than yesterday or the day before. His riding beast must be tiring. You should be able to catch him just before the gets to the Lesser Branch of the Great River."

Gonzalez answered, "Thank you again. We may spot him around midday."

Bianca added, "And please continue to keep in touch, we may still need guidance or warnings once we cross the river. If I may so bold to ask, how are your relations with the folk of Natts' Nohoch Muulo'ob coming along? Any problems? "

"No, both kulkulcano'ob and the small talkative creatures are cooperating well. We can fly patrols both morning and afternoon since the updrafts near the mountains are stronger than over the plains. Yesterday we spotted a small attempted raid by the trolls and were able to warn the people of a nearby town. It took those humans by surprise when my clutch mate landed and told them of the raid. They had been told of the treaty by the small talkative creatures of the town where you and I met. But up until our warning they weren't sure that it was actually true. They heeded our warning however, intercepted the trolls and sent them running back to their holes."

"The small talkative creatures of your town have been busy with their part of the bargain. Several workers have been hard at work building a stone wall around the entrance to two of our more vulnerable lairs. That will be great comfort to us. They do seem to spend some of their leisure time sloshing in the mountain streams with the pans they use for cooking. I'm not entirely sure what that's all about. But both sides are very pleased so far."

"I'm so glad to hear that," said Bianca. "I only hope the agreement continues to work for all of you. The sloshing you mentioned is the workers looking for gold. Make sure they don't spend too much time doing that and not enough time working. Farewell for now, I hope your wings catch the best updrafts. We hope to meet you again later today or tomorrow morning." With that she and the lieutenant returned to the patrol and Ill'yonix took off.

Knowing that the fugitive was close, Gonzalez ordered them into a quick trot. The sooner they caught him the better. A little more than an hour later they spotted him. He had just arrived at the fork in the Great River. The Greater Branch continued west toward the ocean and the town of Puerto Norte. The Lesser Branch veered south toward the capital, then past the city and through the southern forest and into the ocean. That was the river Bianca, the Blankenships and Xander had crossed on the makeshift bridge ten days previously.

Gonzalez immediately ordered an attack. "Catch that bastard, now!" The four guardsmen, with Juan Alejandro in the lead charged at him, trying to prevent him from fording the river. Much to their surprise they were each met with a sudden blast of air that knocked them out of their saddles. They hadn't gotten any closer than ten or fifteen yards. They were totally unprepared for such an attack. They weren't set in the saddles properly and hadn't bothered to prepare their crossbows. They had to pick themselves up and follow their mounts in retreat. Fortunately the unicorns were well trained and returned to their riders rather than escaping into the plains.

Bianca ran up to them. "I'm so sorry. I should have thought to tell you that the wands the members of the Order carry can do more than create a wan light. I'm not experienced or properly trained in its use as yet. But proficient users can also create a narrow blast of air, as you just encountered. If you get much closer, he could cause considerable damage, or even death."

"Thanks for the warning," said Gonzalez sarcastically. "What do you suggest we do?"

"I said I'm sorry. Wands apparently wear their users out very quickly. So he can produce several blasts, at least four that we know about, before he needs to recuperate. I just don't know how many or how forceful they will be. Charging him seems out of the question if he can pick you off one at a time. But I don't think he can both cross the stream and keep us at bay. That would require him to divide his attention and one task or the other would suffer."

While Bianca and the lieutenant were talking the guardsmen could see Xavier busy building a little barricade made of rocks and debris from the riverbank. After looking at the barrier and thinking about the abilities of the wand, Gonzalez decided to fall back a short distance and watch. Xavier couldn't try to ford the stream without risking assault and he couldn't get past all of them if they spread out. One of them would nab him from the side or behind while he would be busy with one of the others.

So began one of the stranger sieges in the histories of both First World and Second World. On one side behind a low wall of debris appeared a very tired, hungry and desperate member of the Order of the Portal. His entourage consisted of one horse which seemed far more interested in the fresh grass growing along the riverbank than any potential conflict. The besiegers consisted of five saddle weary royal guardsmen four of them nursing sore chests due to the wind blasts from the wand, one young girl not at all sure how to use a wand, six unicorns also more interested in the tasty grass than fighting, and two feline cubs more involved in play than anything going on around them. Both sides waited the afternoon away.

As dusk approached Lieutenant Gonzalez called for a conference with the company. They gathered in a group in sight of the barricade, but well out of reach of the blasts of the wand. One of the men kept constant watch while the others hunkered down to talk. Bianca was nearby learning how to play with her cubs.

He voiced his concerns, "I do not think Xavier can ford the stream at night with his horse. He would not be able see any hazards in the water, and he would make too much noise splashing as he crossed. However he could easily slip past us in the dark. We will have to be too widely spaced apart to cover all the ground. Or, he might abandon the horse altogether and swim or float downstream unseen and then come ashore well beyond our knowledge. Does anyone have any idea what we need to do? We cannot let him do a night escape again."

While Gonzalez and the guardsmen were mulling their limited options, Bianca thought for a few moments and came up with a plan.

She approached the group and said, "I have a thought. What if we pretend to attack and start to charge and then feign a panicked retreat, Xavier might become emboldened and come out from behind his barricade to chase us farther away, he then would think he could mount and get free before we could regroup. While he does that you could have two of the guard, one from each side, creep down the berm and along the riverbank and pounce on him from behind."

"Do you actually think that using a pretend rout would draw him out? That's the oldest military strategy known. Do you think he's that foolish?"

"Xavier is a member of the Order of the Portal, not a military strategist or historian. Feigned retreat worked for Hannibal at Cannae, it worked for Belisarius at the siege of Rome, it worked for William at Hastings, and it will work for us."

He had to pause for a moment. "I must admit that actually sounds like a valid plan. How in the world do you know about such things? Very well, it's worth a try. We'll fake the attack in about an hour. That should give one of the guard time to sneak away from our position and roll down the bank and make ready to come up on him from behind. I'll have him mount a bedroll vertically to his saddle. From a distance and in the heat of a fight that might fool Xavier long enough for the trap to work."

"You need two men, one from each side. We can cover the deception by driving all the unicorns around with their bedrolls on their saddles to create a distraction so he doesn't notice the missing men. We then attack on foot to complicate his assessment of the situation. The unicorns are well trained and will stay nearby."

"One man will do."

"No, two are necessary."

"Just when did you become so decisive? Very well, you are probably right. If one man is incapacitated, the other could capture Xavier."

Sunset was approaching, so further delay was not advisable. Just as soon as the men were briefed in their roles the attack started. First one or two would rush forward yelling battle cries, shooting a bolt then retreat. Then another one or two would come at Xavier from another angle. They were careful to stay beyond fifteen or so yards so if they got hit by a wind blast it would only knock them down. After about a half hour Gonzalez had the men start to run back and forth in front of Xavier just out of the danger range and shoot crossbow bolts in his direction at random. Then he ordered them to retreat while yelling how frustrated he was.

Xavier had been using his wand as often as he could, more than Bianca thought was possible. She began to worry that her ruse might not work. But when Xavier saw the pretend retreat, he rushed forward from his security to chase them farther back. Once it looked as if he had scattered them sufficiently, he turned to get his horse.

That was when the two soldiers who had crept along the edge of the river jumped him. Surprise was total. Xavier was tackled to the ground, the wand ripped from his hand and he was tightly bound once again. It was just in time, the sun was setting and night was not far behind.

Bianca's plan had worked perfectly. Gonzalez was impressed and said to her, "Extremely well done. That was a very good plan. Xavier will not escape this time. We'll camp here for tonight, then ford the river in the daylight and make for Puerto Norte. From there we should be able to commandeer a ship to take us to the capital. Then we'll see what this traitor has to say about his brother and why they wanted to sully the name of our king."

Bianca appreciated the military man's endorsement. But she wanted to talk to Xavier tonight. Waiting until they reached the city was not acceptable to her. "By your leave, may I speak with him now? He's not going anywhere and I want to know why I was such an essential part of whatever they had planned. Why me, why not someone else?" She of course knew the king's role but knew better than to argue with the lieutenant at this time.

He had no objection, so she walked over to where Xavier was trussed up and sat down next to him. "Would you like to tell me your goal in all this? Why involve me?"

"I don't want to talk to you or anybody." Xavier was understandably surly. "You killed my brother, I will hate you forever. We were going to be the powers behind the throne and we would have fulfilled our goal. You have destroyed all our dreams. You were supposed to be dead by orders of the king. Personally, we didn't care about you but one more tragic casualty of the kulkulcano'ob would have suited our purposes."

For someone who didn't want to talk, he was being quite chatty. His frustration and despair had clouded his judgement and loosened his tongue. It was almost as if he were drunk.

"Why did the king want me killed? What were your aims?" She had an inkling of the reason for her kidnapping, but wanted confirmation. She had no idea what aims he was talking about.

But Xavier was done. He had clearly said more than he intended. He turned his back on her, reverted to his surly state and withdrew into himself, wallowing in his misery.

Realizing that further questioning was pointless Bianca left him and returned to the others. Juan tried to engage her in idle talk but she wasn't in the mood. There were a few things she still didn't understand and she was preoccupied. So his attempts to draw her out were just as fruitless as her attempt with Xavier.

After a bit she went to play with the cubs and then tried to sleep with them curled up next to her.

Sleep came late. Xavier had been of no help. She would have to find a way to confront the king to learn her role in his plot. The dread of that confrontation kept her awake most of the night.

Morning finally came and she had a brand new problem to worry about.

CHAPTER FIFTEEN
RAIDERS FROM THE SEA

The Lesser Branch of the Great River, Grasslands of Vlogentia
Gregorian calendar: January 13
Mayan calendars: Tzolk'in: 8 Ix
             Haab: 7 Muwan

Bianca had to admit to herself that the start of the day was going to be a little scary. All the perils she'd faced in the past two weeks had been thrust upon her without warning. She'd not had time enough to worry or fear what was ahead. She'd braved the stream at Nats' Seebek Ha' out of necessity, and without planning. This was different. She knew they had to cross the river, and she was not a good swimmer. In fact, she didn't really like being in the water. A bath was her limit.

Lieutenant Gonzalez checked with Bianca and her cubs to make sure they were ready to travel. He then checked to make sure Xavier was secure. He was not going to let the renegade get loose again. Finding a way across the Lesser Branch of the Great River was the next order of business.

He ordered riders to search up and down the riverbank looking for a shallow place to cross. They were near the fork in the rivers, so looking north toward the Greater Branch didn't take long, and was fruitless. Two of the soldiers he sent south along the Lesser Branch's banks found nothing shallow enough to wade across.

He told Bianca, "It appears that swimming the unicorns and Xavier's horse across is our only option. Fortunately the current does not seem as swift as I feared, and the water is still cool enough from the mountains that crocodiles are not the threat they would be further south toward the capital. You need to prepare to ride your mount across. Don't worry, unicorns are excellent and powerful swimmers, just make sure you keep your knees tight on his flanks and you won't fall off. Your cubs will be fine if you secure them in your saddlebags."

"That's all very reassuring," she replied, not really meaning it.

Once all the provisions were secured on the backs of the mounts two of the riders started across. They had tied all the lassos together into one long rope and they carried one end with them while Corporal Juan Alejandro held the other end. The unicorns made it safely to the other bank although a little farther downstream than planned. The two rode back to a point directly across from the rest of the group and stretched the line across the river, which was about thirty yards wide. Bianca and Xavier crossed while holding onto the line as their mounts swam.

The water was cold as it streamed around her legs but she did as she'd been told and squeezed tight to the unicorn's sides with her legs while holding the safety line with a death grip. Her mount cut through the current like it wasn't there. She made it to the far shore faster and easier than she ever could have imagined. "I *did it. Actually, it wasn't so bad,*" she tried to convince herself.

There was no concern about Xavier trying to escape since one of the troopers swam alongside him with hand on rapier. He looked much less than pleased upon reaching the shore.

After they were across the remainder of the detachment swam across holding their end of the rope, which was being coiled as they neared the bank. Finally on the other side the lassos were untied and the company headed west toward Puerto Norte.

Bianca felt relieved, even elated, at completing the crossing. It was a small victory, but proved to herself that she could face a known peril and persevere.

After about an hour's ride they left the grasslands and entered farmlands. Around them were pastures for livestock and fields of maize and sweet yams. Further to the north by the banks of the Greater Branch would be rice fields.

Finally they spotted the houses of the town a mile or so ahead. Something seemed to be wrong, the church bell was tolling furiously and several clumps of people could be seen leaving the town in all directions, some of them carrying or pulling carts of goods with them. The lieutenant sent two riders to gather the folk together and calm them. He confronted the first of the groups he met, "What is going on? Why are all of you fleeing? We are Royal Guardsmen and will take charge of whatever situation is happening. Now settle down and tell me what the problem is."

One of the men stopped long enough to talk to the lieutenant while Bianca and the remaining guardsman herded the others back toward Lieutenant Gonzalez. He was fidgeting, shaking and his voice had the quavering tone of a man in mortal fear. "There is a pirate ship approaching the docks. It will dock within an hour or two and the raiders will start to pillage the town. We are just a trading community and fishing village and have only a little gold and trade goods scattered throughout. We've never had a pirate raid before and have no defense. So we're leaving to save ourselves and whatever we can carry with us."

"Are you sure it's really a pirate ship? How do you know? How big is it and how many crew does it carry?"

"It's definitely a pirate. They fly the black and red banner we've all heard about. It's a huge ship, at least a hundred fifty feet long and must carry three hundred or more crew. We're doomed!"

Lieutenant Gonzalez tried to calm the man as well as the rest of the villagers. "Now, I have heard of pirates traversing the Great Ocean, but never in the Inland Sea bordering Vlogentia. For one thing the Inland Sea is shallow outside the shipping lanes leading to the capital. Large vessels would quickly run aground. For another we would have been told if any seafaring trader visiting the capital had seen such a vessel. All of you stay here while we see what is truly happening."

"Corporal Gomez, take charge of this mob. Keep them quiet and keep them here. Do not allow them to scatter like oak leaves before the wind. I will go to the harbor and see for myself what this pirate looks like."

He dismounted and crept into the side streets of the town on foot. He returned a short time later. "I was able to spy the ship from behind some crates near the dock. It's not anything like he," pointing to the scared villager, "described. It is a much smaller ship and will be a problem only because we are so few. It's a sloop-rigged ship of forty feet or less. It couldn't have a crew of more than twenty or so. It was indeed flying the red and black of pirates. But rather than a deep sea pirate, it looked more like a coastal raider or smuggler that has come down from the north. It's definitely a problem for an unprepared town, but not the ship of the line described to us."

Quite unexpectedly Ill'yonix took this moment to arrive. His sudden appearance threw the villagers into even greater panic. It was all Bianca and the guardsmen could do to calm them down and keep an eye on Xavier, bound to the saddle though he was. She was able to control their fright after a few moments.

Ill'yonix just sat there, watching the strange behavior of the small talkative creatures and waiting to talk to Bianca.

"Please," she begged, "the kulkulcan is our friend and ally. He will not harm any of you. Perhaps the pirates will not be so lucky."

Once the villagers stopped moaning and crying she approached the kulkulcan. "A pleasant blend of days to you. What news do you have? I have some considerable news for you."

"And a strong morning wind to you. I have nothing new to report. I was just going to tell you that since I noticed during my morning reconnaissance that you had captured the renegade"—he looked at Xavier and made a point of showing his teeth and getting what Bianca assumed was the desired response— "and will be taking him back to the big city of yours, there isn't any need for me to fly this far from the mountains any more. I must now return to my lair. The winds are dying down and I will not be able to launch and fly if I wait any longer. Before I leave, what was the news you had for me?"

"*So much for using Ill'yonix to destroy the pirate ship,*" she thought. "We have a situation with some seafaring raiders. We thought you might be able to help. But if you have to get home now you should go. We can handle them." She had just thought of another idea that she hoped would not involve much, if any, killing. "I thank you for your help in our chase of Xavier. We could not have accomplished it without you. Go with our blessing. Any yes, I plan on visiting you often."

"Then for now this is goodbye," he said, "but I want you to visit me soon, and often." With that he spread his wings and leapt into the sky.

"Why did he leave?" asked Gonzalez. "He could have defeated the pirates."

"It is too late in the day for him to stay aloft. Besides, the streets of the village are too narrow for him to engage the pirates when they raid the houses and shops."

"He could have at least burned the ship."

"We can use the ship to sail back to the capital. That would be quicker and much easier than the overland journey. We can also keep Xavier more secure below decks, rather than worrying about him galloping away at the first opportunity. I have a plan. But first I need to know how many pirates we may be facing. It won't work if there are hundreds of them."

Gonzalez answered, "It was not as large a ship as we were told. As I said, I estimate no more than twenty or twenty-five of them."

"Excellent, my plan should work. The pirates are greedy and will want to pillage and get away as fast as possible, before help can arrive. They won't care if there are people sitting on the rooftops. In fact they will think the townsfolk are cowards hiding on the roofs. It may even prove amusing to them."

"Why do you want to put people on the roofs?" asked the lieutenant. "What purpose does that accomplish?"

"In fact the villagers will be lookouts. Whenever they spot the pirates splitting up into small groups of two or three so as to gather the most loot in the least time, the lookouts will signal us to indicate to us where to ambush them. We will stay just outside town and wait for the signal. Then we can take two or three of us along with ten or so armed villagers. The pirates will be outnumbered at each encounter and will either surrender or be easily overcome and captured. The villagers know the streets of the town better than the pirates. Once they have a location from the lookouts they can lead us and their team to the appropriate spot, conduct the ambush, and quickly get out before other pirates arrive. Then we return to our place here to detain the bandits."

She could see him mulling over the idea. "This might work. I'll want large enough ambush parties to ensure little or no resistance from the pirates. We'll need a signal from the spotters to let us know how many looters we will be trapping."

"Yes, we'll need to know that as well. We conduct an ambush and capture or disable them and bring them back here. We then wait for the next signal to grab some more raiders. It may take some time to capture all of them and there will be some property damage and the loot will have to be returned to its owners. But the chance of anybody getting hurt is much less than fighting a pitched battle. What do you think?"

"That actually sounds like a good plan. Once again you have come up with a solution to a dangerous confrontation." Gonzalez looked at her as if he was beginning to form a vastly different opinion of her. "You are not at all the silly young girl I originally thought you were. I must admit I am a little impressed."

"Thank you, but we better prepare for the raiders."

Lieutenant Gonzalez assigned several men from the town to spots on the rooftops, carefully chosen to keep the entire town under surveillance. Semaphore signals were agreed upon and they hurried to take up their posts.

The rest of the assembled villagers were divided into three groups of eight to ten able looking men, with at least one of each group knowledgeable of his local street layout. One or two soldiers were assigned to each group. Bianca insisted on participating and Gonzalez relented, although with severe reservations.

The rest of the townsfolk were assigned to monitor Xavier and the prisoners as they were brought out of town. Bianca found a couple of women willing to tend her cubs.

The ambush groups were positioned at critical points outside the town limits, and the stage was set.

One of the lookouts signaled that the ship, aptly named The *Unlucky Lady*, had finally docked and begun to discharge its crew. He reported that what was probably the captain stayed by the gangway along with his executive officer.

Upon receiving this news, Bianca turned to Juan and said, "Let's take a few men and creep into the town, near the docks. I want to know if my plan is working, and if it is we can descend on the pirates from the rear when they're confronted by one of our ambush groups. That will make the trap more effective and the raid shorter and less destructive."

Juan was shocked. "By the old false gods, are you insane? I won't let you put yourself into peril like that. When did you become so reckless? You'll stay here and wait for the raid to be quashed."

"Put myself into peril like this? Facing an angry kulkulcan trying to kill me isn't perilous? After that this is nothing. You and three or four stout men will be with me. Are you coming with me or not?"

Her mind was made up. She motioned for three of the strongest looking men to follow her and off she went, looking over her shoulder at Juan.

Juan looked at the lieutenant, who resignedly signaled for him to follow.

One of the townsmen led the other four through the alleyways. They wound up behind some crates near the docks, possibly the ones the lieutenant had used. They could see, and hear, the pirate leader and his mate standing by their gangway getting ready to address the crew. Everything else was quiet, much quieter than one would expect during a pirate raid.

There was no resistance or activity at the docks.

The pirate captain motioned with a dismissive wave of his hand and said to his companion, "What cowards they are." He spoke the common tongue of raiders and merchantmen in Second World. "At least the last town we raided up north put up a fight."

He turned to his men. "You scour the town and grab as much loot as you can. It would be best if you split into pairs to cover more territory. Meet back here in three hours."

The crew dispersed as instructed and headed off into the streets to see what they could find. They were walking into Bianca's trap.

The captain and his second in command waited by the *Unlucky Lady*. There wasn't much to hear at first, just some doors being battered and windows breaking. After a while, they and Bianca's group started to hear some yelling at a distance.

"It seems the cowards decided to put up a little resistance after all," said the captain.

"It would seem you are correct, sir."

They waited, and waited, and waited. None of the crew was returning with loot. This was obviously unexpected and they began to look worried and pace back and forth. Hours passed. Finally two of the crew appeared, looking considerably worse for the wear. They were followed by four soldiers wearing the livery of the Vlogentia Royal Guard and several dozen townsfolk. The soldiers carried swords and the townsfolk carried miscellaneous implements. His crewmen carried nothing, no loot and no weapons, and did not look at all pleased.

The outcome was obvious to Bianca and Juan. The pirates were defeated and only two of them were walking. Her group's assistance had never been needed, much to Bianca's delight.

She stepped out from behind the crates, strode to five or so feet from the two raiders and said, "Captain, all your crew has been killed or made prisoner. There are only"—she turned to Lieutanant Gonzalez with a questioning look. He held up some fingers—"six left standing. Your raid is over. You may surrender or suffer a far worse fate."

The two pirates acted stunned. Their mouths were agape, their eyes were wide and they held their hands in a defensive position. They stood as if frozen for a few seconds before accepting the obvious. They surrendered. All the folk broke into a cheer as the last pirates were led away.

Lieutenant Gonzalez asked for the town's mayor or headman.

A portly, middle-aged man stepped forward. Apparently this was the required appearance for provincial mayors in Vlogentia. "You have saved us. We are eternally grateful. What do you need or want us to do?"

"You need to find a way to detain the pirates. We will send a ship from the capital to collect them so they can spend some considerable time in the capital's prison. All we need from you is the use of their ship and a few sailors from Puerto Norte to take my detachment to the capital. We would like to set sail in the morning."

"I will assign ten men to sail the ship for you. For tonight, please accept our hospitality at our inn. Is there anything else we can do?"

"No, I don't think so. Just let us spend a night in decent lodging and stable our mounts. If you don't know unicorns, they can be difficult to manage."

The mayor, nor anyone in Puerto Norte, knew anything about the care and feeding of unicorns. They were happy to let the soldiers tend to their mounts, but were more than able to prepare a proper feast for the hungry group. Followed by a night's sleep in real beds. Bianca kept her two cubs in her room. Xavier got to sleep with two burly townsmen just outside his door. His window was barred by the innkeeper, so escape was again impossible.

For the first time in four days, they slept well. The next morning they boarded the sloop with the ten sailors. The pirate flag of red upper half and black lower half was lowered and the sky blue flag of Vlogentia was raised. It had three thin silver stripes running from the upper corner near the staff to the far lower corner. It had an eight pointed silver star, the four cardinal points longer than the other four, in the upper right corner away from the staff. The guardsmen saluted as it was raised. The unicorns were stored in the holds below. Xavier was locked in what they assumed used to be the captain's cabin. Bianca kept the cubs in a makeshift cage on deck with her since she had been unable to find anyone in Puerto Norte willing to keep and care for them. She was beginning to regret suggesting a sea voyage to the capital.

Before they cast off the mayor of Puerto Norte hurried to the side of the ship. "Some of the pirates were overheard by our guards talking among themselves during the night. It seems that there is a base on one of the barrier sand islands where they stay between raids on our neighbors along the northern coast. They have another ship they use to carry their loot to other kingdoms across the Great Sea to trade for supplies and food. If that base is left alone they may use that other ship for both raiding and trade. Can't you do something to stop them?"

"Did your guards learn on which of the five barrier islands their base is located?" asked the lieutenant. "How many men are presently there and what defenses do they have?"

"That we did not learn. But based on their comments about raiding just to our north it seems likely the base is on the northernmost isle. If the raiding party consisted of most of their fighters, then there shouldn't be very many men stationed there," responded the mayor.

"That's mostly guesswork, although reasonable. Give me some time to confer with my men to see what we might decide to do." Gonzalez turned to his soldiers and Bianca for a conference of war. They had only the five guardsmen, ten sailors from Puerto Norte, and Bianca with her two cubs. Not exactly an overwhelming force. Nonetheless, they decided that a scouting mission would be feasible. If they were spotted by the pirates stationed on the base they could escape long before the pirate ship could give chase.

Gonzalez turned back to the mayor. "We can afford a few days to explore the islands to see what needs to be done to eliminate the pirate threat. That is our duty as guardsmen. Just in case, do you have any additional men that might prove useful in a fight?"

"No trained fighters, but a few more hardy sailors that won't mind knocking a few pirate heads. I'll see how many we can recruit." He left and about a half hour later returned with ten more very stout looking men spoiling for a fight with the raiders.

"Thank you. We will see you in a few days," said the lieutenant.

The unicorns were offloaded and left with a livery stable that promised, with trepidation, to take good care of them. The extra men boarded. The *Unlucky Lady* cast off and headed west into the Inner Sea to search for the pirate base.

CHAPTER SIXTEEN
THE COUNTERATTACK RAID

The Inland Sea
Gregorian calendar: January 16
Mayan calendars: Tzolk'in: 11 Kab'an
                  Haab: 10 Muwan

With the prevailing west wind against them it took nearly two full days to sail close hauled across the Inland Sea to the northernmost of the barrier islands.

Bianca spent the time on deck, most definitely regretting her decision to join the expedition. *"What was I thinking? I don't like the water, I don't like sailing,"* she mused to herself, *"I'm letting my fury with the king and my impatience to get back to the capital cloud my judgement. I'm getting careless and impulsive. This isn't like me. It must stop."*

Juan sat next to her. "How are you doing?" he asked. "Are you seasick?"

"I'm not sick, it's just that the boat tilts so much every time you tack the sail, if that's what they call that maneuver. Is that really necessary?"

"The ship's master told me it is. He also said that it's fortunate that this sloop is much quicker than the usual square rigged flat bottomed boats used by our people or the trip would take yet another day. Don't fret, once we get near the barrier islands the sea will calm and you'll be fine. How are your cubs?"

"Better than I am. How much longer will this take?"

"Not much. We're almost to the first island. Just stay here by the mast, keep out of the way and listen to the crew. That might teach you more about sailing and help alleviate your fear of boats."

"I'm not afraid of the boat, I just don't like being on the water. Don't worry, I'll be fine."

Early on the third day out of Puerto Norte the lookout spotted a cove on the west, leeward, side of the northernmost isle. Across the mouth of the cove was a floating barrier, probably with a metal net hanging below it to keep out the merpeople and the rare shark. Moored inside the little port was a square-rigged ship a little larger than the *Unlucky Lady*. A few shacks littered the shore with a larger building behind them.

"I bet that's their warehouse," said the ship's master pointing to the building. "This is definitely an anchorage and a port of some sort. I don't see any people though. Perhaps they're not up yet."

"How fortunate for us," said Lieutenant Gonzalez. He ordered the *Unlucky Lady* to reverse course and drop anchor well to the north of the harbor and out of sight. He then called a meeting of the crew, including Bianca, to decide how best to capture the small port.

Fortunately the merpeople weren't near where they anchored.

The master said, "They are concentrating near the entrance to the cove in hopes of snatching any careless pirates. That could be our way in. We can pretend we're repelling a merpeople attack and signal for help. The pirates in the cove will come out to fend them off while they lower the barrier to let us in. They will be preoccupied and unprepared for our attack."

All agreed that sounded like a viable strategy. The lieutenant added a twist. He had the sailors use the ship's small boat a few times to ferry ashore twelve of the men, led by two of his guardsmen. Before the landing party disembarked he told them, "I do not think we've been spotted since we saw no activity anywhere in the harbor. I want you to creep inland, use the scrub for cover, and attack from their rear when I raise our flag. We will pretend to have trouble fending off the merpeople outside the barrier until you signal with your mirror that you're in position. Once they lower the barrier to let us in the port, be ready."

After the landing party was safely ashore the ship weighed anchor and set a tack for the entrance to the small bay. Gonzalez then lowered the flag of Vlogentia and raised the pirate flag. They were to all appearances the looters returning from a successful raid.

Just outside the barrier they found that pretending to repel merpeople wasn't necessary.

Bianca had learned about those denizens of the Inner Sea in her classes. They were mammals, they had long grey-brown human-like hair flowing from their heads but flukes like a whale. Their front flippers had become short arms with webbed fingers and short claws. Their faces closely resembled a human's with a nose and a mouth and rudimentary ears. Their teeth were sharp and pointed. They were air breathers. They were slimmer and lighter than other sea mammals like the whales and dolphins that plied the oceans. They preferred the shallow, quieter leeward side of the barrier islands rather than the more turbulent windward side. They were also very aggressive and attacked any people in their waters. Ships traversing the Inner Sea were careful to keep moving and maintain a sharp lookout.

The attack came at the ship from all sides, swimming from underwater and trying to leap onto the deck. Since they had short arms and no weapons except teeth and claws they showed no desire to capture the ship. They simply wanted a fight and the opportunity to pull a sailor overboard and drown them. It was fairly easy to push them away from the gunwales, but every so often one or two were able to pull themselves aboard. The crew had to pick them up and throw them back. Grabbing them by their flukes and flinging them into the water worked best since they didn't weigh too much.

During all this Bianca had stood in the center of the deck with her rapier in hand ready to fight any attackers that got past the crew. Her cubs stayed by her side growling and snarling like they were ferocious adults. Fortunately, neither she nor they were needed.

Lieutenant Gonzalez was heavily engaged, but he must have somehow noticed the reflected signal from the landing party." If we can get past these troublesome merpeople our trap can be sprung," he panted, out of breath.

By now the land-based pirates had noticed the frenzy surrounding what they assumed were their colleagues returning from the raid. They rushed to the stone breakwaters on either side of the barrier and started shooting crossbow bolts at the assailants.

Finally the merpeople gave up and swam away, waiting for another chance on another day. Once they were gone, the barrier was opened so the sloop could enter the harbor. The netting was then again strung across the harbor entrance and the brigands started to gather at the pier to welcome the ship. There were about twelve of them.

Just before the ship reached the dock Lieutenant Gonzalez lowered the pirate flag and raised the standard of Vlogentia. This appeared to confuse the land-based buccaneers. That action might mean that the sloop had captured some important person or loot, or it might mean they were under attack. Of course, the latter was correct.

The ship touched the dock and the crew and guardsmen leapt onto it and charged the outlaws. At the same instant the landing party charged from the brush behind the settlement. The trap was complete. Outnumbered, surprised and surrounded the pirates made the only reasonable choice. They surrendered. That is, all but three. They broke away, eluded the landing party and ran along the beach, heading south along the axis of the isle.

Bianca saw them and immediately and without thinking leapt off the boat and pursued the getaways. "Stay there and guard the prisoners. I'll run those men down and capture them myself!"

As she vaulted over the gunwale she heard the lieutenant shout to Corporal Gomez and one of the crew to follow her, "You two follow and assist her, I don't care what she thinks she is doing, one against three is never a good idea."

Bianca chased the men for a hundred yards or so before she realized just how foolish she'd been. Her zeal had overridden her good sense, just like at Puerto Norte. Just as she started to come to a stop the fugitives came to a brush pile and started to pull the camouflage off a small boat hidden underneath. They were trying to escape the island. Where they were headed after that was a mystery to her.

She came to a stop and tried to think what she should do. At that instant one of the men saw her and attacked with his sword. She parried his thrust and countered. He wasn't much of an expert with a sword and she quickly disarmed him. One of the other two also started toward her but never got close. Unbeknownst to her the cubs had followed her and immediately jumped the person they perceived was attacking Bianca, They knocked him down and proceeded to bite with their huge canines and claw every part of him they could find.

The third pirate was now occupied with Juan and the sailor. His fight was equally brief. He tried to thrust at the sailor before the guardsman could enter the fray. His attempt was futile and he was stabbed and cut down by Juan. The fight was over. Two of the pirates were dead and the third nursing a slice on his sword arm.

The sailor escorted him back to the dock and Bianca, her cubs and Juan followed. He was irate. "Did it not occur to you to let trained soldiers and sailors do the fighting? Are you trying to get killed? Do not ever do that again! I could not live with myself if you did something this foolish and were injured or, our good God forbid, killed."

"I'm sorry. I wasn't thinking. I let my emotions get the better of me again."

"No you certainly weren't thinking. What's come over you? You've never been this reckless or impulsive before. Where's the girl that just wanted to play pitz and visit with friends? Don't do something that foolhardy again."

"I said I was sorry. Ever since Ill'yx I can't seem to control my rage. But I won't let it happen again, I promise." She looked at him, imploring him to understand.

He huffed, "I don't want to talk about it anymore," and stormed off to the ship. He was clearly furious with her.

Left behind she scooped up her charges and carried them back to the ship. "You bad cats. You shouldn't be chasing around like that." She placed them in the crate on the ship that she'd prepared for them. They looked smug. *"And I shouldn't be chasing around like that either. I did it again,"* she thought.

After the fugitives were reunited with the other bandits Bianca spoke to the lieutenant. "Those three were trying to escape in a hidden boat. That tells me there must be a hideout on another island. But the captives at Puerto Norte indicated that this gang had only the two boats. What do you think that means?"

Gonzalez was not sure. "After we send this bunch of criminals back to Puerto Norte in the hold of the second vessel I think we need to search the islands some more. Let me detail some of the sailors to sail the prize ship and the prisoners back to Puerto Norte and you can return with them to the mainland. I'll take the rest of the men and the *Unlucky Lady* and do some more reconnoitering."

"No. Xavier and the original gang are safely imprisoned. There is no need for me to be there until you return with this ship so we can sail to the capital together. When we reach the capital we need for all of us to be present along with Captain Mendez and my friends so we can convince the authorities of the danger to our kingdom. That was our original plan, and I think we should stay with it." She didn't bother to mention that her main reason was that she wanted to stay close to Corporal Gomez.

Gonzalez relented. "Alright then, take your place by your cubs. But stay out of the way. I need to see to the prisoners." He turned to leave but immediately bumped into Corporal Gomez.

"I just gave your friend"—pointing to Bianca—"permission to accompany us on our search. I'm not sure what's come over her. She gave me some lame excuse for coming but she could just as easily wait for our return at Puerto Norte and then sail with us to the capital. But she is stubborn and I don't feel like arguing. Besides, those cubs might prove useful again."

Juan replied, "I don't know what her problem is either. I thought she didn't like sailing. If she wants to come, let her. I don't want to talk to her right now." He stomped away from his lieutenant and from Bianca.

"Just what we need, a lovers' quarrel," said Gonzalez to no one in particular as he walked back to amidships.

Bianca overheard the entire conversation. She decided it was most likely a deliberate act by Gonzalez to impress on her the gravity of her actions. It made her feel even worse than when she was arguing with Juan. She didn't want to worry Juan or get in the lieutenant's way. But she could no longer stay in the background like she used to do. That part of her had changed when she learned of the enormity of the king's plot.

It took a while to situate the prisoners below deck. While this was going on two of the guardsmen examined the warehouse. They reported back that it was filled with precious items as well as the more mundane things such as food and supplies. There was no room on either ship to load all the treasure, so the lieutenant decided to secure the building as best they could and leave it for later. "If we get rid of all the pirates in these waters, the treasure and goods should be safe for a few days until the officials in the capital can send a ship to load it and send it to the Royal Treasury in the capital. There are very few trading ships on the seas at this time of the year, so this gamble is a safe bet."

Finally, all was set. The prisoners were locked below deck and the second sloop set sail for the mainland. Gonzalez, his guardsmen, the ten sailors originally assigned to the mission and Bianca and her cubs set sail for the south. They left the barrier intact after leaving the cove. No point in risking the merpeople causing damage to the warehouse or the dock. It wasn't likely, but it was a precaution.

The next day a lookout spotted a couple of shacks in the center of the next island south. They anchored and sent the boat ashore with a couple of men to investigate. They reported, "It is uninhabited, with the barest of provisions inside the shacks."

"This must be where those three were headed," said one of the sailors. "My guess is that they hoped to hide here until another ship sailed by and they could signal it and claim to be castaways. Not much of a plan, but a plan nonetheless."

There was no danger, so the lieutenant, Juan, Bianca and two sailors got into the skiff to investigate further.

As they followed her into the craft, Bianca overheard Gonzalez whisper to Juan, "You two work out your differences or I'll leave both of you here."

Juan nodded understanding.

Bianca realized she was causing a problem between the two. That was the last thing she wanted or needed. *"I have been rash. I'll try to find time to talk with Juan,"* she thought.

The party explored the meager encampment. The two huts were of fairly recent origin, made from palm trunks with thatched roofs. They had no facilities, not even facilities for cooking. The sailor had been correct. What the three pirates had planned to do at this place for any length of time was unclear. They probably hadn't thought that far ahead.

While searching the site for treasure or anything of interest one of the sailors noticed that there used to be remnants of a much older settlement. All that was left were the indications of foundations of ten or so houses, possibly of several rooms in each house. The outline of the ruins was that of Mayan houses. No indication of exactly how old the ruins were.

Bianca asked the lieutenant, "Who do you think left these ruins here? They must have been a people, possibly from First World, that we have never known. Do you think they are still somewhere near Vlogentia?"

"I have no idea," he replied, "but this site is older. Perhaps they didn't survive. Perhaps they somehow arrived and then left the island for other places. We simply cannot know. But this is a mystery for some other time. We need to return to the ship and continue our search. By the way, isn't that Corporal Gomez over there?"

She looked over at Juan, nodded to the lieutenant and went to talk with him.

Finding nothing else of note the explorers left the site and set sail for the other barrier islands.

Searching the islands further south turned up nothing of interest. Finally, Lieutenant Gonzalez ordered the ship to turn northwest and head back to Puerto Norte.

The wind was behind them, so it only took a day to reach their destination. They docked early in the day on the twentieth of January by the Gregorian calendar. I was two Imix' by the Tzolk'in ritual calendar. Imix' is the day of return so everyone on board felt good fortune was with them.

The mayor met the ship as it docked.

"Welcome back. That took longer than anticipated but the results are wonderful. I learned about your successful counter raid from our crew of the captured pirate ship when it docked here with the additional prisoners. Well done, well done indeed. Will you need to spend the night before leaving for the capital?"

"No," answered Gonzalez, "we need to make haste for the capital. I have dallied more than I intended. We are late for a meeting with my captain. We need the prisoner Xavier and our unicorns on board as soon as possible. We will make sail this afternoon. Keep the other prisoners under guard until a ship arrives from the capital to take them to jail. Leave the pirates' nest on the island alone. We'll arrange for another ship to take care of that problem."

The unicorns were retrieved from the livery stable. They appeared in good condition, the grooms had done an excellent job with the unfamiliar creatures. Xavier was brought on board and locked in the captain's cabin. Bianca and her cubs once again situated themselves on deck along with the guardsmen, including a certain corporal once again by her side, and the sailors.

The afternoon wind allowed them to set sail. The trip down the coast to the capital's port took only rest of the day and the night, the sloop was definitely faster than their usual vessels.

The soldiers got a much needed rest, Xavier fumed in his cabin, and Bianca spent most of the trip chatting with Juan and playing with her cubs.

The next morning found them docking at the capital's port.

Bianca looked at the city as the *Unlucky Lady* was tying to the pier and wondered what the king was doing now. Was he aware that his plan was in shambles and, if so, what would he do about it? She wondered what she could do to stop him and save the realm, her home, from disaster. The time was rapidly approaching when something needed to happen, but she had no idea what that might be. She felt desperate.

CHAPTER SEVENTEEN

THE VILLAGE

On the sacbe toward the capital, Kingdom of Vlogentia
Gregorian calendar: January 10
Mayan calendars: Tzolk'in: 5 Chuwen
             Haab: 4 Muwan

J ason and Margaret rode on the seat of the medical supply wagon as it brought up the rear of the column as the troop started down the sacbe. Jason felt he was getting quite adept at driving a wagon. At least he had something useful to do. Margaret kept him company and tried to manage the horses on occasion, but just couldn't get the proper feel of the reins.

Captain Mendez had organized the column as before. He rode in front, this time with a sergeant alongside him and the rest of the guardsmen behind them.

As the detachment rode away Jason and Margaret looked back at Bianca and the five guardsmen left behind and waved goodbye. Margaret yelled, "Good luck, and be careful."

Bianca waved back and replied, "You be careful, and may the two moons show you the right path."

The rest of the day passed uneventfully and the seventeen of them made good time. Jason and Margaret could hear and understand some of the conversation between the soldiers due to their translators, but spoke sparingly since the doubling of their voices bothered and sometimes confused the Vlogentians.

They camped as usual that night. The soldiers were cordial to the Blankenships and they all sat together as they ate. But they had little in common with the couple from First World and were frankly baffled when Jason tried to tell them about their home and life there.

Margaret scolded him. "You're confusing or boring them. They don't care about First World, it's almost a myth to them. You need to try and view things from the soldiers' perspective and understand their interests and knowledge of their world. For instance, try this approach."

She turned from Jason to the nearest soldier and asked him, "What do you know about Bianca? We have just met her and have come to like her, but don't really know much about her other than she can be resourceful. Killing Ill'yx proved that. But when your column arrived at Natts' Nohoch Muulo'ob we sensed you knew more about her than that she was Juan Alejandro's sweetheart. Why is that?"

"She's well known in the city," answered the sergeant, "due to her unusual appearance and her friendliness with just about everyone. She also is a good pitz player. Of course we know about her and Corporal Gomez. We pretend not to notice. That's really all I can say."

"Thanks for the information," said Jason, "that helps a bit. But what exactly is pitz?"

The sergeant's response led to a long and confusing answer.

Jason decided that pitz was the Vlogentian version of the Mesoamerican ball game he had learned about on some old television documentary. .

Sunrise saw the company already fed, saddled, harnessed and on the sacbe again. They were still making good time. It was late afternoon when they started to pass a small village on the left of the road. It was so small it didn't even have a name, according to one of the troopers. Just as they reined to a stop, four of the men came running out of the village and hailed the captain.

"Please stop and help us. We were attacked yesterday by a gang of bandits. They injured several of us, burned some of our homes and ransacked our church. We need help for our injured and it is your duty to bring the brigands to justice."

"We have been warned of the brigands," the captain told them, "this must be one of the towns the last village told us about. Don't worry, we're here to capture them. Tell us exactly what happened, when it happened, and where they went."

"There were ten of them. They rode in from the south around midafternoon yesterday and assaulted the priest, our headman and some others trying to defend them. Then they called everyone else into the center of town and told us to give them all our valuables. We didn't have much. That angered them so much that they set fire to the nearest houses and defiled the church, taking the few items of any worth. They rode back south when they were done, around sunset. We don't have any trained healers, just our old shaman to tend to the injured. Please, can you help us?"

Captain Mendez told them to wait a moment and rode back to Jason and asked, "Did you understand what he said? Can you work some of your healing magic on the injured?"

"Of course I can. Just show me where to take the wagon and bring me the wounded. I have a more than adequate supply of magic potions." He deliberately used the phrase 'magic potions'. He had heeded Margaret's advice and was learning how to live in Vlogentia.

"Excellent. However the bandits were riding donkeys and will not be as fast as our unicorns, so we will wait until sunrise tomorrow to chase them down in the daylight. I'm sorry, but you your return to the capital will have to wait until we have dealt with this gang."

Both Jason and Margaret were more than willing to help.

Jason said, "No problem for us. Help me get this wagon into the village so I can get to work. After all this time, one more day won't make much difference."

It took several minutes, but with all the soldiers' help the wagon was soon over the road's sidewalls without having to empty it this time. Jason parked it in the village center and went to check on the patients with Margaret serving as his nurse. The church was small but intact, though ransacked inside, but big enough to handle the six patients.

The priest, father Pedro Lopez, had a stab wound in his shoulder, but was in surprisingly good spirits.

Jason asked him if they could use the church as an infirmary.

After a moment of disbelief upon hearing Jason's translator say in Yukatek whatever Jason had just said in some foreign language, he replied, "That is an excellent idea. Please feel free to do whatever you need."

Jason nodded thanks and went to work examining his patients.

Fortunately all of the wounds were not overly serious. Either the bandits were careful not to injured potential future victims or were simply incompetent. Jason tended toward the latter view. It did take the rest of the day, but he was able to clean the wounds, all of which were shallow stab wounds, and apply dressings. Each man got a good dose of antibiotics, but Jason still had an ample supply. He spoke with the shaman and told him how to care for the men. One of the women was pointed out to him as the best seamstress in the village. He asked her to visit the men in the morning to see if she could work the same stitching magic Mia had done in Natts' Nohoch Muulo'ob. She agreed.

Morning saw the patients doing extremely well. Jason removed the dressings, applied some of the topical antibiotic and set Maria, the seamstress, to work closing the gashes. Her work was just as good as Mia's had been. He was pleased.

He told the captain, "All of the men are doing well. They should heal completely in a few weeks. Will you start after the bandits now?"

"Yes, and you are coming with us in case we have wounded to tend. Pack your wagon and follow us. Your horses are not as quick as unicorns as but still faster than donkeys laden with spoils."

This was not what Jason and Margaret were expecting. He'd had hoped their adventures were over. All they had anticipated was a slight delay to tend to the wounded, a trip to the capital, a sail to the Portal isle, and then back to Florida. Now they were off chasing bandits through the countryside.

Margaret sighed, "Once again I ask, will this never end? What will we have to do next? Overthrow the king?"

"Let's hope not," said Jason as he hitched the horses to the wagon. "I don't think I can take any more escapades. That one night at the inn in the town Bianca called Natts Seebok Hah, or something like that, is starting to look like the high point of our journey. Besides, I don't have an unlimited supply of medicines. I hope they won't be needed."

They followed Mendez' men south out of the village.

Travel was rougher after they left the village. The road was no longer a sacbe, but a common rural dirt track. Thankfully it didn't have wheel ruts, but the dirt thrown up by the cavalry in front made riding on the wagon a disaster. Jason could hardly see to drive. Margaret gave up entirely and just covered her eyes and face with a rag. Both of them were choking on the cloud of dust created by the unicorns. Jason tried lagging a little farther behind to mitigate the discomfort.

"Keep up you two," Called Captain Mendez. "I don't want you getting lost and wasting our time while we have to search for you."

So Jason tied a kerchief around his face to keep out the grime like in the old western movies. He soon realized that was the real reason cowboys wore bandanas. But he was able to keep up with the others.

It wasn't until the afternoon that the company caught up with the bandits. At first, the raiders didn't notice Captain Mendez and his men, but that didn't last long. They started to run, but couldn't bring themselves to leave the donkeys behind. That slowed them even more. The captain ordered his men to split into two seven man columns and ride to either side of the bandit band. They would then close in and attack. This worked as planned, except two of the band managed to escape on foot into the forest to the west of the trail before they could be captured. The others surrendered.

After securing the eight prisoners, Mendez detailed four of his men to guard them. He then ordered the rest of the company and Jason, without the wagon of course, to accompany him.

"I want you with us in case you need to tend any wounds. Get what supplies you may need and can carry. And hurry up about it. Your wife will stay behind and help watch the prisoners and their donkeys."

"I'm so honored," she said, and plopped down on the ground in the shadow of the wagon and refused to budge. "I wanted to venture into the woods and out of this stifling heat." She stared sullenly at the prisoners and they stared equally sullenly at her.

Jason had no choice. He gathered what he could and fell in behind the guardsmen as they entered the forest. The trees were a mixture of mature deciduous and palm. Their crowns loomed far overhead and blocked most of the sunlight, but not all. Because about half were palm, the underbrush was not as thick as is usual in a purely deciduous forest. Dead fronds lay about mixed with fallen leaves. That made the ground soft but not muddy. The air had a pleasant odor and the humidity was low. Walking through the woods was actually quite pleasant. There were enough leaves strewn across the ground to show the disturbance left by the fleeing bandits. It looked like this was going to be easy.

That misconception didn't last long. About a hundred yards into the woods they were suddenly swarmed by thousands of the fairies that Jason had learned about from Bianca. Except this was worse than anything she had described. They were everywhere, diving and even ramming into the men and Jason. They were so thick that it reminded Jason of the dust cloud kicked up by the unicorns. He actually could not see more than a few feet in front of his face.

Based on what Xander and Bianca had told him about the fairies he began to worry about being stung multiple times. The guardsmen seemed to be equally worried. They were swatting at the pests with their rapiers and hats and trying to cover their faces with their hands. Ahead of them, perhaps a hundred yards or less, they could hear the bandits yelling and screaming as the stinging began.

Captain Mendez started to order a retreat. Just as he yelled, "Fall back and ..." Jason remembered a trick his grandfather had told him about beekeeping.

"Wait," he said, "if we can light some of these fronds they should create a lot of smoke. Pests like these don't like the smoke and will avoid it and us. It won't be pleasant, but much better than being swarmed and stung to death."

His notion was quickly seconded by Private Colon. "That's right! My mother's sister-in-law's brother is a beekeeper. He's told me that they use fumes and vapors to control and tame the bees so they can collect the honey. I think the First Worlder's idea is a good one. We should try it."

Mendez agreed to try the idea, since trying to make it back out of the woods before being stung did not seem likely. Jason and he told the men to gather fronds as best they could with the swarm about them, and light them with their flint and daggers. The men were desperate and made very quick work of getting some makeshift torches going. The combination of flames, more fire than Jason expected, and smoke had the desired effect. The fairies fell back several yards giving the captain's party room to maneuver freely.

Once they had rid themselves from the cloud of fairies, they were able to make way to the bandits who gratefully surrendered. Being prisoners of the guard was better than the torment they were currently experiencing. The two had their hands bound and, surrounded by soldiers carrying smoldering palm fronds, they and the guardsmen made their way safely out of the forest and back to the wagon and the others.

Back at the wagon Margaret asked Jason, "What is going on? Why are the men carrying torches made of palm fronds? Did you have any trouble with the capture?"

Jason told her what had happened and added, "We were lucky my grandfather was a beekeeper and that I spent summers visiting him on his farm. None of us was injured, but the bandits were stung several times so I need to treat them. I'll be back as soon as possible. How did it go with you?"

"Nothing to report. We just sat here waiting. Now I'm glad I wasn't part of the chase."

Jason went to examine the two prisoners. Fortunately, none of them exhibited an allergic reaction to the stings. All he had to do was instruct them to use cool compresses from their canteen water and not to scratch. To help that he gave each of them a jar of cortisone cream to apply to the stings, he had a lot of that, and made them swallow some ibuprofen for the pain.

"Magic potions," he told them. He was beginning to like that phrase. He was also counting on a marked placebo effect.

After the injured were treated the captain ordered the column and the prisoners to begin their return to the village. Back on the trail Jason noticed the captain looking over the captives.

They were all young men, not past their early twenties, if that much. He asked the one he gauged was the ringleader, "Who are you, where are you from, and what made you want to raid a village?"

"We're from one of the villages farther to the south. We were bored with village life and wanted to have some excitement. We thought becoming highwaymen would do that. We were going to hide out in the woods and live off the land and the spoils we took from the neighboring villages."

"Well, you've had your excitement haven't you? Didn't it occur to you that raiding villages would bring down the royal guard?"

"We thought we'd be safe from them deep in the woods. We didn't know about the fairies. Nobody we knew ever ventured into the woods so we thought no one would ever look for us there. "

"Maybe if you'd asked one of your village elders you might have learned why no one ever went into the forest. As it is you will now be able to spend some time viewing the sights of the capital, but not participate in the festivities. You'll be inside a jail cell." The captain rode on.

The procession made its way back to the village the band had raided.

The convoy arrived back at the village late in the day. The residents gathered in the central plaza and cheered the capture of the bandits and the return of their possessions. Even Father Lopez was pleased. All of the items taken from the church were recovered. After the villagers claimed their possessions the captain gave the donkeys to the village as partial compensation for the damage and insult they'd experienced.

Camp for the night was set up just outside the village and by the sacbe. As the soldiers sat around their recounting the day and praising Jason on his idea one of the village elders approached the group.

"We are grateful for your capture of the bandits. However, there is one other topic I'd like to discuss. Our village has an old legend that we'd like you to investigate. Since you are the first Royal Guardsmen to stop here in many years we think it is also your duty to determine the truth or falsehood of the folklore."

"What is it?" asked Mendez. "I do not wish to delay our journey to the capital any longer without a very good reason."

"Our forefathers have handed down a tale of a city of gold hidden in the forest to our west. The same forest your captives tried to escape into. Supposedly this fabulous city is protected by the fairies and a pack of woods trolls. The tale also goes on to tell of a group of five members of the Order of the Portal who went searching for the city more than a hundred years or more ago. Only one returned to our village with his tale of the expedition and he died shortly thereafter. He did say before he died that their five wands were captured by the trolls. Can you imagine? A city of gold! Even if that were not true, wouldn't the Order pay dearly for the return of five lost wands? But, a city of gold. We'd all be rich!"

All of a sudden the troop was very interested, even the captain.

"We have our duty to return to the capital," he said, "but a delay of at most a few days seems minor compared to the momentous discoveries we might find. As the elder mentioned, just finding the lost wands would justify the interruption. Also, Lieutenant Gonzalez has agreed to wait at the rendezvous spot for several days and since both Xavier and the couple from First World are needed to confirm the existence of the nefarious plot to start a now useless war I foresee no problem with a slight delay on our part."

Jason had understood most of the discussion and even he became excited. Finding the fabled El Dorado was the sort of adventure that becomes legend.

Margaret didn't act quite as excited. She whispered to Jason, "Really, we're going to look for a city of gold? Are you sure?"

"Oh yes," he replied. "Where's your sense of adventure?"

"I left it in Natts' Nohoch Muulo'ob."

"Give us a moment to consider your request." Said Captain Mendez to the elder. It actually took less than a minute to arrive at a unanimous agreement of the troopers.

"We will set off in the morning to look for this city. As I stated we are on a mission critical to the king so we cannot take more than a couple of days or so before we leave for the capital. Will that will give us enough time to verify the truth or not of your tale."

"Yes, I believe that it will," he replied.

"Very well. Return tomorrow morning to meet with us to finalize the details of the search. Until then, goodnight."

The elder returned to his home in the village.

The guardsmen continued to talk excitedly among themselves.

Jason tried to settle down for the night. The anticipation of finding an actual city of gold made that difficult. He slept very little. He couldn't wait for the expedition to start. He didn't mind putting off the voyage home for a day or so for an opportunity such as this.

He, along with everyone else, rose early the next morning.

"Well, we're here," said Jason as he, along with Margaret and the village elders, joined Captain Mendez and his men for a council of war. The decision to search for the lost city of gold had been made. Now they needed to learn more about the legend and where to look for it.

CHAPTER EIGHTEEN

THE HUNT FOR EL DORADO

The raided village
Gregorian calendar: January 13
Mayan calendars: Tzolk'in: 8 Ix
                    Haab: 7 Muwan

The captain started by grilling one of the elders, "First we need to learn from you which direction to take, then how far away the site is and what obstacles we're going to face. So, according to your history where did the one surviving member of the Order come from when he left the forest? What exactly did he tell you, or your forebears?"

"Our legends are vague since they're so old. If the Royal Guard had visited us years ago our information would have been more recent and accurate. But we believe he came from the southwest, the same direction you took yesterday. So the city of gold must lie deep in the forest but directly southwest of where you captured the bandits."

Captain Mendez rubbed his chin, apparently deep in thought. "This seems almost too convenient. If you know approximately where the city lies, why haven't you searched for it yourselves?"

"We're poor peasants. We don't have the equipment or skills to conduct a search. We'll leave that to the professionals, you."

"I'm still not so sure. Fetch the bandit leader to me. I want to hear what he says about the land and forest to the southwest."

The bandit leader was marched out of the shack his group were housed in and thrown down in front of the captain. "Where exactly where were you headed when we intercepted you?"

"We had a hideout a little south of where you captured us. It was in a small copse of trees just outside the forest. That's where we felt we could stay hidden from pursuers like you. It's not in the forest so we never had to deal with those awful fairies. We didn't know such beings existed."

"What else? What did you see? Did you explore anywhere?"

"No, we didn't search the area. But a couple of the men did notice what looked like an old path leading into the woods. If we'd had more time we might have reconnoitered the trail."

He looked at the captain, and then at each of the guardsmen in turn. His hands and eyes were pleading, "Be sure to tell the judge how helpful I am. You will tell him, won't you? I don't want to spend the best part of my life in prison."

"An old path, hmmm. This still seems awfully convenient," said Mendez as he ignored the pleas of the raider. "Where did you think the path led? How old is it? Is it maintained or overgrown? Give me some details."

"We have no idea about any of that. I said we never got around to investigating. If we had gone into the forest we'd have been attacked by the fairies and driven back. All I can say is that the entry looks overgrown and is apparent only because the brush and trees are much shorter and seem to be a different foliage than the rest of the woods."

"All right. How far from where we captured you is this hideout?"

"About two miles. If we'd had just a little more time we would have been safely hidden."

"With all those donkeys your gang couldn't hide in an unlit cave. " Mendez sent the criminal mastermind back to detention. He thanked the village elders for their input and sent them home.

They left with pleased looks on their faces.

"They think they've got us hooked, "said Jason to Margaret.

"Oh, they most certainly have you on the line," she replied.

The captain faced the meeting, "Despite the vagueness of the information, the bandits' presumed hideout sounds like the place to start our search. What do you think?"

One of the men pulled a map out of his gear and unrolled it for all to see. "It is possible that the group from the Order cut a swath through the forest as they went. If it's still visible after all this time they must have cut down everything in their way and salted the ground or something to prevent new growth. That would have made their return journey easy to follow."

"Wait a minute," interjected Jason, "I don't care what they did to the path. After a hundred years it should be so overgrown that it'd be invisible. It wouldn't even exist anymore. This doesn't sound right."

"You're right. It can't have been a hundred years ago. No trail would last that long. The villagers' legend must be wrong. Perhaps it was just one generation ago, or less. Small villages like this one don't bother to keep accurate track of the time."

"Look at the map." The trooper pointed to a spot on the map deep in what appeared to Jason to be the depiction of a forest. "If I were to build a city or town, especially one made out of gold, I would want it near a river or stream for easier transport of materials. Note that if there is indeed a path starting from where the bandit indicated a route directly southwest would take you to the bend of the Lesser Branch of the Great River. The forest is dense in that region so a city, even one made of gold, built even a short way off the river would be unnoticed by the traffic going up and downstream."

Captain Mendez and the men studied the map for a considerable time. It was not very detailed. "I wish Vlogentia had better mapmakers," said the captain, "this doesn't show us as much as I'd like. But Jesus' idea seems as good as any to start with."

The decision to follow yesterday's trail to the hideaway and then penetrate into the forest along the presumed path didn't take long for all in the meeting to approve.

The captain rolled up the map, put it in his saddlebag and started to issue orders.

"This time let's be ready for the fairies. Collect any old rags the villagers don't want. We'll get them damp so they'll smolder but not burst into flame. We do NOT want flame inside a forest."

"Why not," asked Jason, "in fact I haven't noticed an open fire the entire time my wife and I have been in Vlogentia. Even the cooking stoves are tightly controlled. Why?'

"Fire in Second World is an extreme hazard. It burns with such ferocity and is so hard to control we avoid it at all costs. It is rare that an open fire is needed, so you're fortunate that guardsmen carry flint for an emergency. Almost no one else does."

Jason had to be satisfied with the partial answer since it wasn't clear to him why fire was so dangerous in Second World. He got busy rearranging the supplies in the wagon. The trail was nowhere as smooth as the sacbe and things had gotten jumbled the day before. He made sure all was secure for what he thought would be a bumpy trip. Margaret helped him.

She had insisted on coming along. "Now that you truly are off on your golden goose chase I want to see for myself. I doubt that such a city exists, but I can't pass up the possibility that it does. So I'm riding with you."

"Welcome," he said.

Captain Mendez ordered four soldiers and their mounts to stay at the village and guard the prisoners. "The rest of you will follow me on your unicorns until we reach the anticipated path through the forest. Jason and Margaret, you follow on the wagon, again. Once at the entry into the woods, the unicorns and wagon with its horses will be left with three more guards and Mrs. Blankenship. The remaining seven men and Jason will accompany me along the anticipated path. I plan to be gone no more than three or four days. I know that's a day or so more than I had said last night. But I think we can afford the extra time, especially if we discover what we hope to find."

The troopers started to organize despite considerable grumbling by the men detailed to guard duty and therefore not part of the group that would find the legendary city.

Margaret threw a fit. "You are not leaving me behind. Jason has agreed that I can ride with him. I deserve a chance to find the city of gold as much as any of you. Besides, if you leave me outside the forest I **will** sneak a ride on a unicorn, your rules notwithstanding."

"Very well, you can come. But you better not slow us down." Conceded Mendez.

"I won't. Just you watch."

Off they went. As usual the captain in front. The troopers behind him and the wagon with Jason and Margaret trailing. Since they had a good idea where their destination was they made very good time and arrived at the aforementioned copse of trees in mid-morning. The entrance to the path through the forest was as described by the bandit leader. Most of the rest of the woods was a mixture of tall trees and palms with significant but passable underbrush. The entrance was definitely marked with much smaller trees and a different, greener ground cover.

"Your man was right, "Jason told the sergeant riding alongside the wagon, "this looks much more recent than a hundred or more years past."

"I agree," said the sergeant. "I think this path has been used much more recently, within the past year or two. We'd better be careful. There might be persons or things in there that are unfriendly, to say the least."

The copse had a small pond in the center and lots of grass for the animals. The three men ordered to guard the site set up camp and secured the wagon.

"Wait for us for five days," ordered Mendez, "no more. If we are not back by then return to the village, collect your colleagues, proceed to the capital and report directly to the colonel. Understand?"

"Yes, sir. Are you certain we cannot join you? The wagon and animals will be fine for a few days by themselves."

"You know better than that. Just follow orders. We'll tell you everything when we get back."

"Yes, sir."

Backpacks were outfitted for the exploratory group. Mendez made sure Margaret carried her fair share.

Jason told him, "Don't think you can deter her. You are mistaken. She exercises regularly at home. She can carry her burden as easily as the rest of the group."

Smoke torches were prepared and the group started into the forest. It was the same as the previous day. Pleasant at first, soon followed by a horde of the fairies descending on them like an avalanche. This time they were prepared. The torches were lit and the procession made its way along the path without incident. The trail was starting to become overgrown but still obviously recent enough to be easily followed. The fairies hovered just outside the smoke cloud, acting as if they were very annoyed. The smoke was itself a bother to the hikers, but tolerable. Much better than a bombardment by the flying pests. Margaret appeared to be enjoying herself.

The trail led them in the direction they expected, southwest toward the bend in the Lesser Branch of the Great River. Travel was easy and they made excellent time. There was nothing else to see as yet, but that was anticipated. If the map and their idea where the lost city of gold were correct it would be miles before they reached their goal. They marched the rest of the day with frequent stops for rest and water and snacks.

Toward sunset the captain called a halt and ordered camp to be set. "We've made fantastic progress today. If our calculations are correct we should reach the city by tomorrow evening. That will give us a day to explore our discovery and two days back to the stand of trees. This will make us late to our planned rendezvous, but Lieutenant Gonzalez knows to wait for us. The look on his face when we tell him what we've found will make the delay worthwhile."

Camp for the night was pleasant. The weather was warm. They uncovered a small lantern they'd brought for security purposes. Apparently the fairies didn't like the night or the light of the lantern. They disappeared. A few night insects of some sort chirped in the distance, but otherwise all was quite.

Day two on the trail of the lost city was like day one. The way was easy and the fairies kept at bay by the smoking torches.

Very early in the morning things suddenly changed. The nice, obvious trail came to an end. Lying there were bodies of two men. They had large swords like machetes that they had obviously used to cut through the brush. They were clad in remnants of leather armor from neck to foot and leather helmets, presumably to protect them from the fairies. They appeared to have been savagely attacked by something. Bite marks covered their bodies from head to toe and their leather armor was ripped to shreds.

"Well, we now know why the path was so easy and recent up to now," said Mendez. "But it looks as if our way ahead is going to be more difficult, and we have enemies of some sort. It seems to me that our villagers may not have been entirely honest with us. I think these two are from there and when they didn't return the elders saw us as their backup plan. I'll have a nice chat with them when we return."

They took the time to bury the two unfortunate explorers.

Progress was now much slower. Brush had to be cut down and trees notched to mark the return journey. It was not long, less than a couple of miles, before they came to a large clearing in the forest. It had to be a hundred yards or so across. In the center of the clearing were twenty or so houses surrounding a large central building like a church or temple. Behind the building was a golden stele, square in shape with faint carvings on its sides.

"We found it, the fabled city of El Dorado," said Captain Mendez.

CHAPTER NINETEEN
EL DORADO FOUND

In a southern forest by a tributary of the Lesser Branch of the Great River
Gregorian calendar: January 14
Mayan calendars: Tzolk'in: 9 Men
Haab: 8 Muwan

The spectacle was amazing. It may not have been a huge city teeming with rich denizens but it was golden. All of it. Every one of the homes, the church/temple and the stele were gleaming bright gold in the sunlight that poured down on the clearing. Every square inch of every building was shining the bright, beautiful, rich color of gold.

Everyone in the patrol stood transfixed looking at the wonderful sight.

The captain kept repeating, "We found it, we found the lost city of El Dorado."

"*Well,*" thought Jason, "*the lost village of El Dorado.*" But he noticed that nobody acted as if they cared about the distinction.

Even Margaret appeared awestruck, and she hadn't the gold fever the rest of them had.

They were so distracted they didn't even notice the fairies were gone.

After a few moments marveling at the sight. Captain Mendez said, "There have to be residents of this place, and we know they're not welcoming to uninvited guests. Form a square with me on the front and move cautiously toward the nearest house. Jason and Margaret, stay in the inside of the square. The rest of you keep a sharp lookout, an attack will probably come any instant from any direction. I know this is a most unusual tactic, an infantry square is meant to be a stationary defensive formation to repel attacks from all sides. But we were few in number and any other formation would leave us exposed if we are flanked and overrun. Proceed!"

They maintained formation as they crept slowly toward the nearest golden house.

The houses and church/temple continued to shimmer brightly in the sunlight. The approach felt to Jason like it took forever but the formation finally drew adjacent to the nearest structure, an apparent home about twenty feet on all sides, a door on the side facing the village's center, and a roof that looked to be made of gold tile. Soldiers nearest the wall extended their arms to feel the precious metal.

That was when they received the greatest shock and disappointment of their lives. It wasn't gold at all. None of it. The building, and presumably all the rest of the village, was completely engulfed with a climbing vine that had incredibly densely packed tiny gold colored leaves. The leaves completely hid the stems of the vines so the appearance of the wall from more than a foot away was of solid gold. A slight breeze made the leaves rustle slightly, causing the look of shimmering metal. It was a crushing revelation. The group stood nearly as stationary as they had a few moments previously, but now with total disappointment rather than elation on their faces.

It was at this moment that the trolls who seemingly lived in the village of false gold attacked. They poured out of the other huts and rushed the patrol. The guardsmen were well drilled. They immediately broke square and formed a defensive line in front of the home's false gold wall.

These trolls were not like the mountain trolls. They looked like four foot tall canines except that they walked and ran on two legs. Their fur was reddish brown on their backs, but white on their bellies. The muzzles were long and armed with sharp teeth. Their ears looked like normal, pointed and erect canine ears. They had short arms instead of front legs, and paws that looked like hands. They carried short sticks that they used like jabbing spears and they could pick up and throw a rock. Their chief means of attack however was the bite. They growled and yammered in what sounded like a primitive speech, but the attack was uncoordinated.

The soldiers drew their swords and stood shoulder to shoulder. They used the fronds as makeshift shields. The trolls could not break through the line and fell back after a few desperate attacks. Not one of the soldiers was hurt, but the trolls had taken quite a few casualties.

Captain Mendez feared a standoff. A situation his squad could not long sustain, they would eventually be overrun. Jason looked at Margaret. "First trolls that look like giant lizards, now trolls that look like werewolves. Don't worry, the captain will get us out of this." He hoped he sounded more reassuring than he felt.

Both sides stood looking at each other. Neither made a move. Suddenly one of the men let out a heavy grunt and went down like he'd been shoved backward. Jason noticed one of the larger trolls/werewolves standing about twenty feet away pointing a wand at them. He realized it must be one of the five missing wands the elder had told them about. Somehow that troll/werewolf was able to use the wand for a weapon. So that part of the legend was unfortunately true.

And that troll knew how to use the wand although not expertly enough to cause real damage. Another man grunted and fell back, but got up right away. Both men were obviously winded and not able to perform at their usual level of expertise. This could be disastrous. If the trolls attacked while a man was down, the line would not hold and they'd be overrun.

Jason had an idea. "Quick, light some of the smoke torches and hurl them at the troll wielding the wand. The smoke will blind him and disrupt his aim. It may also dissipate the force of the blow."

Margaret grabbed a torch and lit it from one of the smoldering remnants they had brought with them from the forest, swung it around to get it smoking and tossed it at the troll with the wand. It landed in front of him and the smoke rose into its face. It worked. The troll started coughing and forgot about attacking them with the wand.

Captain Mendez had Jason and Margaret light more torches and throw them at the trolls. The smoke must have been unfamiliar and threatening to them, it was blinding and the smell must also have been disagreeable to their sensitive noses. They broke and ran. The troll with the wand dropped it and also took flight. It looked like that the attack was over. A prolonged fight would have proved disastrous.

Before the enemy could regroup one of the men ran out and retrieved the wand. The trolls had disappeared in a literal blind panic into the woods in every direction since the smoldering fronds created a veritable wall of smoke between the group and the edge of the forest.

Captain Mendez told the group, "I think they will need a considerable time to regroup for another attack, if they bother at all."

Since it appeared that they had the time to perform some reconnoitering of the village the Captain decided to do just that. He detailed two exploratory groups of three people each. Jason would be a member of one of the groups and Margaret would accompany the other group. He and the remaining three soldiers would stand guard at the edge of the village.

"Stay together and report back to me as quickly as possible, or immediately if you hear us raise the alarm."

The two groups spread out and searched most of the nearby homes. Nothing much of interest other than the dwellings had obviously been occupied by humans in the past. Mayan humans at that. The interiors looked exactly like most peasant homes in Vlogentia with the same sorts of furniture and wall decorations.

Margaret's group entered the large central structure.

She gave Jason and the captain a detailed description of what they found when the patrol regrouped.

"The building turned out to be a church. The soldiers told me the interior looked like any other church in Vlogentia that had been neglected for years. We found the other four missing wands lying on the remains of the altar. Behind the altar there was a door in the back of the church that was bolted from the inside. It had never been breached by the forest trolls. One of the soldiers used his sword to force the lock and we crept into the dark room."

"Another of the soldiers had a lantern with him, so he uncovered it. The room was about eight feet square with a table and chair in the middle and shelves with books and codices stored on them. A skeleton was curled up in a corner. That person must have locked himself in the room to record whatever disaster had descended upon the village. Next to a lamp filled with dead fireflies was one of the books lying open on the table. It was the diary the unfortunate writer had used for his last entries. It was in Spanish so I asked one of the soldiers to translate it into Yukatek so my translator could render his speech into English. It wasn't the best of solutions, but it worked."

"That sounds sort of complicated," said Jason, "but you were able to learn what the diary said?"

"Yes, I did. The story in the journal was alarming, to say the least. It wasn't entirely clear to me but some of the older entries indicated that the people of the village were outcasts from the original settlers of Father Sebastian's village in the Yucatan. During the initial series of transfers from First World to Second World the exiles noticed that the portals would appear to become unstable if too much was brought to Second World at any one time. The orbs would pulsate and often a rainstorm would form above them."

"Wait a minute. What do you mean the portals are not stable? What happens then?" asked Jason.

"Let me finish," she said.

"Father Sebastian and the elders apparently did not share their concern and banished them so they'd not frighten the rest of the emigres. The castaways sailed first to one of the barrier islands bordering the inland sea. They resettled here when that isle could not support them. They formed a truce with the forest dwellers, the trolls, and lived alongside them in peace for many years."

Margaret digressed from her recount of the outcasts' story for a moment. "To answer your question. I took an astronomy course as an elective in college. We learned the basics of black holes and there are theories that small ones can become unstable and eventually disappear in a cataclysmic event. If the portals are black holes that have been stable but can be destabilized, perhaps by overuse, then the doors between our two worlds are in jeopardy. Who knows what would happen to either or both our worlds. I don't think the outcasts realized the true danger, though. They didn't say anything more and just accepted their exile. But if my theory is even partially correct the Order of the Portal needs to be told. We all could be in danger."

"Oh, that doesn't sound good, we definitely need to tell somebody when we get to the capital," agreed Jason.

She finished the tale of the diary. "The last entries related the end of the humans of the village. Five members of the Order found them just a few years ago, not the time long past the elders of the raided village had said. Instead of greeting their fellow humans they proceeded to kill everyone they could find. For no reason the chronicler could discern. His last entries were that he would preserve the history of the village. His last recollection of the village before sealing himself in the room was that after the slaughter of the humans the forest folk, what we call forest trolls, had fought the invaders. He had no idea of the result."

Margaret finished by saying that she had told one of the soldiers, "We have to take these journals back to the Order. They need to know the danger."

"He told me that we don't have the time to gather and package the texts for transport. Their weight would just slow us down. We resealed the room and later expeditions will have to retrieve them."

Her tale worried Jason and alarmed the captain.

"Yes, I agree with your husband. You must tell your thoughts to the Master of the Order once we reach the capital," said Mendez.

A little further exploration of the village by both groups found nothing else of interest except that they discovered it had been built on a tributary of the great river. That explained why they found it sooner than expected, the town was closer to the edge of the forest than anticipated.

But now it was time to leave before the trolls might attack again. The captain ordered the patrol and the Blankenships to retreat to the woods and start back along the path they'd used on their way into the clearing. They didn't feel the need to run, but kept close watch for any attack from the trolls until they were past the burial sites and back on the trail cleared by the unfortunate villagers.

After a brief hike he called a halt for a much needed rest and regrouping. There was no sign or sound of pursuit. The undisturbed appearance of the trail indicated that the forest trolls did not venture this far from their homes.

They settled down for a very uncomfortable night. A guard was posted in shifts throughout the night and everyone else tried to get some sleep.

The next morning a bunch of stiff, sore, grumpy soldiers and the Blankenships got back on the trail to the copse where their mounts and wagon waited. Some of the men still had flint, and they all had their weapons, so finding and lighting fronds to smoke away the fairies was not a problem. At least something was going right.

Progress was good and they finally reached the edge of the forest and met the three guardsmen tending the animals. Despite the expedition's bedraggled appearance the first question was, "Did you find it? The city of gold? Is it like the fables say?"

Captain Mendez said, "Look at us. Do we look like we've been celebrating in golden halls with golden cups and plates?" He then gave a brief account of the events of the expedition, leaving the disappointing news about the false golden village to the last.

Needless to say, the three appeared disappointed at that news. But the look on their faces at the appearance of their comrades convinced Jason that they were glad they hadn't gone on the trek.

The captain made the decision to rest for the day and return to the village located by the sacbe tomorrow.

That afternoon the captain came over to Jason. "I think the forest trolls attacked the renegade members of the Order as they slaughtered the humans in the village. Only one of them made it out of the forest and his rantings before he died must have planted the idea of a city of gold deep in the forest. The elders used us to find the treasure. I bet that they planned to loot the site after we disposed of the forest trolls and before another patrol would arrive from the capital. I will discuss my impressions and opinions with them once we return there." His tone and the look on his face implied that the 'discussion' would be loud, long and one-sided.

Jason answered, "I believe you're correct, but other than some time in the near past I have absolutely no idea when that happened. The trolls are just a pack of semi-intelligent wolves. Except for one of them accidentally learning how to use a wand they didn't seem very sophisticated. I'm not sure they had a language much more advanced than normal wolves. You are probably correct about the fate of the original villagers and the five members. I guess the myth of El Dorado, at least for Second World, can be laid to rest."

"I agree. But we did recover the five lost wands. That at least is something. The Order will be happy to get them back. If we are right and the village elders did not stretch the truth too much the trolls must have taken over the false golden village a few years ago. We'll need to start patrols this way to keep those vermin in the woods and away from the farmlands."

"I agree with you. What next?"

"Tomorrow we head back to the village. I will have my talk with the elders. They will not be happy after that. Then we resume our belated journey to the capital. With your assistance in retrieving the lost wands, I cannot see the Order doing anything but getting you home as soon as possible as a reward."

"Margaret will be so happy to hear that. Let me tell her. Until tomorrow then." With that Jason went to her and gave her the news.

She was too exhausted to be very excited, but said, "I so want to believe our nightmare might actually come to an end. Let's pray it finally does." They both were sound asleep in minutes.

The next morning dawned clear and bright. It was as if nothing untoward had happened the previous day. Jason and Margaret hitched their horses and climbed onto the wagon. The captain and the ten guardsmen mounted and the group hurried to the village. They arrived around noon.

The captain was in a hurry to get back on the road. He realized how much time he'd wasted on the futile hunt for El Dorado and wanted to get back on schedule, or as close as he could. The captives were collected and secured together so none could run away without dragging the others along.

He ordered the village elders into the church, which doubled as the village meeting hall. Nobody outside the church could understand what was being said, but it was loud and only Mendez' voice could be heard. He exited a few moments later, made sure his crew were ready and ordered them onto the sacbe and toward the capital. Jason saw no sign of the elders leaving the church as they departed. He guessed they'd wait until the captain was well out of sight.

Once on the road Mendez sent one of the troop galloping ahead to tell the colonel and king what had transpired at Natts' Nohoch Muulo'ob and in the forest. The prisoners had to walk so the rest of the unit and the Blankenships had to take a much slower pace.

The messenger was scheduled to arrive at the palace the next day.

The others took three days to reach the capital. Then the truth of the plot to ruin the kingdom of Vlogentia would finally come to light.

CHAPTER TWENTY
FELIX' QUANDARY

The palace, capital city
Gregorian calendar: January 17
Mayan calendars: Tzolk'in: 12 Etz'nab'
            Haab: 11 Muwan

Felix paced furiously around his study. He was wearing his new coat with the overabundance of buttons, but it looked disheveled and dirty. He had been pacing for the past two days and had not bothered to clean up or even eat. The doors to the balcony were open to let badly needed fresh sea air into the room. His desk was cluttered with papers, all of which were covered with his attempts to write the speech to the Grand Council of Towns and Villages that would save his magnificent plan. The speech was not progressing well, not well at all.

Two days ago the messenger from Captain Mendez had arrived at the palace and was shown into Felix' presence. His news could not have been more disturbing. The one kulkulcan was dead, that was good, but according to the message the other kulkulcano'ob had made a treaty with the people of the town.

Without kulkulcano'ob to fight Felix could not call the realm to arms, there was not going to be a war. Even worse, that girl was still alive and apparently the cause of all this misery. He had asked the guardman, "Are you sure? Couldn't you be mistaken? Surely one girl couldn't kill a kulkulcan?"

"It is certainly so, your majesty. Surely this is good news. Now we won't have to fight the kulkulcano'ob." The relief in the soldier's voice was apparent.

"Yes, yes," Felix lied, "that is good news. Have you told this to anyone else?"

"Oh yes, sire, I told several city folk as I rode into the city, as well as the staff in the palace, and of course I reported to the Colonel of the Guard. Then I came straight here."

"Wonderful," said Felix. The man obviously didn't notice the sarcasm in his voice. "You may leave me now. Return to your barracks or duty station or guard post or whatever. Just leave."

The guardsman saluted, turned and strode out of the study.

Ever since that audience, Felix had not known what to do. He had been tormenting himself day and night on how to fix this mess. Damn that girl. Double damn her. Why didn't she die the way he'd planned? Now he'd have to figure another way to deal with her.

He then had to make another mental note to himself to tell the priest at confession that he had cursed. Just one more thing to add to his woes.

Just when Felix was about to give up his uncle Ronaldo, the Duke of Ki'pan, entered the room. As always, he didn't bother to knock. As always, Felix pretended to ignore the insult.

"What's bothering you so much?" asked Ronaldo. "You and this room look like a storm has blown through here. You should be preparing for your declaration of war to the Grand Conclave."

Felix realized that Ronaldo had obviously not yet heard the news since he'd been in the countryside tending to his estate.

He related the news the messenger had brought. Then he added, "I don't have any idea what to do next or what to announce to the Grand Conclave. This is a mess, a disaster. What should I do? Tell me what to do!" His voice was shrill and wavering. He threw his hands up in the air, then down by his side, and then up in the air once more. He wandered around the room aimlessly.

Ronaldo seemed almost as disturbed as Felix. He put his hands to the side of his head and shook it back and forth. He looked up and then down again and again. Finally he started to move and said, "Let me think for a moment."

He then started pacing around the room in time with Felix. The king thought the two of them must look like a couple of frightened chickens running around the barnyard in lockstep.

After a half hour or so Ronaldo stopped, slapped his forehead, and said, "Of course! Why are we so concerned? The solution is obvious. All we need to do is amend our list of enemies. Instead of fighting just the kulkulcano'ob we will tell the Conclave that some of our towns are in open rebellion and allied with the kulkulcano'ob. That will sound better to the members of the Conclave than just fighting kulkulcano'ob. Fighting other people sounds much easier. We still have the captive who can poison the kulkulcano'ob, don't we?"

"Yes, I believe the messenger said he is still with Captain Mendez and on his way with the captain back to the capital."

"Excellent. When he returns to the city we will confine him and his wife and force him to formulate a potion for the kulkulcano'ob. We can use his wife as incentive. With the kulkulcano'ob out of the way our, I mean your, new army will hone its abilities on a few border towns and then be ready for conquest. In truth this is actually better. The army will be better trained and prepared for war."

"Your idea is excellent, as always."

"Yes, if I say so myself," said Ronaldo. "You are an eager and good student of true regal thought. But often your ideas and plans are not fully fleshed out. I still have so much to teach you. About the only good idea you've had recently was getting rid of the girl and I felt obliged to clean up the loose ends. But you are learning, and learning well. I have high expectations for you."

"Thank you," said Felix. He was not at all sure he'd just been given a compliment.

"*Oh well, he's my uncle. That's just how he is,*" he thought.

Ronaldo strode to the desk piled high with the stack of unfinished oration. He had lost the uncertainty of moments before.

"Clean that mess off your desk. I will help you write the speech."

With that they pulled chairs up to the desk, swept off the useless attempts at a speech and went to work. There wasn't a lot of time to waste.

CHAPTER TWENTY ONE
REUNIONS

The dockyard, capital city
Gregorian calendar: January 21
Mayan calendars: Tzolk'in: 3 'Ik
           Haab: 15 Muwan

The sloop arrived at the capital's port in early morning. Bianca was standing at the rail looking at the warehouses and the palace off to her right. The city was the same as it had been three weeks previously, but it looked different to her. Somehow everything looked more sinister. The westerly breeze was the same, but if felt colder and less welcoming. The smell of the docks was the same, but seemed fouler to her. Everything felt different, and not in a good way.

It took a while to offload the unicorns and saddle them.

Then it was time to pull Xavier out of his room. He was now completely broken, he had no resistance or will left in him. He didn't even wait for the ship's captain to start offloading him. The entire plot spilled out of him to everyone in hearing distance like water from an overfilled pitcher.

Lieutenant Gonzalez, Juan and the four guardsmen stood stock still in apparent shock.

"I am appalled," said the lieutenant, "that our king would be involved in such a deceitful plan. Such treachery has never entered my mind. I don't know how to react to this awful news."

Bianca suggested, "Lieutenant, you and you men need to take Xavier directly to the prison and locked in solitary confinement. For now, do not talk to anyone or let him talk to anyone. We don't know who else may be in on the intrigue. Keep him securely away from anyone else but you four. Once I and Juan meet with Captain Mendez, his men and the Blankenships we may devise a plan of our own. Perhaps Jason or Margaret will know of some First World strategy that has been used that will solve our dilemma."

"What about you?" asked Gonzalez. "What are you going to do?"

"Juan and I need to find someone to tend my cubs for a while."

"Then I want to visit and talk to Daniela. I want to know why she participated in my abduction and what they promised or threatened. I want her to know that I'm alright. I pray that I will be able to tell her I hold no grudge against her."

"Finally I need to find the headquarters of the Order of the Portal and tell them of Xander's death, his involvement in the plot and that I have some limited use of his wand. I assume they will need to debate among themselves what to do about me. Nothing bad I hope."

"After that we will meet you at the campsite."

"I see," he said, "but I'm afraid I can't let the corporal accompany you. He needs to come with me to file his report with the rest of us. Any deviation from our usual procedure might look suspicious to the wrong eyes. You could come with us to the prison and then go about your tasks."

"But," she sputtered, "can't you make an exception in this instance? I need to get it all finished today. I don't have time for a detour."

"No, as I said his absence from our patrol might look suspicious to someone in touch with the palace."

"It's alright, dear," added Juan, "I'll help take Xavier to the prison, fill out my report and then pretend to go on leave. I'll meet you at the agreed site. Just be careful and wear a cloak. No one in the city knows we're here, so you'll be safe."

"If you think that's best," said Bianca, "then alright. Please hurry."

She gave him a big hug for several seconds then let him go.

He gave her a quick kiss and left with the lieutenant.

They went back to the ship and collected the other guardsmen and Xavier and headed off to the prison.

The *Unlucky Lady* cast off and headed back to Puerto Norte with a promise that a larger vessel would soon be sent to transport the pirates to prison in the capital. The harbor master arranged for another ship to be sent to the pirates' lair to retrieve the treasure.

Bianca watched the ship and Juan and his comrades with Xavier leave. She picked up her two cubs, one under each arm, and headed for a livery stable she knew. She had to walk since her unicorn had been sent with the others because a rider other than a guardsman wandering through the town on a unicorn would raise too much attention. In order to minimize her unique appearance she grabbed a cloak from the ship's locker before it departed and threw it over her back and head. She was even able to hide the cubs under the sides of the cloak. She carried Xander's rapier strapped to her back.

The livery stable was on the far side of the warehouse district and away from the port. It was right at the edge of the city so horses and livestock could have some paddocks to roam around in. It was still morning and the offloading of ships' cargos in the port had yet to begin so Bianca made good time past the nearly empty warehouses and arrived at the stables around mid-morning. She knew the proprietor from when she been allowed to take riding lessons before her real mother died.

Standing at the main door to the barn she called out, "Pedro Marroquin, where are you? It's Bianca. I have an unusual request for you."

Pedro came out of one of the stalls and threw his arms open for a great bear hug. He was a big man with strong arms and just a little paunch. "Bianca, may the moons grant you a blessed blend of days. I haven't seen you for several years. How have you been? How are you doing now, with both parents gone?"

"A good blend of days to you, as well. I'm alright, but the last few days have been a struggle." She briefly reported her adventures of the last twenty days, and ended with, "I want to ask you if you can care for a couple of youngsters for me for a few days. They're not your usual guests, and will require special accommodations." Opening the sides of her cloak brought two sets of inquisitive feline eyes.

Pedro jumped back. "You weren't kidding when you said they were unusual. Just like you. But I think my wife can prepare one of our spare stalls for them. Of course, they won't be able to go outside, but the stall should be large enough for them. That is, until they start to grow. Are they weaned?"

"Yes, they've been eating scraps of meat from our meals, and drinking water. They obviously don't know how to hunt yet, so your small animals around here should be safe if they get out. Actually, they're very playful and your wife ought to play with them every day. I think Marta will come to like them. They're just big kittens."

"Very big kittens. What are you going to do with them? They won't stay small for very long."

"Once they're big enough to fend for themselves its back to the grasslands for them. I can't imagine they'll make nice pets after they learn to hunt for themselves." Just how they would learn to hunt hadn't occurred to her yet. "I will be back in a few days to see how things are going, and settle up with you. I need to be off on another errand now. Please give my apologies to your wife for not greeting her today. I hope to have more time to visit next time."

Until then, be well," said Pedro.

Next on her list was the one she dreaded the most. She had no idea how that meeting would go, but it had to be done. Daniela's home was about halfway across the city, and she was still covering her face and hair with the cloak. Knowledge of the king's scheme was making her suspicious of everyone. It took more than an hour to reach Daniela's abode. It was a typical worker's home with a thatched roof and red, yellow and blue stucco exterior walls.

When she got there the house looked unkempt. That struck her as odd since Daniela's parents were particular about the appearance and cleanliness of their home. It wasn't in a state of disrepair, it just looked dingy like it hadn't been cleaned for a few days. A few weeds were growing in the flower boxes.

Curious, Bianca knocked on the door. No answer. She knocked again, and again. She called out. Still no answer. While she was standing there in a bewildered state one of the neighbors came over to her.

"Who are you and why are you knocking at this door?"

Seeing no alternative, Bianca pulled back her hood and asked. "Where are they? They should be home."

"Oh, it's you, Bianca. I hope your blended days are blessed. We haven't seen you or Daniela's family for almost twenty days. Where have you been?"

"And blessed days to you. You say you haven't seen any of them recently?" She deliberately did not answer the question.

"No, not since the New Year's Festival night. Daniela got home late that night, and was sobbing. I could hear her even through my door. Then later that night three men came to the door and entered. I don't remember hearing anything else. But the next morning the house was empty. I checked. The door is unlocked, you can look for yourself. I called for the city guard but they said they had orders from the Duke of Ki'pan not to investigate.

This sounded bad, very bad. Bianca thanked the neighbor and gently opened the door. The main room was a mess. Two chairs were on their sides, the table was upside down and a few dishes were lying on the floor. The beds were messed. Everything was dusty, as if it hadn't been cleaned for the twenty days she'd been gone. The closet was ransacked and some blankets were obviously missing. A cold shiver ran down Bianca's back, she feared Daniela and her parents had been abducted as she had been. But their fate seemed much more ominous. This was how the Duke paid the people who did his bidding.

A cold, furious rage started to well up inside her. Gone was the carefree girl who loved playing pitz and meeting her friends at Joaquin's. That girl had been gone from the day she faced Ill'yx. But now she felt the need for revenge. She wasn't sure she liked her new self. She started to cry.

Bianca walked out of the home, still sobbing.

The neighbor asked, "Is everything alright?" Her face said that she knew full well it was not but was hoping for a better answer.

"No, it's not. Just shut the door. Leave everything as it is. I will get someone to come and clean in a few days."

The neighbor went back home talking out loud to herself, "I'm locking my door at night from now on. What is happening to the city?"

Bianca wandered around the streets for a while then came back to her senses. She could do nothing for Daniela now, she had other things to do.

Revenge could wait, but it would happen.

The headquarters of the Order of the Portal was in the city center near the administrative offices. Bianca debated with herself if going there would be a good idea. She finally decided that it would be safe enough if she used one of the gaps in the ceremonial wall nearest the offices and kept the hood over her head. Off she went, with a more determined stride than usual for her.

Upon arriving at the headquarters she knocked on the ornate door. It was a double door at least ten feet tall and seven feet wide set in an archway. The building was classic Spanish colonial with second floor balconies, iron grates over the first floor windows and a bright stucco exterior with a tile roof. Bianca wondered why it had grates over the windows, since no other structures in the capital had such features. Probably to protect their secrets, she guessed. The door opened and a member of the Order greeted her.

"Who are you and why do you come seeking counsel from the Order?"

Bianca threw back her hood.

"I am Bianca and I have news of two of your order and seek advice on matters directly pertaining to the use of these." She took two wands from her sash, the one she had taken from Xander and the other she had confiscated from Xavier.

The member stepped back, surprised. This was not an ordinary visit. He led Bianca into the building, up a flight of stairs that faced the entry, and into an ornate office in the middle of the second floor.

"Grand Master, I have a very unusual supplicant for you to meet. She must have a most interesting tale to relate, please grant her an audience."

Bianca stepped into the room which was about twenty feet deep and thirty feet wide. It had filled bookshelves on opposite walls, and a double door leading to a balcony overlooking the ocean behind it. In the center of the room was a large desk with two chairs for visitors. Sitting behind the desk, with his back to the double doors, was an elderly man with grey hair and a beard wearing the usual garb of the Order.

"Enter and be seated, please. Tell me your tale," said the Grand Master.

Bianca sat and told him everything that had happened to her since her kidnapping. She told him about the Blankeships and why they had been abducted from First World, she related how she killed the kulkulcan, how she found Xander's wand, how she learned from Senora Sacniete what the wand was and how she could make it produce a small light, how she helped capture Xavier and everything else. It took quite a while.

When she was done the Grand Master got up and walked around the desk and asked her to give him the wands. He examined them carefully, then asked her to stand and try to produce the light she'd described.

Bianca took Xander's wand and did as Sacniete had instructed. A pale, small globe of yellowish light glowed at the end of the wand. He then switched wands with her and told her to try the same thing with Xavier's. Nothing. No light, no effect at all.

"Only certain people have the ability to use a wand to travel between worlds and to produce the effects you describe," said the Grand Master. "But it takes much practice to be accurate and adept at their use. Once trained an acolyte will usually work with just the one wand that seems best attuned to them. But they can use other wands as well, just not as efficiently. I suspect you have always had the innate ability to be a member of the Order, but you will need much training and work. If you would be interested that could be arranged."

"Perhaps I could be persuaded," she said. "Is there anything I need to tell you?"

"Oh, yes, I have a serious problem. We need to learn everything we can about those two brothers and how they came to violate the most sacred principles of the Order. Tell me everything you know, or think you know, about their activities and their thoughts. We need to weed out such miscreants from our ranks. To do that I need to know why they would want to do such things."

Bianca told him everything she could think of about both of them. How and what they said, how they acted and how they treated others.

The Grand Master asked many questions. Some she could answer, some she could not.

Finally, he was finished.

It was her turn. "What will you do with Xavier?" she asked.

He said, "For now, he should be put in the jail. That will serve him right. We will inspect him later. You should go to your meeting place with your comrades and let them know what I have said. The captain has his own worries. Something will have to be done about the king and his plan. You and I will meet later to discuss any future you might have. But I need to keep those wands."

She handed them over, curious whether she'd ever handle one again, or even want to. She thanked the Grand Master for his time and advice.

The member of the Order she had encountered at the front door was waiting for her outside the office and escorted her to the street. "Be careful and go quickly. God be with you."

She donned her hood and scooted along the streets toward the rendezvous spot. Along the way she unexpectedly and fortuitously ran into Lieutenant Gonzalez and Juan on their way to the rendezvous from the prison.

"I'm so glad to see you," she said as she hugged Juan, "I really wanted you with me."

He hugged her back. "I knew you'd be alright. How did you errands fare?"

"I fear Daniela is dead, by the order of the Duke. He will have to pay for that. My other meetings went well, I'll tell you about them later. What about you?"

"After we took Xavier to the prison I left the other three guardsmen as his security," said the lieutenant. "I don't think they are needed at the meeting place, and I'm was pretty sure I can count on them spreading word of the plot to anyone within listening distance. That, of course, is exactly what we desire. Let's go, we have much to relate to Captain Mendez."

When they arrived at the agreed site they found the wagon with Jason, Margaret and Captain Mendez waiting for them.

"We've been here for two days," said the captain, "and were beginning to get worried. We're so glad so see you. Did you capture Xavier? Is everyone alright? What happened that took you so long?"

"Yes, we got him," said the lieutenant. "But we have a tale to tell you."

"And I bet we have a greater tale to tell you."

Everyone was relieved that they were back together and safe. After warm greetings all around the captain related their adventures, giving full credit for Jason's part in the capture of the bandits and the fight with the woods trolls and the discovery of 'El Dorado'.

Lieutenant Gonzalez took his turn and told the tale of Xavier's capture and his confession about the plot.

Captain Mendez sat down with a thump, a look of shock and surprise on his face. "Never in my worst dreams could I conceive that the king would do such a thing."

Bianca then took her opportunity to tell the captain, Jason and Margaret about the cubs, her fears about her friend and what the Grand Master of the Order had told her.

Margaret had nothing to add, but simply hugged Bianca and said, "I'm so sorry about your friend."

Juan was intrigued. "What will you do if they want to induct you into the Order?"

"It's still to be determined that I would even be considered," she replied. "We have many other much more immediate problems to worry about. Just forget about that for now." She hoped her tone made it obvious the matter was closed.

She addressed the captain, "If your messenger reached the king, then he must be beside himself. He knows his plan has failed. He most likely does not know that we are aware of the plot. Let's stay here for the night, then decide in the morning what we need to do. I am thinking we should try to get an audience with his holiness the Vice Pope."

The captain sat in consternation. "I still have trouble believing the king would do such a thing. I don't know how to respond to this news." But after a moment of thought he agreed to her idea.

The next morning Bianca stood outside the wagon looking at the overcast morning sky and getting wet. It had started to rain overnight, which was unusual.

December, January and February were the hot, dry months of Vlogentia's year. But the storms blowing in from the sea, some said from the portal isle, had been a frequent fixture for the past few months. The unusual weather made Bianca wonder if that was an ill omen for the remainder of the day.

CHAPTER TWENTY TWO

RAINY DAY

Adjacent the Sacbe, just outside the capital, kingdom of Vlogentia
Gregorian calendar: January 22
Mayan calendars: Tzolk'in: 4 Ak'b'al
Haab: 16 Muwan

The rain made Bianca think about Margaret's story of the false town of gold and the outcasts' worry about the portals. Margaret had said that the exiles felt that overuse of the portals caused a rainstorm above them. Is it possible that the recent weather in Volgentia was related to the portals somehow? She remembered the strange voices of the fairies. The thoughts concerned her, but she had greater worries this morning. She didn't know what Felix was up to. He was the immediate danger. She shook herself off and went back into the wagon.

The rain had started around midnight so the six of them had crowded into the wagon for shelter. There was more room than previously since Jason had used quite a lot of the supplies. It was cramped quarters nonetheless.

The rain picked up in intensity. By midmorning it was a downpour. While the rest waited in the wagon, wondering if it was worth venturing out, Juan went into town to see what was happening.

He came back about an hour later with disturbing news. "The day after New Year's the king called for a Grand Conclave of the Towns and Villages. It is scheduled for tomorrow, the Tzolk'in date of the founding of Vlogentia. In celebration of the creation of our kingdom he was going to make some grand announcement that the Conclave was supposed to approve. The king is obviously counting on the fact that the Conclaves have always approved a royal proclamation. Some of the other guardsmen I met said that the rumor was that he was going to declare a war on the kulkulcano'ob."

"We know that's not going to happen," said Bianca. "What is he going to say or do? What possible way could he use the situation to further his goals?"

"I don't know. But the Conclave has not been cancelled and is still scheduled for tomorrow. In fact, they are now setting up pavilions in the Grand Plaza for the assembled delegates from all the towns in Vlogentia. They will meet this afternoon in the Plaza for a celebratory feast before the assembly tomorrow. Perhaps we could learn more then."

"This news is curious to say the least," said Bianca. "According to Captain Mendez his messenger should have been apprised the king of the failure of his plot several days ago. That gave him plenty of time to cancel the Conclave. So what could he be planning?"

Jason had an idea. "Let's split up and do more scouting through the town to see if we can find anyone that might know anything useful. Captain Mendez, Juan and Rodrigo should concentrate on the royal guard. They know you and be more willing to tell you what they know. Tell them you need the information so you'll be able to perform your duties. Margaret, Bianca and I will wear cloaks to blend in with the crowd and concentrate on the workers erecting the pavilions. They may have heard something. Bianca can move around freely as long as she stays cloaked. Margaret and I shouldn't talk since our translators will give us away, but we can listen just fine. Let's meet back here in a couple of hours."

"That's a good plan," said Juan, "but I need to go with Bianca."

"No, you don't." said Captain Mendez, "if she's wearing a cloak on a rainy day such as this she will blend in with the crowd much better than if she has a guardsman by her side. Besides, you are part of my command and would be expected to accompany me. You're coming with me. We'll all be back together here soon enough."

"Very well, sir." Juan's voice sounded less than enthusiastic.

Bianca said, "I think he's right, Juan. I'll be fine and see you in a while."

She squeezed his hand in sympathy and patted him on the shoulder.

Before leaving Juan arranged for a local farmer to watch the wagon and the horses. He, Lieutenant Gonzalez, and Captain Mendez then mounted their unicorns and headed for the barracks inside the city center.

Bianca had the farmer obtain cloaks for Jason and Margaret and a dagger for each of them. She still wore the rapier over her back, but her cloak prevented easy access and a dagger offered quicker and subtler defense.

"What are these for?" asked Margaret carefully turning the knife over in her hands. She was careful to not touch the blade.

"You may need protection," is all that Bianca would say.

Jason added, "They're just a precaution. If we stay quiet and keep our heads down we won't need them."

He then turned to Bianca, "Which way do we go, and what are we looking for?"

"That way," she pointed toward the city center, "you'll see a low wall with multiple gaps in it demarcating the ceremonial center of the city. The palace will be beyond the wall toward the seafront and the area for the pavilion will be in front of the palace and between it and the wall. There will be other official buildings, but don't mind them. Just wander around looking at the sights and try to hear something useful. Don't worry, you will be fine. Everyone will think you're out-of-town visitors."

"Then that's where almost everybody in town is gathering," Jason said as he clambered out of the wagon. "Our best chance for information is there. We'll try to listen to the workers setting up the venue."

Seeming somewhat reassured Margaret left the wagon with Jason and headed for the city ceremonial center.

Bianca had no trouble reaching the Plaza. She knew the city, after all. The appearance of the city was far less impressive to her than she remembered. It looked drab and much less colorful than the twenty or so days ago when she was last there. Perhaps it was the rain, or the downcast mood of the people or her frame of mind.

She heard a lot of rumor, and all of it sounded as if the king was going to demand his war after all. How they knew that wasn't clear. Most likely it spread from the palace staff to the workers in the Plaza to the general population. After a while she had heard as much as she wanted and headed back to the wagon.

Jason and Margaret returned to the wagon only a minute or so after Bianca.

He reported, "It took us quite a while to find our path through the crowded streets to where the pavilions are being set up. Along the way we tried to stay inconspicuous but listened as best we could. The translators jumbled a lot of the conversations of the crowds, as they always do. But now and then we could make out something intelligible. But we never heard a hint of a rumor of an imminent war. We really couldn't make out anything useful other than a general impression that the populace is unhappy. I'm sorry."

"That's alright," said Bianca. I felt the same impression. I heard nothing specific, but the tone was that there was going to be a war."

Margaret added, "Your city is amazing. All the shops and houses are so colorful, despite the downpour. Once we reached city center I was amazed. There is a magnificent cathedral to the left beyond the ceremonial wall, the Grand Plaza is front and center, and there's a curious structure to the right that looked like some sort of open air arena. The Palace was behind the Plaza as you described. The pavilions are now almost fully erected and tables underneath the canopies are being set up for what look like several hundred delegates. We mingled for as long as we could, picking up what rumor we could. It wasn't much and as Jason said and it didn't seem useful. After a while we gave up and headed back to the wagon. What a wonderful city you have."

"Thank you," responded Bianca, "it's my home and I like it."

A few moments later Rodrigo, Juan and the captain rode up to the wagon. It was their turn to relate what they learned.

Captain Mendez reported, "We arrived at the barracks in good time. Naturally we were wearing our cloaks and were soaked and a mess. The sergeant on duty didn't recognize us, he must have thought we were returning from an extended patrol. He ordered two grooms to tend our unicorns and then ordered us to get cleaned up and into new uniforms. He had no idea he was bossing around superior officers. We followed the 'orders' and changed into fresh enlisted men's uniforms so we could spy a little less conspicuously."

Lieutenant Gonzalez took up the account, "Of course we heard a great deal of rumor from the other men not yet on duty. Some of the men had heard the king practicing his speech while they were on guard duty. If they were right our worst fears were realized. His majesty is going to declare a state of rebellion by the border towns which have formed an alliance with the kulkulcano'ob. Apparently the war is on after all."

Juan finished the story, "That's all we needed to hear. We snatched some cloaks, snuck out of the barracks, took some horses so as to be less obvious and headed back to the wagon."

Next came the debate on what to do. Ideas filled the air like flies at an outdoor fiesta. Bianca finally said, "I don't see we have any choice. We must get to the Conclave and tell the attendees what we know. We will talk to them individually if necessary. I only hope we can convince enough of them. From what we have learned the general gist of his speech is common knowledge, and the general public are not happy. If we can persuade enough delegates, the Conclave may not approve the king's declaration. That would be a first, I know, but it is the only chance we have."

No one had a better idea. Not that she realized that it was a good one, but it was better than anything else they came up with. As she had noted, the Conclave had never in known history overruled a reigning monarch when he or she had asked for approval. The consent had always been just a formality. Her hope was that this time would be different.

They donned their cloaks and set out for the Grand Plaza.

Rain was still pouring when they reached the Plaza. It was now late afternoon and the attendees were gathered for the welcoming feast. To everyone's surprise King Felix made an appearance, parading from the palace entrance toward the pavilion.

Standing at guard between the pavilions for the feast and the palace was the mercenary company hired by Duke Ronaldo. They were his private army and Bianca had seen them prove useful in intimidating several merchant gatherings in the recent past. The duke never used the royal guard for his efforts, he clearly trusted his hired band more. So far the company had never resorted to force, their presence was enough to persuade people to do what the duke wanted. But she knew their presence in Vlogentia was greatly resented.

Felix exited the main doors of the palace, followed by his seneschal, and strode down the steps toward the pavilion now filled with delegates. He was wearing his newly cleaned dress coat and carrying the ceremonial Sword of the Realm. He paraded through the pavilions, stopped in front of the canopies and turned to face the delegates, temporarily standing in the rain so both the attendees and the general populace could see him.

Seeing him posturing there so proud of himself was too much. Bianca remembered having to face Ill'yx because of him. She recalled the plot to slaughter villagers to further his ambitions. She simply could not contain herself any longer. Her rage at his callous and self-serving plot and the fate of Daniela boiled inside her like a furnace out of control.

She ran from where she and her friends were standing, about twenty yards from the king and behind the ceremonial wall, throwing her hood back so she could see where she was going. The rain drenched her hair and thoroughly soaked her partially open cloak. Her shoes quickly became waterlogged, so she shed them and proceeded barefoot. Her sudden appearance took all present by surprise, nobody even tried to intercept or stop her.

She raced right up to the king's face and stopped just inches from him, her feet splashing in the puddles and her hair tied atop her head matted and soaked throughout.

Felix appeared astounded. His mouth gaped wide and his eyes were as open and he could make them, his pupils were fully dilated. He was speechless. Although he worked his jaw, no words came out.

She placed her right foot between his legs and behind his left foot so he could not step back, or anywhere for that matter. She then grabbed him by the collar with her right fist and held his right sword arm, which he had raised over his head in a defensive posture, with her left arm straightened so he could not wield the sword. He was immobilized and overwhelmed.

She spoke, with a rage loud enough for everyone within the pavilions to hear even through the roar of the downpour.

"You incredible fraud. You pretense of a monarch. You think yourself a great ruler. You want your subjects to call you 'sire'. Do you know what 'sire' means? It means that you are the father and protector of the realm and its people. That is your true responsibility. It means that you guide and lead by example. It means you nurture and encourage the populace. It does not mean that you may decide to destroy a village or have subjects slain to serve your vanity or your search for glory. It does not mean that you have a mandate from God to do anything you want. You have been granted rule by God and his holy church to protect and govern justly. Fail that and you lose your mandate."

She could hear the crowd and the delegates utter a huge gasp of astonishment.

"You imagine that you will become a great leader of armies and march to fame and magnificence. You will not. You will destroy this realm and slaughter its people. You will not become known as Felix the Great, Felix the Conqueror, or Felix the Magnificent. Your ambition is folly. You will instead be known to history as Felix the Foolish, or Felix the Inept, or Felix the Incompetent."

Now the multitude laughed aloud.

"Look around at your subjects. You won't see any honor for you here. You won't see any admiration for you here. You won't see any praise for you here. Look closely at their faces. You see no respect for you here. You see no esteem for you here. You see no welcome for you here. You are not even wanted here. Leave this spot. Go back to the palace to think about what it takes to be a true monarch. Go!"

Bianca freed her right leg and backed up slightly and let go of his collar.

Felix shook loose and dropped the Sword of the Realm. He looked at the assembled crowd and must have seen that Bianca was correct. Their faces showed contempt. He said nothing. He stood for a few seconds and then turned and fled back into the palace.

Everyone stood frozen. Now, there wasn't a movement or a sound anywhere except for the patter of the raindrops on the pavement.

Bianca noticed the ceremonial Sword of the Realm lying on the wet ground.

"Seneschal, this sword is the symbol of the heart and honor of the people of this realm. It is the physical symbol of the soul of our land. It cannot be allowed to lie in the ground like a piece of trash. Pick it up and take it to the king and remind him of what it means."

"But only the monarch can touch the sword. No one else may handle it. It is the symbol of royal authority," said the hapless official.

Bianca though for a few seconds, then strode forward and snatched a dagger from the seneschal's sash and used it to cut a swath of fabric from her skirt. It was about four inches wide and three feet long. She bent over and carefully placed one end of the fabric over the hilt of the sword and carefully picked it up without actually touching the hilt. She then wrapped the rest of the length around the hilt and part of the blade, picked the sword up by the wrapped hilt and held it in front of the seneschal.

He didn't move.

She stepped forward and practically shoved the hilt into the man's face so that he had to put up his hands to protect himself and wound up grasping the wrapping holding the sword. She said nothing but gestured with a hand toward the palace.

He took the hint and ran after the king holding the sword in front of him.

Rain was still pouring down and Bianca was thoroughly soaked. The Conclave members were dry under their canopies, but standing in shocked silence. So were the populace beyond the ceremonial wall as were the mercenary company and Duke Ronaldo.

Bianca didn't move for several seconds before realizing what she had just done. She feared she had only made things worse by embarrassing the king. She turned and made for the sanctity of the cathedral. Her companions followed her. A general clamor started to flow through the assembled throng. Nothing like this had ever been seen before.

On the way to the cathedral she heard Margaret remark, "I think Bianca just sent the king to his room without supper."

Jason nodded and said, "And I wonder what will come of it. This isn't exactly what we had planned."

As Jason and Margaret were ending their conversation Juan confronted Bianca.

"What were you thinking? You did it again. Did you pay no attention to what I said after you chased after the three pirates? You could have been killed just now. What if he'd tried to use the ceremonial sword? What has happened to the girl I've known forever who shied away from the public except for pitz? I am terrified of what might now happen to you and furious at you for your recklessness. I couldn't live with myself if anything happens to you. Please be more careful."

"I couldn't let Felix get away with his plan. Anger at him and my rage for what he tried to have done to me and the kingdom consumed me. I've seen and experienced too much since those days. I'm not the girl you once knew. "

She looked at Juan defiantly and then strode toward the cathedral.

The five of them followed Bianca into the cathedral stunned at what she had just done. What would happen next was anybody's guess.

CHAPTER TWENTY THREE
THE DUEL

The Grand Plaza, capital city, kingdom of Vlogentia
Gregorian calendar: January 22
Mayan calendars: Tzolk'in: 4 Ak'b'al
            Haab: 16 Muwan

Bianca and her friends gathered in the narthex just inside the large double door of the National Cathedral. The took off their cloaks and hung them on wall pegs meant for that purpose and then entered the nave to sit on the pews in the back, away from the sanctuary. They began to discuss what to do next. Bianca was determined to find a way to prevent her rashness in embarrassing the king from causing even greater problems.

She said, "We need to go back to the delegates while they are still in the pavilions and convince them the king is everything I said he is. If they disperse now and do not congregate again until tomorrow they may dismiss or forget the substance of what I said and heed his diatribe. I will have accomplished nothing."

Captain Mendez disagreed. "No, we need to rally the royal guard and neutralize the mercenaries. Then we can deal with the king and the duke." Lieutenant Gonzalez agreed. So did Juan.

Jason said, "Margaret and I have no opinion about the politics of Vlogentia and have nothing useful to add. We don't know who the powerful people are or how to motivate them. All I can say is that it would be best to avoid a pitched battle. How to accomplish that is beyond me."

Captain Mendez offered a provisional notion. "Let Lieutenant Gonzalez, Corporal Gomez and myself go out and scout around the plaza. We need to know if the delegates are dispersing to their quarters or not. We need to know the mood of the populace. I also would like to know what the mercenaries are doing. We cannot make plans without adequate information."

"A good idea, captain," said Bianca. "Jason, Margaret and I will wait here until you return."

Juan gave Bianca a quick squeeze of the hand as the three soldiers donned their cloaks again and went out into the rapidly slacking rain.

"I'll be back soon, wait here and be safe," he said.

The three friends sat in a pew and debated the merits of Bianca's and the captain's ideas and waited for the soldiers' return.

In the midst of the discussion Ronaldo threw open and stormed through the doors into the narthex, brandishing his rapier.

"I have finally had enough of you," he bellowed at Bianca. "I will put an end to your insolence and show the rabble outside what happens when anyone questions the will of a king."

Bianca rose from her seat and stood in the aisle, feet apart, arms on her hips.

"Not even when the will of a king is foolishness? That is when his councilors should question him and give him guidance. Instead I think you have encouraged this idiocy. That means you are as much at fault as he is."

"Disarm yourself," she added, "you cannot use a sword inside a church. That is sacrilege." She had forgotten she still wore her sword across her back, it had been there for so long.

"I will use my sword when and where I will. I am the Duke of Ki'pan and no one can question me or my decisions." He advanced toward Bianca with obvious intent.

She finally remembered her rapier and drew it.

"You little fool, I am the greatest swordsman in Vlogentia," he boasted. "I have defeated twenty three opponents without as much as a scratch. I am the number one sword in the realm. This will be a pleasure."

The sun had started to shine through the parting rainclouds as it set in the west. The downpour had slackened to almost nothing. The sun's rays shown through the eight large stained glass windows on either side of the nave with their biblical scenes and images of Saint Sebastian and the founding of Vlogentia and poured through the open doors facing west, illuminating the two oppo-nents with a kaleidoscope of warm colors. It looked like a scene from a dream, a deadly dream.

Ronaldo assumed his dueling stance. "Prepare to witness the best sword in the realm."

Bianca held her sword pointed at him, level with her eyes, wrist up in fight-ing position and assumed her stance. "Prove it."

Both had rapiers. Swords with long narrow blades usually with an elaborate hand guard. Ronaldo's rapier was the usual forty one inches long and one inch wide made of tempered steel and sharpened along both sides of the blade all the way to the hand guard. Bianca's rapier had been taken from Xander and was not meant for someone skilled in dueling. It was slightly shorter, at thirty seven inches, also one inch wide and made of tempered steel but sharpened only half-way down the sides. She had no elaborate hand guard, just a simple hilt.

Bianca knew that Ronaldo had been trained in the gentlemanly art of duel-ing with the rapier, called destreza. She had been trained, in the years before her mother had died, in the ungentlemanly art of making sure her opponent couldn't continue.

He started by trying to thrust past her rapier. She slapped his blade to her right as she danced to her left, spun past him and cut a slash in his right cheek as she went by. They changed places. He thrust again. This time she started a dodge to her left and reversed direction and darted to her right and past him. He missed completely and she put a cut in his left cheek as she went by.

They switched places again. He tried to feint. She intercepted him in mid-movement and caught his blade with the flat of hers. As his sword rebounded she closed inside his thrusting distance and shoved him in the chest with her left hand. He staggered slightly and threw up his left hand for balance which gave her the chance to slash a deep gash in his left palm as she once again rushed past him to her right.

He turned to his left to face her, she countered by dancing again to her right and circled him yet again.

Ronaldo's face began to show frustration and concern. He tried a full thrust, blade fully extended and pushing off with his left foot. She skipped to her left and pivoted to her left so his blade missed, passing harmlessly past her back.

This time she countered his thrust with one of hers as he started to recover his position, her blade plunging deep and through his right shoulder, severing both nerves and tendons. As Ronaldo fell back, now completely unable to use his right arm, she made one final thrust to his right knee, crippling him.

It was all over in far less than thirty heartbeats.

Bianca stood looking down at a bleeding wreck of a man. Ronaldo was lying in the aisle of the nave moaning in agony, his blood seeping from multiple wounds.

She said, "Actually, sir, you are now number zero."

She gave the formal salute to an opponent, sword pointed out, then up to the face, and down to the right with a slight bow. The need for revenge was gone, it left when she saw what she had done.

She turned to Jason, who had been standing in the narthex with Margaret. The entire event had taken place so quickly and so unexpectedly that neither of them had even tried to react.

"Please, sir, this man urgently needs your expertise."

"But he tried to kill you." Said Margaret.

"Yes, but he is no longer my enemy. Please help him."

Jason went to bind the wounds and stench the bleeding. Using strips of cloth from the fancy coat Ronaldo was wearing, he managed to stop the loss of blood. There was nothing he could do for the right arm or right knee. The left palm would heal, but with a significant scar.

Bianca felt relief that Ronaldo would no longer torment the young men of Vlogentia.

Margaret, awestruck, approached Bianca, "You carved him up like a Thanksgiving turkey. Where did you learn to do that?"

"I started to learn how to defend myself with a blade when my mother was alive. She was acquainted with some true swordsmen and persuaded them to teach me. As it is, the rapier is not my best weapon, but I'm competent with it. By the way, what is a Thanksgiving turkey?"

'I'll tell you later." Margaret, still stunned, went over to help Jason.

Bianca sank slowly onto one of the pews. She had wanted revenge for Daniela, and she had achieved it. For that she was glad. But the sight of the moaning Ronaldo, former Duke of Ki'pan, lying there in his own blood, disturbed her.

A commotion at the main door caused Bianca to look up. She was thrilled to see Juan and the two officers enter the cathedral. They saw Ronaldo being tended by Jason and Margaret, obviously deduced what had transpired and rushed over to commend her.

"I've always known," Juan marveled, "since our childhood, that like many of the children in the capital you'd had some instruction in swordplay but I had no idea that you are that capable."

While Jason and Margaret tended Ronaldo and the soldiers were congratulating Bianca, Father Radames come over to her.

"You know fighting in the church is forbidden. It was obvious that you were only defending yourself, but still forbidden. You will have to serve some penance, although not as severe as it could be."

"I know, Father. I will do whatever is required of me."

One of the soldiers, she thought it was the lieutenant, finally said something pertinent. "What about those mercenaries standing outside? They're waiting for the Duke to reappear and tell them what to do. Does anybody have an idea about that?"

Except for the moans of Ronaldo, the church fell silent. Even Father Radames, who almost always had something to say, was mute.

After a few moments of contemplation Bianca stood up, walked to the door, and looked out at the mercenaries. They were still standing at attention where the Duke had left them, facing them was a crowd of city folk. All of them seemed to be waiting for Ronaldo to reappear.

She turned to Jason and asked him, "Can you bind his wounds sufficiently for him to be carried out of the church for a little while? The mercenary company needs to see his current condition."

"Yes," said Jason, "it's not advisable for any length of time but a few minutes won't hurt him any more than you already have." He paused for a second as a worried look crossed his face. "I'm sorry, I shouldn't have said it like that."

She flinched at the remark, but continued, "Good, patch him up as best you can. As soon as he is ready, I would like the two of you," she gestured to the officers, "to carry him out just far enough for the company and the crowd to see. I am going to talk to the captain of the mercenaries and they need to see what has happened to their employer."

She turned to Juan. "This time I am not rushing ahead without thinking. I know what I am doing and what needs be done."

With that she replaced the rapier across her back and donned her cloak. She exited the cathedral and strode directly to the aforementioned captain. It had started to drizzle once again. When she got to within five feet she stopped and spoke the language of sea traders since she knew that was their preferred tongue.

"Your situation has changed for the worse. Much worse. Your employer, your patron, is no longer capable of fulfilling his side of your bargain. He is no longer capable of much of anything."

As if on cue the captain and lieutenant carried out the ruined Ronaldo. They stood about ten yards behind Bianca, but close enough to make his conditions obvious.

"You are no longer in a position to receive lucrative businesses from him," she continued, "and you no longer will get rich landed estates. You will no longer be placed in positions of influence. In fact, he will not even be able to pay you what he owes you. He started a duel in the cathedral, and his holiness will confiscate all his properties, businesses and wealth as punishment for that act."

As if on cue Ronaldo let out a low, mournful moan.

"You are now faced with receiving nothing for your time of service. If you think you will just pick up and leave our fair land, you are mistaken. The people here resent your presence and will fight you as you try to leave. Do not think that your retreat will be like the Anabasis of the ten thousand leaving Persia. No, it will be more like the rout of the Spanish from Tenochtitlan. The few of you that make it out of here will always be marked as men who went to work for a ruler who would kill his own people for his own glory."

Bianca looked at the faces of the troop and saw concern and worry.

"I'm convincing them," she thought.

She continued, "However, I have a proposal for you. If all of you would sign a solemn and binding oath to never attack or harm Vlogentia or any of her citizens, or to aid, encourage or abet such a venture I will try to persuade the Colonel of the Royal Guard and His Holiness the Vice Pope to grant you safe and quick passage from here. Each of you will also be given ten gold reales as compensation. If you agree this arrangement will prevent useless and pointless bloodshed, pay you for your time and let you go about your lives away from here. What say you?"

"Who are you to make such a promise?" asked the captain.

"Just a girl with an idea that would prevent a lot of unnecessary violence and bloodshed. If you will let me try to approach and implore the Colonel of the Royal Guard and His Holiness. I think they will appreciate the fairness of my proposal. Again, what say you?"

The captain of the mercenaries turned to his second-in-command and said, "If this girl can persuade the authorities to accept that proposal it might get us out of an untenable situation. I also wonder just exactly what happened to our employer. He was supposed to be good with the blade. Perhaps one of the men with her was better."

The second in command was clearly not so inclined to consider an offer of amnesty.

"Are you going to listen to this old woman?" He waved a hand at her white hair. "We are the Company of the Wolves. We don't back down from anyone. We can fight our way out of here with no problem. She obviously doesn't even like fighting. Why should we listen to her?"

Bianca said, "You misunderstand me, sir. I truly abhor violence. I don't want bloodshed. But I never said I wasn't good at it."

As she was uttering those words she reached to her back with her right hand and drew the rapier she still wore under the cloak. The rapier flashed almost faster than could be seen and before he could react the second in command had the point of a sword at his throat.

"Do not move and you will not be hurt. But make no mistake, I know how to use this weapon. I have placed the tip of my blade exactly where I wanted. It is neither a hairsbreadth closer or farther from your throat than I intended."

She addressed the captain again. "I await your decision, sir."

"Now I understand what befell our former patron," said the leader of the mercenaries. He slowly, so as to not alarm her, reached out and gently pulled the rapier away from his man's throat. "We will consider your idea. What do you want us to do?"

"Return to your barracks for now. Let me have time to counsel with the authorities I mentioned. If you and your lieutenant would come to the cathedral in an hour and a half, I should have an answer for you."

He nodded agreement and ordered his men to face right and march to shelter.

As they passed, she asked the second in command, "Are you alright, sir?"

He nodded.

Ronaldo had already been carried back to the cathedral even before the negotiation was finished. Bianca slowly followed.

On the way she told the crowd and delegates still milling around and waiting to see what would transpire, "There will be no more activity this evening. Go home. Have a meal. Enjoy the night."

Once in the narthex she asked the Father Adames to please ask His Holiness to grant an audience with her.

She also asked Captain Mendez to go and request the Colonel's presence. Everything depended on those two seeing the wisdom in her plan and signing the pact with the mercenaries.

The priest and Mendez had overheard everything she had said to the mercenaries, and knew what to tell their superiors. They went off to summon them.

Bianca had one last item. She approached Margaret.

"If I remember correctly you made a tremendous difference helping compose the treaty between dragons and people. I think your skills would be extremely useful now in creating a contract between the mercenaries and us that would be binding and agreeable to all. Would you be willing to help draw up such a pact?"

"Of course I'll be thrilled to help. Thank you for asking me."

With that she sat in one of the pews and started to scribble on some scrap paper the priest had found for her.

One crisis had been averted. Everyone looked relieved.

Everyone but Bianca, who knew the king would not back down after his public humiliation. Something had yet to be done about him.

CHAPTER TWENTY FOUR
FELIX' RANT

The Palace, late afternoon, capital city, kingdom of Vlogentia
Gregorian calendar: January 22
Mayan calendars: Tzolk'in: 4 Ak'b'al
                 Haab: 16 Muwan

Felix bolted from his encounter with Bianca. They had been standing in front of the pavilions in the pouring so rain he had to pass under the canopies and through the assembled delegates and Ronaldo's mercenary company standing at attention before the palace. He felt their stares boring into him from all sides. The feeling was unbearable.

He pushed past the attendants trying to close the great palace doors, shoving both of them to the sides, and dashed through the atrium and then up grand staircase to his study on the second floor. He didn't even notice when or where he had dropped the ceremonial Sword of the Realm.

He and his beautiful new coat was soaked. He threw open the door and hung the finery on a peg and began to pace frantically around the room. He was clasping and unclasping his hands behind his back as he moved from the door to the desk and back again, head down and his hair dripping onto the floor.

He was furious. Furious at himself for allowing such a public humiliation. Furious at her for scolding him so pointedly and loudly. *"I am the king,"* he thought. *"Nobody questions or talks to a king like that. She is so wrong, I am supreme in this land. I need no mandate from God."*

Even worse, it seemed as if the people agreed with her. That simply could not be possible. He must be mistaken, they must be angry with her for being so disrespectful of him. But he could still not rid himself of a feeling of intense embarrassment.

A servant cautiously entered the study, "Is everything all right, sire?"

Felix had noticed the Duke following Bianca into the cathedral while he was retreating into the palace. "No it is not. I need to confer with Duke Ronaldo as soon as possible. Bring him to me the instant he arrives."

Ronaldo would undoubtedly dispatch her before coming to the palace. Her demise would at least ease some of the sting of his discomfiture.

The servant left, and Felix resumed pacing.

A few seconds later, the seneschal entered the room gingerly carrying the ceremonial sword. "You left this behind, sire, and I brought it for you. Notice I didn't actually touch the sword."

"Put the thing down over there." He pointed at a side table.

"Are you sure, sire? That is not where it should normally be displayed."

"I don't care. Just put it there and leave."

The seneschal did as ordered and left as quickly as decorum allowed.

Why was his uncle taking so long? Surely he would have dealt with her by now. Pacing did not help calm him.

Just when he was ready to order someone to summon Ronaldo, the servant re-entered the study. He was literally shaking like a leaf and looked terrified.

"I have terrible news, sire. She came out of the cathedral by herself and approached and spoke to the captain of the mercenaries. While she was addressing him two others came out of the cathedral carrying the Duke. He was maimed and a bloody mess. He had to be carried since he apparently was crippled. He looked as if his right arm was paralyzed and his left hand was bandaged. He had gashes on both sides of his face. I fear he is ruined!"

"That is not possible!" shouted Felix. He grabbed the servant by his lapels and shook him. "Tell me you are mistaken."

"No, sire, I am not. The Duke is finished. To make matters worse the mercenary company just left their post and returned to their barracks. I think she finally went back into the cathedral."

Felix could not believe it. His uncle was effectively gone. For the first time in his life he felt frightened and completely alone. He couldn't even talk with his mother, the queen. She was out of the city at a rural estate.

He dismissed the unfortunate servant and ordered him out of the room. He then resumed pacing, even more frantically than before.

It took him a long time to calm down. He had to decide what to do and his uncle was not there to counsel him. The debate raged inside his mind. Do this. No, do that. Nothing new occurred to him. Finally he decided the only thing he could do was stay the course.

He would demand the Grand Conclave grant him the army he desired. He would have the captive eliminate the kulkulcano'ob. He would raze a couple of worthless villages to prove his prowess and then begin his campaign of conquest. He would finally take revenge on Bianca.

He had hated her ever since she had rejected his interest in her at their first brief encounter. He thought she probably didn't even remember that meeting. She apparently preferred that useless corporal. Other valid reasons for wanting her out of the way were of no consequence to him.

She would pay.

They all would pay.

He would reign triumphant. Just wait until tomorrow.

CHAPTER TWENTY FIVE

BIANCA HAS AN IDEA

The Cathedral of Vlogentia, capital city, kingdom of Vlogentia
Gregorian calendar: January 22
Mayan calendars: Tzolk'in: 4 Ak'b'al
  Haab: 16 Muwan

Bianca and Margaret didn't wait for long before His Holiness, Father Augustin Alanzo, came to meet them.

He had been in his office next to the cathedral's chancel and chapels when Father Adames went to request his presence, so it was a short walk down the aisle in the nave to the narthex. He was tall and slender for a Mayan but not very muscular with grey tinges in his black hair. His demeanor had all the authority and gravity expected of the highest church official despite the fact he was wearing casual clothing.

"Greetings, my children. May you have a blessed blend of Tzolk'in and Haab days."

"And a fortunate blend of days to you, Your Excellency," replied Bianca. She knelt and kissed the ring on his right hand.

"Greetings, sir," said Margaret. She simply stood politely behind Bianca.

He waved his hand in a gracious manner and nodded at Margaret.

"Rise, child. Father Adames tells me that you, of all people, have brokered a deal to rid us of the mercenary company. He also told me you had a duel with

Duke Ronaldo in the nave. I sincerely hope you can enlighten me as to the circumstances of the former and have a satisfactory explanation for the latter."

Bianca stood. "I believe I do, your holiness. The duel was because the Duke attacked me without provocation inside the cathedral. He gave me no opportunity to escape and I had to defend myself."

"As I hear, you defended yourself superbly. If what I have been told is true we won't have to fear the Duke's machinations any longer."

Bianca got the welcome impression His Holiness was not a supporter of Ronaldo or his activities.

"You will have to give me your confession so I can assign your penance. It may not be too severe." That was a most unusual statement for any priest, let alone the Vice Pope. "Where is the Duke and what is his situation?"

"Thank you for your kind words. The Duke is just over there." Bianca pointed to where Jason was tending him. "He is gravely injured. He is in dire need of capable healing. Can you arrange to have him taken to the nearest healing house?"

"Yes, that will be done." Vice Pope Alanzo signaled to Father Adames to take care of the Duke. He in turn summoned one of the junior priests to arrange transport for the Duke to a nearby infirmary.

Bianca continued, "As for the proposal about the mercenaries, please let me introduce my friend. This is Margaret Blankenship. She was abducted from the First World by a renegade member of the Order of the Portal and forced to support the king's treachery. She is a specialist in constructing contracts and has helped me compose the agreement that will suit both us and the mercenaries."

Bianca motioned Margaret to her and had her read the contract. It was in sea trader talk, of course, but the Vice Pope was fluent in that tongue and followed the train of thought quite well.

"That is an excellent idea, my dear. My only concern is where is the money you promised them?"

"For his sacrilegious attack on me in the cathedral you can confiscate his lands and wealth. You can pay the mercenaries from the church's treasury now and replenish it with the proceeds from the sale of his estates."

His Holiness said, "So, in effect, Duke Alonzo is still paying for his hired soldiers. I like that. So that the contract will be binding on both parties, I will have Father Adames translate a copy into Spanish. The mercenaries can have a copy in their tongue, we will keep the Spanish version for our archives."

Colonel Emmanual Alanzo chose that moment to enter the cathedral. He was also tall and thin but more muscular than the Vice Pope and had the bearing of a professional soldier. He was in the formal sky blue and silver uniform of the royal guard because he had been on duty for the feast. Bianca had noticed him attending the delegates when she confronted the king,

"I was witness to your remarkable performance this afternoon. I heard rumors of the king's plan and I very much disapprove of such an enterprise. It would ruin Vlogentia and I was elated than someone finally told him so. Now I hope he will rethink his actions and put the welfare of the kingdom foremost. But that is not why I am here. Tell me about this treaty with the Duke's mercenary company you have proposed."

Bianca had Margaret go over the contract once more. The colonel nodded approval as she read each clause.

"Do you agree with this?" he asked the Vice Pope.

"Most definitely, we should proceed as soon as their captain arrives."

As the two officials consulted one another, Margaret asked Bianca, "What's with those two? The colonel seems awfully casual with such an august personage as the Vice Pope."

"They're cousins. I hear they grew up together," she replied.

"Apparently nepotism is alive and well here as well as at home." Whispered Margaret to Jason, who had moved beside her.

He nodded agreement.

The two cousins and Father Adames withdrew to the office to complete the translation. There wasn't much time.

Bianca thanked Margaret for her assistance, hugging her warmly. Margaret was ecstatic at the outcome of the day and that she was again doing something useful. "I'm grateful to be of help. But the day belongs to you. You were so incredibly fearless. Telling the king just how foolish he is and facing down the mercenary company. That was heroic."

That remark caused a sudden release of some of the feelings that Bianca had kept carefully controlled for the past twenty days. She'd been kidnapped, thrown to a kulkulcan, fought trolls, chased Xavier across wild grasslands, publicly scolded the king and faced a company of mercenaries. She found herself collapsing on a pew and sobbing uncontrollably. It felt like a tidal wave of emotion had crashed upon her and was sweeping her away. She sat on a pew and began to cry. The tears kept coming and wouldn't stop no matter how much she wanted them to cease.

Margaret was confused. "What's the matter? Are you alright?"

Through sobs Bianca replied, "I'm so tired of everything that has happened to us the past few days. I did not and do not want to be anyone important. I just want to be plain, ordinary Bianca."

Margaret and Jason appeared puzzled by that statement, but the soldiers nodded understanding.

"I'm not fearless. I was so scared. While I was standing before the company fear ran through my veins like ice. My body went cold. It took all of my control to not to flee in a blind fit of panic. I'm no hero, just a silly girl who lets her anger control her actions and then has to figure a way out of the mess she's created."

Captain Mendoza walked over to her and knelt by her side. "We can understand that you were terrified, but I have a problem with your opinion of yourself. When all was said and done the mercenaries were doing the retreating and you were the one left standing alone in the rain. I call that courage."

Everyone else nodded agreement.

Margaret put her arm around Bianca. "Jason and I have been through almost as much. We know how you must feel. Let us support you."

Her sympathy comforted Bianca. She stopped sobbing and stood up and began to regain her composure.

After a moment of thought, she said, "There is still a major problem facing Vlogentia. Does anyone think a public scolding will deter the king from his plot? I don't. He will go before the Grand conclave tomorrow and still devise a pretext to declare a great war with somebody, anybody, which will require the enlistment in his army of every man and boy in Vlogentia. Many will obey the order despite hating it just because the king issued it. Many will refuse to obey. I foresee a tremendous civil strife that will tear our realm apart. Vlogentia will either embark on a ruinous campaign of conquest or an equally ruinous civil war. Either outcome results in disaster for us. What do we do about that?"

No one had an answer. For several moments all was quiet.

Almost simultaneously the captain of the mercenaries and his second in command entered the door of the cathedral as the Vice Pope, the Colonel, and Father Adames returned to the narthex from the sanctuary. The two groups met at the back of the nave and went over the contract in great, time consuming, detail. Finally the five of them nodded in agreement, shook hands, and signed the documents.

The Vice Pope told the captain, "Your gold is on its way to a ship we have hired to transport your men to whatever destination you desire."

The captain promised that his men would board at first light and depart as soon as all were aboard.

As he left he turned to Bianca. "My compliments. You have avoided a bloody situation."

She returned a curtsy. "Be safe on your journey, sir."

Surprisingly, the second in command nodded at her as he exited. "Be safe yourself. I can't believe I'd ever say that to someone who'd held a blade to my throat. Your resolve impressed me. Perhaps we'll meet again in much friendlier circumstances."

She curtsied a second time for him.

"That was marvelous," said Colonel Alonzo. "I wish all our documents were so thoroughly examined before being inked. Our king despises signing papers of any kind and never reads anything requiring his approval. He just signs it, usually without even a cursory glance at the contents. We get all sorts of confusing drivel because some clerk was in a hurry and didn't proof his work. The king signs it and sends it to us to figure out what really needs to be done."

That statement caught Bianca's attention. Felix' aversion to the written word was fairly widely known. But the Colonel's mentioning it struck a chord within her. A plan started to form.

As Bianca mulled over her newest idea, the Colonel said, "I will take Lieutenant Gonzalez and Corporal Mendes with me to our barracks to report. The rest of the guardsmen will need to know what has happened today and what might happen tomorrow. I will have someone bring fresh clothing for the three of you. You look like you've slept in them for at least a week."

"It's been well over a week. But thank you. We will appreciate a fresh set of clothes," Said Jason.

Juan and Bianca gave each other a brief hug. Then the three soldiers left the cathedral and headed to their barracks.

That left Jason, Margaret and Bianca in the narthex since the Vice Pope and Father Adames had retired to their offices in the sanctuary. No one seemed to have noticed that the three had not retired to a place for the night. Jason and Margaret went to rest on one of the pews while they waited for the clothes to arrive. Then they could decide where to go. Bianca, however, sat on another pew deep in thought.

It was only a few moments before a messenger arrived to deliver a fresh set of clothes for the three of them. He bowed casually, put the bundle on the floor and left.

The clothes were the standard everyday dress of the Mayan public. Since the cathedral was empty except for Jason, Margaret and Bianca they changed behind one of the pews.

"Look, I feel like I look like one of the residents," said Jason. "So do you, Margaret. I feel like a new person."

All was quiet for several moments. Then Bianca stood. It looked to Jason and Margaret that she had fully regained her former composure.

"Would both of you wait here for me? I have an idea that might solve our realm's problem. I must beg another audience with His Holiness before he retires for the night. I will be back shortly."

"What are you up to?" asked Jason. He and Margaret exchanged confused looks.

"You'll see, I hope."

Bianca practically raced along the aisle to the Vice Pope's office hoping he was still there and awake. She knocked on the door. She was in time for the door opened and she went in.

She spoke with His Holiness for an hour or more. Finally she left the office and returned to the Blankenships.

"Margaret, would you please come with me? We have need of your expertise yet again. There is an edict that needs very, very careful composition. I know I am asking a lot of you, but your knowledge will prove invaluable. Jason, I ask that you remain here in case anyone comes for us."

"I'd love to help," she replied. "This is great, actually being able to do something useful twice in one day. Let's go."

"Well, I'll just stay right here," huffed Jason. He was clearly miffed at being left behind.

Bianca escorted Margaret into the Vice Pope's office.

Two hours passed before Bianca and Margaret exited the office.

"Thank you, your excellency," said Bianca. She curtsied.

Margaret curtsied as well. "I'm glad to have been of assistance."

The two of them rejoined Jason at the front of the cathedral.

"I have never seen you curtsy before," Jason said to Margaret. "You do it quite gracefully. What happened in there?"

Margaret looked puzzled, cocked her head for a second and then shrugged. "It seemed like a lot of bother over nothing. They just wanted some document about Vlogentia ceding some real estate. Bianca and His Holiness were very insistent on the exact wording. I cannot imagine why this was so important when we have to worry about the king going before the Grand Conclave tomorrow. There were a couple of other documents that Bianca said were routine and didn't need my input. I almost feel like it was a ruse to make me feel appreciated."

Bianca heard this, of course, and said, "You're very wrong. That document is important. You are more valued than you realize. Both of you are. But tomorrow will be a critical day and you need to be very careful. Come what may I want you to go to the headquarters of the Order of the Portal as soon as you can. It's in the city center across the palace from here. They know about you and your plight and will arrange for your return to First World."

"What about you?" asked Margaret.

"If my idea works there is a possibility the king can be prevented from declaring a war. In order to achieve that result he must be prevented from making his pronouncement. The Vice Pope has agreed to deliver a speech that will divert the king's attention but he also feels my presence at the Conclave will add to the king's distraction and help accomplish our desired result."

"I bet your presence will distract him," said Jason. "He'll probably try to kill you! Just what are you thinking?"

"He will undoubtedly not try anything in the presence of the delegates. In any event I must do this to save my land and its inhabitants. My part is necessary. But this is not your fight. You didn't ask to be abducted and forced to participate. You need to return home and forget all this."

"That's not going to happen," said Jason. Margaret nodded in agreement. "We're in this with you and will attend the Conclave to see what happens and to assist you if we can."

"If you must attend, you can watch from the upper gallery. Your new clothes will let you blend in with the crowd. But make sure you have an escape route should it prove necessary. If everything works as I hope, war will be averted and your aid won't be required."

"We'll be there," said Margaret.

Jason nodded agreement with his wife. But he couldn't help adding, "If I could offer an unsolicited, and probably unwanted, opinion. This is the consequence when you get a monarch determined solely by who his father was. Obviously this system can lead to some extremely unfit men in power."

Bianca demurred. "It's not like that at all for Vlogentia. Other realms in Second World may do that, but we don't. Firstly, the Maya have a history of ruling queens. Not often, but it has happened twice since we've been in Second World. Secondly, when a monarch dies or leaves the throne a Grand Conclave is assembled to choose the next ruler. In fact, that is almost the only time a Grand Conclave is called. It is up to them to consider the available choices and select the best candidate. That person is then crowned by His Holiness. It has almost always been a son or daughter of the late king, but that is not required. "

"What happened in this instance? If the Grand Conclave is tasked with choosing the best available candidate, how did Volgentia wind up with Felix? Wasn't there some other heir or relative that should have been chosen?" asked Jason.

Bianca seemed reluctant to answer his question. But after a moment of reflection she said, "Felix is the stepson of Javier, the late king. His first queen died, quite suddenly and unexpectedly," she paused and sighed, "and Duke Ronaldo's sister was recently, and conveniently, widowed so he convinced the king to marry her. Thus Felix is Ronaldo's nephew and the son of Javier's second queen. When the Grand Conclave met to name King Javier's successor the Duke managed to convince them that Felix was the logical choice since there was no acceptable heir. It probably didn't hurt his argument that the mercenary company was stationed just outside the palace where the assembly was meeting. So we got Felix. At the time no one thought it would turn out this badly."

"There was no acceptable heir? Then there was another to choose from. Why were they unacceptable?" Margaret asked.

Bianca sighed again, "They said I was too young."

CHAPTER TWENTY SIX
TO THE PALACE

The Cathedral of Vlogentia, capital city of Vlogentia, very late in the evening
Gregorian calendar: January 22
Mayan calendars: Tzolk'in: 4 Ak'b'al
Haab: 16 Muwan

Margaret started to say, "Well, if the acceptable heir was too young, why not appoint a regent until …" It suddenly dawned on her which pronoun Bianca had used. "You mean you're the heir? You were next in line? But you have always acted as if you didn't want a public presence or acclaim. Nobody calls you 'Your Highness' or bows or anything. Why not? What happened?"

Bianca looked down as she wrung her hands in her lap. "When my father married Andrea, Felix' mother, it became obvious to me and everyone else that Duke Ronaldo was manipulating the king and wanted to be the power behind the throne. To be honest, I didn't mind. I was never interested in affairs of state or royal protocol, and after my mother died I lost what little interest I ever had in being a princess or whatever position official etiquette required."

"You don't like being a princess?" asked Margaret. "I don't understand."

"I loved being the person you met that first day. Everyone that knew me or knew about me realized that's what I preferred. Everyone also knew that Felix was probably going to be king. They let me pretend I was simply Bianca and not Bianca Carlota Maria Tlalli Yaxkin Ryoko Castellano Ueyama. I still wish for that simpler life, but the past twenty days have ruined everything. Now, as King Javier's only child, I will have to assume the appearance of a princess at least until the situation with Felix is resolved. What happens after that is any-one's guess."

Margaret was stunned. Jason appeared equally surprised. This was not at all what she had expected. But now it made sense. Of course Felix would want a possible claimant to the throne eliminated. That's why Bianca was abducted.

"So the king was trying to get rid of Princess Bianca Carla and whatever other names you said you have. That is a lot of names. He is afraid you're a threat to his position," said Margaret.

"Actually I don't believe that thought ever occurred to him. He hates me because I never showed any interest in him when we first met. He doesn't handle rejection well. And, yes, royal families like lots of names." Bianca paused to collect her thoughts. "So tomorrow I will appear at the Grand Conclave as the Crown Princess as well as his public tormentor. The hope is that he will be distracted sufficiently for my idea to work."

Jason added, "As I said before he is likely to try to kill you then and there. I now think that is even more likely. What protection will you have? What should we do to help? We want to be there."

"No, I told you he would not attempt anything so bold at the Conclave. He isn't daring enough to perform such an act. Also, the Colonel of the Guard and several of the Royal Guard will be there. They will protect me. The worry is what might happen later. But now I need to get ready for the Conclave. Since you want to attend why don't you come with me to the palace? I would very much appreciate having my friends with me this evening."

"Of course we'll come to the palace with you," said Margaret. "Being invited to a palace by a princess in a magical land is something out of a novel. I can't believe this is really happening. We are going, aren't we Jason?"

"Yes, of course. Let's go," said Jason.

The dire nature of the situation didn't faze Margaret at all, at least for the time being. Bianca didn't bother to change out of the rags she was wearing into the attire brought by the messenger since she'd need to change into appropriate attire to look royal for the Conclave. They left the cathedral and walked the short distance toward the palace.

The sun had set by the time they left the cathedral and the all-day rain had left a dank and dense fog over the city. The firefly lanterns cast a weak glow on the pavement around them. The city center and the streets were deserted except for the occasional night watchman making his rounds in the distance. The city was silent.

The three of them walked along the path from the cathedral to the palace like ghosts, apparently unseen and alone.

On the way Margaret felt that she had to ask, "Some of that long list of names you have don't sound Spanish or Mayan. Am I correct?"

"Yes," Bianca answered, "they are Japanese. My mother was from the Second World realm of Japanese expatriates. Ryoko was her given name and Ueyama her family name. It was an arranged marriage, for political purposes, but my parents were quite happy with their union."

"She died when I was sixteen, four years ago, and up until then I tried to play princess to please them. As I said, once she died and Andrea became queen and Felix my stepbrother I lost any desire to try to act the part any further. I became the Bianca you met twenty-one days ago. I would prefer if you just call me Bianca."

This explained a lot to Margaret. Some of the odd comments and reactions of the people around them now made sense. The inhabitants knew who she really was, but also knew what she really wanted to be. It even partially explained some of her unusual appearance. But not the color of her hair or eyes. She guessed partial albinism, but that did not fit with what she knew about the condition.

Margaret walked alongside Bianca wondering what other revelations were in the offing. Jason trailed behind them in what she knew was his protective mode.

They neared the palace. It had a wall surrounding the palace grounds was that higher than the ceremonial wall around the city center It was at least six feet tall.

Bianca told them, "It's to keep uninvited people out. It has three sets of wrought iron gates, one double gate at the main entrance leading to the palace's main doors and a single side gate at either end of the palace. Each gate has six foot tall stele set on each side but with Spanish and transcribed Yukatek inscriptions rather than Mayan glyphs. The main gate was open earlier this evening. You must have noticed that when Felix fled through it after his encounter with me. It should now be shut with guards behind it. The two side gates will also be shut and have patrols present with a small office for the duty officer. We need to pass through the nearest gate to get into the palace. Follow my lead."

Bianca and Margaret approached the nearest side gate with Jason still trailing behind.

The corporal on duty at this gate will know me, of course," said Bianca, "but he will also have strict orders. I have an idea."

As they neared the gate, which was open in contrast to what Bianca had said it would be, the guardsman in command ordered them to halt.

"I'm sorry," said Corporal Enrico, Juan's friend and Bianca's acquaintance, "but I cannot knowingly let you pass. The king has commanded that no one enter the palace this evening. He seems angry, although I can't imagine why." He had his hands behind his back and was rocking back and forth as he addressed them. Margaret guessed that he was being facetious.

"I understand," said Bianca, "you have to follow orders. I think that to obey them to the fullest you should have your men patrol up and down the outside of the wall to make sure no one tries to scale it and get into the palace. They would need to walk at least fifty feet along the wall, one group going west and the other going east. You would need to tell them to keep their eyes on the surrounding areas, there might be a disturbance tonight. Also, don't you have some duty rosters to fill out? While your men are patrolling the wall wouldn't it be a good time for you to catch up on that paperwork? By the way, do you know where Juan is or what he's doing? "

The corporal stood for a few seconds and then nodded in comprehension of her true intent. He immediately turned to his six soldiers and said, "You three go west along the wall as she suggested, the other three go east. Make sure you keep a sharp watch for any possible intruders coming from the town." He pointed away from the gate. "I will stay here in the guard office and finish this infernal paperwork."

He turned back to Bianca. "Juan was ordered to the barracks by the colonel. I haven't seen him since but I assume he's fine."

The men saluted and took off on their assigned patrols, being careful to watch the town. Not one tried to look back at the gate. The corporal sat down in the office and turned his back on the gate so he could concentrate on the duty roster, all one page of it.

"Thank you, I appreciate the news," replied Bianca.

"What was that all about?" asked Jason.

"The corporal and his men are following the letter of their orders," said Bianca. "They cannot be accused of neglecting their duties. But we get into the palace. I need to clean and change into something appropriate for the Conclave.

I imagine you would like to freshen up even though you have now have new, clean clothes to wear. Please wear those same clothes tomorrow, they will help you blend into the crowd and give you a measure of anonymity."

The three of them quickly passed through the gate and entered a side door to the palace.

Once inside the palace they were in a great hallway that ran the entire length of the building, from the south end to the north end. Halfway along the hallway on the right side was the palace's huge main double door, flanked on either side by two large arched stained glass windows. Another door like the one they'd just entered was at the far end of the hallway. To their left was an ornate staircase leading to the second floor. Margaret could see a similar staircase at the far end of the palace. Across from the main door were another set of arched double doors. On either side of those doors were smaller staircases leading to the second floor.

"This stairway," said Bianca gesturing to the nearest one to their left, "leads to a second floor hallway flanked on both sides by five rooms, living suites on the right and offices, with doors leading to balconies overlooking the sea, on the left. At the end of that section of the second floor hallway is a railing separating it from the smaller staircase that leads to the galleries overlooking the great room. Thus, people using that staircase to reach the gallery cannot enter the hallway to the rooms and offices."

"Follow me and let me make contact with my staff. They know and trust me and would expect me to spend the night in my quarters. The king undoubtedly did not bother to tell them about his orders to keep out visitors, so they won't think anything about my bringing some visitors I met while I was absent. I'll tell them why I've been gone so long and to not inform the king or any of his retinue that we're here. I want my appearance at the Conclave tomorrow to be a surprise to him."

Bianca led Jason and Margaret up the near staircase and accompanied them to the third door on the right and opened it. It was a medium sized suite with a poster bed and a hammock, several dressers and wardrobes, two nightstands, a desk for writing and a window overlooking the courtyard, which still had the pavilions in place. It even had a bathroom with a tub.

Margaret felt that was the best part.

Bianca said, "Please wait in here. I will have one of the staff I trust draw a warm bath for you. Please rest as best you can for the rest of the night. Tomorrow should be a busy day. After I talk to the staff I'll be next door in my room if you need me. Just knock."

"Thank you, this really is a dream come true," said Margaret, "A night in a real bed, and a bath, and in a palace. Let tomorrow be tomorrow. The rest of this night is to be enjoyed."

"You're very welcome. Someone should be here in a few moments to tend to you."

After the bath was drawn Margaret and Jason washed and dressed for the night. The suite's wardrobe even had fresh linen bedclothes. They would get to sleep in a decent bed in a magnificent room for the first time in Second World.

Before turning in Margaret went to the suite next door and knocked on the door.

"Bianca, its Margaret. May I come in for a moment? I want to tell you that you have our unwavering support, come what may tomorrow."

Bianca opened the door and let her in. Margaret was surprised, Bianca's room wasn't as large as theirs. But that fit with what she was learning about her new, unwilling royal, friend.

"It's not huge but more than adequate for me," said Bianca. "I'm glad you're here. The staff have all retired for the night and I need an opinion."

She opened a wardrobe full of gowns and dresses. "I need to find the best outfit for the Conclave." She took out one floor length gown with full sleeves. It was white with blue embroidery along the hem, midriff and sleeves. "What do you think? This was my mother's coronation gown."

"It looks great. You should wear it."

"Then that's settled. I'll wear my mother's jewelry and her tiara. For once I'll do my best to look like a princess. Not for long, I hope."

Margaret hugged her and said, "You'll do fine. Everything will turn out the way you want. We'll be there for you, as will everybody else."

They said goodnight and Margaret went back to her room. She wasn't anywhere as sure tomorrow would be as fabulous as she pretended.

CHAPTER TWENTY SEVEN
THE GRAND CONCLAVE

The Palace of Vlogentia, capital city, kingdom of Vlogentia, morning
Gregorian calendar: January 23
Mayan calendars: Tzolk'in: 5 K'an
                 Haab: 17 Muwan

T he January sun rose early since Vlogentia lies in the southern hemi-sphere of Second World. But Margaret and Jason did not. The past three plus weeks had taken a toll on their bodies and their emotions. They needed a full night's rest and more. Then it became a frantic race to get ready for the Grand Conclave.

For Margaret preparation consisted of another warm bath and donning her new clothes. A quick look in the mirror convinced her that she indeed appear like a local. Jason took quite a bit longer since he hadn't shaved since their arrival at the portal isle. Finally he was ready as well. They entered the hall to wait for Bianca and sat on a bench next to their door.

Bianca must have had somewhat more to do. She didn't leave her room for several more moments. "I'm sorry I took so long. I had to rummage through the back of my wardrobe to find some of my mother's jewelry to wear. I have to say, though, that the two of you look for all the world like a local couple attending this unusual Grand Conclave. You'll blend in perfectly."

Margaret sized up Bianca's appearance. She was wearing the floor length gown apparently made from the silk of her mother's homeland. It was off white

213

with the usual Mayan elaborate embroidery, a mix of light and dark blue stitching. She wore a necklace, bracelet and earrings of diamond and deep blue sapphire gems that matched her eyes, all set in silver. The gems made her eyes seem even more intense and striking than usual.

Her crown was made of the same materials, about two inches high except in the front where the large central blue sapphire made a peak of three inches. An attendant must have helped with her hair, it was braided down her back. She looked very much like a royal.

"What do you think?" She asked Margaret. "Do I actually look acceptable? Do you think I will distract the king? Everything rests on that."

"You look marvelous," said Margaret. While thinking to herself, "*If time and circumstance permit I must have a talk with Bianca about her self-image.*"

She still wasn't at all sure why distracting the king was so critical. But anything to put him off point sounded like a good idea.

The Conclave was scheduled to begin immediately after the noon meal and it was just about that time. The three off them spent the few minutes left to them chatting about nothing.

"*As people tend to do before a major event,*" thought Margaret.

Before long the herald stood at the double door to the great hall and began to call the attendees to order.

"You should go mingle with the crowd," Bianca told Margaret and Jason. "I'll enter the hall last, after the delegates are seated and the other dignitaries have been introduced. Before we left the cathedral last night the Vice Pope told me that he would this morning inform the herald that I would be attending the Conclave, but not to say anything to anybody until I am announced. That way I will be a surprise to the king, and not give him time to react to my presence. Let's hope it works."

Just after midday the upper galleries started to fill with spectators. Jason and Margaret had gone down the side stairway they'd used the night before, exited the side door of the palace and mingled with the crowd before entering the main doors of the palace. As they entered the palace with the crowd they heard rumors, their translators for a change allowing them to understand some of the talk, being whispered about the king's announcement and most of the stories didn't sound good.

Juan was standing guard outside the doors to the Great Hall. Margaret tried to surreptitiously nod to him as they went by, but he either didn't notice them or pretended not to.

They went up the left balcony stairway and managed to situate themselves toward the front of the Great Hall, near the dais set at the opposite end of the hall from the double doors. The main floor was filled with chairs for the attendees, several hundred of them placed in the space between the rows of columns supporting the balconies. Stained glass windows toward the front of the hall and behind the columns and behind the balconies let in plenty of light.

After a few more stentorian announcements from the herald the attendees finished filing into the hall and took their seats. Everybody, delegates and audience alike, appeared to Margaret to be filled with trepidation.

At last all the emissaries were seated and quiet. The herald then began to introduce the king and the dignitaries who would preside over the Conclave.

First he introduced the king, of course. "Honored guests and delegates, rise and welcome our most august majesty King Felix Necahual Alarcon Estrada of Vlogentia."

Felix entered through the doors at the back of the hall and strode toward the dais. His staff must have managed to recover the splendor of his new coat and he looked impressive. He went up the three steps onto the platform, turned to the gathering and sat on his throne situated just to the left of the center of the dais as he faced the hall.

"Wow, look at all the buttons on that coat," whispered Margaret to Jason, so as to not be overheard by others. "What on earth, either First World earth or Second World earth, could anyone need with that many buttons?"

Jason just shrugged his shoulders.

Next the herald announced His Holiness the Vice Pope who entered wearing the full regalia of his office, mounted the stage and sat to Felix' left.

The chair to the right of Felix, meant for the Duke of Ki'pan, was left empty.

The Queen Mother entered likewise but sat behind and to the right of Felix. She was a tall and stately woman, apparently in her early forties with the Mayan complexion and dark hair tinged with streaks of grey. She wore a light blue gown with dark blue trim.

Then the Grand Master of the Order of the Portal entered, wearing the grey and blue trimmed robe of the Order, and made his way down the aisle and sat to the right of the empty chair. Next came the introductions of Felix' seneschal and castellan. They stood behind the Queen Mother.

Felix prepared to rise and deliver the speech Margaret, Jason and outwardly everyone in the hall and galleries both anticipated and feared.

Before Felix could stand the herald announced in his booming voice, "Honored guests and delegates, please welcome Her Royal Highness Bianca Carlota Maria Tlalli Yaxkin Ryoko Castellano Ueyama, Crown Princess of Vlogentia."

She stood for a second in the doorway then proceeded deliberately toward the dais.

As she strode down the aisle the gathering turned to face her. At first there wasn't a sound from them or the gallery. Then a murmur started at the back of the assembly and followed her as she approached the dais. It grew to a muffled roar of apparent approval by the time she mounted the stairs to the platform. Then it died and all was silent once again.

First she faced the Vice Pope and curtsied, then the Grand Master. Lastly she faced Felix and gave an almost imperceptible curtsy, turned her back to him, walked to the side of the stage to the right of the Grand Master and turned to face the attendees. She was motionless, like a statue.

Felix' face was contorted in a scowl. He uttered not a word or a sound. He stood with his fists balled up at his sides and glared at Bianca. He obviously couldn't conceive what he should do next.

Before Felix said or did anything the Vice Pope rose and addressed both the Conclave and Felix. "Your majesty and honored guests, allow me to make a proposal. Yesterday your majesty was subject to a slight that a king should not endure."

Margaret, and presumably the rest of the audience, knew he meant Bianca's public scolding of Felix.

"That was tragic. Sometimes a mere king must endure such discomfitures. But no one would ever consider speaking to an emperor in such a manner. That would be truly unthinkable. An emperor is so much more commanding and majestic than a mere king. Therefore, it is the opinion of the church and the officials of Vlogentia that Felix should be an emperor. Such a title would signify to all just how majestic he truly is and how they should bestow on him the veneration he deserves."

At first Felix was paying little attention to what His Holiness was saying. He was fixated on Bianca. But the stentorian voice of the Vice Pope seemed to override Felix' hostility and he turned to fixate on the Vice Pope. Felix the Emperor must have sounded wonderful to him, given his obvious desires for fame and glory.

His Holiness continued, "Accordingly the cardinals of the church and I, in accordance with the Colonel of the Royal Guard, have written several documents that will allow us to proclaim your majesty an emperor. Not just as the emperor of Vlogentia. That is just one kingdom and not worthy of an emperor. Emperors rule more than one land. You will become the emperor of a land called New Byzantium, named after the thousand year descendant of the glorious empire of Rome. Your majesty will be the supreme ruler of New Byzantium and no one will question your authority or your word in that realm."

This speech caused considerable confusion among the delegates to the Conclave and the visitors in the galleries. An undercurrent of whispering spread throughout the delegates and the galleries. From what Margaret could make out from her neighbors few of them knew what any of this meant and if some thought they knew they most likely didn't like the sound of it.

Margaret was horrified. 'The Vice Pope has betrayed Bianca," she whispered to Jason. "He seemed so nice last night, and now he does this. What do we do?"

He looked at her, shock and surprise in his eyes. "I don't know."

His Holiness added, "In order to crown you the Emperor of New Byzantium, first you must designate the lands that will comprise that empire. We have composed a royal edict for that purpose. Once that is signed we will present you with the Church's holy decree naming you emperor. Of course, an emperor cannot also be a king."

Margaret was confused. "Is that true?" she quietly asked Jason.

"No, I don't think it is. Why would the Vice Pope say such a thing? Doesn't the king know better?" he responded.

The Vice Pope continued, "You must first give up the kingship of Vlogentia so we can crown you the emperor of the grander realm of New Byzantium. Our decree is carefully worded to protect you. Unless you are named Emperor of New Byzantium you will remain king of Vlogentia."

He handed three documents to Felix.

"Here is the decree naming you Emperor of New Byzantium for your perusal. Also are the two decrees establishing the lands of the empire, and your renunciation of kingship of Vlogentia so you can become emperor. Do you need to look them over?"

This was a long oration even by the Vice Pope's standards. It achieved its purpose.

Felix appeared transfixed by the concept and eager to accept his new title and acclaim. He looked at Bianca with a self-satisfied expression. He briefly looked at the titles of the three documents and read them as much as Margaret had learned he usually did.

"Give me the edicts. Let's get this paperwork out of the way so I can be crowned emperor. Then the real business of this Grand Conclave can begin."

He first signed the edict naming the lands of New Byzantium. This was the one that Bianca and the Vice Pope had Margaret help compose.

When Margaret saw Felix sign it, she began to understand. She tried to suppress a smile and nudged Jason. "I think this is what Bianca had in mind."

Jason looked even more confused and worried than before.

The edict needed not only the king's signature, but required the signatures of two witnesses to ensure that he signed it willingly. The Vice Pope and the Grand Master obliged. Next came the abdication proclamation, followed immediately by the coronation decree. Those also required two witnesses attesting to the king's voluntary agreement.

Once finished, the Vice Pope asked Felix to kneel so he could remove the crown of Vlogentia and place in on the seat of the throne. He then placed a makeshift crown representing the new empire on Felix.

"Rise Felix Necahual Alarcon Estrada, Emperor of New Byzantium."

Felix started to step forward to address the Conclave.

But before he could say anything Bianca also stepped forward, stood in front of the empty chair, and spoke first. Her voice was loud, clear and surprisingly forceful.

"Your pardon, sir, but you are no longer king of this realm and have no standing at this assembly. You are merely a visiting dignitary observing our ceremonies. Please stand aside."

Felix stood dumbfounded, hands at his side, mouth agape. He sputtered for several seconds and then finally managed to say. "What impudence. How dare you speak to me yet again? I am now the emperor. Emperor of not only Vlogentia but any other lands I will conquer."

"Yes, you are an emperor. But not of Volgentia or any of her remaining lands or any other realms of Second World. Your realm consists of, and only of, five of the barrier islands of the inland sea. Before abdicating the throne you signed a decree ceding those islands, and only those islands, from Vlogentia to create the dominion known as New Byzantium."

"That is preposterous," he sputtered, "I would never intend to do such a thing. This cannot be true."

"Nevertheless that is what you did. You should have read what you signed."

"But those islands are barren and devoid of inhabitants. They are not a proper empire." Comprehension of what he had done and the dire position he was in spread across his visage.

"You're wrong. The islands have rather large populations of sea turtles, sea lions and sea gulls. You should do quite well there."

Turning to the Colonel of the Guard who had been standing beside but off the dais she said, "Sir, would you be as kind as to escort the emperor and his retinue to a ship to take them to their domain. Make sure they depart this day. Also be sure to supply them with sufficient provisions and shelter."

Felix looked at Bianca, the Vice Pope, the Grand Master and the assembly. The realization of defeat slowly crept through his posture. He slumped his shoulders and put his face in his hands for several seconds.

The Queen Mother, Andrea, had an equally astonished look. She started to look around wildly as if to ascertain that this was all a grand hoax. She also was speechless and immobile like she was frozen to her chair.

Felix started to follow the Colonel out of the hall. As he went down the steps to the main floor, followed by his thoroughly confused and distraught mother and castellan, the seneschal rushed Bianca.

He endeavored to attack her with the dirk he kept in his belt. Bianca jumped back and reached through the slit in her gown to draw the dagger she had strapped to her thigh.

There was no need. Before the seneschal could get within six feet of her he was struck by a concentrated blast of air created by the Grand Master and his wand. He fell, dropped the dirk and grabbed his chest.

"He should have only had a couple of cracked ribs that will heal," said the Grand Master, "but is out of action for now." He bowed toward Bianca. "I take it this was a plan of yours. My compliments"

She gave a brief curtsy.

"I am glad to have been of help to your highness," said the Grand Master. "Perhaps we should meet later and continue our conversation about the proper care and use of wands."

"Thank you. I appreciate the aid and your offer. I must decide if I really want to learn those skills." She gave the Grand Master a proper curtsy.

The assembled delegates and the spectators in the galleries were stunned by the turn of events. In some cases they were speechless. Others suddenly couldn't stop babbling.

Vlogentia no longer had a king and the events of the past several minutes were unprecedented according to the conversation Margaret was able to overhear and understand. She further gathered that all in attendance agreed the lack of this particular king was a good thing and speculation as to what would come next was on everyone's lips. .

Jason and Margaret hugged each other in glee.

"Her idea worked," said Margaret. "I had no idea why that document I helped compose was so critical but it worked. The king essentially sent himself into exile." Their relief at the result of Bianca's plan and her safety was profound.

Amid the near chaos spreading throughout the hall Bianca moved to the center of the dais and tried to speak. She was drowned out by the turmoil. Finally the herald, who as a prerequisite for his position had a voice that could penetrate a thunderstorm, was able to be heard above the tumult.

"Silence. Her highness wishes to address the Conclave."

It took four tries, but the din finally subsided.

"Firstly, I want to say that I regret the deception that was necessary to protect this land from a disastrous course of action. I can only hope that history will decide it was the correct choice."

Her statement was greeted by a unanimous round of applause.

"Secondly I want to thank all of you for your attendance at this Grand Conclave. However, the purpose of this assembly has changed. No longer will you be required to endorse a plan to raise an immense army. Now you are tasked with deciding the future of Vlogentia."

She paused to look around at the now silent crowd.

"You must decide how our land is to be governed. In order to properly come to an agreement on the destiny of Vlogentia you must not rely only on what has been done before. Instead look through history to see what has been done by others. Look not just at kingdoms and empires and our history but at what all the past has to offer. Study the ancient Athenians, the early days of Rome and the tribal councils of our ancestors."

Now she stepped forward and lifted her hands in appeal to the delegates.

"While considering these options you must put aside your biases, your wants and needs, and your personal preferences. Those considerations pale beside the needs of everyone living in Vlogentia. Instead consider the welfare of all the citizens from the highest city officials to the farmers in the fields. Do all this and you will achieve strength and prosperity for our land. This is now your charge. Do you accept this charge?"

The confusion among the delegates made it clear that this was not what the assemblage was expecting to hear. Puzzled murmurs spread throughout the crowd. They were trying to comprehend what she was telling them to do. It was a novel concept. For a few moments nobody said anything about agreeing to accept her charge.

Finally the Vice Pope asked, "Do you accept this charge?"

He had to ask it three times but the entire assembly finally answered, "Yea, we accept the charge!"

At this Bianca took a step back and said, "Then I will leave you to your deliberations. I will ask His Holiness to mediate. As for myself, the past days have taken a toll on my body and especially on my emotions. I am spent. I need to step back and take time to recover. Perhaps my honorable uncle will invite me to visit my mother's homeland. Perhaps I will visit the home of my friends." She looked in the gallery for Jason and Margaret. "Or perhaps I will visit one or two realms of Second World. But I will return. Vlogentia is my home and place I wish to live."

A few scattered cries of, "No, stay with us," came from somewhere in the crowd.

She shook her head no and took another step back and carefully removed the crown from her head and placed it carefully on the seat of the empty throne next to Felix' crown. She straightened and descended the steps from the dais and strode out of the hall.

As she went through the doors Margaret could see Juan waiting for her. They hugged.

The colonel must have permitted him to wait for her.

The doors closed and the Grand Conclave got to work.

Chapter Twenty Eight
Surprising News

The Palace of Vlogentia, capital city, kingdom of Vlogentia, late afternoon
Gregorian calendar: January 23
Mayan calendars: Tzolk'in: 5 K'an
                 Haab: 17 Muwan

Bianca had surprised everyone. As she started to leave the Great Hall she turned to look back at the disorganized crowd. Delegates were milling back and forth, constantly bumping into one another. Their voices created an unintelligible din among the delegates on the main floor that even drowned out the booming voice of the herald. Confusion and pandemonium reigned everywhere.

The galleries were no less confused, but she could actually hear some of the talk over the racket. Spectators were offering varying opinions of everything from what form of government they should have to what the weather was going to be tomorrow.

It took a while for the clamor to subside but the representatives finally seemed to settle into several discussion groups and actually began to deliberate their options. The gallery started to empty.

Bianca took that opportunity to greet Juan and give him a hug. She was crying tears of joy and relief and shaking with excitement.

"It worked, it actually worked. Felix cannot drive the kingdom into ruin," she exclaimed to him. "This ordeal is finally over. Let's go somewhere, maybe to Joaquin's to celebrate."

"I had no idea what was going on until you sent the king on his way," said Juan. "Was that your plan? When did you devise it? You said nothing about this last night when the Colonel ordered me to the barracks. But later he must have had a hint, perhaps from his cousin, since he stationed me by these doors today. It was a brilliant idea. Felix is no longer able to lead Vlogentia into devastation and no blood was shed. You really are not the shy girl of a month ago. I cannot believe what you've accomplished in the past two days. I am so proud of you."

He gave her another congratulatory hug.

"I'm happy the result is so good," she said in between sobs of relief. "Now let's go celebrate."

She hoped to spend a quiet few more momenets with Juan and then go meet with her friends.

But they had only a moment before the Grand Master found them. "Pardon me, your highness, but I wonder if this might be a good time to continue our discussion from the other day? I think you should consider learning more about portal wands, what First World is like, and why the Order is so important to the security of Second World. Could you spare some time?"

She decided that he was well meaning but not the most astute observer of human nature. With her moment with Juan disturbed Bianca was, for her, rather curt.

"No, I think we should pursue that topic some other time. Please call me Bianca, I'm not so sure about being a princess."

"As you wish, but sometimes we don't get all we desire. Outside influences, call them fate if you wish, may force us on paths we would not voluntarily choose."

"Perhaps you are right. We shall see." She thought for a few seconds, then added, "Do you remember my mention of the couple abducted from First World? Second World is not their home, they are out of place here and they want to return to where they belong. Could you be persuaded to grant them that favor? They have been subjected to unimaginable sufferings and performed bravely and admirably. They have earned every consideration you can give. Please help them. If you do I might reconsider your offer."

"Of course the Order will do everything necessary to return your friends to their rightful home. We would do so whether you agreed to instruction or not.

If they are available, we should speak with them now. The sooner they return to First World, the better."

"Dear, I need to take His Prominence to Jason and Margaret," said Bianca. "Can you come with me?"

"No," answered Juan, "I need to return to the barracks and report. I couldn't have gone to Joaquin's with you now anyway. But rest assured I will find you later, you may rely on that. Then we will really celebrate."

"I will be waiting for you. If I'm not here you know where to look. Do not take too long!"

She led the Grand Master to Jason's and Margaret's suite on the palace's second floor. She assumed that's where they would go after she left the Conclave. They were, in fact, quietly sitting in their suite and just looking out the window.

"Jason, Margaret, for a change I have good news for you. May I introduce the Grand Master of the Order of the Portal. He has agreed to have the Order take you back to your home in First World. I assume that is what you'd like. Am I correct?"

"Oh, yes. We desperately want that. Vlogentia is a wonderful, magical place. But we belong in Miami doing our regular jobs," said Margaret.

Jason added, "How soon can we leave? As my wife said this place has been an adventure of a lifetime, not entirely in a good way. The resolution was great, however. Your plan and your performance were marvelous. But now all we want is to return to our normal lives in, what is to us, a nice and sane universe."

The Grand Master said, "Excellent, be ready to travel at daybreak tomorrow. I will have some of the Order escort you to our ship that will sail you to Portal Isle. Once there we'll send you back to First World and then take you back to where that rogue Xander kidnapped you. Will that be sufficient?"

"Yes, thank you. We greatly appreciate it. We'll see you tomorrow morning," said Margaret.

With that the Grand Master turned to Bianca, "And I would like for you to come to my office the day after tomorrow, if you can. Good evening to all of you." He departed for his office in the adjacent building.

"Tomorrow will be a busy and happy day for you. I wish you a safe and, for once, a boring trip to your Miami. Whatever that is," said Bianca.

"It's a city. It's the city where we live and do our work. Not anywhere as exciting or dangerous as Vlogentia, but it's where we want to be," said Jason. "But we will miss this land and especially you. We will always remember our time here."

Bianca said, "I sincerely hope that will be true." She had her doubts.

"But now, please forgive and excuse me. I have a short errand to attend to. I wish to speak with that miscreant Felix before he's sent off to his new 'empire'. I'll be back shortly. Please wait for me, I want to spend our last night together as friends should do."

She left them in their room talking excitedly about their so long anticipated return home. She came back about an hour later.

"I'm sorry for that. My conversation with Felix was unpleasant but necessary. Now I have a surprise for you. Please come with me, I want to show you the cubs you've undoubtedly heard so much about. You will love playing with them and we can talk about our adventures while we were apart."

Bianca left a message with one of the housemaids for Juan telling him where they would be. The three of them left the palace and Bianca requested a carriage to take them to Pedro's livery. They spent the next few hours talking and laughing and recounting their interesting times while trying to put their disagreeable memories to rest. Jason and Margaret were thoroughly enchanted by the cubs who seemed to accept them as friends of Bianca.

Margaret got around to telling Bianca about her discoveries at the village of false gold in the forest.

That tale totally astonished Bianca. "I'll need to see if the Grand Master or anyone of the Order knew about the danger to the portals! If they did, why didn't they tell anyone? If they didn't, then they need to protect the portals even more than before. Rogues like Xander and Xavier simply cannot be allowed in the Order or even near the portals. Are you sure of your suspicions?"

"Yes, I am. If not careful the portals could vanish, and they probably won't just go 'poof'. Their destruction could result in a disaster of unimaginable magnitude. Life in either or both worlds would be devastated. But I think that all the Order needs to do is manage the portals carefully and no harm will come to anyone."

"I hope and trust you are right," said Bianca.

Margaret then looked slyly at Jason and nudged him. "Do you think I could ask her now?"

"You can try, I'm not sure any time is the right time," he replied.

Margaret took a deep breath and faced Bianca with a most serious look on her face. "Since I know you understand the potential danger to the portals and that you'll make sure nothing untoward happens to them, I'd like change the subject to a different and, to me, an important question. I never got to ride a unicorn. Unicorns exist only in legend in First World but I have been fascinated by their stories ever since I was a child. Once I saw them here I was ecstatic. I couldn't stop wanting to ride one. I really, really want to do that. Could that be still be possible?"

Bianca thought for a minute. "The law is that unicorns may be ridden only by the royal guard or the royal family. That's why I was allowed to ride one on the way back from Natts' Nohoch Muulo'ob. I'm so sorry." But an idea was forming in her mind.

Margaret nodded in reluctant agreement and sat quietly for a while.

The conversation between Bianca and Jason continued and Margaret gradually recovered her excitement about their return home. They all promised that they'd somehow keep in touch if the Order permitted. Jason and Margaret, based on what they thought they'd been told, were certain it was true. Bianca feared it was not.

They chatted about many things and about not much of anything. Jason and Margaret tried to describe what life was like for them in First World. Bianca wasn't sure she understood everything she was being told and was equally unsure she'd like anything about First World. It was no great wonder to her why the Order was so protective of the portals.

It was nearly midnight when Juan burst into the stall where they were petting the cubs. "I have been searching for you for hours! Whatever are you doing hiding in the back of a stable…"

He noticed the cubs. "Oh, I see."

"Didn't you get my message from the maid?"

"No, I was in too much of a hurry to chat with the staff."

He paused and looked around, as if afraid to say what came next. "I'm afraid I have very bad news. Xavier has escaped again!"

CHAPTER TWENTY NINE

XAVIER PLOTS REVENGE

The prison of Vlogentia, capital city, kingdom of Vlogentia, around noon
Gregorian calendar: January 23
Mayan calendars: Tzolk'in: 5 K'an
               Haab: 17 Muwan

X avier was pacing in his cell trying to figure out what to do. He was rapidly becoming desperate and hopeless.

He gathered from the actions of his guards that something unexpected had happened at the Grand Conclave but he had no idea what it was. Did Felix actually put his plan of conquest into action? If so could Xavier hope that the king would release him and ask for his assistance? That didn't seem likely since the excuse of a war with the kulkulcano'ob was no longer an option. The king and Ronaldo no longer needed his involvement. What could he do? How could he implement his and Xander's plan for revenge on the Order from inside a prison?

It had all started so well. They were able to work their way into the confidences of the king and his uncle with the pretext of accepting sweeping authority in the administration of Vlogentia. All the while what they really wanted was to incriminate the Order as traitors in league with the kulkulcano'ob. That would have resulted in the obliteration of the Order and exacted revenge for the humiliation of their father. Now he saw no way that could happen even if the war was declared.

His pacing grew more frantic and he started to hit the walls with his fists in frustration. He was so distracted by his misery he almost didn't hear the commotion outside the cell. It took several moments for a newcomer to attract his attention.

When he finally did look his spirits took a turn for the better. It was Mateo, one of his cousins who had helped capture the Blankenships and escorted Xander and them to Natts' Nohoch Muulo'ob. The guards were unconscious or dead and Mateo was unlocking the cell door.

"What happened to you?" Xavier asked. "Where have you been? What's going on out there? Did the king get his war after all? Can we still somehow get our revenge on the Order? I need to know everything."

Mateo said, "Come with me. We need to get you out of here before any more guards arrive."

As he finished unlocking the cell Mateo related the story of how he and his brother Matias, Xavier's other cousin, had escaped Natts' Nohoch Muulo'ob and managed to surreptitiously make their way back to the capital. He told Xavier about the Grand Conclave, Felix' ruin and Bianca's role in the whole sorry mess.

He added, "The king and the duke are no more, the war will not happen and no one knows who will be in charge of the kingdom. I don't see any way we can fulfill our vengeance on the Order. We need to escape to some other land to start over. Matias has seized an unmanned boat at the docks and the three of us can use it to get out of Vlogentia before your escape is discovered. Hurry."

Xavier assimilated Mateo's news. "Stop, Wait for a minute while I think." He paused just outside the cell for several seconds. "Our original plan to implicate the Order in a treasonous plot with the kulkulcano'ob is no longer possible. I have a better idea. We'll sail to the portal isle. The members of the Order won't be expecting trouble and we will be able to surprise and kill or imprison them. Don't you remember the destructive First World weapons we secreted when we were smuggling the medical supplies here? Those devices can kill hundreds at a time and destroy entire sections of the city. We stored them in case our original plan failed. Well, that has come to pass. The time for subtlety is over. We will bring those weapons to Second World and simply destroy the Order and kill as many of them as we can, and anyone who gets in our way. Then we can escape during the panic and confusion we create. "

"Won't that likely result in our destruction as well? We won't be able to fight everybody forever."

"No, we won't need to fight everybody. As I said, the devastation leveled by the First World weapons will shock everyone. They won't know what to do or how to respond. They will be so afraid and confused that they won't even notice when we make our departure."

Mateo thought for a bit and agreed, "Revenge for our family will be worth it. Let's go."

They hurried down the corridor of the prison and left by a side door and hurried to the docks where the boat Matias had commandeered was waiting for them. No one paid any attention to them since they were dressed in the robes of the Order. Once on board the boat they cast off and sailed westward toward the portal isle.

The boat was a single masted scow and they were sailing into the prevailing west wind, so they had to tack frequently. The voyage seemed interminable. That gave the three of them time to make plans. They finally decided that once ashore Xavier would go to the portal and start to bring the First World weapons to Second World. That might take many trips but he hoped the wagon he had secreted would still be there so he could pile on the boxes and crates and have to make only one or two trips.

Matias and Mateo would take care of anyone they met at the dock and then go to the dormitory and imprison or kill the rest. They expected that only four or five members would be stationed on the isle so the element of surprise should be sufficient for the two of them to secure the site and then go help Xavier.

Once the weapons were brought to Second World they would load them onto the boat and sail back to Vlogentia. Some of the weapons were shoulder mounted rocket launchers so Xavier thought they could stay aboard the boat and blast the headquarters of the Order and the palace from the water. Once that was done and the panic set in they could land and continue the mayhem if they so desired.

The voyage to portal isle finally ended. They tied up to the dock just before dawn. As Mateo was securing the boat two of the resident members of the Order approached them. Before they could even ask who the crew of the unexpected arrival were Matias leapt over the gunwales and killed them with his knife. Mateo raced to the dormitory to find any others.

While Matias and Mateo were taking care of the residents of the Second World isle, Xavier waited by the portal. His wand had been taken from him when he had been imprisoned so it was nearly impossible to travel between the two worlds. A fact he'd forgotten.

" *How stupid of me,*" he thought, "*I'd better be better organized or this sortie will degenerate into a mess.*"

He waited for his cousins to finish their tasks. Once they reunited with him he then had to send Matias back to the dock to retrieve a wand from one of the dead members.

"What happened to the members you found?" Xavier asked Mateo.

"I surprised them at dinner. As you know we are not members of the Order and cannot use the wands. So, I jumped them, knocked them unconscious, and tied them to their chairs. Nature will take its course, we won't have to worry about them anymore."

Xavier took the three of them to First World.

Once there they surprised and killed the three members stationed there and went to the shed marked 'For Use by the Grand Master Only. Prior Permission Required for Access'. That of course was a ruse employed be Xavier and Xander. Surprisingly, it had worked.

Xavier unlocked the padlock and they began to load the crates onto the wagon, trundled it to the portal's pit and used the winch attached to the wagon to lower the cargo into the pit. It took just two hours to move the weapons from the shed and position them back on the wagon next to the portal. The total mass of the cargo had to weigh at least two or so tons. Finally they were ready, Xavier brandished the wand, Mateo and Matias pushed the wagon forward and they were back in Second World.

Now all they needed to do was load the boat. Before they could get very far from the portal it started to pulsate rapidly and its color changed from a blue to a dark purple, then to a bright red. The hum increased in volume and pitch. A tremendous thunderstorm formed over the isle faster than any storm they had ever seen. The cloud grew from nothing to a great grey thunderhead reaching to the heights of the atmosphere in just seconds. But the storm formed only over the island. The rest of the sea and sky were calm and clear. The downburst gust of wind knocked them off their feet. The rain pelted down so hard they thought they might drown. Hail the size of small stones pummeled them. Lightning lit up the sky like a million or more Vlogentia lanterns. This was not natural.

Xavier forced himself to his feet and urged his cousins to do the same. It seemed imperative to him that they needed to get away from this unworldly storm as fast as possible. They started toward the boat again, cowering from the force of the rain and hail. They had only progressed a few yards when Xavier looked toward the pier.

Just when things couldn't be any worse, he saw a newly arrived sloop tied up to the dock and fighting the storm. On the deck were several people, one of which was a woman with white hair.

CHAPTER THIRTY
CHASE TO PORTAL ISLE

Pedro Marroquin's livery, capital city, Vlogentia, late evening
Gregorian calendar: January 23
Mayan calendars: Tzolk'in: 5 K'an
                  Haab: 17 Muwan

Corporal Juan Alajandro Gomez finally found Bianca, with her friends the Blankenships, playing with her cubs in Pedro Marroquin's livery. He had been searching for her for most of the afternoon and into the evening after learning of Xavier's escape and plan from the guard who overheard Xavier's conversation with his cousin.

Hours before, Juan had arrived to relieve the guards on duty at the prison and immediately sprang into action upon hearing of the escape.

"Take this man to a healer," he told his aide "and then inform the Colonel of Xavier's escape. There must be at least two other men aiding him. Tell the Colonel to send patrols to the shipyards to intercept the getaway. I also fear that Xavier may try to find Bianca and kill her before he escapes from Vlogentia. I will find and warn her."

With that he raced to his unicorn and began the hunt for his dearest companion.

When he found her and her friends he told them what he knew about the escape. "The guard told me that he had been wounded by Mateo. He played dead so they wouldn't finish him off. While lying in the hall near the cell he heard their revised plan for the destruction of the Order, and possibly all of Vlogentia. After Xavier and Mateo left the prison he managed to stagger to the officer of the day's post to warn of the escape. That's when I learned the horrible news."

Bianca was aghast. "By the evil of the old gods! By the light of a moonless night! May the wrath of Saint Sebastian rain down on Xavier! We've got to chase him down and stop him!"

Juan had never, in his entire life, heard Bianca swear before. Until that moment he didn't even think she knew how.

She sat down and took a deep breath. "Does this mean everything we've done has been a misguided waste of time? I thought that Felix and Ronaldo were the most evil Vlolgentia faced. Getting Felix to abdicate and stopping his foolhardy war was all I thought we had to do. Now you," facing Juan, "tell us that those accursed renegade brothers are a far worse threat. Will this nightmare never end?"

"That phrase sounds familiar to me," said Margaret, "I seem to remember saying the same thing once. I sympathize with you."

Juan sat down beside Bianca and put his arm around her to console her. "None of us had any idea of the brothers' ulterior motive. You did all you could to stop the war, and you succeeded. For that you should be proud. But now we must take action yet again."

"You are right, we have to pursue Xavier and stop him before he brings those weapons into Second World. We know where he's headed. I fear it will take the Colonel and the others too much time to organize a pursuit. If the officer of the day did not locate the Colonel quickly enough they might not be assembling the hunt even yet. We can't afford to wait to find out. There isn't time to waste. I heard that the sea raiders' sloop has returned. It's a fast ship. Let's get to that ship and catch him before he can put his plot into action!"

Before anyone could move, Margaret exclaimed, "It's worse than you think Juan. It's much more serious than I told you, Bianca. The portal itself is in more imminent danger than I realized!"

She started pacing back and forth, her hands waving frantically in front of her, her voice shrill and full of fear.

"I told Bianca earlier that if Xavier, or anybody, tries to transfer too much weight at one time the portals become unstable. But this sounds as if Xavier is now going to try to bring a very, very large cargo to Second World. So large that it may completely destabilize the portals so much so that they may not return to normalcy. We don't have time to warn the Order about the danger. Even worse, if the weapons he wants to bring here have electronic components the electro-magnetic interference between them and the field around the portals might make them even more unstable and lead to unimaginable catastrophe."

"What a bunch of unintelligible words. Why not say it's magic? " thought Juan. "He would not need to use his weapons to rain destruction on all of us," continued Margaret. "As I said, both portals could vanish in a flood of destruc-tion in both First and Second Worlds that you cannot imagine. We must get to him before he transfers those weapons."

Juan and the Blankenships sat for a few stunned and frightened seconds before Bianca leapt to her feet and exclaimed, "The consequences of delay are unthinkable. We must act now. Let's get going. Where's the sloop, Juan?"

The four of them, along with the cubs who refused to let Bianca and their new friends out of sight again, gathered what they could and hurried to the port. Along the way Bianca had an idea to help lighten the somber mood, especially Margaret's.

"Juan, Margaret has wanted to ride a unicorn since Natts' Nohoch Muulo'ob. Let her ride in front of you on your unicorn. Jason and I and the cubs will use the carriage. That way the law is obeyed since a guardsman will still be in control of his mount, but Margaret will finally get a chance to ride."

Juan agreed and offered his hand to Margaret and pulled her up in front of him. "Just sit in front of the saddle and hang onto his mane. Unicorns can be testy, but he knows and trusts me."

He put his arms around her to hold the reins and off they went.

Bianca was right, Margaret was delighted during the ride and the others actually found the sight amusing. They needed that small bit of levity to par-tially counter the sense of doom they felt.

Juan was right about the ship. The sloop was there when they arrived at the port. Bianca, Jason and Margaret boarded and stowed the limited amount of equipment they'd been able to find in their hurry. They all, even Margaret, had rapiers and daggers as well as Juan's crossbow. The sloop had a copious supply of rope which they hoped would prove useful. Juan cleared their departure with a harbor guard and arranged stabling for the unicorn and the carriage horse. He boarded and they set sail late in the evening and set out after Xavier.

Jason was pacing back and forth across the deck with quick and forceful steps. He worried that he might wear a path in the decking.

Margaret sat near the mast, unusually quiet for her. "I can't believe it. I'm so afraid I can't even get seasick."

Bianca stood at the prow of the sloop. She looked at Juan, "I'm trying to will us to the portal isle. Can't we go any faster?" she asked.

"We're making good time, don't fret. How are you feeling, I thought you're afraid of the water?"

"I'm not afraid, I just hate being on or in water, but I find that I hate Xavier more."

The ship actually was making good time across the inland sea. Juan knew that it was faster and could tack closer to the wind than the square-rigged scow that they'd learned Xavier had commandeered.

He told Bianca, "I figure we've gained about a half day on the fugitives. We left about a half day after Xavier. We should catch them in time."

"I fervently hope you're right."

They finally arrived at the isle. The scow was moored there, for how long Juan didn't know.

Just as they were tying up to the dock next to the scow a thunderstorm formed. Not a natural storm. This one developed out of nothing and grew upward into a massive dark storm cloud faster than a crossbow bolt could fly. The hurricane force gust of wind, torrential rain, hail and blinding flashes of lightning started almost immediately. It was worse than any storm he'd ever seen.

Through the downpour Juan made out three men with a heavily loaded wagon just a few yards before them on the path from the portal to the pier. It had to be Xavier and his cousins. On the dock lay two members of the Order. They didn't look good.

Margaret moaned. "Oh my god, they've done it. They've started the collapse of the portal."

Juan peered through the torrent at Xavier and his cousins as he tried to assess the situation.

"Those must be the weapons! We're not too late!" exclaimed Bianca.

"This storm is horrible, I can barely see. It's so much worse than the journals in the false gold village described," exclaimed Margaret. "What should we do? If they go back through the portal, it will kill us all!"

Nobody moved for what felt like an eternity.

Juan was the first to act. He unsheathed his sword. "We're wasting time. We need to act. We need to act now."

He leapt over the gunwale and charged the nearest cousin, pushing against the rain and the wind which were doing their best to impede his progress.

Jason and Margaret, without a second's hesitation, followed alongside him. They were yelling something incoherent as they unsheathed their swords.

Bianca, who had been standing in the prow of the ship, also vaulted onto the dock and joined the attack, pausing only to snatch a wand from one of the fallen members, and approached the other cousin. Her cubs followed her.

As they closed the gap Xavier turned and fled back toward the portal. The cousins stood their ground.

Bianca's man drew his sword and lunged toward her.

The cousin facing Juan and the Blankenships instead drew a strange looking device from his cloak and pointed it at them. Over the roar of the storm Juan heard a series of sharp noises as flashes of light erupted from the device.

"That must be a First World wand," he thought.

He felt a sudden sharp pain. He let out a surprised cry, staggered forward and collapsed in a heap.

CHAPTER THIRTY ONE

THE STORM OVER
THE PORTAL ISLE

Portal Isle, Second World, early morning
Gregorian calendar: January 29
Mayan calendars: Tzolk'in: 11 Ok
Haab: 3 Pax

Bianca saw Juan go down and for an instant her heart stopped beating. Then she heard him let out a low moan as he grasped his left leg and tried to stand. He fell again and stayed down. She desperately wanted to run to him, but Xavier was getting away. For a brief moment she was torn between competing emotions.

Jason cried, "Watch out, everybody get down. That's a First World weapon!"

Before he could say more the renegade used his device again. There were several more flashes from its tip.

"Xavier must have taught them how to shoot a sidearm," yelled Jason, "Bianca, get down, get down:"

Bianca heard several loud bangs over the roar of the storm and then felt whizzing, unseen things passing by her. She ignored Jason's warning.

She had realized what she had to do, Xavier had to be stopped at all costs. She continued her charge at her adversary.

The renegade to her left had tried to use the First World weapon again but this time there were no more flashes. He threw the gun at Jason and Margaret and started to draw his sword.

It was too late, he'd wasted time fooling with the contraption. They were upon him before he could wield the rapier and Jason thrust at him as Margaret swung at him in a hacking motion. They both connected and he went down, apparently mortally wounded.

Bianca closed with the other cousin who already had his rapier drawn and they crossed swords. He was adept with swordplay and fended off Bianca for a few parries.

He never had much of a chance, however. The cubs, sensing danger to their new pride mate, jumped him. He got off a quick thrust at the male cub, but the female sank her fearsome canines into his throat. He gurgled and collapsed like a burst balloon.

Bianca, now desperate to catch Xavier before he could get away, tore past the fallen man and followed Xavier along the path to the portal, stopping only to look at the carnage behind her before she continued her pursuit.

Both cousins lay dead and bloodied on the ground. Jason and Margaret stood motionless aghast at what they'd been forced to do. Juan let out a low moan. The male cub lay lifeless alongside the traitor as his littermate tried to rouse him.

As she turned to carry on her pursuit she saw Jason come to his senses and go over to Juan. Margaret still didn't move.

Bianca raced onward. She got to the portal just as he extended his wand and was beginning the approach that would take him to First World. Whether he was trying to escape or obtain more weapons she didn't know.

She could see him clearly. The deluge and lightning were worse and the torrential rain beat against her like she was being pummeled by small rocks. Her face stung with the fury of the onslaught. But the pulsating portal illuminated him with an eerie purple glow making him stand out from the dark background of trees like a specter from the underworld.

She screamed at him trying to be heard over the roar of thunder. "Stop you murderous coward. Stand and face your fate. Your crusade of hate is finished."

Xavier glared at her with hatred in his eyes, then turned to continue through the portal.

She rushed him with her rapier extended, aiming for his heart.

He dodged away from her thrust and away from the portal, faced her and propelled a blast of air toward her with his wand.

Bianca managed to evade the brunt of the attack, but lost hold of her rapier when his gust struck her outstretched hand. Her sword flew behind her, well out of reach.

She backed away a few feet and tried to fashion her own blast of air from the wand she'd picked up. But it wasn't one she'd become used to and she wasn't very adept at the use of wands in the first place. The storm didn't help. Xavier got a mild puff of air in the face.

He responded aiming another blast of air at her, powerful even through the sheet of rain and the gale force wind. Bianca saw as he raised his wand and leapt to the side just before his second, more powerful, gust blew apart the rain where she had just stood.

She brandished her wand again but this time tried a blinding light, something she was a little more familiar with. All she could produce was a wisp of light, not enough to discomfort Xavier.

He threw another bolt of air at her. She dodged yet again.

She attacked again. He counterattacked again. They went back and forth for several rounds, Bianca unable to generate enough force to take down Xavier but able to evade his counter attacks and keep him from getting to the portal due to her quickness.

That is until she slipped on a tuft of drenched grass, twisted her left ankle painfully, and failed to dodge in time to avoid Xavier's latest attack. The blast struck her full in the torso, knocked her flat and winded her.

As she lay on the ground Xavier walked around the portal to get within killing distance.

"You miserable spawn of the dark gods of the Maya. You have caused me unmentionable pain. You killed my brother. You stopped the puppet king from starting his war. A war my brother and I would use to get revenge for our father. You're even trying to stop this," gesturing toward where the wagon with the First World weapons sat, "final act of reckoning for both my father and brother. Now at least I'll get some slight satisfaction with your death. Then I'll destroy the Order and get my retribution after all."

He raised his wand. Bianca couldn't breathe, but her mind and her reflexes were just fine. She tore the dagger she kept strapped to her thigh free of its sheath and flung it with all her strength at his heart. The gale took it. She missed. It sank deep into his throat instead. Blood spurted from his throat and his mouth and spewed down his front as his thrashing caused the knife to fall from the gaping wound.

For the briefest of instances Xavier had a look of total surprise. He tried to let out a muffled gasp but nothing passed his lips as his eyes rolled up and he staggered lifeless backward. He fell into the influence of the portal. A brief flash and he was gone. A dead body transported to First World. It was over.

The tempest had continued unabated during their duel, but after Xavier's transport through the portal a sudden and immediate calm fell over the isle. The great storm cloud dissipated faster than it had developed. Except for the soaked ground, it was as if there had never been a storm at all. The portal no longer pulsated but gave off a steady blue light.

She thought it might be smaller than when she first saw it, but that was difficult to tell.

Bianca recovered her breath and rose and stumbled back to see what she might be able to do for her friends. She found them by the weapon laden wagon. Jason was tending to Juan. Margaret was kneeling by the dead cub and stroking the confused other cub.

"I couldn't see everything. What happened?" She asked.

Jason related the encounter and finished with, "Juan was wounded by the First World weapon. He has a wound in the left thigh, but the bullet, that's what we call the projectile from the First World weapon, passed completely through him. That's good. He's lost a lot of blood but I was able to stem the flow and I think nothing vital was hit. He will recover if I can get him more complete healing attention soon. For now he seems to be alright."

Bianca knelt by Juan. She looked at him, then at Jason. "He was injured by one of your terrible First World devices. You can't pretend that its magic isn't fatal no matter where it strikes. Is my Juan going to die?"

She was sobbing as she said the last.

"No, his wound is not fatal. It was not a magic weapon. I repeat, it was NOT a magic weapon. If I can get his leg cleaned and properly bandaged he will live. "

She let out a sigh of relief. "Are you truly sure? Juan will be alright?"

"Yes, I'm sure. As I said I could use some better bandages and some water to clean his wound, however."

"What about Xavier? What happened with him?" Jason asked. After a brief moment, he added, "Never mind, you're here, He is not. That tells me what I need to know for now."

Juan smiled weakly and tried to make light of his injury. "I'm going to be fine. It's only a leg injury and we know just how good a healer Jason is. You don't need to worry. We'll be strolling along the coast path by the palace in no time."

"Don't talk, save your strength for now. There'll lots of time to talk later," she said as she stroked his brow.

"I'm afraid one of your cubs is not alright," said Margaret. "He was killed by one of the cousins during the fight."

"I know." She stroked the female cub which had come to her side when she returned from the duel with Xavier. She stayed by Juan for a few heartbeats, holding his hand with her other hand.

Then she left him in Jason's care for the moment and hobbled to where the male cub lay. She picked him up cub cradled him in her arms. He'd died trying to protect her. Tears ran down her face although she made no sound. She gazed back at Juan and let out a barely audible sob and then regarded the sister, who'd now lost both her mother and her brother. The cub looked at her as if to ask if everything was going to be alright.

"No, love, I don't think anything will be alright ever again."

She led the cub back to Juan, knelt and held his hand.

Bianca was stunned as she looked around. So much death. So much hate. She wanted it all to stop here and now.

She knelt motionless for several moments, but was roused from her dark mood when Jason interrupted the silence.

He asked of no one in particular, "Isn't there a dormitory or something on this island? It was nighttime when Xander first brought us here but I thought I noticed something like a building on one side of the island. If it contains any healing supplies I need them to properly care for Juan's injury. I'm sure he will be grateful if one of you could find them."

Bianca stirred from her melancholy and replied, "Yes, I think there should be a house for the members somewhere nearby. If Margaret would be so kind as to search for it and find something to treat Juan I will be grateful. I would go look myself, anything to help my Juan, but I need to stay here with him and my ankle hurts so much that I'm afraid I can't do much more walking."

She looked at Juan and squeezed his hand again.

Margaret nodded agreement and rose and headed off to the south part of the isle. "I think the building was in this direction. I hope I that's where I remember seeing it during our first, frightening, visit."

After she left, Jason looked up while he treated Juan and asked Bianca, "Could you tell me a little more about Xavier, the storm, and what happened to you?"

She conveyed to him in as much detail as she could tolerate about their duel, Xavier's demise, the portal and the storm.

She ended with, "I think the portal is somehow back to normal, or almost so. I don't know why. I wasn't paying a great deal of attention when I first confronted Xavier, but I think it appears smaller than when our duel began. As for the storm, his being sucked into First World stopped whatever horrible magic was happening."

She stopped talking and looked at Juan and the cub and started sobbing.

Juan patted her hand. "I told you, I'm going to be fine."

Jason wanted to console her but couldn't find adequate words. All he could say was, "I'm sorry for all this."

Margaret had been gone for about only a few moments, although it felt like ages.

As she returned she said, "Look who I found."

CHAPTER THIRTY TWO
AFTER THE STORM

Portal Isle, Second World, afternoon
Gregorian calendar: January 29
Mayan calendars: Tzolk'in: 11 Ok
                  Haab: 3 Pax

Bianca looked up from Juan as Margaret repeated, "Look who I found, three members of the Order. They were tied up in the dormitory. Please meet Alexander, Ignacio and Vicente. After I freed them they told me that one of the cousins had surprised them, bound them to their chairs and left them to starve or die of thirst. But good news, they have lots of supplies to treat Juan."

The three members greeted everyone and profusely thanked Margaret for freeing them. They carried swaths of bandages, some jars of salve, supplies to close a wound and water to clean Juan's injury and immediately went to work assisting in his treatment.

Jason eagerly accepted the medical provisions and the aid of the members as they continued his ministrations.

While they were tending to Juan, Bianca held his head in her lap and wiped his forehead with a damp cloth. She didn't detect a fever as yet.

They had brought some ointment Vincente said would help prevent the wound from festering. The three had even had brought some of the Vlogentia suture that Bianca remembered had so impressed Jason in Natts' Nohoch Muulo'ob when he was tending her injury.

After a few moments Jason sat back. "I think that takes care of it. Juan, you should be healing well in a few weeks. For now you need bed rest. In a few days you can try a little movement, but not too much. It was a clean wound, but it needs time to heal completely."

Margaret knelt alongside Bianca again and put her arm around her. Neither said a word for a few moments.

Bianca finally looked up, satisfied that Juan was indeed on a path to recovery, and asked Margaret, "I suppose you want to know what happened to Xavier and the storm?"

"Yes, I do. Tell me if you can."

Once again Bianca related Xavier's fate. Somehow the second telling made it easier to accept that she'd killed yet again. She hated the act but realized just how necessary it had been. The storm was over, the portal seemed stable, and Xavier's threat to Vlogentia was over.

She felt a little justice for her wounded Juan and the poor cub. She finished with, "The portal is back to normal if what I've always been told is true. I did seem to me that it is just a bit smaller than before. Does that mean anything to you? You studied the journals from the false gold village. Did anything in those pages mention changes in the portal?"

"They related that a small storm would form whenever something heavy, like a boat, was brought from First World to Second World. But those storms were nowhere as severe as the one we experienced today, no more than a shower, and they always vanished right away. Xavier must have brought enough weight or something else to throw the portal into extreme instability. Whatever he had on him when he fell into the portal must have reversed the process. I have no idea what that might have been. I think I was correct in fearing the portal would have destroyed itself, along with the portal in First World, if the instability wasn't stopped. If he'd tried to bring more across, I'm certain disaster would have ensued. You did that, Bianca. You prevented horrible destruction in both worlds and kept the portal open"

"I have no idea why that happened. I was just fighting for my life and to stop him from bringing more weapons here."

"Nonetheless, you did it."

Now Jason came over to examine Bianca and join the conversation. He had finished cleaning up after treating Juan and left him in the care of the members of the Order.

He inspected Bianca's left ankle, proclaimed it no more than a sprain, and proceeded to wrap it while saying, "You did wonderful, Bianca. Margaret is right, I think you kept the portals from annihilation. Now we need to take these tools of death back to First World and somehow dispose of them."

"That's a horrible idea," said Margaret, "a very horrible idea. If bringing the weapons here caused this amount of instability in the portal, taking them back will be just as awful. We may not be able to reverse it again. The weapons stay here."

"Now that's just as bad an idea," said Jason. "Leaving these things lying around for some other villain to find simply cannot be allowed." He thought for a minute or so. "What if we take the weapons out of their cases, dismantle them as much as we can so as to expose their inner workings, and then drop them into the deepest part of the ocean we can find. Salt water is incredibly corrosive. The weapons will be rendered useless in almost no time."

"Not bad Mr. Blankenship," said Margaret. "I think that's the best solution."

"If you think that will destroy whatever those magical things are, then that's what we'll do," agreed Bianca. "But what if Xavier had or still has accomplices by the First World portal? That's where he was trying to go when I caught him. Why else would he do that? What do we do if they come here? How do we stop them?"

"I don't think we have to worry about that," said Ignacio. "The three of us here are well acquainted with the members stationed at the First World portal and I can swear that none of them would be disciples of that renegade. If there were any of his henchmen there, don't you think they would have come exploring when the portal's storm suddenly ceased? I know our counterparts would have. I know they should have. Nobody has passed the portal. That sadly tells me there may be no one left alive there."

"Perhaps you're right," said Bianca, "but we need to know for certain. Maybe Xavier was simply attempting flight. Can one or more of you pass through to First World and find out what transpired there?"

Now it was Jason's turn to enter the debate. "That is absolutely correct, we need to find out what happened there. I have done all I can do for Juan at this moment, so I volunteer to accompany one or two of the members there. Bianca, you and Margaret can stay and tend to Juan. I think all he needs now is rest and your company."

"No you don't, Mr. Blankenship," exclaimed Margaret. She stood and put her fists on her hips and got face to face with her husband. "You will do nothing of the sort. Chasing after rebels is not something I will allow."

"I'll have Alexander or Vicente or Ignacio with me. They know how to access the portal and they know the layout on the First World isle. Plus, I'll have this."

He held up one of the First World weapons for Bianca and all to see.

"You haven't ever used one of those things outside a firing range," argued his wife.

"What's a firing range?" asked Bianca, trying to quell the argument.

"Nevertheless," Jason argued back, "I know how to use it and we may need it if there are associates of Xavier still over there. If it looks too dangerous, we'll return immediately. But I agree with Ignacio. If anyone was left there, we'd know about it by now. Ignacio, are you and your companions ready?"

"We are."

"Good. Help me carry Juan to the dormitory and put him in a proper bed. You girls come stay with him and we'll report as soon as we learn what's going on there."

Both women bridled at his comment.

"We're not girls," they said almost in unison.

However, arguing further seemed of no use to Bianca. She could hardly walk, and Juan did need care.

Jason and the members fashioned a makeshift sling to carry Juan to the dormitory while Bianca limped alongside still holding his hand. Her cub followed her.

Margaret picked up the male cub and helped Bianca accompany the procession to the dormitory.

"What about the poor men lying there," she asked.

"We'll see to them once we return," said Alexander. "They'll be buried at sea."

"Along with the weapons," added Jason.

They found a well-appointed room on the first floor of the building and carefully placed Juan on the bed. Vincente fetched a bowl of water and some additional bandages for Juan should he need them.

Bianca and Margaret sat on either side of the bed. Juan didn't say anything, he was obviously exhausted from his ordeal and promptly fell asleep.

Jason told Bianca and Margaret as he and the members went out the door to the portal, "We'll be back as soon as possible."

That left them and the sleeping Juan and cub in a room by themselves wondering, and fearing, who might be coming back through the door, and when that would be.

CHAPTER THIRTY THREE
OLD FRIENDS AND NEWS

Portal Isle, Second World, late afternoon
Gregorian calendar: January 31
Mayan calendars: Tzolk'in: 13 Eb'
                     Haab: 5 Pax

Bianca spent the time waiting for the return of Jason and the members by alternately pacing around the room or sitting to hold Juan's hand and check his brow for a fever. So far he had none, which was a good sign.

Margaret copied Bianca, pacing when she sat and sitting when Bianca paced.

It felt like an eternity, but was only a short while before Jason, Ignacio and Vicente entered the room.

"Are you alright?" asked Margaret. She jumped up and ran to Jason to hug him. "What did you find? Are the portals in good condition? How are the members of the Order who are stationed on the isle in our world?"

"We discovered the body of Xavier," said Jason in between hugs from Margaret, "a few feet from the First World portal. He is dead. Your knife severed the artery in his neck, Bianca. We searched him and found his wand, which Alexander took. He also had a cell phone, of all things, that was turned on. Why he had that is a mystery to me. I left it on him. I was afraid that an activated electronic devise might be the trigger that caused the changes in the portal's status. If so, bringing it back here could be disastrous, besides being useless."

Bianca thought, *"I've been around Jason so much I'm getting used to his First World explanations for everything. He just can't accept that magic exists."*

"We searched the rest of the island and found the bodies of the members in their dormitory. They'd been strangled. There was also a shed that had been demolished by the storm where Xavier must have kept the stash of weapons. He'd disguised it as a repository exclusively for the use of the Grand Master. The rest of the island is just like the one here, sunny and bright and wet. So Alexander stayed there to man the station and Ignacio and Vincente came back with me to help inter the deceased and dispose of the weapons."

"I'm so glad you're well," said Margaret.

"So am I." Said Bianca. She turned to face the members of the Order. "And I'm sorry for the loss of your comrades, both here and there. The evil the renegade brothers brought upon Vlogentia and Second World cannot be forgotten. The Order must never allow such happenings again."

"I'm sorry for your losses as well," added Margaret.

"Thank you for your sympathy," said Vicente." We could not agree with your assessment more."

"Now we need to get to work here," interjected Jason. "There are men that need to be buried at sea. There are weapons that must be dismantled, disarmed or whatever we can do to them and disposed of at sea. Would the two of you"— pointing at the members—"accompany me to the wagon so we can get started?"

They exited the room en route to the wagon, leaving Bianca and Margaret with Juan once again. This time Bianca was far less worried, she no longer expected traitors to burst through the door and Juan was fully awake and in good spirits.

It was only a few moments before Jason rushed back into the room.

"There's a ship approaching the dock. I don't know if it's friend or foe."

"Does it fly a flag," asked Bianca. "If so is it a blue flag with three diagonal stripes and a star in the upper corner?"

"Yes, I think that's so"

"That's the flag of Vlogentia. They're friends. I should probably go greet them."

"Juan, are you alright if I see what this new arrival is about? It may be the Colonel or the Grand Master or anyone. I'll be right back, I promise."

"Go," he said, "I'm doing as well as can be expected. I feel fine except for the soreness in my leg. I'll be here waiting for your return."

"Thank you, dear." She gave him a quick kiss and followed Jason to the site of the battle.

Margaret stayed with Juan.

"I'll take care of him until you get back," she said as Bianca left the room.

Vincente and Ignacio were in the process of wrapping the corpses for burial at sea when Jason and Bianca joined them.

The brig *Vlogentia* approached the isle and tied up at the dock. Colonel Alanzo, ten guardsmen, the Grand Master of the Order and four other members of the Order debarked. The soldiers, fully expecting trouble, fanned out and started up the path with swords or crossbows at the ready. Jason went to meet them.

"Welcome to the portal island. I'm afraid you're a little late. As you can see we have eliminated the danger. Xavier and his men are dead, the First World weapons are in our possession and we were about to render them harmless."

"Just exactly what happened here?" queried the Colonel. "This morning we witnessed the most terrifying storm while we were still miles from the isle. Then it suddenly disappeared as if it had never existed. We feared the worst, for you and for what Xavier was attempting. Are you alright? You say Xavier is dead. How did that happen? Are the weapons, or whatever they are, still dangerous?"

"Are you alright, princess?" The Colonel turned to address her. He seemed confused, worried and not just a little frightened.

The Grand Master added, "What about the portal? Does it still exist? We need to know a lot more than you've 'eliminated the danger.'"

Bianca understood their fear and concerns. Sweat beaded on the brows of the newcomers, their pupils were so dilated she could see them from where she stood. Some of the soldiers were trembling, the members of the Order were nervously fidgeting with their wands and rocking side to side and the Colonel and Grand Master were now attempting to appear stern and resolute, without success.

"I meant what I said, everything has returned to normal." Jason related the events of the day, assured them Xavier was truly gone and the danger to the portal and Vlogentia was over.

He finished with, "Bianca is well, in fact there she stands"—he pointed to her—"in fine health. As I said, she is the one who slew Xavier. Juan was seriously injured by a First World weapon that fires small metal projectiles, but is recovering in the dormitory over there." He indicated the general direction of the dormitory.

"We were just starting to prepare the two conspirators and your deceased members for burial at sea and to take apart the weapons so we could drop them in the ocean. That should insure that they'll never be found, but if that unlikely event happens the sea will have corroded them into uselessness. Those arms will be no longer be a threat to Vlogentia."

"Xavier brought weapons that use fire? Was he crazy? He could start a firestorm that would engulf the isle, not to mention what would happen if he used them on the mainland," exclaimed the Colonel.

Bianca knew that the thought of weapons that used fire was anathema to everyone in Second World.

She moved forward to stand beside Jason and said, "I don't know if Xavier was crazy or just so consumed by his desire for vengeance that he didn't care. All I know is that he is no longer a threat and Jason assures me the armaments will be destroyed."

Jason added, "I don't think a pistol, that's what we call the weapon he used, puts our enough heat to start a fire but the rain was so violent that there was no possibility of a conflagration in any event. It will be destroyed along with the rest of the arms."

The Grand Master wanted to know, "What happened on the First World isle? Are there more weapons there?"

"Jason and three members from here that weren't slain have been to the First World isle," said Bianca. "They found more slain members there, but no more weapons or traitors. One of your men stayed there until you can send relief. As Jason said, the danger is over."

Jason added, "Since you are here with additional help, why don't you have some of your men help finish preparing the burials at sea and I'll show the others how to dismantle the weapons so the sea water will destroy them. Then I'll take you to Corporal Gomez."

"Very well, I will accept your suggestions. But I must see how Corporal Gomez is recovering and speak with Her Highness privately as soon as possible."

The Colonel was recovering his composure and Bianca thought he wanted Jason to realize just who was in charge.

As the soldiers got busy with the dead and the weapons Jason whispered to Bianca, "I got the hint the Colonel wants me to use more formal terms of address, both to him and to you, but I'm sure I'm going to play along. I think the he is something of a stuffed shirt and I'll bet Margaret agrees with me."

Bianca pretended not to notice but whispered back, "You're right."

Once the bodies were ready and the guardsmen had been shown how to disable the weapons and load everything onto the brig, Jason led Colonel Alanzo and the Grand Master with his acolytes to the dormitory. Bianca walked alongside the two officials followed by Ignacio and Vicente and the other members of the Order.

As the Colonel marched into the room, followed by the rest, Juan was able to sit up and present a passable salute given his infirmity. Margaret sat beside him. Bianca's cub slept at her feet.

"Greetings. May you have a fortunate blend of days," said the Colonel. "I need a report from you as soon as possible."

He then faced Bianca. "Your Highness, may I speak with you in private?"

"Of course, Colonel. Please follow me." She led him into an adjacent room. "What can I do for you?"

"I have important news for you. The Grand Conclave has elected, despite your obvious intent, to name you queen of Vlogentia."

"I'm not sure I appreciate the honor," she replied. "Are they sure that is the correct and proper decision? What makes them think I can be the ruler they want me to be?"

She took one step back and crossed her arms in front of her.

"You are far more capable than you realize. You have the strength of will and determination to lead. You know and care for the populace. They know and care for you. I think you will surprise yourself just how able a ruler you will be."

She wanted to argue some more, but realized that would be fruitless. It might be better if she spoke with the delegates of the Conclave directly. Bianca pretended to accede to his wishes. "If that is what you and the kingdom feel is best, than I will try my best to be the ruler they deserve."

"Thank you, Your Highness." He bowed.

They returned to the main room. Bianca excused herself from the Colonel, who went to speak with Juan.

She joined the conversation the Grand Master was having with Jason and Margaret.

He was telling them, "The two of you have acted valiantly and with great service to Vlogentia. I realize that your stay here was nothing like you were promised or anticipated and I apologize for the dangers and fear you have experienced. There isn't much I or any of us can do to atone for that. I can, however, promise a safe journey back to First World. I will have one of my acolytes take you through the portal tomorrow morning and ensure you a safe journey to your home. Would that meet with your approval?"

"Oh, yes. That would be perfect," said Margaret and Jason together. Jason was grinning from ear to ear and Margaret clapping her hands together in joy. "What do we need to do to prepare?" she asked.

"Nothing for now. Just be ready to travel in the morning. Get some rest for now."

Jason and Margaret sat on a small sofa next to the room's wardrobe and embraced. "We're going home in one piece after all," said Margaret. She put her head on Jason's shoulder and started to cry softly.

The Grand Master and the members of the Order stood in a corner in deep discussion. They appeared concerned.

Bianca sat back down beside Juan Alejandro and reached out to hold his hand. He squeezed it and gave her a reassuring gaze.

The Colonel had a self-satisfied grin on his face as he strode to another chair and sat in his most important pose to wait for the guardsmen to report.

A short while later the guardsmen entered the dormitory and reported all was ready for the voyage back to Vlogentia. The weapons were dismantled according to Jason's instructions and ready to be dumped into the deepest part of the ocean they could find. The four bodies were also ready for disposal.

The Colonel signaled approval and sent them back to spend the night on the brig. He then strode over to the Grand Master and spoke with him for several minutes before retiring to the brig as well.

The Grand Master related his decisions to everyone in the room. "Tomorrow I will arrange for the Blankenships to return to their home, with our total gratitude. Several of the members will stay and station both isles. The rest of us will take the sloop back to Vlogentia where I understand your highness has some business to attend to."

"Apparently so. I suppose I'm ready to try," said Bianca.

Juan laid back in his bed and let out a satisfied sigh. "You will be a great queen."

The members hurried around preparing for their posting to the portals.

Jason and Margaret were so elated all they could do was hold hands.

Bianca went to Juan and sat by his side, watching the frenetic activity. She hoped the next day would be joyous for her two friends. She hoped the trip home to Vlogentia meant the beginning of the end of her travails. All that is except for a conversation with the Conclave and whatever would come of that.

CHAPTER THIRTY FOUR

JASON AND MARGARET RETURN HOME

Portal Isle, Second World, morning
Gregorian calendar: January 30
Mayan calendars: Tzolk'in: 12 Chuwen
Haab: 4 Pax

J ason and Margaret enjoyed the best night of sleep since arriving in Second
World. The memories of the past month's traumas paled in comparison to
one fact: they were going home.

They rose early and prepared to travel. Their luggage they'd brought with
them from Miami had been found in the closet on the First World cruiser and
brought to their room in the dormitory so they were able to dress in their Florida
apparel. There wasn't much else to do, just clean and wait for their escorts.

A knock on the door revealed two members of the Order, a man and a
woman, who asked, "Are you ready?"

"We are," answered Jason.

Bianca met them one last time as the members started to escort them out
of their room.

"Once again, be safe and may God lead you down a righteous path. Farewell."

She hugged both of them and they hugged her back, waved farewell to Juan as they passed his room and petted the cub one last time. It was surprisingly emotional for all of them. .

One of the escorts, who called himself Pablo, asked, "Would you like breakfast or hot chocolate before we leave?"

"Just a cup of that excellent chocolate to take with us, if you don't mind. We just want to get on our way," answered Jason,

They sipped their drinks as they followed the pair of members to the portal in the clearing. Once again they found themselves holding hands as Pablo walked them close to the glowing orb. Jason felt the weird sensations again, just like the previous day. Then they were standing in the underground chamber they'd been in more than four weeks previously. They were back in First World.

"We're here, we're really here. I almost can't believe it," said Margaret.

Jason looked around the chamber, at the alien-looking orb and at the ladder to the outside and said, "Well, I can believe it. and I can't wait to get out of here and back to Miami. Let's go."

Margaret scrambled up the ladder followed by Jason before Pablo could even start to move and raced as fast as the wet path would permit to the dock where the cruiser waited for them. Pablo brought up the rear at a more sedate pace.

Everything appeared almost too serene to Jason. Except for the occasional puddle there was no indication that a violent storm had inundated the island the day before. It was almost too much to believe. Their adventure was nearly over and his relief was palpable.

Back on board the cruiser, the journey to Key West couldn't go fast enough. Jason kept asking, "When will we get there?"

He felt like when he was a child riding in the back seat of the car when his parents took him on a road trip. The journey was exciting, but not as exciting as getting to the destination.

Pablo steered the boat and said, "Our trip will take the same amount of time as your last voyage. Relax and enjoy the trip."

The Caribbean was a little rougher than the journey to Portal Isle but not too bad. This time Margaret stayed on deck and apparently enjoyed the trip. She no longer exhibited seasickness.

They were just about to dock in the marina in Key West when Pablo offered them a last meal from Second World. They really weren't hungry but felt obligated to eat a little in celebration.

Jason felt mentally disoriented for a few minutes after the snack but then regained normal equilibrium. He attributed the discomfort to the food and the motion of the boat. Margaret, he noted, felt the same.

Once tied up at the dock they got off the cruiser and the crewman, dressed in an odd looking greyish robe, brought their luggage. "I hope you enjoyed your vacation to our little out of the way island. We were honored you chose to spend your leisure time with us and hope to see you again."

Jason said, "We had a very relaxing and fun visit doing almost nothing but relaxing on the beach and drinking rum cocktails. We most certainly will be back." He meant and believed what he said, but somehow it didn't feel quite right.

They picked up their luggage and headed for the taxi stand to take them to the airport. The instant they entered the cab Jason turned to Margaret and said, "I can't believe I've already forgotten the name of the boat we were on. Do you remember it?

"No, as a matter of fact I can't. It isn't important, anyway."

The cabbie turned in his seat and spoke to Jason. "Welcome to Key West. What have you been up to and where have you been? Did you have a good vacation?"

Jason answered him, "We took an exclusive charter to a pleasant, out of the way isle for a four week vacation. It was great. We got lots of beach time and swam in the ocean and had a nice, peaceful getaway."

That's what he believed, although a nagging unanswered question hovered in the back of his mind.

They purchased tickets to Miami at the airport, spent the night at a local Key West inn, and flew to the Miami airport on Friday.

The trip to their house was the usual traffic snarl with everyone eager to start the weekend. The ride seemed dreary and confining inside the cab, not at all the way he ought to feel after a month's vacation. He noticed that the air felt somehow staler and less much less invigorating than it should have. "*The disadvantage of living in the city,*" he thought.

Finally the cabbie dropped them off at home. That, at least, felt right to Jason.

As they were unpacking someone rang the doorbell.

He introduced himself, "Good morning." It didn't sound as if he meant it at all. "I am detective Sean O'Connell of the Miami police. Mrs. Blankenship we received a call from your law office a few days ago. They said you hadn't been in touch with them for several weeks. Your secretary insisted that isn't at all like you and your staff are worried. We've been searching for you for days, and today

I get a phone call from your neighbor telling me that you showed up today as if nothing has happened. Could you explain why?"

He sounded angry. His voice was loud and raspy, his eyes darted back and forth and he was noticeably jumpy. He stepped back out of reach and kept his hands in a distinctly defensive position close to where Jason assumed he kept his sidearm.

Jason reacted quickly but tried to sound calm to defuse any possible confrontation. "We're so sorry. We simply took an extended vacation and lost track of the time. Also our cell phones didn't work on the little island resort we stayed at. So, we had no incoming or outgoing phone calls. We were having such a good time that we neglected to call in. Please accept our apologies."

Once again he fully believed what he was saying about their absence.

"Can we do anything to make amends?" said Margaret. She seemed a little anxious due to the detective's behavior.

"No, I guess not," he replied with a sour note to his voice. "But don't do anything like this again. You had a lot of people worried and looking for you. You better call your people and let them know you're alright." He left, still very visibly annoyed.

Margaret said, "I'll call my secretary and fill her in. I bet I get an earful. At least you had some accrued vacation time. We'll have to show them pictures of our trip to mollify everyone." She got on the phone.

Meanwhile Jason started to unpack. Much to his dismay he found their cameras in the back of the suitcases, obviously unused.

"We never took any pictures. How can we show them what we did?"

Margaret shrugged as she dialed her office. "They'll just have to take our word for it."

Jason finished unpacking. Along with their usual clothes and personal items were two grey robes with bright blue trim. He didn't remember ever wearing them or even ever seeing them before, but they must have been part of the resort's all-inclusive vacation package. He decided to keep them as souvenirs and hung them in the back of the closet.

After Margaret finished calming and reassuring her secretary, she decided to boil some hot chocolate instead of coffee.

"I just felt like making something different today. Hope you like it."

She brought the mugs onto their veranda and the two of them spent the rest of the day relaxing. Margaret took a sip of her brew and remarked, "This is okay chocolate, but I seem to remember having some that tasted better. But not when or where that was. Isn't that odd?"

"You're right. This isn't quite as good, but I don't remember the details either. That really is odd. Oh well, it's no matter."

That Monday they went back to work. Everything was back to normal.

Two weeks later a package arrived at their door via UPS. There was no return address. Jason picked it up and carried it inside the house. The package was unusual, it was long and very light.

Margaret came over and asked, "What is that?"

He opened it and found a feather. It was deep blue on the surface and a lighter blue-grey on the underside. What was remarkable was the size, it was at least five feet long and more than eighteen inches wide. Inside the package was a note.

It said, *"This was delivered to me after you left. I thought you might appreciate it. Your friend, Bianca."*

"I don't remember anyone named Bianca, do you?" asked Margaret.

"No," he replied, "and I don't remember seeing a bird this big. We must have had an awful lot of rum cocktails to forget a peacock of that size. Well, chalk it up to a great and well-earned vacation,"

He hung the feather over the mantel and promptly forgot about it.

Life in Miami went on as usual.

CHAPTER THIRTY FIVE

RETURN FROM PORTAL ISLE

Portal Isle, Second World, morning
Gregorian calendar: January 30
Mayan calendars: Tzolk'in: 12 Chuwen
Haab: 4 Pax

Bianca watched her new friends leave with the two members of the Order. She stood by their doorway like a statue for a few moments thinking about them and their trials and adventures together, from the day she awoke in the carriage facing two strange, shackled, people to the final confrontation with Xavier. So much had happened and she knew she'd never be the same pitz-playing girl of a month ago.

Finally she put her hands together and wrung them as if washing the blood of Xander, Ill'yx, the mountain trolls and Xavier from them and then turned and returned to Juan's bedside.

He was sitting up in his bed and wearing a robe of the Order since Jason had cut up his guard attire when first examining and binding his wound. His left leg was wrapped from hip to knee with a clean dressing and propped up with four or five pillows. He was eating a tamale with considerable gusto and drinking water. He appeared in good spirits and Bianca believed he would heal completely, much to her enormous relief. She wasn't sure she could face the Conclave without him by her side.

She asked him, "How are you feeling? You are looking well on the way to a full recovery."

"I'm getting better, although my leg does hurt quite a bit. Before he left Jason told me how to care for it and what to do to speed my cure. I think I was right, I'll be back to my usual self in almost no time."

Bianca sat next to him and caressed him on the shoulder. "I believe you're right."

While she was administering to Juan, the Grand Master entered the room. "How is he doing, Your Highness?"

Juan looked at Bianca. "He knows I'm awake, doesn't he?"

She patted him on the arm. "Of course, dear, but I think he wishes to address me for the moment."

She turned back to the Grand Master. "He's doing very well. Jason is an excellent healer and we expect a full recovery in time." She was going to have to get used to being addressed as such. That also would take time.

"If you don't mind and have a moment I would like to speak with you about your experience near the portal during the tempest. Also, what did Mrs. Blankenship tell you about the threat to the portal? I gathered from your conversation last night that there is something I should know."

"There most certainly is." Bianca related all that Margaret had said about the journals the expedition found in the village of false gold. She related what Margaret had told her about the battle with the forest trolls and how Margaret learned about the trolls' relationship with the banished ones. She told how the portals become unstable, shrink in size and create storms if too much weight is transferred at one time. She described the unusual color and the pulsation of the portal during the storm. She ended with the cessation of the storm with Xavier's transferal to First World. She finished with, "I think the Order needs a much greater level of protection for the portals. We, that is all of Second World, cannot let this happen again."

"Yes, I think you are right. We had no idea about the fragility of the portals. The history of the renegade sect was lost to us due to their banishment by Saint Sebastian. We will have to retrieve those journals, make peace with the forest trolls and increase security for the portals. I have already spoken to Colonel Alanzo about that. He will organize an expedition to the lost village, contact his counterparts in the other realms and arrange for more protection on both isles."

"Thank you, your highness, for all you have learned and all you have accomplished. That said, I still feel you need considerable instruction in the ways of the Order and the use of wands. Once back in the capital, please visit me so I can make such arrangements."

"I will, as time permits."

With that he rose from his seat, bowed and left the room.

Bianca stayed seated beside Juan. "Don't worry, he's not usually that curt. He's worried about the portal and what Xavier may have done to it."

Later that afternoon Bianca, Juan, the Grand Master, the Colonel and some of the guardsmen boarded the sloop to sail back to the capital. The remaining members of the Order and the rest of the guardsmen were left to protect both portals. The wind was with them, the sea was as smooth as glass as if it realized a peril was past and all was well. They made fast work of the trip home and docked at the port late in the afternoon.

After the ship tied up at the dock Bianca instructed three of the guardsmen to take Juan to the healer's room in the palace.

"I want to bury my poor cub in the grasses of his home," she told him. "Will you be alright for a while, or would you rather come with me?"

"I'll be fine at the healer's room for now. Take care of him and I'll see you soon."

She arranged for a carriage to take her and her cubs to Pedro Marroquin's livery. The others went to their barracks or headquarters.

Before he departed the Grand Master reminded her, "Don't forget to come and see me as soon as you can."

"I said I would. Please excuse me, I have an important chore to attend to."

He nodded understanding. "Just reminding you, Your Highness."

The hired carriage sped through the cobblestone streets to Pedro's livery. Bianca wanted and appreciated the hurry, but the ride threatened to chip some teeth and break some bones. Her female cub spent the entire trip whimpering and trying to curl up in Bianca's lap, a difficult task considering her increasing size. They arrived in one piece after all.

She met Pedro as he exited the stable. "A lucky blend of days to you. I need your help. I have to bury one of my cubs and I want to put him to rest in the grassland behind your barn." She had to take the time to relate how and why he'd died and all the rest of the events on the portal isle.

"I'm sorry to hear about your cub. I know how much you cared for them. You've endured so much but I'm glad that you're well and all is good with the kingdom. Come with me."

They walked a few yards from the back of the barn and buried the cub in the ground beneath fresh grass. Bianca decided not to leave any marker, she just wanted to return him to his rightful home. She knelt for a minute by the grave. The female cub sat quietly beside her.

Afterwards she and Pedro, with the female trailing, walked back to the carriage. She ordered the carriage to the palace but at a slower pace this time. Once there she made sure Juan was comfortable and still healing well, gave him a goodnight kiss on the forehead and then retired for the night with the cub at the foot of her bed.

She rose early the next morning planning to visit the Grand Master after attending Mass in the palace chapel. She checked to make sure Juan was still doing well, left the cub with him and exited the palace by a side door and the side gate, wearing a hooded cloak hoping to avoid a large crowd.

The day was fine with a crystal clear sky as blue as her eyes and a warm brisk west wind. It was going to be a good day, she thought. But as she exited the gate she encountered the crowd of city folk she'd hoped to avoid. They instantly recognized her in spite of the cloak and crowded around her demanding to know the truth about the rumors of the king's abdication and how she was involved. She at first tried to deflect the questions but finally had to relate her version of events. Just as she was finishing her tale the morning sun was blocked by three great shadows rushing overhead. Everyone immediately looked up and recoiled in alarm.

Gliding in for a landing as silent as a secret were three kulkulcano'ob. They soared over the palace and the Order's headquarters, banked to the left and started to descend. They appeared to be heading for a spot just outside the residential areas of the city to the east, along the sacbe.

Bianca excused herself from the throng and sped toward them. Along the way she tried to reassure everyone she could find that the arrivals were friendly. "Tell all you meet the kulkulcano'ob mean us no harm. They are our allies, the king's lies were meant to start an unnecessary war. There is no danger. They are our friends".

The crowd reacted with the expected panic combined with curiosity.

Bianca ran as fast as she could to meet the flight, but it was a long way and the crowd impeded her progress. It took nearly an hour for her to reach them. The kulkulcano'ob had landed just outside the city.

When Bianca finally got to the landing site she saw the three arrivals patiently sitting with their wings folded along their sides. Waiting for her, she surmised. They merely looked at the assembled throng, which looked back curiously but from what Bianca surmised they hoped was a safe distance.

Finally she got to the touchdown area. She was winded and couldn't speak for a moment. The crowd stood stock still and marveled as Bianca approached the nearest kulkulcan. He raised his feathered crest as she approached.

"Greetings, little one, "said Ill'yonix, "the wind from the west is strong today, so I thought it would be possible to fly to your big settlement to learn what had become of you and what happened to the evil small talkative creature you caught. We were concerned at first when we didn't see you with your white crest. That's the only way we can tell you from all other small talkative creatures since they look the same to us. But we decided to wait for news about you. Obviously you are here now, so may I assume your return voyage was successful?"

"It was," she answered, "but then we had still more trouble from him." She then tried to tell Ill'yonix all that had happened since they had last met. Most of it appeared to be of no consequence to him, but he listened politely. Until she told of the portal and the storm.

"We saw the storm from the peaks of our mountains. It struck us as very strange and we wondered if it had anything to do with the odd ball of fire of our ancient myths. Does such a thing truly exist? "

"It does. There was a danger it might disappear or something worse. But all is safe now. You knew of the portal?"

"Only in legends handed down for innumerable generations, and we live for a very long time. Perhaps it is just as well we didn't know of the peril. What else is there?"

"Nothing more. How goes the alliance between the border villages and your clan?"

"We are doing very well, thank you. Your small talkative creatures have constructed several walls around our lairs and have even helped defend us from some troll attacks. Our flying patrols have spotted three additional attempted raids by the trolls and our warnings have foiled the attacks. The trolls should not cause much trouble from now on."

"As a display of our thanks for what you have done for us, we have brought you a gift. Here are two flight feathers from the wings of Ill'yx to symbolize our bond and recognize your bravery."

One of the other kulkulcano'ob handed her the feathers he'd been carrying with his forelegs. "Now, if all is well with you and your fellow small talkative creatures, we need to get back in the air before the west winds abate. Stay well, little one, soar with the morning breeze and we shall meet again soon."

"Thank you. I look forward to future meetings. For now, fly safe and high to the mountains."

The great beasts leapt into the air, unfurled their wings with the usual downburst of air and headed east toward their home. Bianca turned to the assembled crowd of city inhabitants and tried to explain to as many as she could why the kulkulcano'ob were visiting the city, and that more visits in the future were likely. She asked those who heard her to tell others that people and kulkulcano'ob now were allies.

Bianca heard the nearby crowd start to spread the news of her involvement in King Felix' abdication and the pact with the kulkulcano'ob throughout the city. She realized she was fast becoming a celebrity. It was obvious from their demeanor and conversations that folks who knew her would no longer think of her as just a playful royal, she was becoming a hero. That, of course, was not what she wanted.

She made it back to the palace in good time despite the multitude, the feathers securely and safely in her grasp. One feather was given to a messenger with orders to wrap it and make sure it would be sent to Jason and Margaret at their home in First World. She even added a brief note, in hopes they might remember her. From what she had been learned about the Order, that wasn't likely but she hoped for the best.

The day wasn't starting out the way she had planned. Her visit to the Grand Master would have to wait.

So, she decided she that now would be the time to confront Rolando and tell him that he would be joining Felix and the rest of their conspirators and where that would be. So she went to the jail's healing room where Ronaldo was being kept. That conversation wasn't very going to be pleasant.

As she entered his healing room/cell he shouted from his bed, "You meddling little fool! Vlogentia would have been rich and powerful if you'd left well enough alone. Now I am a cripple and ruined royal. Things could not be worse."

"You mean you think you would have been rich, powerful and famed. You never truly cared about the fate of Vlogentia or its people. Had I wished you might also have been slain, but I did not want to do any more killing. Besides, what about all the citizens of Vlogentia that would be killed or maimed as a result of your scheming? Did you ever consider them? What about my friend, Daniela, and her family?"

"Your friend and her family? Pah! They were peasants. Don't you understand, that's what peasants are for? They serve their purpose and then we can forget about them. Your silly friend had completed her usefulness and I had her taken care of before she caused any problems. There are all sorts of other peons you could make friends with, what's your point?"

Bianca couldn't contain her disgust any longer. She slapped the duke hard across his face, reopening the wound on his right cheek.

"She was my friend. Now I am glad I didn't kill you. You'll get to live as a broken and maimed man for the rest of your life. Enjoy your exile on the isle of 'New Byzantium.'"

She stormed out of the room, crying. She hated that man, but she also didn't like the person she thought she was becoming. Being controlled by anger and hate was not how she wanted to be. For the umpteenth time she wondered why she couldn't go back to being the girl who took such joy in winning a game of pitz? As she left the prison she ordered the guard to have Ronaldo transferred to the new 'Empire of New Byzantium.' She was so upset that she didn't notice how easily she gave the order.

Back at the palace she vented her fury to Juan.

He tried to console her. "I'm feeling so much better. I think I can walk a fair distance if I am careful and deliberate and use a cane. I may need to rely on you as well. So, let's go to Joaquin's restaurant. You always enjoyed the people there. A visit might cheer you."

"You may be right. Yes, let's go."

They left the cub in Bianca's room, closed the door to prevent it from following them and strolled out the front gate of the palace. This time the crowd let them pass quietly.

They took a measured pace to Joaquin's place. Juan was traveling surprisingly well, much to Bianca's delight. She walked with her head down still furious with Rolando. The crowd appeared glad she was walking through the city.

Once they arrived at the cafe Joaquin rushed to her and gave her a big hug. "We were so worried about you after you disappeared. When we saw you thirteen days ago confronting the king we were elated. You were alive and, even better, telling him what he should have known all along. All of us were relieved and proud. Come, sit down. Some of your other friends are here. He seated her at her usual table. Julieta and Renata sat down and expressed their relief at her safe return and their pride of her scolding of the king.

Julieta said, "We didn't know what happened to you and to Daniela. And then you show up out of nowhere and proceed to scold the king in front of the entire populace. It was wonderful. We thought you didn't care about politics or ruling a kingdom. Tell us what happened."

Bianca gave a brief account of her travails. She didn't want to go into the full, sad story again. She said, "I could no longer stand back and watch my step-brother destroy Vlogentia." She had to take a moment before continuing. "I'm sorry, but Daniela and her family are dead. They were killed by Duke Ronaldo after he forced her to arrange my kidnapping."

"Oh, no. Not Daniela. Not poor Daniela," wailed Renata. "Where is the Duke and what will you do about him? What punishment will be leveled on him? He deserves death!"

"He is crippled, ruined financially and broken in will and spirit. He will go into exile with Felix. He is no longer a threat to us and will serve a lifetime of pain and agony for his crimes." Again, she wasn't sure she liked being so vengeful. "Please, enough of this. I need some happy news. Tell me about yourselves and the pitz games."

There wasn't a lot to relate, but Julieta and Renata appeared to understand Bianca's mood and did their best to cheer her. The four of them, along with Joaquin, spent the rest of the day trying to relive happier times. They talked until it was time for Joaquin to close the restaurant. Bianca hugged all her friends and Juan carefully walked her back to her room in the palace.

He was looking and acting more and more like the Juan she'd known since childhood and the man she'd come to admire and adore.

He kissed her and said, "I'll see you again tomorrow. Get some rest and try to move forward with your life."

He returned to his room with only the slightest of limps.

Bianca closed the door and sat on her bed with conflicting emotions boiling inside her.

"I'm afraid I won't be a good queen, if that's what is in store for me. I don't like the anger that simmers inside me from time to time. I didn't like having to kill. I just want a quiet, peaceful life."

She sat for a long time before cuddling her cub and crying herself to sleep.

Early the next morning she was wakened by a knock on her door. She thought it would be a messenger from the Grand Master requesting her presence for the meeting he wanted. Instead it was a palace page.

"Good morning, your highness. The leaders of the Grand Conclave and His Holiness would like for you to attend their morning conference. Pease follow me." It almost sounded like a command.

She dressed hurriedly, insisted on leaving her cub with Juan and then followed the page. This was going to be a meeting not of her liking.

As she entered the Great Hall His Holiness, looking a little bedraggled after many days of negotiations rose to greet her. The rest of the delegates were in their chairs and stood as she walked down the aisle to greet the Vice Pope.

She curtsied to him before she climbed the steps and turned to face the hall. He said, "Please take a seat on the throne."

Now she was sure what was coming. The Colonel had informed her of the Conclave's decision, but that had been just news. This was reality.

"The Conclave have spent the past two weeks considering your advice, and then waiting to see if you would return from the portal isle, and fearing that you might not. But that has not changed our resolve. We have decided that we want you, in fact we need you, to be our queen."

Bianca looked over the faces of the delegates. Their visages indicated the Vice Pope indeed spoke their unanimous decision.

"You have proven yourself several times over. You have shown great courage, resourcefulness and the ability to lead. Do not doubt your talents, you will make a fine ruler and we look forward to many years with you governing our kingdom. This is what we all desire. If you do not accept this charge, we have no idea what to do or where to look for leadership. We have always had a king or queen stretching back to well before the Spanish arrival and don't wish to experiment with other forms of government at this time of crisis. You will provide the stability and leadership Volgentia needs. "

Bianca had thought about this moment ever since her conversation with the Colonel. She looked at the faces of the delegates and realized what must be accepted. If she had to become queen she would make some demands of her own.

"If I accept this honor I must insist on some changes in the way we administer Vlogentia."

"But your highness…" began the Vice Pope.

"Please, your holiness, let me finish. I think you will like what I'm about to say."

She turned back to the delegates. "A monarch can rule well only if given good counsel and information. Therefore, I propose that on the first day of every month of the Haab calendar, with the exception of the short 'month' of Wayeb of course, a Lesser Conclave be assembled. It will consist of three delegates chosen from each of twenty of our villages. They will meet here and discuss their concerns with me and my ministers. It will be my task, and the task of the royal council, to listen to them and try to address or alleviate their problems. Each successive Lesser Conclave will have representatives from twenty different villages until all the villages have been heard. Then the process will repeat, but with the requirement that new delegates be chosen each time a village attends a Lesser Conclave. There must be no repeat of the village's delegates. I must insist on this new arrangement for the monarchy or I will not accept."

His Holiness looked at her, then at the delegates. Their relief at her acceptance and her proposal was obvious. She knew her reluctance for public notoriety was well known. The delegates looked elated that she would overcome that unwillingness for the good of the kingdom. They shouted approval in unison.

"Then we are in agreement," announced the Vice Pope. "Your proposal is eminently reasonable. Further proof of your suitability as a queen. I will make the announcement on the steps of the palace tomorrow morning. You should be there as well. Do not fear, you will be a successful queen and accomplish much more than you think. You are much more able than you ever realized."

Bianca curtsied to the Vice Pope and left the dais to mingle with the delegates for quite some time.

He finally came and took her aside. "You need to begin to appoint and organize your ministers. And you need to prepare for your new role. I suggest the coronation be held on February thirteenth by the Gregorian calendar, day thirteen Chikchan by the Tsolk'in calendar, the day to pray for strength, health and the banishment of anger. How appropriate."

"As you wish. I insist that the ceremony be held outside in the Grand Plaza for all to see. If that venue was good enough for Felix' gathering, it's good enough for me."

He nodded agreement. "Go and get some rest. This has been a long and worrisome two weeks for us followed by the events of today. No doubt an equally trying time for you as well."

"Thank you, Your Holiness, you are right. I'll be with Juan Alejandro in the healer's room should anyone need me.

On her way out of the Great Hall she met the Grand Master of the Order.

She said, "You were right, sir, events have taken me down an unforeseen path. I only hope I can master the task."

"You will do well, make no doubt about that. I still think a little instruction on the use of wands would serve you well. Let me know when you can work that into your now busy schedule"

"I will. This has been a busy morning and I need some time to gather my thoughts. I will try to come to your office early tomorrow."

"As you wish, Your Highness." They went their separate ways.

Bianca returned to the palace to tell Juan about the meeting.

He was ecstatic. "It is nothing less than you and our kingdom deserve. I know you never believed you had the ability to lead, but look at what you've accomplished in the past month."

He sat up on the side of the bed and gave her a big hug.

"Thank you. I hope you're right. But there is so much to do tomorrow, and the next day, and the day after that. I'm not sure where to begin."

She curled up on a settee next to Juan's cot, the cub at her feet, and spent the greater part of the night talking and napping. She went to her room late.

The next morning she was up late and sitting on her veranda when some-one knocked on her door.

It was a messenger from the Order.

"If it pleases your highness, the Grand Master requests an audience with you. He said the two of you have much to discuss and you have some training to attend. Please come with me."

"Just a moment."

She went back into her room, donned her everyday clothes and followed the messenger to the Order's headquarters.

The Grand Master rose to greet her as she entered his office. "A fortunate blend of Tzolk'in and Haab days to you. Are you ready to begin?"

"And a fortunate blend of days to you. I suppose I am."

CHAPTER THIRTY SIX
A WALK ON THE BEACH

Northernmost barrier isle, Empire of New Byzantium. Late afternoon
Gregorian calendar: February 3
Mayan calendars: Tzolk'in: 3 Men
                  Haab: 8 Pax

Felix paced up and down the sandy beach much like he'd done for the past seven days since arriving on this forsaken place. He and his entourage, which included his mother and his toadies from the palace, had been loaded onto a ship the evening of the Conclave and taken to this deserted island.

To make matters worse Felix had no idea what seasickness was until the voyage to his new 'empire'. He was so glad when the journey ended even if it meant being stranded on this desolate islet. It occurred to him during the journey that he would have had to endure the nausea and dizziness if he'd actually embarked on his campaigns of conquest. It was a thought that had never bothered him before.

The trip had taken three miserable days. They went ashore late in the third day at a run-down shantytown inside a cove with a barrier across the entrance. He was told the net was to keep out the merpeople.

"Wonderful," he thought, "it gets worse and worse."

Surprisingly, after a day or so he actually began to enjoy his lonely treks along the beach, just as long as he stayed well away from the surf. He'd been told by the sailors during the crossing about the antipathy of the merpeople and had no desire to find out if it was true.

The time spent on his strolls gave him time to think. He was beginning to realize that what he'd been told by his mother and her brother, Ronaldo, was not the glorious adventure he'd always thought it was going to be.

That awareness started the afternoon of the Conclave. He had been sitting with his head in his hands in a locked and guarded room in the palace waiting to be sent into exile when he received a most unwelcome visitor, his step sister, Bianca.

She had stood in the doorway appearing contrite. He looked up and glared back at her. That didn't make him feel a bit better, but he couldn't help himself.

She said, "I want you to know, although you undoubtedly will not believe a word of what I say, that I am sorry for your fall from grace. I wish it had not been necessary. But if you had gone ahead with your plans it would have destroyed Vlogentia entirely. I could not let that happen."

"How can you say that? I would have made Vlogentia the grandest kingdom of them all. You were just being petty because I was made king, and you never liked me either."

"The first statement is completely untrue. The second only partially so. I did not dislike you at first. That came later when you wouldn't accept Juan as my beau."

"How could you prefer him," Felix interjected, "when it was I who would be leading my grand army to victory after victory?"

"What do you think would have happened," she continued, "if you had amassed such an overwhelming multitude? How would it be trained and organized? How would it be supplied and fed? What were you plans for the campaigns?"

"The army would be fed and supplied by the people of the kingdom, of course. What do you think?"

"But you were going to require every man and boy in the land to enroll so you could amass an army great enough for your visions of conquest. You were going to need thousands of women to feed and tend the soldiers. Who was going to be left to raise the crops, weave the cloth for the uniforms, forge the weapons and administer the kingdom? Who was going to organize and train the troops? No one, that's who. The realm would fall apart, there would be nobody left to run things."

"But that's what peasants do. That's what Ronaldo and mother always told me."

"There wouldn't be any peasants left. They'd all be in the army. Didn't that occur to you?"

Felix began to realize he'd never understood the ramifications of his plan. He had to think for a moment. He didn't like where that thought was taking him.

He had to change the subject.

"You humiliated me in public. I can never show my face again. I don't care what your reasons were, you should never have done that. You wronged me. I will always hate you."

"No, I corrected you. You would not have listened any other way. Besides, you tried to have me killed. I consider that a much worse wrong. The scale of justice tips in my favor. Even so, I don't hate you. I pity you for being so misguided."

Bianca paused for a moment.

Felix took that brief interlude to think about what she was saying. He was finding it difficult to counter her arguments.

She continued, "However, if you would renounce your ambitions, I am sure the people would welcome you back. You could do much good for us if you would devote your talents to the benefit of everyone."

"You mean I could be king again?"

"I doubt that. But you might hold a high office in whatever government the Conclave chooses. They are debating that topic as we speak. Think about that. You don't have to be a great military leader to be important. If you ever decide you want to return to Vlogentia and serve the realm, just let the Conclave know."

With that she turned and left without any formal curtesy.

"I'm still furious at you for my public embarrassment," he shouted at her back as she walked away. He knew he could never forgive her for that. But a seed had been planted. He couldn't get it out of his mind.

That conversation had weighed on his thoughts every time he took his walk along the shore. He was understanding for the first time all the ramifications of his ambitions. It frustrated him that she had been correct. That hurt, but it was still true.

Because of that realization he hadn't figured out what he wanted to do next. So he continued his strolls.

Even with all that clogging his thoughts, he had to admit he liked these walks. The sand felt warm and soft beneath his bare feet as the sea breeze whispered through the brush. It was pleasantly peaceful and the scenery was attractive.

He had to admit to himself that he actually liked being here. There were no more boring edicts to sign, or servants or officials begging for a moment of his time, or tedious meetings to attend. He hated to admit it, but being king wasn't as much fun as he'd thought it would be. For now, being stranded on an uninhabited island was one of the more pleasant chapters of his life. Uninhabited, that is, if you ignored the sea turtles, sea lions and sea gulls.

Felix turned back to the shack he was occupying. On his way his mother intercepted him.

"You need to have someone make me my dinner. I'm starving. And when are you going to get us off this desolate spot and return me to my estate? When are you going to start behaving like the son of a celebrated queen and do what I tell you to do? I don't understand why I have to put up with this. I am too important for you to allow this to happen to me."

For the first time in his life Felix saw his mother for what she really was. A self-centered, selfish and vain woman who had only wanted him for what he could do for her.

He suddenly felt disgusted. "For now, dear mother, we are stuck here. You'll have to learn to live with it."

He walked away, leaving her fuming and perplexed. He didn't care.

He had to pass by Ronaldo's abode. He could hear his uncle loudly moaning inside the room in hopes someone would hear and attend to him. He wasn't moaning from pain, although he had to have some of that. No, he was complaining that he was no longer the true power behind the throne and that fate had treated him unfairly. He had been saying the same thing ever since he was deposited on the island that morning. Felix and the few others that had been sent with him were already tired of listening to him and pretty much ignored him. That seemed to make the former duke even more miserable.

Felix realized, just as he had with his mother that he had never meant much to his uncle except as a means to an end. He felt as if his world was turned upside down. He wasn't liking this realization.

He arrived at the shed he was living in. Inside hanging on a peg was the coat that he'd commissioned for the Conclave. Someone, he suspected his step sister, had arranged to have it cleaned and pressed. He put it on. There was no mirror but he could imagine what it looked like.

He liked this coat, it made him feel like he was really worth something, even if it was just a coat. He liked the buttons and the color and how it fit so well. It reminded him of the brief time when he felt good about himself, before he was sent into exile.

He sat outside on the warm sand with the rough palm trunk to his back, faced away from the cove, folded his coat on his lap and watched the sun set while the evening breeze brought the tang of the salt air to his nose.

He wondered what he could or would do next. Perhaps he could escape to the mainland and raise his army. Perhaps he could return to Vlogentia and become someone of importance and respect, as long as he didn't have to sign any documents. Perhaps he could retire to an estate and live like landed gentry. Perhaps he could live in one of the larger villages and become mayor. Perhaps he could leave this island and explore the Second World. Or, perhaps he could stay here and enjoy walks along the beach and sunsets. He had much to consider.

Among those thoughts was one that surprised him. Perhaps his step sister was right. He still hated what she had done to him but he understood why she thought she had to do it. Perhaps he secretly admired her resolve. Perhaps he might come to appreciate her after all.

CHAPTER THIRTY SEVEN
RESOLUTIONS

The Cathedral of Vlogentia, capital city, Kingdom of Vlogentia
Gregorian calendar: February 13
Mayan calendars: Tzolk'in: 13 Chikchan
Haab: 18 Pax

Coronation day was finally here. The past week had been so frantic for Bianca that she relished this day. Once this ceremony was over she could start to settle into her new, originally unwanted, role.

Breakfast was out of the question. Too much anticipation and nerves. She needed to prepare for the grand occasion. It was scheduled for midday in the Grand Plaza so as many people as possible could attend. The weather was bright and clear. There had been no great storms for at least a week. She took that as a good sign that the portal was back to normal.

A podium had been built in front of the palace, in the same spot that Felix' pavilions had been erected twenty-two days ago.

She decided to wear the same dress and jewelry she'd worn to the Grand Conclave. After all, it was her mother's coronation gown so wearing it today was appropriate. In addition to the gown she wore her mother's coronation cloak and train. It was sky blue with silver embroidery that draped over her shoulders and trailed at least ten feet behind her. She found it difficult to maneuver or even walk with all that following her, but the attendants insisted that it be worn. It was part of the tradition of coronation of a new monarch.

She did not yet wear the crown. That would be added by His Holiness during the ceremony. He had told her that the symbolic gesture of leaving her tiara behind as she left the Grand Conclave had not been lost on anyone. But the delegates to the Conclave had convinced themselves, and then her, to accept the responsibility of the crown even though that was not her original inclination. They told her it would be for the good of the kingdom. She hoped they were correct.

Finally the time to begin arrived. The crowd spread across the plaza and beyond the wall delineating the city center. There was a choir to the left of the podium singing some hymns.

Several Mayan shamans were in front of the podium performing the traditional coronation rituals. They burned incense. They chanted for the four winds of the north, south, east and west to symbolically meet at the wooden rod placed upright in the center of their alter to bring prosperity to the kingdom. They were accompanied by the traditional clay flutes, hollow log drums and conch shells.

His Holiness, the Colonel of the Guard, the Grand Master of the Order, and a few of dignitaries of the capital and some of the nearer towns crowded onto the stage. It had to have been made rather large to accommodate them all. Lastly, a throne sat in the center, with an attendant standing behind it holding a case containing the Sword of the Realm.

After the choir finished their hymns, His Holiness gave a prayer asking God to grant health and protection to Bianca, the kingdom and all inhabitants. He then gestured for Bianca to appear. She exited the double doors of the palace and walked, rather shakily and slowly due to the annoying train, down the stairs, across ten feet or so and then up the back steps onto the podium. She stood in front of the empty throne while the Vice Pope announced her to the throng.

"Citizens of Vlogentia, allow me to present your newly nominated monarch, chosen by the Grand Conclave of Vlogentia in accordance with our ancient traditions. Should she take the Oath of Acceptance of Rule, hold the Sword of the Realm and wear the crown she will become our twenty fifth monarch and govern our land in fairness and justice."

Bianca recited the traditional oath, "I swear before God and his representative and the people of Vlogentia to serve all of you as your monarch to the best of my ability. I accept this onus willingly and vow to rule fairly and justly." She turned, picked up the ceremonial sword from its case, turned again to face the crowd and held it point upward, hilt even with her eyes. She then replaced it, faced the crowd once again and knelt.

The Vice Pope first tied the bark-paper headband with her throne name, Nohoch Chakmool Ix K'uhul Ahau written in Mayan glyphs on it. That had been prepared for her by Father Adames. The Vice Pope then raised the traditional ceremonial crown, adorned with eagle and parrot feathers, from the seat of the throne and placed it on her head. He offered another prayer for her continued health and the wellbeing of the kingdom.

She rose and this was the signal for the crowd to break into the expected cheers while the choir started another hymn. Bianca stood still until all was mostly quiet again and added, "This is an auspicious day, but there is much work to be done. Ruling a great realm such as this requires more knowledge and ability than one person has. I will need assistance from all of you. I promise to hear and accept advice from all corners of Vlogentia. I will not be the queen of Vlogentia, I will be the queen of and for each and every one of you. This is a day of new beginnings for Vlogentia. But for now, let us celebrate."

She could tell from the expressions on their faces that was not exactly what the throng expected to hear. But it must have sounded good since they cheered some more.

Bianca shed the cumbersome cloak and curtsied to the assembled dignitaries on the podium and went down the steps to mingle with the crowd. That was obviously extremely popular. She spent about an hour or so greeting as many folks as she could, and finally had be rescued by some of the guard.

They escorted her back to her room in the castle and allowed her some quiet time. She used the respite to reflect on all that had transpired in the past week.

It had begun with the messenger who had escorted her to the Grand Master in his office.

He had welcomed her warmly. But after their greetings he cautioned her. "You have much to do in the next few days. But I must insist that you spend as much time with me as possible. We have never had a monarch be a member of the Order and you need to learn how to balance those different obligations. Are you ready to begin?"

"I suppose so. What do we do first?"

He handed her a wand. It looked like the one she'd taken from Xander. She felt the same sensation as before.

"First you need to know that the wand is merely an instrument. It focusses the innate energy, what the learned ones in the First World call neural electric signals, in you so you can control the very atoms in the air around you. If you can learn to control your energy you can force the air to heat to a point where it will glow. Or you can force the air to produce a concentrated blast, like a small wind from a hurricane. In some cases you can make the air blow toward you, thus allowing you to attract small objects and waft them back to you."

"*More nonsense phrases from First World. Why do First Worlders need to make things sound so complex? Now even the Grand Master is quoting them,*" she thought, but kept to herself.

"But beware, all of this considerable requires energy and that must come from within you. It is as if you are pushing or pulling the air with your arms. You can only use the wand as long as you have the effort and strength to wield it. When you tire, you cannot do any more."

Bianca looked at the wand. It didn't appear so potent.

"When you use the wand to pass through the portal to First World, things are different. Then the energy for the journey comes from the portal itself. You just use the wand to link you and whatever you transport with you to the First World and back again. That is not as hard as it sounds, but still requires practice. We will have to return you to portal isle sometime in the future for that training."

"I have to admit I'm not eager to return to that place," she said.

"I understand, but it will be necessary. I'm sorry."

"If you insist, but please put it off for a while."

"Of course."

He continued, "I heard with interest your descriptions of how you tried to use Xander's wand. You obviously have some innate knowledge of how to wield a wand, you just need instruction and practice in focusing your efforts. I also was amused by your description of Xavier's capture outside Puerto Norte. I suppose you didn't know that he had undoubtedly used all of his energy when he created the blasts of wind to discomfort the guardsmen. For the next few moments, until he regained his strength, he would have been helpless to repel his attackers. You have to learn the strengths but also the limitations of the wands."

"That is most definitely something I wish Sacniete had taught me. It would have been useful knowledge at the time we confronted Xavier after his first escape. It would have saved considerable effort on our part. But I suppose it all worked out to our benefit."

"She undoubtedly told you as much as she thought you could absorb at the time."

"I suppose."

"It should also interest you to know that we have searched our ancient records to find any mention of the sect banished by Father Sebastian. We did find one document from just after Vlogentia was founded. It detailed the claim, which the chronicler of the document clearly felt was ridiculous, that the portal showed ominous changes if used too heavily. It went on to state that those people were considered disruptive and therefore were banished. It made no mention of where they went."

"Of additional interest to both you and us was an addendum in one of our more recent record books that one of our Order, Axel by name, had studied the ancient document and wrote some notes in the margin that he would find the descendants of those heretics and eliminate them."

"Is that where Xavier and Xander enter the picture?" she asked.

"Yes. The Grand Master at that time, my predecessor, somehow found out about this threat and banished Axel and his four associates from the Order. Axel was the father of Xander and Xavier. He must have been one of the five who found the village of false gold and carried out his deadly threat, but at the eventual cost of his own life."

"But due to the warning from Mrs. Blankenship we now realize the danger to the portals and will take appropriate measures."

Bianca had to take several moments to assimilate all this information. She'd never heard the Grand Master say so much at one time. To be fair, she'd never been privy to many of his conversations in the past. They'd been the part of royal life she avoided.

"So that's why they concocted their elaborate revenge," she finally said. "Look what it accomplished: so much death and the near destruction of the portals. They must not have believed that the portals were that fragile."

"What do you want me to do now?" she added.

"Come with me to our training room, we will start now."

He led her to a large first floor room with no windows and with padding on the walls and a reed mat on the floor. It reminded her of the room in the palace her mother had prepared for her when she was young, so she could practice the Japanese art of kendo, and learn how to use the rapier.

The Grand Master handed her off to one of the instructors and they spent the next several hours trying to get her to focus the energy from her mind and down her arm into Xander's wand, which now seemed partnered with and a part of her. It was exhausting and not very successful at first.

The instructor was encouraging. "You clearly have the idea of what to do. I usually have to spend much more time explaining the concept of personal effort. You just need the practice. We will meet for three or four hours every day until you master the talent."

"Wonderful, I can't wait." Said Bianca. She was totally exhausted. Nevertheless they agreed to meet at the same time the next day.

After leaving the headquarters Bianca returned to the palace to bathe and change into another everyday dress. She then headed to the cathedral to meet with the Vice Pope and his staff to make arrangements for the coronation. She also wanted to arrange a mass in Daniela's and her family's honor.

The rest of the week had been a whirlwind of activity. She spent mornings training with the instructor of the Order, afternoons with the ministers of state, evenings with the clergy planning the coronation, and finally evenings with Juan and/or her friends.

It had been draining and she was glad it was finally all over.

The coronation had gone well and it was finally finished. She was exhausted, the populace were dancing and singing in the streets in celebration and she was planning to spend a quiet evening with Juan and her cub.

They met in her room in the palace. The supposedly ferocious cat had become very fond of her and Juan and gamboled about as they tried to pet her. As they played with the cub, which Bianca had named 'Cuddles' in an ironic attempt to make her sound less threatening, she took the opportunity to talk to her beau about their future.

"Juan, you and I have been so very close since we were children playing in the palace gardens. I love you and I think you love me. Why won't you court me like we both want you to do? In fact, why won't you propose marriage? I need your support to be successful as a monarch. Please tell me you love me and that we should be together."

"You know how deeply I feel about you." He replied. "But I have always felt intimidated by our difference in social status, even when you were pretending you weren't the daughter of our king. I loved you for that and how you make everyone like you. And for the woman you have become. But I feel the people would not accept their princess, and now their queen, being married to a mere corporal of the guard. They expect you to marry some prince form another Second World land."

"I do not want some forced marriage of political convenience. My father and mother were happily married for years, but we both know such arrangements are almost never very pleasant. My parents were the exception. But I need to be happy in order to be the queen everybody wants me to be. I want to be with the man I love. That man is you."

She stood and crossed her arms in front of her. "Besides, if I am the queen, I can marry anyone I want."

"You know I love you. I will marry you in an instant if you think the populace would accept our union. So, "he got down on one knee in the traditional pose, "I know this is not the traditional Tzolk'in day for this, but will you agree to marry me?"

She pulled him up, kissed him, and said, "Of course I will marry you. How could you think otherwise?"

They spent the rest of the evening on the veranda discussing plans for the ceremony. The sky was ablaze with stars, the Haab moon was waxing crescent and the Tzolk'in moon was waxing gibbous.

It was a perfect night in Bianca's opinion. The evening ended with them holding hands and gazing contentedly at the night sky and thinking about the future.

So much had happened to her, and so much had changed within her. But whatever transpired next she knew she was ready for it.

• •

Bianca's Throne Name:

"Nohoch Chakmool Ix K'uhul Ahau" is her throne name. It is usually shortened to just "Nohoch Chakmool" if it is used at all. She prefers to be called Bianca.

The literal translation is: "Great Jaguar Divine Lord (Lady)", "Ix" is a feminine marker. The short form is: "Great Jaguar".

The phrase divine lord or lady was used by the Maya to denote the ruler of the city or land. "Ahau" simply meant one of the elites.

"Ahau" is the older form of transcription from Yucatek to English or Spanish. The more modern form is "ajaw". The older form is used in this book since that is the way Sesbastian, and his successors, would have written it.

Great Jaguar is what the people of Vlogentia call the saber toothed cats of the northern grasslands. Her name is in honor of her bond with her saber toothed cub.

Epilogue

The Blankenship residence, Miami, Florida
Gregorian calendar: June 12

Margaret got home late. She had been busy at her office with some new contracts that needed revisions. Jason had been home for about an hour and had started to prepare dinner, as best he could. As they sat down to eat the doorbell rang.

"Who could that be at this hour?" wondered Jason.

Margaret answered the door.

Standing on the front porch was a most unusual looking young woman. She had snow white hair. It looked natural, not dyed or bleached. That made her complexion look a little darker than it actually was. Her eyelids had pronounced epicanthal folds but her irises were the most intense blue imaginable. She was wearing a simple dress, which somehow seemed out of place to Margaret.

"Hello, my name is Bianca. I'm from the place you visited six months ago. We just want to know how you are doing and what you thought of your visit. We met while you were there. Do you remember me?"

"Oh, you must be the one who wrote the note that came with that odd feather," said Margaret. "No, dear, I'm afraid I don't recall ever meeting you."

Jason nodded agreement.

"But we did enjoy lolling on the beach," continued Margaret, "apparently drinking a whole lot of rum punch. We had a wonderful, relaxing vacation. Thank you for asking. You can tell your management they did a wonderful job. Oh, and thank them for that remarkable feather souvenir. It's quite the memento."

"You really don't remember me at all? You don't remember where the feather came from?"

"No, I'm sure we don't. Is there anything else we can do for you?"

"I suppose not. Thank you for your time. Enjoy the rest of your evening."

It looked to Margaret like the girl was going to cry as she turned and walked back to a waiting car.

"That was really odd," said Jason. "I wonder what it was really all about."

"I'm sure I don't know. Let's get back to our dinner," said Margaret. They sat down to finish the meal and thought nothing more about the strange visitor.

• •

Bianca heard the door shut behind her.

They really did not remember any of their adventures in Vlogentia. That profoundly saddened her. She'd hoped the Order would have left Jason's and Margaret's memories intact. But she understood the necessity for preserving the secret of Second World.

She walked slowly back to the contraption the member of the Order called a 'car'. Not that it resembled anything that she would call a car.

As she reached the side of the vehicle the member of the Order, who also served as her driver, asked, "Is everything all right, ma'am? Do you need anything?"

She looked around at the strange and, to her, over built homes. She listened to the awful cacophony of the city and could almost taste the foul air.

"No, everything here is not alright. Take me back to the boat so I can return to Second World."

With that Her Royal Highness Queen Bianca of Vlogentia got into the 'car', sat next to her husband, Sergeant Juan Alejandro Gomez Mendes, and began her journey home.

"I never want to visit First World again."

APPENDIX A
SOME NOTES ABOUT NAMES AND PRONUNCIATIONS

Vlogentia: The official court language is Spanish, and Father Sebastian Vlogentia Garcia Lopez was a Spanish Dominican priest. No one is sure where he got his second given name from.

Consequently, the name of the kingdom and a few of the towns are Spanish.

The "g" is soft and pronounced very much like the English letter "h"

The accent is on the second to last syllable.

Vlogentia is pronounced as: Vlo-hen-TIA-ya

Ill'yx: is the Spanish attempt to pronounce the kulkulcan's true name.

The double "l" is pronounced much like the English letter "y"

So his name is pronounced "ee-y'-YIX" in Spanish or English. Accent on the last syllable. His name has a double 'y' sound with a slight pause between the y's.

Ill'yonix: is also the Spanish attempt to pronounce the kulkulcan's true name and is pronounced "ee-y'-YON-ix." Accent on the next to last syllable. As with Ill'yx his name has a double 'y' sound with a slight pause between the y's.

Kulkulcan: is the Yucatek word for "feathered serpent" as well as the name of the ancient feathered serpent god of Mesoamerican myth. More commonly known in English by its Aztec name: Quetzalcoatl.

The translator given to Jason and Margaret was not able to find a link between the English word "dragon" and "feathered serpent" so it didn't bother to translate the Yucatek word. So Jason and Margaret heard "kulkulcan" in their earpieces whenever they overheard a conversation between residents of Vlogentia.

Kulkulcano'ob: is the Yucatek plural of kulkulcan.

Naats' Seebek Ha': lying somewhat in the hinterlands, this town is known by its Yucatek name. It literally means "nearby swift water." The Yucatek speakers of Father Sebastian's village had no word for "river." Other peoples near the Yucatan called rivers "traveling water" but this stream is mountain fed and quite fast so the Vlogentians use this term for it.

In English, think of it as "Riverton".

Naats' Nohoch Muulo'ob: lying far to the east of Vlogentia and adjacent to the dragonland mountains, this town is also known by its Yucatek name.

It literally means "near tall (great) hills". The Yucatek speakers of Father Sebastian's village had no word for "mountain."

In English think of it as "Mountainside".

SOME NOTES ABOUT CALENDARS

Gregorian Calendar

The Gregorian calendar, the one used today by most of the world at least for business purposes, was promulgated by Pope Gregory XIII in October of 1582. Until that time the European nations and their colonies had used the Julian calendar, named after Julius Caesar. The two calendars are very similar in design: the same twelve months with the same number of days in each month. The difference is in the calculation of leap years. The Julian calendar assumed that the solar year, the time it takes for the earth to make one complete circuit around the sun, was exactly 365.25 days. To account for this the Julian calendar had two February 24th s every four years.

In fact the solar year is just slightly less than that. That's not a big deal for a few years, but after approximately 1500 years the difference added up to too many leap years and the dates of the solar equinoxes (the starts of spring and fall) and the solar solstices (the start of summer and winter) were off by about ten days. This was a major concern of the Catholic Church since the determination of the date of Easter relies on the vernal (spring) equinox. It also meant the start of the seasons, both by the calendar and by the weather, was off by the same ten days.

So, the Pope decreed that ten days would be eliminated from the year 1582. In addition the extra day in leap years became February 29th. All of the Catholic nations and their colonies quickly adopted the new calendar. By the time of

Father Sebastian, the Spanish colony in the Yucatan was using the Gregorian calendar. The protestant nations followed suit, but much later. Some not until the 1700s, and some even later than that. The Russians did not adopt the new system until 1918. Greece was similarly late to the party in 1923.

Since the solar year is not a convenient fraction of 365+ days, not every fourth year is a leap year in the Gregorian system. It gets more complicated than necessary for this appendix, but the years evenly divided by 100 are not always leap years.

The Maya Calendars

The Mayan people, and most of the other Mesoamerican cultures by the time of the start of the book, actually had three interlocking calendars. The dates recorded on their steles always had the date of its construction in all three calendars. The three principle Maya calendars are:

The Long Count Calendar
The Tzolk'in Ritual Calendar
The Haab, or semi solar, Calendar

Add to these the Calendar Round, the combination of the Tzolk'in and Haab calendars

The Long Count Calendar

This is actually the simplest of the three systems to explain. It is merely the number of days since the originators of the calendar thought humans were created. It actually predates the Mayans, they adopted it along with most of the other Mesoamerican peoples. Calculations based on astronomical events left by the Maya on inscriptions that also included the long count date put the generally accepted start of the long count on 11 August 3114 BCE.

The people of Vlogentia did not use the Long Count Calendar since they had the Gregorian system and they counted the start of their time from the day the kingdom was founded. The distant and mythical date of creation meant little to them. This discussion is included only because most descriptions of the Maya calendar will describe the long count. Omitting any mention of it may confuse the reader.

The only complication is that the Maya used a base 20 numerical system, not the base 10 system we use today. So, instead of numbering the days in thousands, hundreds, tens and ones the way we do, they used a totally different grouping of numbers.

The Mayan number groups are:

K'in = 1 day
Uinal = 20 k'in or 20 days
Tun = 18 uinal or 360 days
Katun = 20 tun or 7200 days
B'ak'tun = 20 katun or 144,000 days

Note that this is not a purely base 20 system. The tun is only 18 uinal long, probably to coincide a little closer with the observed solar year.

Also note that these names may not be the ones actually used by the Yucatek Maya. The B'ak'tun had fallen out of use by the time the Spanish arrived, so that name at least is a reconstruction by modern historians and archeologists.

The usual method of displaying the long count is: whole number of b'ak'tun followed by the whole number of katun, followed by the tun, then the uinal and finally the k'in. The number groups are separated by periods. So, January 1st 2019 would be recorded as: 13.0.6.2.2

One final note. The Long Count Calendar did not predict the end of the world in 2012! That was simply the time when one b'ak'tun ended and another began. Nothing more. The Long Count was/is designed to continue counting days for as long as there are days, much like the Gregorian calendar.

The Tzolk'in Ritual Calendar

This is the most complicated of the three system to explain. They had names for the days, just like the Gregorian calendar does. Instead of Sunday, Monday, etc. they had 20 day names. The days were also numbered much like the Gregorian system. We have seven day names and anywhere from 28 to 31 days in a month. So, when the week ends, say on a Sunday the 7th, Monday becomes the 8th. The Tzolk'in calendar does much the same except that they started on the 1st, but quit numbering on the 13th. The next named day in sequence would be the 1st.

The 20 names of the days are, in their proper sequence:

Chuwen, Eb', B'en, Ix, Men, K'ib', Kab'an, Etz.nab, Kawak, Ajaw, Imix', Ik', Ak'b'al, K'an, Chik-chan, Kimi, Manik', Lamat, Muluk, Ok

For example: if today is 1 Chuwen then the sequence progresses to 13 Ak'bal and the next day is 1 K'an. This continues to the last of the 20 day names at 7 Ok. But the numbers continue to increase to 13 even though the day names start to repeat. So the day after 7 Ok is 8 Chuwen, then 9 Eb', then 10 Ix, then 11 Men, then 12 K'ib, then 13 Kab'an and then 1 Ajaw and so forth. This cycle continues until we reach 1 Chuwen again and then it starts all over again. The cycle takes 260 days to complete (20x13 for math aficionados).

The reason for a 260 day calendar is not clear. Some theories think it may be related to the planting/harvest cycle of maize. Others think it relates to the human gestation cycle. It may have some astronomical basis, the Mesoamericans and the Maya in particular were careful observers of the heavens. Not only of the sun but also the moon and Venus.

It is often referred to as the ritual calendar since many Mayan festivities were based on it. For instance the founding of Vlogentia is always celebrated on 5 K'an even though the Gregorian date was April 3rd, 1586.

In addition to festival dates, each of the names in the Tzolk'in calendar had specific activities that were best performed or acknowledged on that day. For instance, B'en is the day for triumph, as noted by Xander when he urges Ill'yx to attack Natts' Nohoch Muulo'ob. Eb' is the day for listening to the ancestors, another reason to celebrate the founding of Vlogentia. It is also the best day to propose marriage, as referred to by Juan Alejandro when he does propose to Bianca on the less auspicious day of Chikchan (the best day to pray for strength and health). Men is the best day for business or trade. And so forth.

Lastly, each day name bestowed certain traits on those born on that day. In that sense the Tzolk'in calendar was the Mayan horoscope.

The Haab Calendar

The Mesoamerican cultures, which obviously include the Maya, knew the year was longer than 260 days. That was obvious from the cycle of the sun. The older cultures used a complicated system to allow for this. The Maya took an approach closer to the Gregorian system. They also had a calendar that closely correlated with the solar year. This calendar had 18 months of 20 days each. Since this is only 360 total days they also had a period of 5 days added to the end of the year. They did not seem to have a leap year, so over a period of many years their Haab calendar would no longer be in sync with the equinoxes and solstices. For this reason modern scholars often refer to the Haab system as the vague solar calendar.

Each month had its own name, of course and the days were numbered from zero (the Maya were probably the first or one of the first people the world to use the concept of zero) to 19. Unlike the Tzolk'in system the first day of the month was always zero and the last day was the 19th.

For the record the Yukatek names of the Mayan months in their proper order are:

Pop, Wo', Zip, Zotz', Tzek, Xul, Yaxk'in, Mol, Ch'en, Yax, Zak', Keh, Mak, K'ank'in, Muwan', Pax, K'ay'ab, and Kumk'u.

Since each of these months are 20 days long, the generic name for a Haab month is uinal, from the 20 day period of the Long Count Calendar.

The five day period added to the end of the year was called Wayeb'. Unlike the 18 regular months these days are not numbered. Many modern historians say the Mayans considered these days unlucky and prone to danger. Some dispute this analysis and feel this period was a time for rites preparing for the new year. The Vlogentians simply considered these days to be the end of the Haab year and attached no special significance to them.

The Calendar Round: Tzolk'in and Haab Calendars together

Longer periods than a year could be accounted for easily in the Mayan system of calendars. Each day had a Tzolk'in date and also a Haab date. Since these two calendars had different numbers of days the start of a Haab year would not coincide with the start of the next Tzolk'in year. Not until both calendars cycled through what is called the Calendar Round. It took 18, 980 days, or approximately 52 Gregorian years, for the day 0 Pop and 1 Chuwen, for instance, to coincide once again. Rather than centuries, this is how large units of time were reckoned if the Long Count was not used.

This relationship between the two calendars is often depicted as two wheels. The larger outside wheel is the Haab calendar, with each spoke representing one day of that calendar. The smaller inner wheel is the Tzolk'in calendar with each spoke representing a day of that calendar. When the two wheels meet at the same starting spokes, one Calendar Round has occurred.

An analogous concept for the Gregorian calendar would be the amount of time between when January 1st falls on a Sunday and the next time Sunday and January 1st coincide.

Interestingly, despite the fact that the Haab months are twenty days long and the Tzolk'in calendar has twenty day names none of the references the author consulted mentioned a ritual or otherwise reason for this coincidence. It seems too much of a coincidence to be ignored. Most likely it is due to the fact that the Maya used a base twenty system of numbers rather than the base ten of our system of counting, so they naturally grouped things in units of twenty.

If this is confusing, don't feel alone. There are many websites that explain the Maya calendars. Feel free to find one that does a better job than this appendix.

APPENDIX C
SOME NOTES ABOUT ALTERNATE UNIVERSES

Magic exists. Not the sort of magic where sorcerers cast spells forcing people to perform unusual or perverse actions. Not the sort of magic where sorcerers can transform things, animate or inanimate, into something entirely different. Not the sort of magic that allows sorcerers to project bolts of immense power or move heavy objects at a distance. These things violate the basic laws of the entire cosmos. Energy, both dark and visible and therefore mass, both dark and visible, must be conserved. Angular and linear momentum must be conserved. Time is unidirectional and invariant. There are four basic forces. These basic laws apply to all universes of the cosmos. The magic that does exist sometimes allows transfer from one universe to another, if conditions are right. The magic that does exist allows for subtle differences on how physical actions may occur in one universe when compared to another universe.

For instance, different universes may have variances between the values of the four forces. Different universes may have varied proportions between dark and visible energy and matter. Sometimes the differences are so great that the two universes are totally incompatible. Sometimes the laws are nearly identical, so the existences are virtually, but not quite, identical. Therefore physical actions or reactions that are impossibilities in one universe become possibilities in another. Magic in one universe is an ordinary event in the other.

APPENDIX D
SOME NOTES ABOUT SECOND WORLD

When the comet created the portal in our, First World, it also created a portal in a universe so nearly like ours, but not exactly, that the two are inexorably linked (or possibly they are really the same portal existing simultaneously in the two universes). Second World is a planet orbiting a star like our sun, with the same size and mass and year. But life never evolved there since the two smaller moons did not have sufficient tidal forces to stimulate biogenesis.

The larger of the two moons, about one half the size of the moon seen from First World has a period of almost twenty days. Hence it is called the Haab moon. The slightly smaller moon has a period of nearly thirteen days. So it's called the Tzolk'in moon. Because of their different periods it is extremely rare for a night to have no moon at all. This is the reason for one of the curses a Vlogentian occasionally uses.

Once the two portals were created life migrated from First World to Second World on occasion. Nothing much happened at first until some plant spores and seeds blown by the wind took root, literally, on Second World. After a relatively short time span, geologically speaking, Second World was covered with greenery. Trees of all sorts, grasses and aquatic flora flourished. The oxygen content of the atmosphere rose to an incredible thirty percent, much higher than present First World and similar to previous eons of First World. This allows for the creatures that came relatively soon after the formation of the portals while the ocean levels were low due to the impact of the comet, such as theropod dinosaurs and the insects, to evolve into larger forms and with different morphology than a First World person would expect. It allows for much greater physical exertion and strength. Creatures than came later, like the mammals during the last ice age when the ocean levels were also low, did not have time to develop such dramatic changes.

So, the dragons have size but also the strength to fly, as long as they are near the updrafts and winds of the mountains. They can fly, mostly soar, away from the mountains only if the winds are strong enough to keep them aloft. The fairies are the largest wasp like creatures imaginable. The fireflies used in the lanterns are much larger and more robust than the ones in First World. But later arrivals from the time of the mammals such as the mammoths, saber toothed cats (called great jaguars by the Vlogentians), other creatures of the grasslands and the unicorns are only slightly larger than a First World resident would expect. Animals recently knowingly imported by the Mayans and the others, such as cats, normal horses, dogs, chickens and the like, are the same as they are in First World. Other creatures such as rats and iguanas are also recent but unintentional Second World residents.

Since the atmosphere of Second World is so high in oxygen content, fire is much more hazardous. An uncontrolled fire will spread like, well, wildfire. Even small fires can develop into disasters. Consequently, the residents of Second World do not use fire for lighting or heat. Vlogentia and the other realms are all located in the tropics and subtropics, so heating is not a problem. The fireflies negate the need for flame lanterns. Cooking is very controlled in very carefully designed stoves and ovens to keep loose flame from escaping. Everyone is always vigilant about the danger of fire. Firearms are considered too dangerous due to the risk of backfire or cinders. Metal work is also tightly controlled. Forges are walled off from the outside and kept as safe from escaping flame as possible.

Finally, the air of Second World smells purer than First World. Less pollution? More oxygen? Or just different? Whatever the cause, the difference in the air between the two universes is noticeable to most people.

SOME NOTES ON THE MESOAMERICAN BALL GAME

The Mesoamerican ball game, known as "pitz" in Yucatek is probably the oldest team game in the world. It was played for at least two thousand or more years in all the cultures in what we now call Mexico and Central America. The Maya adopted the game and made it their own. To them it had great religious significant since the game played a pivotal role in the Maya creation myth.

The religious significance was of no importance to the citizens of Vlogentia, to them it had become what it appears in the book, a spectacle and entertainment.

Of course, being played in so many different cultures and eras means that there was no one set of rules or mode of play. There seems to be a wide variation in the number of players involved, all the way from one per side to four. In fact the exact rules for any version of the game are not well understood or agreed upon. There are references to a ceremonial conch shell used to start the game and possibly some sort of official. In some versions the head might be used, in others it would not. The ring on the sides of the ball court are apparently a late addition to the original sport. The usual assumptions is that putting the ball through the ring would win the game.

Sacrifice of one of the sides was seemingly practiced on occasion. Again, it is not clear if it was the victors (as a reward to be sacrificed to the gods) or the vanquished. It probably depended on the culture and the religious circumstances of that particular game. On the other hand there are references that indicate that there were professional teams supported by the elites that would play often.

The Spanish who witnessed the game were impressed by the skill of the players. They could keep the ball, which was classically much larger than depicted in the book and made of solid rubber and could cause serious injury, in the air and not hitting the ground for long periods of time.

Unfortunately, the Spanish were so captivated by the play, they didn't bother to write down the rules.

So, the game depicted in the book is one that evolved over the four plus centuries of the kingdom of Vlogentia. It may, or may not, have much resemblance to any game actually played in the Yucatan in 1582. But it seems to work, at least for this story.

APPENDIX F
SOME IMAGES OF MAYAN DRESS

Some examples of modern Mayan apparel. The people of Vlogentia would wear identical or very similar clothes.

Men's wear

Everyday women's wear

Women's formal wear

CAST OF CHARACTERS

The Yucatan

Father Sebastian	Dominican priest	Leader of his village
Vlogentia Garcia Lopez		
Balam	Village elder	
Cuauc	Village elder	
Ekchauh	Village elder	

Capital city

Bianca	Pitz player	Kidnap victim
Julieta	Pitz player	Team captain
Renata	Pitz player	
Daniela	Pitz player	
Joaquin	Café owner	
Juan Alejandro	Bianca's boyfriend	Corporal in Royal Guard
Gomez Mendes		
Father Adames	Priest, teacher	Aide to the Vice Pope
Pedro Marroquin	Livery owner	
Enrico	Juan Alejandro's friend	Royal Guardsman

The palace

Felix	King of Vlogentia	
Ronaldo	Duke of Ki'pan	Felix' uncle, chief counsellor
Javier	Late king	
Augustin Alanzo	His Holiness, the Vice Pope	Emmanual's cousin
Emmanual Alanzo	Colonel of Royal Guard	Augustin's cousin
The Grand Master	Head of the Order of the Portal	

Key West, Florida

Jason Blankenship	Biochemical scientist, Physician	Kidnap victim, Margaret's husband
Margaret Blankenship	Lawyer	Kidnap victim, Jason's wife
Xander	Rogue member of the Order	Conspirator, brother to Xavier

Natts' Nohoch Muulo'ob

Franco Estrada	Mayor	AKA: Calhuka
Father Tomas Reyes	Local priest	
Jorge Perez	Captain of town guard	AKA: Uichikin
Mia	Town's healer	AKA: Ixik

The kulkulcano'ob

Ill'yx	Rogue kulkulcan	In league with Xander
Ill'yonix	kulkulcan	Bianca's friend

The relief column

Xavier	Rogue member of the Order	Conspirator, brother to Xander
Captain Angel Mendez	Officer in charge	
Lieutenant Rodrigo Gonzalez	Second in command	

Others

Sacniete	Retired sister of the Order of the Portal	Resides in village along the sacbe
Father Pedro Lopez	Priest in raided village	
Mateo	Cousin to Xander & Xavier	Henchman to Xavier
Matias	Cousin to Xander & Xavier	Henchman to Xavier

ABOUT THE AUTHOR

W m Somers is retired and quietly living in central Florida with his wife and two dogs. Although he's never had to transit between parallel universes he has traveled extensively, having visited six of the seven continents of our world, save only Antarctica.

He is a dedicated fan of "hard" science fiction, some fantasy and the works of Clive Cussler.

He has visited Egypt and spent a week on the Nile and crawled into a pyramid (they weren't meant for someone six foot two). He spent time living in Tokyo. He drove a car up the coastal road in Australia and to Katherine in the outback. He's been to Hong Kong prior to the mainland takeover, to Seoul, Brussels, London, Managua, Cairo, Cartagena de Indies and Fiji. He's visited the Panama Canal and Stonehenge and the old forts in St Augustine, Nassau and San Juan in Puerto Rico. His most interesting trip was his visit to Central America and the Mayan ruins, which inspired this book.

The ruins at Xunantunich in Belize

Made in the USA
Coppell, TX
16 March 2022

75067044R10192